Ghost of a Memory

Julie Boglisch

Published by Rogue Phoenix Press, LLP
Copyright © 2021

ISBN: 978-1-62420-612-2

Editor: Deborah C. Day

Dedication

This book is dedicated to my editor, Kathie Giorgio. Without her, this book would not have gotten into a finished and understandable state. Since I'm here, I'm also going to thank my mom and dad, for just being awesome parents. My publisher, Rogue Phoenix Press, for dealing with my constant sending of new books their way. To all the people I talked to about my stories and listened to me as I groaned about how difficult it is to write sometimes.

Of course, you, the reader, how could I forget about you? This book is made for you, to explore and to discover. So, have fun, and join Kieran in this world that doesn't seem... quite right.

Chapter One

The flickering of the bulb as it died jerked me out of my concentration. It took a moment for my sight to adjust to the dim light streaming through the closed curtains of my window as I stared down at the homework before me. I reached a hand over, clicking the switch a few times to confirm that, yes, it was dead, before getting up with a heavy sigh. Walking over to the window, I pulled open the curtain, letting the early morning sun shine through. The reds and golds of a gentle sunrise caught my attention.

A sharp pain thrummed through my skull, making me wince and stumble. One hand shot to my head as the fingers of the other curled into the wood on my windowsill, stinging from how hard they dug in. Taking a few deep breaths to center myself, I peered down toward the sidewalk and froze.

A figure stood below me, white eyes staring up at me from a white face. How I could tell the difference since it was all the same color? I didn't have a clue, but there was a certain depth to the whiteness that gave me the chills.

White wispy hair flowed over white shoulders, with white clothes draping over the figure's legs. I saw someone pass by, no, stepping THROUGH the figure before continuing down the road like it was nothing.

The figure continued to stare up at me, a slight tilt of the head the only indication of movement. I jerked, as the figure, which I could only assume was supposed to be a girl from what I could tell, turned to walk away.

Not this time! was the only thought racing through my head as I turned and raced down the stairs. I hopped over the banister, hearing a startled yelp from my mother as I slammed the front door open with probably a bit too much force. A split second was all I had to notice the familiar young man standing in front of the door, ready to knock.

SLAM!

I felt a hand grasping my waist as I stumbled, almost tripping down the stairs as a voice whined in pain.

"Geez, dude," a familiar voice said with a slightly muffled sound. "I know it's nice to see me, but could you try not to run into me like this?" A faint chuckle sounded in my ear as I righted myself, pulling myself from the other's grasp. I continued peering around, dusting myself off in the process.

She was gone. I mentally cursed and let out a long breath before turning to the person I ran into. "Sorry about that, Felix."

Felix, a blond-haired boy with a few piercings in his ears and a sharp grin, grumbled around the hand holding his nose. I smiled sheepishly as he rolled his eyes. He glanced over my shoulder, brow furrowing slightly. "I'm going to make a wild guess and assume you saw one of them again." I cringed, nodding. He peered back at me and smirked. "Nice PJs, by the way."

"Idiot," I shot back, only half-embarrassed at my attire. "Come on, I know Mom and Dad would like to say hi and we're getting nothing done standing out here."

Felix nodded, gesturing to the still open doorway. "After you, Kieran." I rolled my eyes, but stepped back inside, Felix following suit and closing the door behind him in the process.

"Hey, Mom! Felix is over for breakfast!"

Mom peeked her head out of the kitchen. "Hello, Felix." She turned to me. "And honey, please don't jump the banister like that. You scared me half to death when you came racing downstairs."

"Sorry." I grimaced and she let out a sigh.

To be honest, my mother was a very pretty woman, brown hair pulled into a loose bun and a smile that always seemed to make me feel a little better on those off days. Her hair was lighter than mine, which was a dark reddish-black. I could already smell breakfast wafting through the house, smelling delicious.

"Hello, Mrs. Williams. Sorry for the intrusion. I was coming over to check on Kieran." Felix waved.

"You just wanted some of Mom's cooking," I joked as I headed upstairs to change, getting a snort from Felix as a response.

Once in my room, I found myself peering out the window once more before getting changed. As usual, there were no signs of the figure anywhere, and Felix obviously hadn't seen her either.

When I arrived back downstairs, Felix was happily munching on some waffles with bacon. Mom was just taking a seat, placing my plate down just as I arrived. At the other side of the table, watching in faint amusement as he tinkered with some sort of strange device, almost like a two-pronged baton, was my father.

My father was a strange man, always working on some device or another. He was an inventor through and through. He often tried to show me his inventions, talking on and on about how certain wires led to certain capsules and that auxiliary channels were needed in some cases and, well, to be honest though I am his son, most of it went over my head. All I could really do was smile and nod, something Mom mentioned I should try next time after I upset him by zoning out and not responding.

He was a good man, though, and well-respected in the neighborhood. I couldn't help but admire him, no matter how much I found myself annoyed at all of his experimentation and inventing, even at the breakfast table. Didn't help that all three are aware of me seeing those strange figures that no one else can observe and getting headaches that put a migraine to shame. I thought he was doing more poking and prodding on me to figure it out, though I wasn't sure how well I was handling it.

I pulled myself away from the thought, took a seat, and began munching on the homemade waffles. As usual, they were fantastic. Fluffy on the inside, crispy on the outside and packed with flavor. Had Mom always been this good at cooking? Yeah… yeah, she had. I really needed to slow down, but I found myself devouring the meal in what felt like seconds.

"Man, Kieran. I really wish I could eat like this every day." Felix leaned back, patting his stomach.

I noted the way Felix peered out the window, expression lost for a moment. "How is your mom doing anyway?"

He glanced back at me, a faint, tired smile on his lips. "Better. She was able to get out of the house today. I just—" He cut himself off and shook his head, grin going back in place as he shoved his hands behind his head. "Anyway, Ki, the figure you saw today, what did they look like?"

"You saw another one?" Mother asked worriedly as Dad looked up, watching me carefully behind his square-framed glasses.

"Felix," I growled under my breath, causing him to throw his hands up in a defensive position before I turned to my parents. "Yeah. I saw one this morning, it appeared to be a girl, but..."

"So you can at least distinguish some characteristics now?" Father asked, a strange tone to his voice.

I nodded.

"Should we be worried about that?" Mother asked, hands to her mouth as she peered between us.

Father hesitated, gaze flicking to Felix before turning back to me. "I don't think so. Just keep an eye on yourself, okay?"

"Don't worry." Felix reached over, hand swinging over my shoulder and half-pulling me out of the chair in the process. "I'll watch him, with Mira's help. The both of us should be able to keep track of him."

Father chuckled and nodded, a tired smile on his lips. "Please do, Felix."

"Now, enough of that. Finish your breakfast and get going, you two are going to be late as it is." Mother pointed out, gesturing toward the clock. "It's almost the end of your sophomore year of high school. Really, you should know better by now."

Felix glanced up with a faint chuckle. "Yeah, sorry about that. Thanks for having me over Mr. and Mrs. Williams, even though it was quite short notice."

"Felix, you're always welcome here; you and Mira." Mother smiled, picking up the dishes. "Now get going."

"Yep." Felix turned to me. "I'll wait outside. Don't go slamming into me this time, will ya?"

"I don't do that all the time."

"So you say." Felix grinned, arms crossing over his chest. "That's why I'm able to catch you as you almost stumble down the stairs. I'm quick, but not that quick."

I rolled my eyes and headed upstairs to grab my things before coming back down, attempting, and failing, to take an easy-going swipe at Felix as we left.

The air was crisp and warm, a gentle breeze flowing through the streets as we walked and talked.

It was mostly just about random things, the latest video game, difficult schoolwork and what we were planning to do for summer vacation.

It was hard to believe that was only a week away. How time flies.

Chapter Two

Thankfully, it didn't take long to get to school. I waved good-bye to Felix and hurried to my classroom. It was already filling up, some students gathered together around one desk while others silently worked on last minute projects.

It wasn't hard to spot Mira. She was leaning back in her seat, staring up at the ceiling, lost in thought. Her long brown hair fell over her shoulders as she tilted her head just enough to peer over. Her chair hit the floor with a clack as she fully turned to face me with sharp brown eyes. She smiled warmly as I took my seat behind her. She threw an arm over the back and grinned. "Good to see you up. Late again, it seems."

"Not that badly."

"Yep." She grinned as the teacher stepped into the room, a bell ringing through the halls. "Anyway, we'll talk later." She waved and quickly swung around.

I huffed, but didn't argue as the teacher called attendance and we started the day. I won't bore you with the details.

As the final bell rang with its cheery sound, I let out a yawn, only to feel Mira poking me in the cheek. It helped that we shared most classes together, so she could keep me awake, plus we always found ourselves seated similarly, not that I was complaining. "Hey, there is our familiar sleepyhead. What are your plans now?"

I shrugged and got up, grabbing my things. "Don't know. Even though classes are almost over, I'm still a bit annoyed we didn't get to share any classes together with Felix."

Mira's face lit up and a deep blush formed over her cheeks. A finger twirled her hair into a small knot. "Ah, yeah... you're right. We didn't... Um, can I join you two?"

"Mira, you don't have to ask. I swear, this happens every time."

"Not every... okay, yeah, it does, but..." She glanced around before trying to straighten. "I'm too nervous to talk with him, especially lately, you know that."

I waved it off as I pulled my backpack over my shoulder, heading toward the exit. "Yeah, around the same time you figured out you lov—"

"Ah! Kieran!" Mira darted forward. "Please don't say that out loud!"

"You still haven't said anything? You've been dating for at least a week and have known each other a heck of a lot longer than that." I couldn't help but let a little frustration slip into my words.

Mira winced and smiled sheepishly, finger finally stilling in her hair. "Yeah, I know. It's a bit pathetic, but I'm trying."

"At least you admit it." I continued out the door, people streaming past, paying us no mind.

Mira moved closer to me, letting out a long breath. "I'll tell him soon enough."

I peered sidelong toward her, but kept my mouth shut. This conversation was familiar, just from Felix's lips, not Mira's. These two were annoying with that. I peered forward once more. Spotting a piece of familiar blond hair, I waved. "Felix!"

Mira let out a yelp and muttered something about needing to collect her books before scrabbling away. I couldn't hold in the groan as Felix stepped over, peering past me. "Mira?"

"You two..." I stepped past, Felix falling into step beside me. "I don't know how to deal with you guys."

Felix raised an eyebrow before bringing his arms behind his head. "And that is new, how?"

I snorted, unable to argue the statement as we moved out of the school and down the steps. I spotted a janitor off to one side, happy-go-lucky tune hanging in the air as he worked. I saw a couple, holding hands.

Near the bottom of the steps, one of our classmates met up with a young girl, probably her sister, and picked her up, spinning her as her sister squealed. Felix watched, a strange expression crossing his features before turning to me. A headache pierced through as the image of a large man and a young boy slammed into my thoughts, before flitting out just as fast. Well, that was unfortunate, but at least the pain was gone.

"Hey, hey, want to know who can get the highest score?"

I blinked, parsing through Felix's words. "Highest score of what?"

Felix let out a sigh. "The arcade, man, we were planning to go to the arcade, remember?"

Ah... whoops? I guess I got distracted again, it's happened a lot lately. "Only if you want to lose." I twirled my hand as a faint snobbish accent entered my voice. Felix stared, bemused. I grinned before hurrying down the street, Felix a few steps behind.

Inside, children and teens of all ages were chattering and laughing. I could sense the competitive camaraderie in the air. I joined Felix as we went from machine to machine, waiting for a chance at the newest game. I could spot a small crowd around it and the owner, a short man in his thirties, making sure they stayed in line. After some time, we managed to get on it. It was a shooting game, must have been imported from out of country. I wondered how he managed to get it. Last I checked, there wasn't much trading between America and other countries, though I could be remembering wrong. You could probably notice how shoddy my memory was at this point.

I held the plastic of the gun in my right hand, finger jolting each time as I swept across the screen, grin forming against my will as Felix's frown deepened before he finally threw his arms into the air, pulling on the cord as a "GAME OVER" fell onto his screen. I hummed in accomplishment. I didn't have the highest score, but at least I beat the game.

Felix huffed, pulling me away. "Damn, man, teach me your tricks."

"Maybe someday." I elbowed him. He dodged away, laughter—

there it was again—on his face. I frowned, but before I could say anything, I noticed him cut off, pausing. I turned, glancing over my shoulder, following his line of sight as a faint blush formed on his cheeks.

Noticing where he was looking, I found myself unable to stop from rolling my eyes before placing my hand behind his back and pushing him forward. "Go say hi, you dolt."

He sent me a glare before walking up to the startled Mira, who seemed like a deer in headlights. Her hands were fidgeting as she gripped her shirt tightly. I didn't know what they were saying, I just watched as Felix rubbed the back of his neck, sheepish expression on his face.

I slipped away, walking out through a side door. The alleyway, while darker than usual, was clear of debris and dirt. Must have just been cleaned recently, sweet! I slipped through the alley and peeked around just as Mira pulled back, face so bright red, I was almost looking for the words 'stop' to be written there. She turned and raced away as Felix awkwardly stood there, hand to his face. Unfortunately, from the angle, I couldn't exactly see, but I could assume from the way she had her hand over her lips that they'd just kissed. I saw him turn and stumble forward. A love-struck expression clear even from where I stood, the idiots. He spotted me and seemed to slowly get out of his daze before glaring.

I stepped out, tilting my head. "So?"

"So? So…" He practically growled at me before slumping almost to the ground. "Can you stop leaving me with her? I never know what to talk about! And…"

"She kissed you, right?" I huffed, before letting out a yelp as he draped an arm around my shoulder, almost dragging me down. "Hey!"

Felix pulled back, hands crossed over his chest as I straightened back up. "Fine, I know we said we would date, but it's been a week and I don't know what to do," he trailed off and I leaned forward.

"Too nervous?" I grinned as Felix turned away. "Man, if I didn't know you better, I would assume you had no idea how to act around girls."

"It's just her! I mean…" He glanced to one side, noting as one of our classmates stepped past. He perked up and shifted over. "Hello, beautiful—"

"Felix." I let out a groan as the girl blinked, staring at Felix before she huffed, continuing down the street. I pulled him along as he stared after her, cheesiness practically oozing off him, before he shook his head and returned his attention back to the road.

"Hey, stop pulling me, man, you know I can walk."

"Could have fooled me." My voice showed my amusement even as a frown formed.

He huffed. "Okay, fine." He shrugged and waved. "I can still compliment them. After all, what's wrong with appreciating the opposite sex?"

"As long as you don't do that in front of Mira."

"Hell no!" Felix called, practically flailing his arms off. "I couldn't think of another girl like that, not in that way. I mean, Mira's just…"

"Something else?" I teased.

"You know what I mean, man!" The only reason I heard the slight whine in his voice was because I've known him for forever and a half. "I mean, she's nice, kind, a little crazy at times, but so passionate and her hair is really beautiful and her eyes! They're absolutely gorgeous with the hints of gold against the warm brown—"

"Okay, okay, I get it." I quickly cut him off, waving my hand. I should have expected that, honestly. It wasn't long before I spotted Felix's home. It was a two-story house with a beautiful garden out front. I saw his adopted mother sitting on the porch steps in a wooden rocking chair.

I swear, if both didn't say Felix was adopted, I would assume they were mother and son with how similar they appeared, but considering his mother never got married, well, I didn't want to think of the alternative, especially considering the alternative would mean the 'father' was in jail.

"Oh! Hello, Kieran, how are you today?" Her voice was soft and sweet, almost the exact opposite of how Felix portrayed himself as she turned to face us. She struggled to stand, only to sit back down as Felix ran up, catching her arm. She gave Felix a warm yet sad smile as she got comfortable once more.

"Fine, how are you?" I walked over, feeling somewhat guilty, though I wasn't fully sure why.

She patted Felix's arm as she faced me. "I'm doing quite well. It's nice to get outside for a little while. But enough about me, you should probably head home, I bet your parents are wondering where you are; it is getting late."

I looked at my watch and hissed. *Oh shit!* "Thank you! Feel better and see ya!" I called before hurrying down the lane with a fast-paced walk.

"See you tomorrow, Ki!"

I nodded, waving back. It didn't take long to reach the street we lived on. It was a quiet road, not too much traffic, which was why I was surprised to find a car parked on the other side of the street from my house and... was that Dad talking with the driver?

I pulled to a stop, quickly ducking behind the neighbor's tree. What was he doing? It was too early for him to be back from work, right? I couldn't hear what they were saying, but I could almost sense how frazzled Father seemed. His arms were out on either side of him, like he was trying to explain something and he held something in his hand. Whoever was in the car, which, by the way, was a very nice-looking car that I would definitely want if I wasn't completely broke, didn't seem pleased, considering I saw Father wince, hesitantly handing whatever he was holding over to the person in the car. What the... was that the thing he was working on this morning? Why would he hand that to some random stranger?

I felt a piercing headache and almost cried out, squatting down with both hands jammed to the sides of my head. It surged; in out, in out. Eventually, it faded, but a bit of time must have passed because Dad was gone, along with the car. Was I just imagining things? I rubbed my temple, cringing. Maybe I was just tired. Yeah, let's go with that.

I pulled away from the tree, feeling a little awkward that I'd been squatting in plain sight of the neighbor's house, but at least they weren't home, so, yay? Pushing the thought away, I hurried home. Unfortunately,

Mom was still home and she berated me for being late. But thankfully, she was in one of her chipper moods, quickly forgiving me and placing her infamous pot pie before me. Damn, lucky! I finished it off, licking my lips. A slight headache thrummed through my skull and I frowned. Why were there so many today and so quickly? I shook my head, trying to focus on keeping my breath even and calm. After some time it faded away again. Mom gave me a quiet expression of worry and confusion? Why? She should know what this was. Still, what could I do to tell her that I'm fine? After all, considering how often this happened she wouldn't believe me. At least it wasn't a problem at school. Either way, I was fine. She seemed to realize that because her posture straightened. Her tone and face were cheery once more as she hummed, busying herself with cleaning, though she did keep half her attention on me.

Of course, I should have realized that the increasing headaches and all the other strange occurrences were a warning, but I was foolish and ignored it. I wish I never did.

The next morning, I woke up late. The sun shining through the windows was bright on my face. I winced, oh not again. I quickly darted up and got dressed. I grabbed my stuff and hurried downstairs. Mom was already down there, holding out a bagged lunch and some toast, a fond expression dancing on her lips. Dad was watching, amused. I noticed a bandage around his wrist, but didn't have time to ask as I raced out the door. After I got outside, I returned to a more even jog. I devoured the toast, licking my fingers as I turned a corner, heading to school.

So caught up in my thoughts, I let out a yelp when I accidentally bumped into someone. I stumbled back and… whatever I bumped into was almost like vapor, the form of a human who slowly took a step back as I stared. I opened and closed my mouth, tempted to say something, but also a bit fearful of even catching its attention. Before I could really think about it, I felt an arm land over my shoulder and I found myself letting out another yelp.

"Hey, Ki, what are you doing just standing here?" That voice. I breathed out and glanced toward Felix. Felix leaned his head forward. "Dude, you are totally zoned out right now. Was your mom upset with you last night?"

I shook my head as the sound of faint footsteps rang ahead of me. I looked up as the figure I bumped into raced away. "Wait!" I shouted, shrugging my friend's hand off and stepping forward. Unfortunately, it was already gone. I stared at the corner, feeling foolish.

More footsteps sounded and Felix stepped in front of me, worry shining on his features. "Again? Didn't you just spot one yesterday?"

"Yeah," I spoke quietly, staring down the street where the figure disappeared. "Which is why I wanted to know if I could maybe ask it something. That's the closest I've ever gotten to one of them before."

"Dude, from what I saw, you RAN into this one." Felix's expression was beyond worried as he turned slightly to follow my gaze. "That's not good. If you can run into one, doesn't that mean they can do the same to you?"

I paused at the thought, a hint of terror racing through me. These things... these invisible entities who usually had no impact on the physical world could now touch and possibly hurt me. I felt a shiver run up and down my spine as I ended up pulling one arm close to my chest, grasping tightly onto the other. "I'm not in the mood to try to think about that right now." I spoke quietly before turning and walking back the way I came. "Come on, let's take another way to school."

Felix followed after me, but didn't say anything, just hung by my side as we walked, the morning sun glowing brightly over us. At this rate, we were definitely going to be late for school, but it seemed neither of us really cared.

"By the way, what did this one look like? Was it different than the one you saw yesterday?" Felix finally spoke up as we got closer to school, sparing me half a glance.

I let myself flicker back to the figure, the memory already feeling a little fuzzy in my mind. That was odd and a little frustrating, but... "A young man. Maybe. He seemed way too thin to be healthy."

"Well, maybe he died because of starvation before the new technology."

I frowned, but didn't argue. After all, everyone who knew about me seeing these people, all four being Mom, Dad, Felix, and Mira, assumed that they were dead. Well, I thought they did. Mom and Dad were pretty quiet about their opinions on the matter. After all, no one else could find or hear them: they didn't exist to them. But death, well, it didn't mean anything. No one really died, per se. But now it was just getting complicated. Needless to say, I did NOT think they were dead. After all, how could you run into a dead person? But then, again, they didn't really seem like people, fog or vapor was more accurate, so maybe I was just trying to keep myself from freaking out even more than I did earlier. My heartrate was just starting to go down, thank you. I shook the thought off as we got to school.

Felix dropped his arm and glanced at me. "Just don't do anything stupid." A serious expression descended on Felix's face before he blinked and frowned. "Huh... I wonder why I said that." He shrugged. "Anyway, I'll talk with you later!" He hurried down the hall towards his class. I watched after him before I headed to my own class.

Mira was already there, expression distant, yet fond. She spotted me and waved. I took a seat and we just kind of chilled until the teacher stepped in. I would have asked about the kiss yesterday, but I figured there was no point in starting the day with a flustered version of Mira, so I held off. First class went by without any issue. It was the beginning of my second class when things started feeling weird. As the bell rang, I frowned, a slight headache forming behind my skull. What was going on? The door to the classroom suddenly jammed open, showing one of my classmates coming in, panting.

"Sorry!" A couple girls giggled as the boy took a seat.

However, my gaze stayed on the door as it slowly swung shut. It was one of those vapor figures, head bowed and hands on its knees, as if imitating trying to catch a breath. The thought itself was mind-boggling, so I figured I was just seeing things as its head slowly turned upward. I quickly reverted my attention to my desk, attention specifically on the wood. If I didn't look, it wouldn't find me, right? Hey, I know it was a stupid thought, but I held onto it anyway.

I tried to listen to the teacher, but the sound of footsteps caught my ear, followed by faint breathing. I tried not to, but my gaze slowly turned upward.

White eyes stared down at me and I froze.

I thought I saw its mouth open, words flowing over me like a breeze, barely there and indistinguishable. The warmth of the air suddenly felt chilled and I wasn't sure if it was just because the A/C kicked in, or something else. The thoughts from earlier swam through my mind.

If something happened... if this thing tried anything... no one would know who did it, or would be able to help me.

Panic thrummed through me as part of me wanted to back away. I forced myself not to, to avoid making a scene as my overactive imagination plagued me with thoughts of what could happen. I closed my eyes tightly and snapped my head down, as if preparing for the gallows. Ah, what a pleasant thought.

My heart pounded in my chest as I waited... and waited. Nothing happened for a moment, just a moment where I thought, foolishly, that maybe it was gone.

Water-like fingers brushed against the side of my face in a strange stroking gesture, one that, if it wasn't such a terrifying moment, might have been gentle. My eyes snapped open and I jerked, hand automatically moving to slap the thing away. I felt like I was going to have a heart attack, my heart pounding in my chest out of rhythm, which wasn't helped when the classroom door slammed open.

Before I could do anything, or really react beyond that, the figure, a girl I realized, darted away. I turned to find a police officer standing there, startling the class. "I do apologize." The man bowed just as a faint sound and a crash rang through the room. I jolted, turning toward the sound as some people shrieked, covering their faces as one of the windows broke, shattering to the ground in a rain of glass. I saw the girl jump clear through the window, glass cracking under her feet right before she dived out. I heard footsteps and saw the police officer step up to the window. He peered around before kneeling down. His fingers felt over the glass, pulling back after a moment. He faintly clicked his tongue and stood, turning to the class. His gaze roved over everyone, resting on mine before continuing his perusal. Did his gaze linger? I hoped not. "I do apologize. It seems that there was a problem with the air conditioning system." I blinked and shook my head as the man smiled in a way that should have unsettled me, but didn't. He nodded to the class and left. I heard a few people murmur around me, relief shining on their face.

They believed him. And part of me was confused to find that I did too.

I stared out the window, brow furrowed before I quickly shook my head. That didn't make sense though. I definitely heard the clinking of glass INSIDE the building and the officer obviously picked something up, right? As I thought back on it, I found myself uncertain, that headache still throbbing through the back of my skull, the pain slowly subsiding as I sat there. However, the figure was familiar from the brief glimpses I got of her, it was the same one as the day before. Was she after me? But why? And what actually caused the window to blow out? Because it was definitely not her if the glass was on the inside instead of out. The teacher at the front of the classroom shrugged and spoke, pulling me from my thoughts. "Well, at least now we have a nice breeze."

I heard a couple of faint chuckles and, like nothing happened, the class continued, window shattered and all.

My gaze flitted to the window throughout the class to the point where Mira actually rapped on my desk to get my attention, frown on her face. "You okay?" she mouthed. I nodded and forced myself to pay attention. The fact that she noticed I was out of it when she would need to turn around, was evidence enough of my lack of awareness.

Those figures, I wished they would just go away. After all, I was only able to see them since these stupid headaches started a year and a half ago. Finally, after enduring a few more classes and way too many long hours, the day ended with Mira gazing at me worriedly. Felix walked over, startling both of us and causing Mira to blush or actually, straight up turn into a tomato.

Not in the mood to watch their soap opera, I grabbed their hands and pulled them along. I wanted to get out of school. Now.

After a while, we ended up at the local diner. I could hear Felix asking what was going on behind me, yet I didn't reply until we found ourselves seated at a corner table. Though I did hear some of Mira's speculation. One of which was that I was freaked out about the air conditioner blowing a fuse and thought the whole thing would explode throughout class. I never dissuaded her otherwise. I would have preferred that, to be honest. Once we sat down and I had a clear view of the two exits, I sighed, relieved not to notice any of those figures here. I turned to Mira and Felix who were sitting next to each other, shoulders almost touching and hands inching toward each other, even as they watched me worriedly.

"Hey, dude, you okay? You know the air conditioner is back at the school and not going to explode, right?" Felix leaned forward, frown on his face and I let out a breath, letting my tense shoulders relax as I let out a faint snort.

"It wasn't the air conditioner."

"Why didn't you say that!" Mira threw her hands up, now embarrassed. "That's literally the story I've been telling the whole way here! Wait, Ki?" Her expression shifted to one of concern.

"It was one of those figures." I shoved the words out of my mouth, just wanting to get it over with. They both stiffened, but I found myself continuing to explain what happened during class and the weirdness that occurred with the window.

Felix sat with rapt attention as Mira's expression shifted to shock. "Wait, so you saw one of those figures jump through the window? Because, I swear, I remember hearing the sound of the air conditioner going haywire right before the glass shattered."

"Really?" I frowned, "I didn't recall anything like that, I mean, I did recall hearing a sound, but it sounded sharper, more like a small explosion. I don't know, but definitely not from inside the building, it was a more distant sound."

"Must have been a bug in the system," Mira muttered before shaking her head and scrutinizing me. "So you say it was standing over you? Creepy."

"It didn't do anything, right?" Felix leaned on his elbow, eyes narrowed.

I shook my head, placing a hand up to my cheek. "It didn't really have time. I felt it touch me, but…"

Felix frowned. "So this morning wasn't just a fluke. You ran into one this morning and then later in the day, a figure comes bursting in to touch you as if they were now aware that you could touch them." Felix shivered and glanced around. "So that means that, not only are there more than one, they must talk with each other as well, or whatever form of communication they have."

"That's an interesting thought." Mira leaned back, finger to her lip. "That just leads us to why Ki, here, can interact with them to begin with. You and I don't even sense them, but Ki can? And now he can even touch them and vice versa? Are his senses getting more honed or is it something else?" She let out a sigh, dropping her hand. "I mean, no one else in your family seems to have 'ghost sense' or whatever it is you use to spot these things. So maybe it's something else? Maybe, as ghosts, they are attached to something?" She threw her hands up. "I haven't a clue! This is too confusing."

"No kidding," I muttered as the door to the diner opened. I turned in time to watch an elderly man walking in, paper under his arm. I wouldn't have paid it much mind, if I didn't notice the wispy figure of an old woman right beside him, holding his arm, trying to grasp for him.

I gulped, realizing the old man didn't feel or sense her, which meant—

"Hey, earth to Ki, you in there, buddy?"

I snapped my gaze toward Felix, who was holding up a hand in front of my face.

Mira leaned forward, arms crossed over the table. "Did you spot another one?" Curiosity invaded her voice and she grinned. I didn't know why she always got so excited about this, especially after the conversation we JUST had. It was downright terrifying. My gaze flitted to the 'couple.' The old man sat down with the woman right beside him, sitting there, trying and failing to hold him. I shivered.

"Ghost-crazed girl," Felix muttered, a hint of fondness in his voice as he leaned into her a bit.

"You know it," Mira breathed, forehead touching his before realizing how close they were and pulling back, blushing deeply. "I mean... I just..."

"We get it," I quickly interrupted, waving a hand.

Felix sent me a grateful smile as Mira fumbled with her fingers and calmed her breathing. I chuckled as I realized they were still tightly holding hands even in their awkwardness. Geez, these two.

After a few moments, she turned back to me, expression alight with wonder. "You know, I wish I could see them. I bet it would be really cool! I mean, ghost stories are always fascinating. Where do they come from? Are they from when someone gets angry at another? Is it evil incarnate? So many options."

"You don't think it's from someone who died?" Felix asked before blinking, a frown once more forming on his face as he muttered under his breath, as if trying and failing to piece something together. "Died? No. That's not right, right? Man..."

Mira examined him in confusion as I found myself frowning, a dull thrum echoing in my brain. Mira leaned forward, her face smoothing out in worry. "Died? No one dies. That used to happen, years ago, but now technology is good enough where everyone lives out their lives appropriately. There's no such thing."

Felix furrowed his brow before shrugging. I could feel my own lips turning downward in thought. That was right, but it wasn't, right?

My head hurt, but for a totally different reason.

I heard movement and tilted my head up as the waitress stepped over to us to take our order. I froze. A little boy was standing next to her, clinging to her skirt. A little boy, the waitress and—a headache burst through my skull and I almost cried out as the image of a newspaper clipping sprang to mind, only to be wiped away by the image of a girl holding a tiny child in a mix of disgust, sadness and pain. I forced my eyes open as the little boy before me turned his head and watched me, his gaze piercing. A moment later, the grip tightened before loosening and the boy reached forward, arms stretching toward me, as if asking for me to pick him up.

I think my whole body was frozen except for my pounding heart. I forced myself to move and found myself slowly shifting away as the boy took one cautious step forward and then another.

"Sir?" I snapped out of it, gaze flicking to the woman, who I now realized was only a few years older than us... and familiar. Had I seen her before? No, I couldn't have. Maybe I read about it? Something that happened in another country and thought it was her?

Then why did it sound so familiar? What was it again? A rape incident? A victim forced to bear a child? No. That didn't sound right... that didn't happen here. Death, rape, theft, it didn't exist anymore.

I tried to calm my breath and racing heart as I spoke. "So... Sorry, just remembered I have a major test that I forgot to study for, I must have panicked." I wasn't totally lying, I did have a test tomorrow, but as you could probably guess, I wasn't really worried about that.

The woman nodded, a slight chuckle in her voice as she responded, "Ah, I remember that, I used to panic all the time for those, so I know what you mean." I tried hard not to watch as the little boy placed his tiny hands on the seat and tried to pull himself up, a white piercing gaze glowing from white skin and wispy white hair.

"I'll just have some water," I finally said and she nodded, sympathy flashing on her face before she turned and stepped away. The little boy stopped, gazing back and forth between me and the woman before dropping back down and stumbling after her, desperately grabbing at her skirt and holding on tight once more.

It was only then when I realized I squeezed myself into a corner of the cubicle. I finally let my choked breath out and felt my shoulders slump.

A moment later, Mira was draped in front of me, hand on my head and expression alight in both curiosity and concern. Her shirt slipped down just enough to expose more than I expected and I found myself quickly averting my gaze, jerking slightly in discomfort as she pulled back. "You saw another one, didn't you?" Her voice held some concern, but I could sense the brimming curiosity and excitement.

Lucky her.

Felix had his elbows on the table, fingers clasped under his chin. A strange expression crossed his features for a moment. "You're seeing more of them today, at least more than usual."

"I have been getting more headaches lately. Before, they would only come once every few weeks, but now…" I winced as another one pulsed quickly through my head. My hand darted up and I grimaced before feeling it fade, grateful that they were quick things.

Felix sighed. "Why don't you ever do some research about them? These symptoms? We can just go to the hospital and—"

"NO!" The word came out strangled and a few customers turned my way. I quickly sent them a sheepish grin and waved it off before returning my focus back to my two stunned friends. Felix's head pulled away from his hand, mouth open and Mira sat back, slowly peering between us.

"Why not? I don't get why you're so damn adamant not to find out about them. Hell, even your parents are opposed to it for some reason, your dad especially. Are you all just afraid of hospitals or something? I just… I don't get it. What if these things could hurt you, or us?" Felix's voice was exasperated as his hands fell onto the table with a soft thump. "Honestly, Kieran, I'm worried about you, we both are."

Mira nodded, pulling herself from my seat and joining Felix on the other side. "Come on, Ki, it's been a year and a half, a long time to still be having what many would assume are hallucinations. We might not find anything, but can we just check?"

I wanted to argue, but I didn't know why. A large part of me was terrified, I didn't WANT to know. But another part of me agreed with them. It had been over a year, what harm could come with just a little search? Dad always said not to worry about it, even as he tried to find ways to help me and Mother didn't have much to say either. However, as I thought it through, I found myself… well, as cliché as it sounded, though my heart really wanted to find out, my mind rebelled.

I let out a long sigh and shook my head. "Please, Felix, don't worry about it. I can't say it will go away, but," I shot them a quick grin, "it's not going to cause any problems. After all, I have been dealing with it for a year and then some." Felix furrowed his brow and pursed his lips, but didn't argue. Mira seemed down, almost a little upset at my decision. I hoped they didn't think of doing anything stupid. "Promise that you won't try to research anything regarding this?" Mira nodded, and Felix after a moment of hesitation, leaned back and clicked his tongue. Honestly, that was probably the best I was going to get from those two. "Thanks!"

Felix stared at me for the longest time before he chuckled. "Well, after we eat, want to go to the arcade? I do have to get home early today, but…"

"Sounds good!" Mira chirped, gaze still on me. "After I find out what Ki saw."

"Your mother," I deadpanned.

She gaped at me for a moment and then huffed, returning my comment with her own monotone, "Ha-ha, funny."

I shrugged and she backed off, thankfully knowing me well enough not to ask anymore. I kept my gaze firmly on the table every time the waitress came up, feeling bad because I was being so rude. But what could you do? At least I made sure to leave a decent tip.

Finally, we finished up and headed out. I didn't really have the heart to play any games today and so decided to turn in early, much to both Felix's and Mira's surprise. Though I discreetly noted the way Mira smiled while Felix blushed, stepping closer to her as they walked away.

My brain felt like it was pounding against my skull when I made it home and I grimaced, holding my hand to my head tightly as I stepped through the door. Mother glanced up and almost dropped what she was doing as she darted forward, hands gently supporting me. "Oh, Ki dear! Come on, sit down." Her voice was soft as she led me to the living room, thankfully keeping the lights off and the curtains pulled so only dim light slipped through. She left and returned a moment later with a cup of water, quietly fussing over me. I didn't mean to make her worry, I really didn't. I grimaced as the couch dipped next to me.

"Mom, I'm fine."

"Ki..."

I blinked and tilted my head up enough to notice Mother standing in front of me, confused and a bit nervous, glass in hand.

Wait. I slowly turned, not sure what I was expecting. Only to come face to face with someone, a wispy white figure, sitting on the couch, watching me.

This time, I sure as heck did NOT hold in my scream as it literally ripped from my throat. I scrambled back, falling off the couch in my panic. The figure shot up, suddenly seeming panicked itself, as if unsure what to do. Mother quickly got in front of me, squatting down with her hands on either side of my face.

Worry and concern shone clearly as she held my head. "Breathe, Ki, breathe! You're fine. You're fine, all right?"

I focused on my shaky breath, flowing in through my nose and out through my mouth. My limbs felt locked up and tingly. The hardwood under my fingers was smooth as I curled my hands tightly into my palm, knuckles rapping against the ground from my rattling. At least the pain was gone.

As Mother stood up, I glanced toward where the figure was. There was nothing there.

I let out a long breath and slowly dragged myself to my feet. "I think I'll turn in early tonight."

Mother didn't question it, just giving me her traditional warm smile. Traditional... wasn't it once warmer? "All right, dear, sleep well, okay?"

I tried to give her a confident expression in return, but I knew it didn't quite make it on my face. I trudged upstairs and collapsed onto my bed, making sure my door was firmly shut, along with my window.

I'd be hot tonight, but at least I should hear if anyone entered.

Chapter Three

Thankfully, it wasn't long until the last day of school came and went. I was grateful. My gaze flickered to another white figure running from class to class, flailing its arms as the final bell rang loudly through the halls. I quickly turned away and spotted Felix standing off to one side. He noticed me and waved, walking up to me. Mira, who joined me on our way out, gave a blushing smile. Felix fiddled with one of his piercings before returning his attention to us.

Geez, those two, you wouldn't think either of them could be nervous and here they proved me wrong. Mira leaned forward, peering up at him, causing him to jerk back slightly. "I recognize that expression. You found something interesting, didn't you?"

Felix's expression was more than a little nervous as Mira pulled back. He hesitated, leaning forward, arm draping around her shoulder and pulling her close before glancing at me. "Maybe?"

I hesitated, but followed after them anyway as they headed away from school. Mira playfully pushed Felix away and he fell back, hand to his heart in what was probably absolute melodrama. I rolled my eyes, stuffing my hands into my pockets as he led us down the street. To my surprise, we went past the arcade and toward the library at the other end of town.

Luckily, the town wasn't that big. I mean, it was decent-sized to the point where, if you wanted to get one place to another quickly, a bike would be a better choice, but the suburban layout made it fairly easy to get from one place to another and with the school right in the middle of town, it was not hard to get to places afterwards. Stepping into the cool air of the library, I scanned the room. I hadn't been in the library in ages. The musty smell of old books and the quiet chattering that faintly trailed down from the second floor gave it a quaint atmosphere. Though, I'm not sure why people still come here, what with the fact that you can practically carry ten books in your hand through a simple device. I grimaced, I think you could, right? Felix surveyed the room before stepping to one side, he moved behind one of the large bookcases. Mira scrambled after him, glancing back at me occasionally. I sighed and followed after them, unsure why we were even here.

After some time, we stopped at a computer in the back corner of the library, a lone window shone faint light into the little alcove as Felix took a seat. Mira pulled up two chairs from nearby before plopping into one of them. I sat in the other, leaning over Felix's shoulder as he typed. He was pretty fast, but then, he was always interested in computers, almost as much as girls. Within moments, he passed through the library's restrictions and arrived at a webpage. "So I was searching for your symptoms, because I was curious."

"Felix!" I resisted swatting at his head, sort of. He grimaced as I rapped my knuckles against his shoulder, feeling annoyance and anger surge through me.

His gaze met mine for a moment before returning to the screen. "You wouldn't believe how difficult it was to find anything about it." He was ignoring me!

"Not surprised, not many would want to talk about it," I muttered, glaring at him. "Didn't I tell you?"

"It's not just that."

I blinked and examined Felix a little more closely. What did he mean by that? His expression was a mix of amusement and, underneath that, concern.

"What do you mean?" Mira leaned forward. "After all, ghost stories are quite common, why wouldn't someone mention that they could see them? I mean, yeah, they might seem crazy, but—"

"Do you know anyone crazy?" Felix sent her a strange expression. She closed her mouth, thinking it over before slowly shaking her head.

"What do you mean?"

"Well, there's no crime and technology has developed to the point where we no longer fear death, right?"

I nodded along with Mira, yet a strange feeling welled up in my stomach. Something wasn't right about that.

Felix turned to me. "Well, we don't have any fatal diseases, mental illness, anything. So why is it that you have something that can be analyzed as, well, a mental illness?"

I glared. I knew full well it wasn't a mental illness but that led to a good question.

"So, you're saying that they might heavily medicate him if someone found out?"

"That's only my guess, I don't know. After all, this is the only page I could find regarding it. Too bad I can't connect to anything from foreign areas."

Oh right, that whole disconnect with the rest of the world. I think it was after a pandemic ravaged the world that we closed off our borders. Well, at least we have the technology to keep us healthy. Maybe all those wisps are deceased, from before the development of the technology? I didn't think so, but it was a scary thought. I shook my head as I heard Mira question what the webpage said.

"That's the thing, this was in the underweb." He grinned at us and I couldn't help but give him my best deadpan expression. Why was he searching around in the underweb for my symptoms? His smile faded as he caught my annoyance. "It talks about how if you can see these beings, then you must have a special connection with one of them. I think it's deliberately vague because it's been kind of hard to find as if it constantly changes URLs."

"So, are you saying that Ki has a dangerous ability or something?" She glanced over toward me, a mix of awed and worried.

Felix shrugged and pushed away from the computer as it closed down. He turned to us. "I don't know, I just know that there might be more to why he can sense them. After all, this only started a little over a year ago, right?"

"A year and a half," I replied without much thought.

"Wasn't that when your headaches really started?" Mira put a hand to her lips. "You kept insisting not to go to the hospital, that's around the time when we started wondering if your whole family was afraid of hospitals or something, because even your parents seemed opposed to it, like Felix mentioned earlier."

I frowned, trying to think back to then. I remembered feeling really disoriented, the first few months after they started were very blurred. I think I remember feeling terrified at one point, and pain... a pain different from the headaches I have now, but I'm not sure what it was or if it was just my imagination. "I wouldn't be surprised."

"Yeah, it was kind of funny, you would occasionally beg either Mira or me not to literally drag you there, even when you almost collapsed on us. Talk about scaring the daylight out of us," Felix joked, hitting my shoulder lightly.

I glared at him. "Now you're just exaggerating."

"He caught you there." Mira chuckled, leaning close to Felix's face. The boy blushed brightly, jerking backward.

I stood, pulling them up. "I don't know why you two are so nervous around each other. You've been dating how long?"

"Fourteen days," they said in unison before glancing at each other. Mira grinned as Felix licked his lips. Man, these two were so strange. I wanted to say just kiss already, but honestly, it didn't really mean much.

I face-palmed before letting my hand trail down my face. I gave them both my deadest expression. "This is ridiculous, honestly."

"Hey!" Felix snapped as Mira puffed out her cheeks.

I shrugged. "Well, at least you two aren't oblivious, that would be even worse."

Mira winced as Felix rubbed the back of his neck. "True," he muttered and I couldn't help but laugh.

I gestured and started walking through the bookshelves. "Come on, let's get something to eat and plan for summer vacation."

"Sounds good!" Mira chirped, hurrying up to me.

"Hey! Wait!" Felix scrambled after us.

I glanced at Mira. "Want to make this a race?"

She hummed in thought as Felix skidded to a halt next to us. Felix sent us a look. "You were thinking of ditching me, weren't you?"

"Maybe." I elongated the A for a bit, smirk forming, tugging at my lips.

He huffed, lightly tapping my shoulder with his fist. "Come on, man, that's just cruel, thinking of leaving behind your best buddy."

Mira turned, walking backward as we stepped out of the library. "Hey, you can't say you wouldn't do the same."

"What are you insinuating?" Felix glared and I chuckled as the two peered at each other, walking almost in tandem. I waved my hand between them and they both quickly looked away.

"Now that that's settled." I lay my hand down. "Let's grab some food."

~ * ~

We picked up some snacks as we passed by the diner. I let them go in, observing things from the outside. I could already spot those white forms inside and I really didn't want to deal with them right now, or ever, really. At least the headache was manageable this time, more a throbbing warning than anything. Thankfully, the things didn't seem interested in harming anyone, but they were creepy as heck.

When Felix emerged, he threw me a box which I quickly caught, hoping no food spilled out.

"Felix!" Mira glowered, smacking him lightly. "What was that for?" Felix winced and gave her a sheepish grin as she turned away. "By the way, here's dessert, my treat for this one being such a dolt." She passed me another bag and I took it gratefully.

"Thanks." I shifted the items as we walked a ways down the road, both of them carrying their own boxes of food. We finally found a spot near the school with a couple benches. The sunny sky was clear and bright. The food was hot and fresh as I carefully peeled it open and dug in. Felix was already stuffing his face as Mira cut each item into tiny pieces. She must have been hungry, because those cut pieces were getting steadily bigger with each cut.

I finished and opened the bag for dessert. It was a cake slice and I grinned. Damn, they knew me way too well. The cake had a thin layer of butterscotch cream and chocolate with pieces of Oreo decorating the top.

A fork reached forward and, before I could stop it, Felix swiped a bite. I glared as he licked his lips. "Hey, come on, gotta have a bite, right? After all, we did pay for it."

"I gave you money to pay. You bought this on a whim," I deadpanned, noting as Mira leaned forward around Felix. Was that cake crumbs on Mira's face? I jerked my head down noting that a large chunk was missing from the cake. I promptly pulled it away from the two ravenous thieves. Once sure I wasn't going to lose any more cake, I turned, giving Mira an unamused expression. "You too?"

"No." Her gaze shifted away guiltily before she shrugged.

Felix chuckled, wrapping an arm around her shoulder and leaning into her. "That's how it's done!"

I let out a sigh as I dug into my now half-left dessert. Meh, all well. I finished, listening as the two talked next to me. Once done, I placed the empty container down, watching as a nearby cleaner came over. I handed him the trays and he smiled at us before taking them and bringing them to a nearby trash bin, which he then changed. I watched him go and smiled.

"I don't know how some people like to do that stuff, but, I mean, if it's for society, then I guess it makes sense." Mira turned to me. "So, summer plans. I was thinking—"

"If you say haunted house, know it will be an immediate no, and not just from our resident ghost seer." Felix snapped his fingers and she pouted.

"It wasn't going to be that cliché," she grumbled and I raised my eyebrow.

"Sure… and really, Felix? You still think I'm seeing ghosts?"

"What other explanation is there? How else can you sense something no one else can? I mean, you also describe them as whitish and smokish, right?" He shrugged. True, when hearing it like that then, yeah, it did definitely sound like I was seeing spirits. Lovely.

"I wish I could see them!" Mira clasped her hands together, emotions shining clearly with that distant smile on her face.

At least I wasn't alone this time, Felix groaned at that point and gave me a resigned shrug. I waved it off. After all, I guess I was starting to get used to it.

Mira shook her head and turned to me. "Well, we could also just check if we can find out more about Ki's symptoms. After all, it's pretty suspicious that you had to go to the underweb to find out ANYTHING regarding it. He can't be the only one out there that can sense them."

Part of me wanted to say no again, but another part of me couldn't resist the idea. I really wanted to know who or what those figures were. Why did they keep coming to me? Why did I start spotting them more lately? I was still a little pissed at Felix for researching it, but I couldn't completely blame him. I really wished Dad could figure out how to fix my headaches, maybe then I wouldn't sense them any more. After all, they didn't hurt anyone.

"I guess we could do that, what do you think, Ki?"

It took me a moment to kickstart my brain back into the conversation. Felix, unfortunately, seemed excited at the possibility of more research. Yippee. "Fine."

Both of them grinned before Mira leaned forward. "All right, so that's a thing we can work on, what else do you want to do?"

We continued to talk on just random things. We decided to meet up in a week at the local waterpark and then decide from there.

Chapter Four

The week passed without much to say. I slept in, trying to ignore the increasing strength of the headaches. Felix continued to research my symptoms while Mira scrutinized through the library for anything. At least they didn't ask anyone. That could definitely lead to awkward questions.

Finally, it was the day we were supposed to meet up. I dressed myself in a loose tank top and shorts with a pair of comfy sandals, bag draped over my shoulder. Mira arrived first, ringing the doorbell before stepping right into my house. "I'm here!" she called from the entrance before heading into the kitchen. I peered up from the dining table, finishing up breakfast.

"Oh, hi, Mira." Mother stood. "Did you want anything?"

"Nope, just here to pick up Ki, we're heading to the park today."

"Oh right, he did mention that, didn't he?" She ruffled my hair and I half-heartedly swatted at her. She flinched, confused as her hand darted down toward her waist before dropping naturally to her side. She chuckled. "Have fun, okay?"

I nodded, momentarily confused by her reaction before pulling myself away from the remains of my delicious breakfast. Mira led me out, and toward Felix's home. I wondered if he was up yet, who knew.

"So, are there any?"

I stared at her in confusion before the question clicked. I huffed before scanning our surroundings. Sighing in relief, I shook my head. She pouted. "Ah, there we are." Yep, that was definitely Felix's place. Mira shielded her eyes from the rising sun and called, "FELIX! WAKE

UP!"

I dug a finger into my ear, wincing. "Geez. You could wake up the whole neighborhood at this rate. Did you forget that his mother probably just got home from work and is trying to sleep?"

Mira glanced at me before sheepishly pushing her fingers together. "Whoops?"

I rolled my eyes and stepped up to the doorway to knock. Before I could get there, Felix slammed it open, almost smacking me in the face. Thankfully, I jumped back; if not, that would have really hurt. I went to berate him, only to feel ice lock up my joints. And no, it was summer, it wasn't cold.

No, what caught my attention and froze me in place was the white hand tightly gripping my best friend's shoulder. It seemed to be trying to pull at Felix, as if trying to tell him something. A blue uniform flashed, dancing over the figure's body before disappearing.

"Felix?" I choked, catching his attention.

The figure must have also noticed me staring, because he suddenly stopped. For a split second, nothing happened and then I noticed Felix stumble at the same time as something grabbed me. White curled around my wrists, a vice being looser than this. Damn! That grip was like steel. He was well toned and there was something slung over his shoulder, but I couldn't make out what. He was big, that much I knew, and I could practically feel the panic and fear coming from him.

"Ki!" Felix's voice rang out as he straightened, probably noticing my stiffness. Or maybe the way my arms were LITERALLY being held UP! The fingers gripped tighter as the figure's mouth moved, words whispering to me. I wished I could understand, but I couldn't!

The grip tightened even more, which I hadn't thought possible, and I winced, trying to pull away. Damn, that HURT!

Mira was next to me in seconds, fear shining on her face. "Ki, are you okay? What's going on?"

I tried to say something, but only a grunt of pain came out when the man, because that's what I could assume it was, considering the size, shape and strength, started shaking me.

I felt Felix and Mira step up next to me, grabbing at my upper arms and tugging. For a split second, I found myself wondering if this was what the rope felt like in tug of war, before I was falling, sprawled out on the ground. Mira scanned everything wildly before checking me over. I sat up, massaging my head while Felix stood in front of me, trembling. The man's attention focused solely on Felix, shocked, I think. His hands fluttered and I could tell he was once more panicking.

"Come on, let's go." Felix's voice pitched upward. I nodded and Mira helped me to my feet before we found ourselves racing down the road. I scanned the area, trying to find someplace to go, someplace without those figures. After some time, we arrived at the school and slipped onto the grounds. The trees we sheltered under just a week ago when eating our snacks hid us from sight and it was only then I let out a breath and slumped down. With my heart decelerating, I found myself scrutinizing my wrists. That was strange. I could already spot bruises forming.

Mira was staring at my bruises in shock and fear. "Are those…" She shook her head and touched my arm. "Are you okay? What happened?"

I couldn't help but catch Felix's attention. He seemed to realize, because he took half a step back. "That's why you said my name. There was one of those things in my house, wasn't there?" He clenched his hands, fear clinging to his face.

"Yeah, he didn't seem dangerous, but…" I didn't think I needed to, but I showed them my wrists anyway.

"But he hurt you!" Felix growled, though I could still spot the fear and Mira nodded, anger shining on her own face.

"Guys! I'm fine." I stood, brushing down my clothes now that I got my breath back. Part of me wanted to know why that person was in Felix's house. But another part of me… I gritted my teeth and shifted my attention to Felix. "Did you feel him?"

"What?" Felix furrowed his brow. "Feel… him?"

I shook my head. "Don't worry about it." If he was wondering, then he probably didn't notice anything. "Now come on, if we stay here, we'll never get to the park."

"You are not just going to push this off." Felix slashed his hand sideways. "I didn't know these figures could hurt you or others! Sure, we hypothesized it, but I didn't think it would actually happen! And what do you mean, him? Who was he?"

"They usually don't. They mostly just stay away from people. Maybe he was startled I could see him." I hesitated. "But what do you mean, who?"

Felix stilled confusion clear on his face before he gritted his teeth. "That's beside the point. Just because he was startled didn't mean he had the right to, what, shake you? What was he doing?"

"Trying to get my attention, I think," I said, shrugging. "But he seemed more panicked than anything, desperate, I guess."

"But does that mean Felix and his mother are in danger from him?" Mira voiced, gulping.

"Considering Felix probably didn't feel him, I would guess no," I responded, peering out through the copse of trees we found ourselves in as my arms dropped to my sides. "Still, I really don't know." The last words were spoken in more of a whisper, not wanting to worry the others more. Because, honestly? I really didn't know anything about these… things.

Felix pursed his lips. "And what about you, man? You sure you're not hurt?"

I smiled, thumbs up. "I'm fine! Geez."

He huffed, but didn't bother asking again. "Come on, I guess we should go."

I nodded and turned to head toward the park. I heard both of them follow reluctantly. After a few moments, Mira joined me. "Sorry."

"Huh?" I tilted back, slowing my pace to better match hers as I felt confusion bubble up from my veins.

"I was entranced with the idea of ghosts and seeing one. I didn't really think about how dangerous it could be for you."

I waved it off. "It's fine. You wouldn't be you any other way. Now can we stop thinking about it? I thought we were supposed to have fun today?"

Mira gave me a faint smile. "I wish I had your strength. I was scared when I saw you like that, I…"

"We were both worried." Felix finally spoke up as we cleared the trees and headed down the street once more. "After all, it kind of seemed like you were struggling against air. If we didn't know you sensed figures and such, well…"

I peered over my shoulder to Felix, who was staring at me with an odd expression on his face. I looked away and shrugged. "Fair enough." I didn't know what else to say, really. What could I say?

We made it to the water park in no time at all and I was relieved to see that both Mira and Felix calmed down after that escapade.

I would admit, I was still scared and a little jittery, but I didn't want to worry either of them so I tried hard to portray a calmness I sure as heck was not feeling.

The park was packed, probably due to it being the beginning of summer break and everyone going now that they could. Still, we found time to go on some of the rides.

I was just kind of dragged around. Where Mira had a habit of hopping on the ones that made my stomach drop and flip, Felix was more casual, going for some of the larger splash rides where you got soaked, no matter where you sat. Now if only I could just ignore the abundance of ghost or spirit things around the place. It sent a shiver down my spine whenever we got close to one. Of course, a little less scary and more annoying than anything was the way those two were making love eyes at each other because I was NOT going on the Ferris wheel with those two right now if that was our next option. They could go alone, for all I cared.

It was a little after noon, probably closer to one, when we decided to finally get a rest from all the rides. I let out a sigh, plopping myself into one of the plastic chairs around a well-worn table. An umbrella sat right in the middle, barely shading us from the sun. Felix sat down beside me while Mira, who was the one who ended up getting drinks and food, returned with an arm full of snacks and three drinks. I grabbed my Coke while Felix swiped a Mountain Dew.

"Man, the lines are ridiculous today," Mira groused as she placed the food down and took a seat. "I know summer vacation just started, but geez!"

"No kidding," Felix said around a mouthful of food. "But hey, it's not really a surprise, right?"

"True," I interjected. "After all, it's really close and the only water park within almost a hundred miles."

"Well, no, there is one in the next city over," Mira pointed out.

"That one doesn't count." Felix waved the words away and smirked toward me. "After all, everyone talks about how it's practically haunted, no one goes there anymore. Last I heard, it was abandoned."

I sighed. We always got back to the haunted thing. "So, what do you suggest we do now?" I took a gulp of Coke, enjoying the fizzle that popped in my mouth, soothing my dry throat.

Mira frowned, fingers to her lips as Felix placed his hands behind his head. We sat in silence, occasionally grabbing one of the greasy snack foods on the table. I might have slipped some of the cheese fries closer to me and devoured them, but, meh. I reached for another fry when I noticed Felix shiver. I glanced over and honestly, did I have to say it again?

I tried desperately not to freeze, but I knew my expression betrayed me anyway as I examined the same figure from just a few hours ago. Another person stood behind him, watching their surroundings, or at least it seemed like it. They were set in a pose that screamed watchfulness, but that figure looked more feminine. A woman?

I could see the first figure trying to talk to Felix, fingers curling over his shoulders. Felix jerked, scanning the area with a strange expression on his face before he shook his head and returned his attention to me as if he wanted to say something. I gave him a weak smile and quickly tried to turn away, focusing on Mira. Should I say something? But he wasn't hurting Felix and I honestly didn't want to scare my friend any more than I had to. Since he hadn't tried to go after me first, maybe he realized I couldn't help him?

I did not know where my train of thought was going. I was so terrified, I was not thinking straight.

"So, are you going to just let that cheese drip on your shirt or are you going to eat it?"

I blinked and peered down before letting out a yelp. I had gotten so distracted, I forgot I was holding a whole group of fries. The cheese dribbled down my shirt. That was embarrassing.

I heard chuckling and returned my attention back toward Mira. She was grinning sheepishly. "Sorry, you just looked kind of funny, what's on your mind?"

"Other than the fact that I need to clean my shirt? Not much." I grumbled as I popped the fry into my mouth. I glanced sidelong to Felix, who was chowing down on his own food, as if not even sensing the person holding him, trying and failing to shake him. To be honest, I didn't want to freak him out if I could help it. I just finished having a long conversation. My best bet, honestly, was to see if I could lead this guy away.

Speaking of, how was it that the man could grab me, but not Felix? What was going on? And why the hell was I calm enough to think all of this? I stood up. "I'm going to find something to change into."

"All right, don't take too long." Mira waved as Felix swallowed his food.

He wiped his mouth with an already scrunched napkin before catching my attention. "Dude, want to grab some water?"

"Yeah, yeah." I waved it off, hearing the screech of the chair over pavement as I pushed it out of the way. I stepped past Felix, brushing past the man, who seemed to stiffen. I continued on my way, passing by the woman figure. They turned to face me, scrutinizing me as footsteps started to echo distantly over the pavement. That… wasn't creepy in the slightest. I tried not to turn back and instead picked up my pace. I wove through the crowd, noting as the ghost-like figure followed, barely needing to dodge through the crowd. I gulped and didn't think about it. I hurried around a corner and then another until I was practically barging my way through the crowd before ducking into a small side alley. I let out a breath and turned one more corner, only to come to a halt. I could see the woman, the one with the man. She was standing in front of me. I could feel something push into my chest and I froze. How the hell did she get in front of me?

Pants sounded from behind me—could these things even GET out of breath? —before a voice sounding like the breeze wafted over me. I slowly turned my head, keeping half an eye on the figure in front of me even as I took in the one behind me. The other one was bent over, but quickly straightened, stepping into my line of sight.

Well, this was stupid.

I could see he was speaking and frowned. I slowly tilted my head, trying to pay attention.

One word floated to me. For once I recognized it and my eyes widened.

"Felix."

"How do you know Felix? You don't plan to hurt him, do you?" I growled and the man, who seemed to understand, quickly put his hands up, waving them as he shook his head. Whatever was pushing into my chest was pulled away. I spared a moment to see the woman take one step back, as if shocked. I turned away, refocusing on the man. "What about Felix?"

The man seemed to concentrate before slumping. After a moment, I heard rustling and then yelped as something was pushed into my grasp. It was a piece of paper. Once more, the sound of footsteps rang out and I tilted my head up in time to see both figures retreating. I stared after them in silence before unfolding the paper. Scribbled, unceremoniously and in a hurry, was the word 'Danger.'

Felix was in danger? From what? And why were ghosts warning me? When did they even get the paper or write this? When could I even hear what they were saying? That was the first time I could recall hearing words from them... a distinct word. Was it my imagination or something else?

I shook my head before hurrying toward the nearby store. I bought a shirt and quickly threw it on, putting my soiled one into the bag before hurrying back toward Mira and Felix. They were probably starting to wonder where I was.

I got back to them as Felix was staring at Mira, their faces inches apart and both their cheeks a bright red. Should I interrupt? Part of me didn't want to, but, unfortunately, Mira seemed to notice me and jerked away, blushing brilliantly. Felix almost fell over before spotting me. He scurried to his seat, brushing his hair down. "Oh, hey, man, what took so long?"

I raised an eyebrow, deigning not to respond. I tossed him a bottle, causing him to slightly stumble in his catch. My thoughts were going a mile a minute as I tried to piece through what the figure meant. Should I tell Felix and Mira? Would they believe me if I said I could hear the figures? I was shocked Felix and Mira already believed this much, I'm not sure how much more they can believe before they started thinking I was pulling their leg. It was worrying.

"Dude, are you okay?" The words jerked me out of my thoughts. Felix was watching me with a worried expression, water bottle in his grasp.

I opened my mouth to reply and it was only then I realized how much I was shaking. I closed my mouth and grinned instead, shrugging. I quickly tried to catch my breath. "Yeah, it was just a struggle to get through the crowd." Not necessarily a lie.

"If you say so…"

"Oh come on, lay off him. It's been a crazy morning." Mira stood, waving at Felix before turning toward me. She must have been worried if she wasn't a blushing mess from the almost kiss. "Still, maybe we should go home, you don't look too good."

"I'm fine. We already said we would spend the day out, right?" Yeah, spend the day. Those figures didn't seem to be bothering us anymore and I didn't think we were in danger right now. Plus, what danger would Felix even be in if those things couldn't touch him? No, I would figure this out. I didn't want to worry them.

Plus, another part of me was whispering that I shouldn't involve them anymore. This was my problem, not theirs.

Mira and Felix exchanged looks before Mira let out a sigh and

Felix grinned. "Called it."

"I was almost certain he would say yes to going home," Mira muttered.

It took me a moment to figure out what they were talking about. But when I did, I did not hold back on making sure they were aware of how unamused I was. "Were you two betting on me or something?"

"No…" Mira trailed off before clapping her hands. "Anyway, I think we still have that log ride to do. I call the front!"

I found myself being dragged forward and chuckled. My thoughts flickered to the little note, stuck deep in my pocket. Who? And why? If they could leave notes, why not give Felix or his mother a note?

Something wasn't right about this situation, more than usual.

I wished I had at least some idea what was going on, but I wasn't that lucky. As if on cue, a pounding headache shot through me and I winced, fingers massaging my temples for a moment before I quickly pushed them back down. Now if these damn headaches would just go away.

Chapter Five

Thankfully, the rest of the day went a little better, and by the end, I was able to sort out my thoughts enough that I realized I should probably tell them. Even if they didn't believe me, at least they would know. It was on the way home when I decided to let them know about what happened, especially now that those figures weren't hovering around us. I figured Felix might as well know that he was in danger. Though what type of danger, I hadn't a clue.

Mira stared at me in shock as Felix frowned, his furrowed brow deep and prominent. "So, you are saying the same one who hurt you was right behind me at the park, trying to get my attention? And you decided not to tell either one of us, for the rest of the day?"

I nodded, only to jerk back as he glared at me. "What?"

"Why didn't you mention something sooner? Is this because I researched your symptoms behind your back?"

"No, that's not..." I trailed off, receiving an unamused expression from Felix as Mira watched from behind, neither interfering or helping. She seemed annoyed too.

"Oh. You didn't think we would believe you, did you?" He seemed to realize that a bit too fast... and my wince was enough to show him he was right. He massaged the bridge of his nose as Mira pursed her lips.

"Ki, I'm not sure why you thought we wouldn't believe you." Mira spoke up. "I mean, I get that you were probably worried about us, but..."

I turned away and crossed my arms over my chest. "It seemed

ridiculous, okay? The fact that I could hear those things, that they could give me a warning. That it was for Felix, who they couldn't touch…" I trailed off.

Silence enveloped us, even as we came to a halt at the side of the road, one or two cars passed by, but other than that it was quiet. I heard Felix sigh.

"Ki, I don't know what to tell you." I peered over to see Felix as he ruffled his hair, a pained expression on his face. "Well, other than that was stupid and I get it, but you should have still told us. What if they hurt you?"

"I guess that's fair," I admitted.

Felix sighed, but he let it go. "Hm…" Felix rubbed the back of his neck as he grimaced. "This seems all so complicated. One of them gave you a note with the word danger? And you were able to at least hear them say my name? Other than being ridiculous, as you said, it's kind of worrying."

"Really?" Mira looked curious, glancing between us.

I hesitated, unsure how to respond before I shrugged, continuing on down the street as the others scurried to catch up. "I get why you're worried. I am too. Up until this point, I only generally seemed to sense those things and now they can touch me and I can hear them?" I shivered. "That just adds a whole new level of creepy that I have been trying hard to ignore."

"Could your power, or whatever this is, be getting stronger?"

I winced. "You make it sound like I'm a physic or something."

"Well, dude, you are talking about hearing spirits speaking." That expression couldn't have been any more deadpan. Felix definitely thought I was crazy at this point. Good thing he knew me since we were kids. As crazy as I might sound, at least he'd stick by me, as he oh so kindly reminded me earlier. It was thanks to him, really, that I met Mira a few years ago, as strange as that might seem. Still, the two of them were the best friends I could ask for. Case in point: when Mira put her hands to her lips to think over what I said instead of pushing away the fact that I could now hear spirits.

"Hm… what I wonder is why they gave you a note. Can we see it?"

I shrugged and pulled it out, only to pause and stare at the paper. It was still crinkled from where I folded it, but… I flipped it over and then back before wincing. I slowly tilted my head up toward my two friends. This was not helping my case.

After all, the page was completely blank.

"Okay, dude, that's creepy." Felix was more than a little perturbed, staring at the paper as Mira slowly blinked. She grabbed the paper, fiddling with it.

I was just glad they didn't seem to question whether I told the truth or not, because right now, I wouldn't really be able to defend myself. Mira gave it back to me, humming thoughtfully. After a bit, she nodded. "Maybe it was imprinted."

"Imprinted?" I couldn't help but ask and she grinned.

"You know, like how ghosts can influence things, like flickering lights and moving items? Maybe they imprinted a thought on the paper and it faded after they left? Maybe that's why only you could read it and why it's not there anymore."

At this point, even as farfetched as the idea was, it was the only plausible assumption we had, assuming they were ghosts.

I was definitely starting to believe that was the case, considering they couldn't interact with most people, they were vaporous and seemed to only be able to do certain things to us and others.

"That leads us to the final question, why is Felix in danger? Why just him?" Mira peered over toward him, expression determined and angered, to my surprise. "He hasn't done a thing."

Felix seemed like he wanted to bite his lip, moving it in and out of his mouth before he let out a sigh and shrugged. "No idea. I would think Ki would be in more danger than me, considering he can interact with these things."

"Yeah, but he can also see them and defend himself from them, we can't." Mira pointed out. "Then again, they can't seem to hurt us, right?"

"Not that I've seen," I admitted and Mira seemed to sigh in relief. As much as the girl loved ghost stories, she was not really much for getting completely involved in one. I didn't blame her, it wasn't fun.

"Well, as long as we watch our backs, we should be fine." Felix leaned forward, piercings shining in the evening light.

"But watch our backs from what?" Mira snapped. "It's so vague, we're going to be jumping at our shadows."

Already doing that, thank you. Oh, we were talking about Felix? That too.

"I know, but what else do we do? The only thing I can think of has to do with researching Ki's condition, but then that leads us back to him being in danger, not me."

I frowned, he brought up a good point and Mira seemed to agree, her mouth snapping shut before she sighed, arms going limp. "All right, just stay safe." She drew to a stop. Her house was right beside us, only a block or so away from mine and four blocks from Felix's. It was a beautiful two-story house with white shutters and a pristine lawn. Mira waved good-bye before slipping into the house. A few minutes later, we arrived at my house and Felix turned to me. "Dude, I might advise locking the door," he trailed off before glancing away. "And thanks for getting him away." He hesitated for a long moment before seeming to resign himself. "Do you know how weird it feels? I kept getting this cold chill down my spine, it was freaky."

"So, you could sense him?" I was only partially surprised at that when Felix nodded, returning his attention to me.

"I didn't want to admit it in front of Mira, since it was faint, nothing really concrete, but it was the first time I felt that. If you are dealing with that all the time, then I want to help you. We'll figure out what's going on, okay? Just hang tight." He went to turn before he gestured over his shoulder. "And, hey, trust us next time, will ya?"

He seemed to be waiting for a response. I chuckled. "All right, all right. I get it."

He waved, heading towards his home, disappearing down the street as my smile dropped. I wanted to tell him it was okay, a part of me was screaming to stop him, but I watched him go, feeling my stomach twist and drop.

What else could I do?

Chapter Six

That night, I was restless. I swore I had a dream or something, but I couldn't remember it.

I felt a gentle touch and blearily blinked. Staring down at me was a girl with olive-green eyes in a heart-shaped face, a fond smile sat on her lips, a vaguely familiar glint in her expression that spoke of something. Short black hair that was probably cut by someone without a mirror trailed past her pale face and yet... she was familiar. She met my gaze and for a split second, warmth and joy flooded through me as her lips formed into an ecstatic smile.

She opened her mouth and I furrowed my brow. She was saying something, I knew she was, but...

A throbbing pulse slid through my head and both hands darted up as I cried out. I felt arms around me in a tight hug as I curled inwards. This, it feels...

As soon as the strange feeling came, it disappeared.

For a brief moment I could have sworn I heard Mother call for something, maybe to ask if I was still up, but it was so hard to hear anything through the throbbing ringing in my skull. The pain intensified and as I pushed into whatever was holding me, I could hear another call from downstairs, indistinct. A set of soft fingers traced through my hair, almost comforting as I trembled trying and failing to get rid of the pain.

I faintly heard the pounding of feet before my door slammed open. The arms wrapped around me retracted as another person ran forward. "Kieran!" My mom's voice rang out as I fell onto my side, whatever was supporting me now gone. She reached over and held my head as I whimpered. I couldn't help it, it hurt!

I could still feel another gaze on me. I tried to focus on them, the figures I sensed earlier. They were blurry, but I still spotted someone. Someone wispy and white. How? Was it the same person? No, it couldn't be, but I didn't hear anything else, and they felt familiar. The girl slipped forward, placing a hand in mine and, without really thinking too much about it, I held on tight. The grip was comforting and finally the pain passed and I lay down, panting and exhausted. Mother held me tightly, shaking. I really worried her there.

I felt the fingers retract, followed by footsteps. It didn't take much for me to realize she, that girl, left. Finally, I pulled away from Mom as she continued to hold me. "Sorry."

"Ki…" Mother pulled back, looking me right in the eyes. "I know I promised not to bring you to the hospital, to have your father watch you like he asked, but—"

"No! I can't! I'm fine. See?" The words came out of my mouth, faster than I realized I could even speak. It didn't even sound like me, not with the fluttery and high-pitched voice of panic that suddenly consumed me.

Mother quickly rested her hands on my shoulders, conflicted. "I don't know why you and your father are so afraid of the hospital, you never used to be…" For a brief moment, confusion shone on her face before disappearing. She seemed to mutter under her breath for a second before returning her attention to me.

"I know, I'm sorry, but please? I'm fine now, it was just momentary."

Mother pursed her lips before pulling away. "All right. I'll only agree on two conditions."

I perked up and listened as she raised her fingers, curling them in respectively. "One, tell me whenever you feel a headache or something coming on." I opened my mouth, but she continued, steamrolling over my argument. "And two, I want you to take it easy for the next week or so. No going to the park or doing anything overly strenuous, simple meet-ups are okay as long as you talk to me first, understood? I'll have your father check to make sure you're okay. After that, you're free to do what you want."

I wanted to argue, but Mom was stubborn. I let out a sigh and nodded. She smiled, relieved, and gently rubbed my head. "I know you hate the idea, but I'm just worried about you, we both are, okay?"

"Yeah, sorry."

She nodded. "I was going to ask you something if you were still up, but don't worry about it, okay?" Oh, so she had been calling to see if I was awake. I sent her a tired smile and she gave me one in return before she stepped out the door, closing it softly with a click behind her. I stared at the wooden frame for a bit before slowly laying back down, my gaze turned to the window, thoughts flipping to the figure from before. They had never been that clear before and she seemed... I pulled on a piece of my hair and examined it in the dim light of the moon, inky black, similar to the girl's.

Was it an ancestor? A ghost from before the new technology? What was she doing here and why could I see her? Even for just a brief moment? I sighed and sat up, leaning my elbow against the window sill, chin sitting in my palm as I gazed outside. The moon was full tonight. Its bright light shone through and coated the ground in a silvery layer. My thoughts whirled, unable to let me go to sleep. Who was she? I felt like I should know that person, but why? I didn't know how long I sat there with those thoughts. At one point I could have sworn I heard footsteps as mother headed to bed.

I sighed, realizing I wasn't getting anything done now. I grabbed the landline—why were they even called that anyway? —and pulled it up to my ear. It was late enough that Felix's mom was probably still at work. The dial tone buzzed back at me as I tangled my fingers in the cord. Supposedly, a few years ago, we used cell phones, electronic devices that could be carried around to call others, but they were seen as problematic, causing disturbances, until finally all were cut off and people reverted back to landlines. I wasn't sure if that was necessarily the case, but it didn't bother me. Things still worked.

Finally, Felix picked up with a loud yawn. "Dude, it's one in the freaking morning."

I blinked, noting the time on the nearby clock before grinning sheepishly. "Uh... whoops. Sorry about that."

I could almost hear the sigh and the ruffling of sleepwear indicating Felix was rubbing the back of his neck. "Well, why did you decide to call at this time?"

"I..." Why did I call him? I furrowed my brow before letting out a sigh. "I was wondering, can I get your help?"

"With what?" Felix's tone was more controlled. He was probably scowling, leaning against the wall with legs and arms crossed.

"I think there was another one tonight, but I actually got a chance to examine her, what she looked like. I was wondering if you could help me do some research on people from before the new technology."

I heard a faint humming sound from the other end before he let out a sigh. "Sure, I'll contact Mira. Considering how ghost-obsessed she is, she should be able to help."

"Thanks."

"No problem, I'll call you in the morning, get some sleep."

"Er... right." I grinned and lay down the phone. I felt a little better now that I was meeting up with them tomorrow. Mom said I couldn't do parties or anything strenuous. She also mentioned I could still meet up with them. Hopefully that would be enough for her.

~ * ~

The next day, I threw on a short-sleeved shirt and cargo shorts. A hat sat snuggled on my head, helping against the bright morning sun that gleamed down at me. It took a bit more work than I would have liked to admit to convince Mom that I could meet up with Felix and Mira, but after I promised her I would be back soon and that we were only going to the library, she relinquished, agreeing that it did follow the guidelines she had placed. I crossed my arms, leaning against the gatepost at the end of my driveway. I scanned the road, before spotting Mira. She waved at me, grinning as she hurried up to me. "So you met your ancestor?"

Wow, talk about getting to the point. I shrugged and she perked up, excited.

"Geez, calm down." At least she wasn't blushing this time as Felix stepped up to us, carrying a bag. If there was one good thing about all this, it meant those two actually spent more time around each other. Boy, was I glad that their shyness or whatever was starting to fade. It was a real hassle. Though now I was worried that all I was going to see was them being overly affectionate. I wasn't sure which was worst, to be honest.

He scrutinized me before nodding, more an affirmative than anything. "Anyway, since you decided to call me at some ungodly hour, I decided to grace you with my presence by helping with all of this."

I gave him my heaviest deadpan expression and even Mira seemed unimpressed. Felix shrugged. "Well, had to try." He gestured and, after exchanging looks with Mira, walked down the lane. After some time, we found ourselves at the library once more, right back in the same corner as before. It was busier this time, people wandering in and out of the bookshelves and quiet chatter filling the air. Mira grabbed a couple books and placed them on the table while Felix worked on the computer. There really wasn't much to go on, the books weren't really historical. I believed all our history books were now either online or kept in a governmental building secured for safekeeping.

You would think one might question that and a lot of other stuff, but, well, we didn't and I didn't know why. Finally, Mira let out a sigh and dropped her book before leaning back, arms falling over the back of her chair. "God, this is boring."

I shrugged, flipping through another book that seemed to be talking about ghosts of the past or something. I wasn't really reading it, so much as skimming. Most of the books were junk anyway and the few good ones were either fictional stories or had been damaged because of misuse.

Felix let out a sigh, pushing away from the computer and turning to us. "Well, that was a waste."

"You didn't get anything either?" Mira asked, curiosity clear in her voice.

"Well, I mean, history really isn't important, so no one comments on it and there is not much to find online regarding heritage or anything. Well, not except government-related things and I'm NOT going to try hacking those again." He shrugged. He turned to me. "You mentioned she looked like you. How old was she again?"

I opened my mouth and paused before furrowing my brow. I didn't really know... "She seemed, like, my age? Maybe? Probably our age," I responded, voice hesitant.

Mira's expression softened. "I wonder how she died then, if she died so young."

I shook my head. "Don't know, she seemed really rough, ragged cut hair, tattered clothes, all of that."

"Poor girl," Mira muttered before she sat up, determination shining. "But maybe we can find something! After all, she would have probably died around here, maybe there is a specific space she haunts. I mean, if you spotted her easily, maybe we might be able to sense her!"

I wasn't so sure about that, but I didn't want to argue with Mira when she was in this mood. Even Felix seemed hesitant to disagree. He let out a sigh and shrugged. "It's worth a shot. We're not getting anything this way."

"But how do we find her?" I leaned forward, gesturing. "It's kind of hard to tell them apart when they're..." I didn't want to say ghost-like, so I let my words trail off. They seemed to get it anyway.

"Well..." Mira seemed at a loss. Felix frowned, hands to the back of his neck as he tilted himself backward in the chair, staring at the ceiling. After a moment, he spun and started typing at the computer for a while. Silence enveloped the area as we waited. Mira tapped her chin before she turned to me. "I know you said you didn't want to check out any haunted houses, but..."

I went to open my mouth to argue, then frowned. Honestly, at this point, that might not be a bad idea. I let out a sigh and Mira, recognizing what it was, let out a little cheer. Felix looked up and then, upon spotting our expressions, rolled his eyes. "Good thing I was already looking into it."

He turned the chair, hands draping over the back. "We could go to the haunted amusement park, but that's quite a ways away so the next best thing would probably be this." He gestured toward the screen before continuing, "There's a haunted house, one from before the pandemic, that still stands not that far past the edge of town. It's only about ten minutes away by bike. It's a two story and every time someone tries to knock it down, accidents and tragedies occur, even now. I think that would be a good place to start."

"Is that close enough though?" I asked and Mira frowned before shrugging.

Felix shook his head. "Probably not, but that is the closest occurrence that seems consistent. Maybe from there, we can figure it out?"

"If you say so…" Why did I feel like this would end badly?

"I'll grab some supplies. Why don't we meet up tomorrow and—"

I shook my head and grimaced. "We'll have to wait till next week. Mother is kind of keeping a close eye on me. It was hard enough just to convince her I could go with you two today."

Mira and Felix raised their eyebrows before Felix threw his arms up. "Only you. Geez, all right, so next week, we'll meet up, bright and early, sound good?"

I shrugged, not sure what to say. After making sure we had a set time, we went our separate ways. I trailed down the street, scanning the streets without much worry. There wasn't any ghost in sight, which was a relief. At the last corner before heading home, I spotted a police officer holding a strange device, almost like a scanner. Why did it seem familiar? I winced as the image of my dad holding a similar device flashed through my mind. Had Dad been working on it? But when? I shook my head and noted as the officer spotted me for a second before returning his attention to whatever device he held, continuing on his way. I shrugged and stepped into the house. After convincing my mom that, yes, I was all right and no, I didn't go to anywhere besides the library, I went up to my room and sat down at the desk, staring at the fixed lamp light. This was going to be a long week.

Chapter Seven

Damn, I thought it was bad to be grounded during school; to have an overprotective mother when it was vacation was not fun. Especially since Dad's work had increased lately and he was rarely around. Still, I didn't blame either one of them. I was just bored.

I pulled my bike out of the garage. The tires were still good and the chrome shone under the bright morning sun. After making sure the seat was adjusted accordingly, I slipped on and took off. The wind felt great against my skin; the backpack sat comfortably against my back.

I stopped in front of the school, waiting for the others. Felix arrived right after, a shoulder pack slung haphazardly on. He sent me a wave before slowing to a halt. "Still not here?"

Assuming he meant Mira, I shook my head and turned toward where our friend would be coming from. As I watched, I noticed a police car slowly passing by, almost crawling.

"Why are there so many police around lately?" Felix questioned, watching the car quietly.

"Don't know." I heard the squeal of tires and jerked in time to avoid Mira as she sped toward us, heavy backpack pulling her down.

I yelped as she slammed to a halt, almost crashing into me. She overbalanced for a second before recovering and giving us a wide grin. "Sorry, guys!"

"Damn, woman, did you have to almost run us over?"

"Hey, who knows, might make you look better."

"Burn." I grinned as Felix hissed, clearly annoyed. He wrapped an arm around her shoulder, ruffling her hair. She let out a squawk of protest before giggling.

She turned to me after pushing away from Felix, patting her cheeks to get rid of her deep blush. "You guys ready to go? I have all our things."

I would ask, but I didn't think I wanted to know. Even Felix decided to stay silent, instead taking the lead and heading down the street at a steady pace. I followed with Mira at my side. She hummed, a big grin on her lips. I didn't know how she was so enthusiastic about this.

"This is so exciting! I might even be able to sense a real ghost."

"You're absolutely crazy!" I heard Felix call. Mira stuck out her tongue before returning her attention to me.

I had nothing to say to her and she seemed to realize because she returned to gushing about ghosts and what she would do if she could sense one and all that jazz.

I was only grateful that, if we did come across any of those figures, they wouldn't be able to hurt either Mira or Felix. I wouldn't be half as willing to go, if not for that.

The sunlight overhead faded as we continued on, the sky covered in thick gray clouds with weak light shining through. We left the suburbs and went into an area covered in trees. Another police car zipped by before all of us pulled to a stop. Felix observed the place we stopped which was near the side of the road with woods on either side, frowning slightly before stepping off the bike. He slipped into the undergrowth, gesturing for us to follow. I slid off mine, with Mira, and we both followed him. "The road there is blocked by a wide gate, but I talked to a few people."

"Ah, the ones who said they went there themselves? And didn't find anything?" Mira leaned forward. "I heard there's a gaping opening in the wall to one side. No one knows how it got there, but no one has the courage or time to repair it."

"Exactly, so we'll use that to get in." Felix grinned as he leaned his bike against one of the trees. I followed suit, staying quiet as Mira and Felix led us through the trees. Usually, I would join in the conversation, but I didn't feel good. My head was throbbing and my stomach felt queasy. I hoped I wasn't coming down with a bug.

It didn't take long to cut through the trees. Before us stood a tall brick structure, this must have been the wall they were talking about. Off to one side was a jagged break in the wall, as if someone smashed through it with Thor's hammer or something. I MIGHT play too many games, sue me.

Mira's expression lit up and she ran over, slipping through the opening with Felix yelling after her. I stared at the brick wall, shifting my gaze up to spot the second floor, peeking over it. Cracked windows and creeping vines decorated the once beautiful mansion. There were still hints of what it must have been like before it was abandoned. I followed after them, hearing the stone crack under my boots. The building stood over us, the architecture quite brilliant and elegant, though I couldn't think of a name for half of the architectural stuff even if I tried.

The lawn was overridden with ankle-high grass and wildflowers all the way up to the locked and chained door. Mira grew quiet as we walked. The clouds overhead seemed more overbearing, growing darker as a storm threatened. Those were rare, but not unprecedented. Too bad we hadn't thought to check the weather today. Hopefully, it was just a summer storm. Those were usually pretty quick to pass.

Felix gestured to us, expression downturned into a slight frown. We moved to one side of the house, finding a wooden door where the locks were broken.

Mira crept forward and pushed at the door. "It's open." Her voice grew quiet as we moved. It just seemed to fit the atmosphere.

"Well, let's go." I hurried forward, deciding just to get it over with. We stepped into the house, the wood creaking with each step. Mira followed behind with Felix in the back. The normally brave boy was downright timid as he stepped through the doorway. The hallway in front of us was dark, the only light glowing softly from the entrance and two porthole-like windows. We traversed down the hallway as wind started to whistle through the doorway from the growing storm. Mira reached into her bag and pulled out three flashlights, handing them over.

My surprise must have been obvious when she passed it over to me, because she grinned sheepishly and said, "I might have been planning this for a while."

"That's Mira for you." Felix flung his arm over her shoulder, pulling her into a side hug before lightly tapping the flashlight on her head. "Thanks for these, good work." The bright smile must have made Felix hesitate, because his next few words were stammered as he pulled away and continued, "Now let's explore this place before you go ballistic and leave us to examine this place by yourself."

She stuck her tongue out before all three of us quickly clicked the flashlights on.

The powerful beams pierced through the dark corners, showing a doorway near the end of the hallway. I stepped forward, opening it and peering through. On the other side was a kitchen. Grimy windows sat over cracked porcelain. The weak light shone through, casting flickering shadows. I heard a sound and glanced back. "Hey, did anyone put a backstop against the door?"

Felix stared at me while Mira followed my line of sight, the only one able to properly peer through the doorway. Her face paled and she sent me a guilty expression. Ah, so that sound was the door swinging shut from the wind. I was hoping that wasn't the case. I recollected my worried thoughts and turned to the kitchen. I stepped over the ceramic tiles, hearing the click clack of my boots. Felix moved off to one side, flashlight flickering over the empty, yet open cupboards.

"Who left the house like this?" Mira seemed to be observing everything, curiosity clear in her voice. "Isn't there usually certain parameters when it comes to leaving?"

"Well, except for if they left suddenly, died or something else," I pointed out as I stepped to the other side of the room. I was not going to lie, part of me was relieved we haven't seen any of those figures. Of course, that didn't help the jittery feeling that just seemed to stick with me as the windows rattled from the growing storm. The door was slightly ajar into the next room which seemed like a storage area. Dust lingered in the air as my flashlight moved over the decrepit boxes. I heard a rumbling sound in the distance and the light pitter patter of rain. I gulped and pulled back.

I really wanted to leave. Mira seemed excited though, almost shining in her enthusiasm. "This is perfect! So exciting and intense!"

"If we don't end up hurt," Felix muttered as he joined her. "Though I do admit, this is pretty cool."

Great, two against one. "Let's keep going." I stepped away from the storage room and toward the middle of the room. I passed by the old stove and a couple cabinets before stopping in front of an elaborate door. I glanced at Mira and Felix, who gave encouraging thumbs up in unison. I rolled my eyes, feeling a little better. I turned the handle and opened it. On the other side was a dining room. A table, covered in a white cloth and a few chairs covered in that same grayish white fabric, were set up in the middle of the room. A once pristine crystal chandelier hung from the high overarching ceiling. A line of cracked and grimy windows exposed us to a little bit of wind and rain from outside. I shivered as a chill slipped up my spine. Mold covered part of the floor where the rain had hit over the years, grime clung to the walls and wind moved around the rafters overhead, creating a slight howl.

The room was huge with two more doorways, again: one at the opposite end and one halfway through. I decided to go to the closer one first. I stepped up to it as I heard sounds of awe and curiosity from behind me. I felt the handle, surprised to find it hard to turn. I grimaced, before finally getting a good grip. I turned it and peered through. Now, at this point, I could practically scream how stupid we were being. After all, wouldn't we know if someone was here by now? And if it was someone like the girl from before, wouldn't she seek me out if I was nearby? But I kept myself silent. I checked on what Mira and Felix were doing regarding this situation. Mira's hands were clasped together, a wide grin curling over her lips as she meandered around the table and stared up at the rafters. It was hard to tell whether she was scared and trying not to show it, or if she was truly fascinated by all of this. Felix was a bit more reasonable, examining the room with a slight frown.

"This place is huge—"

"You better not say we should split up," Mira interjected,

stepping up to me as I peered through the now opened door. I didn't hear her next words as I stared down the decrepit hallway. A figure raced past the opposite end of the hallway. I couldn't tell who it was or even whether it was male or female. I opened the door a bit wider and, against my better judgement, proceeded down the hallway. Another figure, this one going just a bit slower, meandered past the end of the hallway. He, I thought it was a he, spotted me for a moment before he kept going. I heard scrambling before Mira grabbed my arm. "What are you doing?"

I glanced back at her before she shone her light forward. I followed her gaze. Before me, inches from where my foot hovered, was a jagged hole in the floor. I gulped and pulled my leg back. Felix came right up behind me, almost resting his chin on my shoulder to spot what we were examining. "That could have been nasty. I forgot how old this place was. There are probably a lot of areas that could crumble at a moment's notice. Still, what were you doing? Mira just said—"

"Not to get separated, I know, but I saw two people at the other end." I shrugged as Felix frowned. Mira pursed her lips, a hint of nervousness showing in her tense posture for the first time since we arrived. "I couldn't tell who the first one was, but the second one seemed like a male." I glanced back at them. "That means there are more here, but…"

I shook my head, noticing the slight frown on Mira's lips before pulling them both back to the dining room. At least we had some light from there. I looked down at my hand, only then noting that the bulb was dying. I lightly hit it against my palm. That was why I hadn't noticed the hole: that, and my distraction with the second figure. Why was he walking by so leisurely when the first was practically racing through the halls?

The light grew once more as I turned toward Mira and Felix. "All right, so I'll leave it up to you two what we do. We can continue and find out why these two are here or we can leave. I will say, the first one I noticed could have been her or someone else, I couldn't tell." I didn't want to scare them more than they already were by mentioning the weird inconsistency of one racing through the halls while the other meandered.

After all, I was barely keeping myself from panicking. What if this was just a huge mistake? I knew they would be all right, but what about me?

I wasn't in the mood to be grabbed and tossed around by some vaporous ghost, no thank you! I wished my tongue worked enough to tell them just to forget about this. I brought it up and all, but I could tell that my words only seemed to excite Mira and even Felix seemed a bit curious. Unfortunately, my tongue was stuck to the roof of my mouth, even as I tried to swallow.

"That's fine, they don't really affect us. So you're the only one we need to watch out for." Felix gestured.

Thanks for the reminder. Not like I had already just thought of it.

Mira shook her head, giving Felix a glare. "Don't you know anything? If it is a ghost, then they should be able to affect the environment. Remember that note Ki got? We have to watch out for that." Mira waved her hand. "Honestly, you need to do more research next time." She shook her head before examining the doorway we just passed through. "All right, so that way won't work. Let's try another way through. Maybe we can find them and figure out what's going on."

Part of me wondered if she was right. After all, if ghosts did affect the environment, then couldn't Mira and Felix get hurt? The thought sent my already semi-frazzled mind into panic, and yet, as terrible as it was, another part of me was fascinated, excited to learn more about the figures. I hoped to find something here, and as such, I moved a little slower, following behind, thoughts swirling as we moved up to the third doorway. Just as Mira pushed it open, I could have sworn I heard something, a cut-off scream. I shivered, pushing away the thought as wind whistled through the rafters above, creating a very similar sound.

I hurried up as Mira's light beamed into the next room, a living room this time. White cloths that turned gray over time covered the couches and side tables, causing the room to gleam a weak silver from the windows. The rain, more a subtle presence up till this point, decided to finally break loose as a crash of thunder sounded outside, coinciding with another sound I didn't recognize. Felix jumped as Mira shone her light around the room. Again, there wasn't much else beside dust, debris and wood. In a way you could almost say it was boring, if not for the driving storm, cloudy darkness and the thought that two people were here that only I could sense.

I gulped as I watched Mira and Felix go in separate directions around the room. I stayed by the doorway, gaze flitting back into the lit dining room, the sharp smell of decaying wood and something that smelled faintly of rot met my nose. There weren't many places we or those other people could go. I heard a loud creak and popping noises and jumped, scanning the room.

"That must have been the pipes," Felix muttered, voice shifting up a few notches. "That's all."

Ah-huh, and I was able to sense dead people from before the new technology. I finally convinced myself to move away from the door as Mira and Felix convened in the middle of the room.

"You know, now might be a good time to call it quits," Felix broke in with a weak smile. "No one besides those people Ki thought he saw have appeared, and this is almost characteristic of a horror story, I mean, stormy weather and all... plus two people at that. Couldn't that mean they're not the people we're searching for?"

Mira pursed her lips and then sighed. "Sorry," she muttered. "I really thought this would help."

I smiled and waved my hand. "It's no problem, believe me, I appreciate the fact that you even believe me."

"Of course we do!" Mira cut in, even before Felix could open his mouth, though from his expression, he seemed like he wanted to say the same thing. "You're our friend! We wouldn't just leave you behind like that!"

I felt the grin widen before a pounding headache slammed through me. I let out a yelp as both hands darted to my head. I heard Mira cry out in surprise as Felix hurried to me. I felt fingers grip my arms as I curled inwards. This wasn't good.

I heard a creak, even through my dazed senses. My gaze was bleary as I forced myself to peer upward.

White gleaming irises stared back at me from a grinning face.

When had I turned around? I stared at the figure standing in the doorway to the dining room. It was the same figure who was moving so leisurely before. Wispy white hair and clothes sat over a tiny frame. He appeared sickly, thin to the point of emaciated.

My attention drifted to his hands. Two thin sharp knives, white as well, sat in his hands, as if they were just a pencil or something. He held them way too easily and... faintly I heard a dripping sound that had nothing to do with the rain. White fell from the knives, slowly disappearing as it descended.

"Um... just curiosity," I managed to choke out as the grin widened and the man cocked his head to one side. "If there was a ghost with knives that might have blood on them, do you think we should run?"

The man opened his mouth, wind whistling through the room.

"Uh... what do you mean?" Felix's voice hitched and it was then the man's gaze flicked to my friend. I barely caught Felix's wavering gaze out of my periphery, his attention swiveling to near where I was staring. Mira was beside me, taking a step forward to stand in front of me.

I didn't think much about it, just grabbed both my friends' hands and scrabbled sideways. I heard a yelp, followed by a cry. My footsteps pounded over the rugged floor as I pushed through a doorway on the right side of the room. Felix pulled his hand out, keeping pace with me as Mira followed behind, her footsteps ringing behind me as we hurried around the corner and found a flight of stairs. Without thinking twice, I bounded up them and through another doorway. Once the other two were through, I slammed it shut, leaning against it with all my weight. A moment later, I heard a loud thud, followed by scratching. A wispy sound reached my ears and I shivered, adrenaline pumping. Felix hurried up, carrying a chair. He pushed it under the handle as it turned. Mira was off to one side, searching around wildly before stepping next to a thin bookcase. She grimaced and then started pushing. Felix seemed to realize because he hurried over. Thankfully, within moments, they had it pushed in front of the door and me out of the way. We stood away from the door, backs pushing into the curtained wall at the opposite end of the room, a thin grime-filled window sat to my left, rain pounding against the glass. After a few moments, the sounds died out and I finally took a breath.

"What the hell was that?" Felix's voice was now pitched as a soprano. I didn't blame him, at least he could talk.

"Ki, what was that?" Mira asked, voice shaking and on the verge of breaking, hand covering her arm tightly as her breaths became more panicked. She was trembling. I blinked, as Mira, who managed to retain her flashlight, watched me with a thousand-yard stare. The light from the beam shone against her skin, showcasing the bead of red trailing down the pale flesh.

I stepped forward, suddenly feeling very shaky. I gripped her arm and she winced, but didn't pull back. "Felix?" My voice trembled as I called out to him.

Felix stepped over and grabbed Mira's light before shining it down at her arm. A thin cut traced over the skin and I realized, like a stone plummeting through my stomach, that those knives, that person, actually managed to hurt her. Which meant... "He can hurt us." My voice might have cracked a bit there, but I didn't particularly care. "That ghost, thing, can hurt us." I was trying to push the thought away by repeating it, but that didn't work considering the panic from earlier was now up to eleven. My head pounded like a final combo in a videogame, the rhythm erratic at best. I could hear stumbling footsteps and jerked, glancing toward Felix who was at Mira's side, plopping down beside her onto the dust covered floor, causing it to billow up as he took her arm and examined the wound.

I guess I wasn't the only one struggling to breathe through my panic; the other two didn't appear to be doing much better.

Chapter Eight

Eventually, Mira took a deep breath and turned to me.

"Thank you." Mira's voice caught me off guard as I glanced up at her. Her smile was shaky, but visible. Felix, who seemed to be out of it for a moment longer, shook his head and reached into her backpack. Mira was definitely as prepared as we thought, because he pulled out a roll of bandages and quickly wrapped them around her arm. Mira quietly thanked him before turning back to me. "If you hadn't pulled us out of the way, if you hadn't seen him when you did—" she gestured to her arm, "—I think this would be a lot worse." She gulped and I turned away.

I wasn't about to argue with her. Even though I was the reason we were there. However, her thanks helped pull me out of my panic attack. I quickly focused on something else, anything else so I didn't slide in again. After all, panicking wasn't going to help at this juncture.

"So, what now? Mister dangerous guy is still outside." Felix pulled away, his own panicked breaths slowing slightly as he stood and moved toward the window. "We can't just sit in here. He probably knows this house better than we do. He will find a way in, or just wait us out. Plus, the only one who can sense him is Ki and I highly doubt he missed that."

Mira nodded, shifting into a more comfortable position on the floor, ignoring the congregating dust. "I know what you mean." She patted the ground and, after a moment of hesitation, I joined her. "It would be suicide to just go back outside without some sort of plan, and Ki can't look everywhere. There has to be some way for us to know."

"Could you hear him?" I decided to bring up, desperately trying to think of any way that I could help them. Mira expression shifted, confused, but Felix snapped his fingers, what I was trying to say dawning on him.

"That could work, it's not as convenient as your ability, but it should help keep us alive while we get out of here."

"From practically the middle of the house too," Mira announced and I winced. Yeah, whoops. Who runs away UP a staircase? Not my best idea. "What do we listen for though?"

"Footsteps," Felix pointed out. "I was able to hear the faint hint of footsteps even with our own frantic pace. After all, the floors still creak accordingly. If we stay close to Ki and pay attention, we might just manage."

"All right," Mira agreed before turning to me. "What about means to defend ourselves though? I thought these things couldn't touch us, nonetheless, with blades."

"I thought so too." Every time I met with these things, what they were, the idea of what they were, was thrown out the window. No matter what I did, I just couldn't figure out how they were, what they were, or even why I could sense and interact with them. Of course, NOW I found out they actually could interact with the world? The thought sent shivers up and down my spine. Did that mean that the man from before could have hurt Felix? That it wasn't just me affected, but everyone? What about my parents? Could they be hurt by the ghosts I kept seeing in our house?

"Kieran!"

That name snapped me out of my ensuing second panic attack. It was only then I noticed my short breath, shaking hands and the sweat beading on my brow. I really had to stop this. Mira was waving her hand in front of me. As soon as I responded, she and Felix let out twin sighs of relief.

"Oh man, you scared me there." Felix reached forward, draping an arm around my shoulder, a source of comfort. "We'll be fine, dude, how could you have known? I mean, for over a year, you barely noticed these things and it's only been recently that you've spotted them more often, right?"

I tried to swallow, failed and tried again before giving a shaky smile. "Yeah. Thanks." The words came out choked, but he got it anyway. He ruffled my hair and pulled away, gaze narrowed at the doorway, though it wasn't hard to spot the sweat beading down his brow, showing he wasn't quite as calm as he seemed to be trying to exude. "Now to figure out how to get past that bastard outside."

I nodded as Felix moved over to the window and stared out. I wasn't sure what he noticed, but from his expression dropping in resignation, it probably wasn't good. I forced myself up and peeked out. I noticed the man from before, his whitish outline stark against the gray backdrop, yet barely visible through the blinding rain. I heard the faint sound of thwacking and took a closer look. Only then did I spot the hammer in his hand, pounding against the wall. How did he get a hammer? I grimaced, right... at his waist. I hadn't really noticed before, but he had a tool belt strapped to his waist.

I froze. Wasn't that where we came in? Through the heavy rain it was hard, but I could just find the opening in the wall a little past that and felt ice slide and sit in my veins.

We were trapped.

I exchanged glances with Felix, who was now as pale as the ghost. He must have noticed the boards. Mira, who got up around the same time I did, swallowed thickly. "You know, I think now would be a good time to find another way out. He's busy, so..."

I nodded and watched as the two hurried over to the blockade we created. They pushed it away as I kept my attention on the guy. He worked steadily, without any rush in his movement, hair blowing in the wind, as if evaporating. He paused and turned his head and stared back at me. He seemed almost casually amused before he turned his head and continued, thwack, thwack, thwack.

"Ki! Come on."

I pulled away from the window and rushed over to Felix and Mira, who were by the door. They pulled it open and hurried out. They grabbed my arms and Mira took the lead, gaze determined. We rushed downstairs and, after a quick glance around the once grand entranceway, Mira turned, moving AWAY from the kitchen.

"There must be another way out, a servants' exit or back door. Something we can use to get out." She glanced over toward me with a worried smile. "Don't worry, we'll figure something out."

I nodded, unable to get my voice to work. We lightly trod through a doorway to the left and I frowned, noting as a strange smell, something I'd noticed up till this point, but ignored, invaded my nose. I coughed, covering my mouth as Mira and Felix flinched.

"Damn, this place stinks," Felix muttered, pulling his shirt over his mouth.

I agreed, but at the same time, the smell was difficult to fathom. Rotting meat and... metal? Maybe? I shook my head, trailing after the others, keeping my attention behind us as we moved. The hallway was dark, only showing flashes of light, and curved to the left. We passed doorways with cracked and warped wood, Felix trying a few before promptly giving up when they barely budged.

"Are you sure we should be going this way?" Felix muttered, sounding like he was trying hard to only breathe through his mouth with the minimal amount of air. At least, that's what I was doing as the smell grew more pungent as we walked.

"It's away from that ghost, so..." Mira was a little more hesitant with her answer before shrugging. "I don't think anything else here can harm us, so as long as we're careful and watch out for any damaged floors we should be fine."

I wasn't sure I agreed, but I also didn't feel the need to argue, my head starting to thrum in a faint hum of pain. I tried hard to ignore it as we rounded the corner, only to stop dead.

Before me, laying over the floor in contorted twisted lumps, were those figures. The white wispy creatures draped over one another, blending and blurring as... was that blood? Blood dripped onto the floor. I could hear a faint sound against the rain, a constant plop, plop, plop. My hand shot up to my mouth as the smell intensified and I took a step back.

"Yikes! It reeks. What up and died here?" Felix groaned, curling into himself. I stiffened, pain lancing through my head.

Died... those figures... they were dead, weren't they? I stared at the hallway, part of my mind realizing the extent of what I was staring at. There were about ten of them, all together, draped along the side, as if thrown. I found myself taking another step back, my stomach churning. Then I stiffened. There, lying not that far from where Mira stood, was the figure I noticed earlier. Even in the flash of lightning and from a brief moment, I could recognize it, the wild hair and loose-fitting clothes... Its neck or no... her neck was twisted, mouth open as something flowed down her back, dripping onto the floor.

"Ki? Kieran!" I jerked, as Mira tugged me around, catching my gaze. "Kieran, look at me. We're fine. Got it? Calm down."

How could I calm down! Those things, those figures, they're dead! How was that possible? Death didn't exist, right? But then, those things weren't human, no matter how much they might appear to be. Right?

"Ki, what is it?" Felix called, backing away from the hallway.

I opened my mouth, before promptly covering it once more, feeling like I needed to hurl. I swallowed harshly, trying again. "You don't want to know," I whispered before taking a deep breath. However, I knew full well that sentence wouldn't satisfy either of them. Noting the annoyed expressions, I let out a breath. "I'll tell you once we get out of here, all right? Just trust me," I pleaded, outright pleaded with them. I couldn't say it, not out loud. I couldn't admit that these things, these creatures that appeared so human, were dead... and I could only presume that the reason they were was the same reason we were running for our lives.

They exchanged a silent conversation before Felix shrugged. "All right, man, we'll trust you. Now let's get moving, I don't think any of us want to stick around here any longer."

Not arguing, I nodded and turned before recoiling. I didn't want to go through there, not in the slightest, but... I took a deep breath and shakily started forward, leading the way. The others followed me, probably aware that I was purposely following a pattern, carefully dodging around the figures. I heard a squelching sound as I took a step too close to one and shivered trying hard not to vomit. I was so glad neither of them could sense anything.

"What is this stuff all over the floor? You got it on your shoe," Mira spoke up, warily. I decided not to look down, knowing full well what it probably was.

"Maybe it's blood," Felix muttered. "With that crazy nutcase outside who knows."

I winced and I'm positive both of them caught it, because they suddenly shut up, their footsteps a lot lighter after that.

Thankfully, it wasn't long before we got down the hallway and through the doorway. I let out a breath, leading us through, before practically slamming it shut.

Part of me was, admittedly, worried that one of those figures would just get up and follow us, so I was grateful it didn't happen. I don't think I could handle it right now.

Mira let out a breath as Felix coughed. "Well, THAT'S over with... and I haven't heard any footsteps or anything, right?" He glanced over to me and I grimaced. I was going to be honest; I wasn't really paying as close attention as I should have. Stepping past dead ANYTHING will do that to you.

They must have noticed my hesitation because they both paled.

"Right, let's hurry." Mira muttered before glancing around the room. She quietly cursed before heading toward another doorway to the left. I peered behind me as we moved through the door and down the hall, keeping quiet. My heart pounded in my chest, sneaking up my throat. My mouth was dry and I licked my lips, trying to keep calm, er, well, to calm down at least. I could feel Mira trembling as Felix scanned everything twice over. We came across another room. The floor was splintered and broken. Mira ignored it, weaving around the degraded floorboards and to a doorway at the opposite side of the room, quietly cursing. She opened it and peeked through. It wasn't hard to assume what she was searching for... a way out.

I could tell Mira was getting frustrated and jittery as we continued through the mansion. Finally, we came to a room with a lot of windows, I wasn't sure what sort of room it once was, but I noticed the rain pounding against the heavily boarded-up glass panes as light from the lightning flickered through the cracks. I noticed Mira frown, gnawing on her lips before turning to me. "Do you think you—"

I heard a creak and whipped around, scanning both doorways as Mira stiffened. Felix took a step back, seeming guarded, wary and outright terrified.

I heard a faint giggle and, without thinking about it, bolted toward the doorway we'd just come through. I slammed my shoulder into it, gripping the handle just as I felt it turn under my fingers.

Terror flared up my spine as a giggle sounded from the other side before a sharp THUNK rang through the door. Felix and Mira took a step back, panic clear on their faces as they realized just how close the guy had been! Holy shit, that was close!

I heard a faint screech and then footsteps. I tensed, digging my feet in just in time as the door jolted.

I stumbled, but managed to hold the door, jerking the other two out of their momentary shock. Felix raced over to help as Mira took in the room.

There were windows everywhere, but not a single one any of us could slip through. What the heck? We might be able to get to the other hallway, but then we'll just be constantly trying to outrun this thing.

If we started fleeing, especially now that the only way out was blocked, we were done. Dead.

I shivered at the thought as my knees buckled slightly from another impact. I heard a shout and peered over in time to spot Mira clambering up to one of the windows, a broken piece of what appeared to be flooring in her hand. I briefly wondered where she got it, but pushed the thought aside as I realized the state of the room once more. She pulled back and then threw the piece into the window. A crash sounded around the room as glass shattered and the storm suddenly grew louder. Wind whipped through the area as water splashed onto the floor. Mira reached up, pulling herself through the gap. Blood trailed down the wood, but I quickly returned my attention to the door as another thud sounded out, along with the shank of a blade.

I was very much glad this door was thick.

"Come on! Hurry!" Mira called, straddling the sill, hands placed on either side. Her hair whipped around her as rain pounded over her shoulders. She extended one arm out toward us.

I turned to Felix and gestured with my head. He hesitated and I sent him a glare. "I'm faster than you and I can sense him, just go! I'll be right behind."

He stared at the door and, after feeling it shake once more, nodded. He pushed away, darting to the window. Mira grabbed his arm and pulled him up, tugging him through.

I heard a thud from the far side of the window and guessed Felix was through. I waited, one... two... THUD. I stumbled, but the door still held. As the footsteps hurried away from the doorway, I bolted. I reached the window in the span it took for me to realize we were almost out. Mira grabbed my arm, tugging me up. Why the heck were the windows so high up? Lightning flashed and a whistle sounded behind me. I lunged forward, partially slamming into Mira. Mira let out a screech, splashing down on the other side as pain blossomed in my shoulder. I barely caught myself, my feet stumbling under my misjudged landing. I gritted my teeth, my hand darting up to my left shoulder. Wetness leaked down my shirt and over my fingers. I glanced back, spotting the figure in what could only be a throwing position.

"Kieran!" Mira must have scrambled to her feet, her head peeking over the window as her hands grasped the sill, reaching inward.

"Go!" I shouted, before turning and racing for the other doorway, away from that guy and the hall of bodies. If that knife hovering in his other hand was any indication, I was NOT using the window any time soon. Hopefully, Mira and Felix would understand what to do. At least, I hoped they did.

I jerked the door open and raced down the hallway, feeling it curve. At one point, I passed a stairwell that was broken beyond repair.

The sounds of shuffling rang behind me... a faint whisper sounding through the air, heard even with the storm.

That fear of death was creeping up on me with each step the figure took, he was too casual, but he always seemed to be right on my trail. It wasn't long until I found myself entering the main foyer. Ahead of me was the front door, bolted and chained. I knew there hadn't been enough time for Mira and Felix to get to the other door, if they were even going there. What could I do? I stumbled and turned, catching the man off guard.

"What do you want?" My voice shook, hand tightly clasping my arm, but it stilled the man, who cocked his head to one side. A sound echoed over the howling gale from outside. I didn't catch many words, if any. But what I did catch was simple. *Intruder... Kill... revenge... death... fun...*

That was pretty simple to understand and did NOT help the chills that were now a constant on my spine.

I took a step back and then another as the man watched me, as if curious. Was he just playing with me? Why would these things play like this?

What WERE these things?

He pulled his arm up, a knife in his hand as he lightly traced over one side of the blade, humming faintly. He opened his mouth, as if to speak, words floated over the room, indistinguishable in the pounding of the storm. I took another step back. He grinned.

The white grin curled and twisted into a gruesome semblance of a smile. The white and DRIPPING dagger was the last straw. What little control I had left fled. I turned and bolted. I wasn't thinking, I was just moving. The hallways all appeared the same to me. No matter where I turned or ran, it seemed like there was no difference. Until finally, to my surprise, I ended up back in the living room. I glanced over my shoulder as I raced into the dining room, slamming the door shut behind me, letting out a breath. I knew he wasn't that far behind me, but it gave me a moment reprieve. This was, to be honest, the only way he could come into this room, considering the state of the other two paths. I caught my choking breath, the gasps loud in my ears.

Silence. There was nothing from the other side, no footsteps, no scrambling, nothing. I gulped and slowly pulled away. I didn't hear him so I peered toward the kitchen and could hear something faint from that direction. Maybe…

I glanced at the doorway once more before scanning over the dining room. I slid away, quiet, and grabbed a nearby chair. I stuffed it under the handle to the living room and let out a breath before turning and grabbing another. I hurried over to the other doorway, doing the same thing. It wouldn't do much and was probably pointless, but it should give me a little extra time. After, I turned and headed with quick steps toward the kitchen. I went through the doorway, past the WAY too empty kitchen and into the mudroom. The door wasn't open, but I could hear something from the other side. I moved fully into the mudroom, noting how the door to the outside was sturdy and well-made. However, the one on the inside was a flimsy swing door which would do nothing to keep an attacker out.

There was no way I could hold him back through that door, let alone avoid getting stabbed through the wood. I shook my head and hurried toward the doorway I hoped my friends were at. I spotted the cracked and grimy glass of the two portholes. I leaned into one and peeked through, spotting Mira and Felix. Mira was holding a hammer, tongs side digging into the nail of the plate. I wondered where she found that. Did he leave it, not expecting us to get this far? They were soaked to the bone, hair and clothes plastered to their skin. I glanced over my shoulder, gulping just as Mira jerked up, noticing me. Determination seemed to flare through her. Her efforts redoubled.

I just hoped it would be enough.

Chapter Nine

I didn't know how long I stood there, how long they both worked at it, but I could feel the blood pounding in my ears, my breath shaking and hands gripping tightly to the sill, ignoring the wound on my arm.

Where was he? Was he behind me? Was he going after them? I didn't know how he got back in so I didn't know if he would go after them instead. I hoped he didn't realize they were out there still. What if he did? They'd be in trouble and there would be nothing I could do.

Panic seared through me and I kept my eyes peeled, through the rain. I heard creaks and groans, cracking and footsteps—I stiffened and slowly turned my head back toward the doorway as it swung open, showing the figure, haggard, tired and... Well, that answered that question.

I pushed myself against the doorway, trembling so hard, I was shaking the door as much as they were tugging at it. The man was focused on me, words whispering from his mouth and anger vibrating from his being. Yeah, I would probably be angry too if my prey kept getting away. Shut up, Ki, not helping! I couldn't even swallow anymore, fingers curling into the wood so tightly, I could hear the screech over the wind and rain.

The man took a step forward before he darted right at me. I ducked, right as a knife sailed through where my head was. Gah! That was way too close! However, my dodging was mediocre at best.

Actually, it was pathetic as I found myself stumbling and slamming to the ground, wincing as I hit my side. I heard a sound and rolled, just as something slammed into the ground where I was. I glanced over, seeing the quivering knife before following the knife up to the person. Shit! I was boxed in. The door was beside me, at my back. The man was almost hovering over me, a second knife, that he must have grabbed earlier, held up to swing down. A grin formed on his cracked lips and for a split second, I swore I saw a pale gaunt figure, bloodshot eyes and ragged teeth decorating a pockmarked visage, before the knife plunged downwards.

Maybe time stood still, I didn't know, because, as I felt the door give, I heard something go off. Glass shattered as I covered my head. The man cried out as the knife went spinning out of his hand. What the hell? Was that a gunshot? Again? I couldn't help the startled cry as I flopped onto my back, staring up at Felix and Mira. Felix briefly glanced toward the window, seeming startled, before he reached down and grabbed me, tugging me to my feet with a surprising amount of strength.

"Close the door!" I couldn't help but screech, my voice crackly and high-pitched. Mira didn't need to hear twice. She slammed the door shut once more, right into the man's startled face.

Steadying my feet, Felix and Mira grabbed my arms and tugged, pulling me through the slippery and mud-filled gardens. I could barely see through the blinding rain, hair and body soaked in seconds. Glass dropped from my clothes, landing on the ground. We stumbled through the gap and hurried through the trees. Felix led the way, keeping a firm grip on us so we wouldn't get separated. Within moments, we came across our bikes.

I was never so happy as I was right now to sense them. I tugged mine out, Mira and Felix doing the same before all three of us hopped on and took off down the road. I could hear the squelching sound and peered back as the white figure slipped from the trees, standing on the road, staring after us. For a brief moment, I wondered who shot the knife out of the man's hands, but that thought was pushed aside as I turned away, curving around the road and out of sight.

Chapter Ten

It didn't take us long to get back home. We all decided to crash at Felix's house, considering he was the least injured and he could talk with his mom to convince her to let us stay over, if she was home.

Taking side streets and hurrying past my and Mira's houses, we stopped in front of Felix's. All three of us were almost the color of the figures, shaking so badly the bikes skidded on the water a few times.

Felix pulled himself off and walked down the lane to his house, grabbing the keys. He opened the door, peered inside, then gestured for us. Unlike him, I practically jumped off my bike, hurrying down the lane and through the held-open doorway. Mira wasn't far behind me.

The hallway was warmly lit as the door swung shut behind us and locked. Felix let out a sigh of relief and leaned against the door. I couldn't blame him, taking in my own gasping breaths alongside Mira. Finally, I got my breath under control and straightened, just to jump as the phone went off down the hallway. Mira let out a string of curses indistinguishable from the rain and my own panicked thoughts. I inched over to the phone and picked it up. Considering Felix was frozen at the door in fear, it didn't leave many options.

"Hello?" my voice squeaked out.

"Kieran? Honey? Are you okay? I saw you riding past just a few minutes ago. What were you thinking, biking out in that storm!" Mom's voice rang through the phone and I almost let out a breath of relief. Mom, as scary as she could sometimes be, I could at least handle. "Why didn't you come straight home instead of going to Felix's? You were supposed to take it easy!"

"Mom," I cut in, stopping her in her tracks. "I'm fine." I tried hard to keep my voice even. "I'm sorry I didn't come home, but we were heading to Felix's house anyway and I guess I just lost track of things."

Silence fell on the other end.

"I'm just going to stay over here for tonight. Nothing else. So, you don't have to worry or try to pick me up or anything. Felix's mom should even be home soon and it's pretty late already."

"Kieran..." After a long delay, a sigh rang over the line. "All right, but I am picking you up bright and early tomorrow. You will have some explaining to do, young man, understood?"

"Yeah. Thanks, Mom." I let out a breath and couldn't stop the faint smile from forming. "Good night."

"Good night, honey, and say hi to everyone for me, okay?"

I nodded, though I know there was no point, before hanging up and letting out a groan. "Well, that could have definitely gone worse." I turned, noting that the others seemed just as relieved.

"Phew... that scared me," Mira admitted, hand to her chest before straightening. "Your mom is ridiculously observant." Her gaze flitted to my shoulder and she frowned. "Now come on, let's get that patched up and then I am going to take a shower. I'm soaked to the bone and need a change of clothes."

"I'm fine." I waved it off and then grimaced as pain shot up my arm. She just gave me a deadpan stare as Felix chuckled.

"Mira, why don't you get a shower and changed, I'll take care of him." Felix gestured toward the stairwell. "We'll talk after."

She hesitated for a moment before nodding and hurrying upstairs.

"And what about your parents?" I called up.

She froze for a second before waving. "I'll call them later, AFTER I'm changed and we get this settled."

I watched her go before letting out a quiet yelp as Felix lightly prodded my shoulder. I sent him a quick glare as he smiled. It was a warm, if shaky, smile. "Good to see this is the only thing that happened to you."

I pursed my lips as we walked to the downstairs bathroom,

pulling out some medical supplies to dress the wound. While Mira's had thankfully been a thin cut, the knife had dug a deep path through the side of my shoulder. No wonder I felt a little dizzy.

Soon enough, I was able to take my own shower and finish bandaging the wounds. Felix was the last to go, as I took a seat in Felix's room, trying and failing to dry my hair with a somewhat wet towel. The clothes, which I borrowed from Felix, sat loosely around me. It was an annoying reminder of how scrawny I was compared to him, but I pushed the thought away.

I heard footsteps and peered over as Mira came upstairs, holding three mugs of hot cocoa. She was dressed in what could only be her spare clothes, which made sense now that I thought about it, considering how prepared she was for everything else. She handed one cup to me, placed one to the side and then sat down in a beanbag chair off to one side, nursing her own cup. We sat in silence, waiting for Felix to finish up.

It wasn't long before he came into the room, already having changed, and letting out a sigh of relief. Mira waved to the extra cup. "Sorry about using your kitchen, and about how cold it probably is now, but I didn't think you would mind."

Felix waved it off, taking his drink. "Of course not, you're always welcome."

A beaming smile crossed Mira's face as Felix seemed to realize what he said and quickly turned away. I chuckled quietly as I took a sip of the now lukewarm drink. Mira seemed to be adjusting her own bandages before following suit with her own drink. As cool as it now was, the warm chocolate felt good going down my throat.

For the longest time, we all just sat in silence, thinking over what just happened. At one point I noticed as Felix and Mira clasped hands. That was almost a calming sight in all this craziness.

"We didn't find her, did we?" Mira's voice was faint, almost depressed. "After all that and we're no closer than when we started."

"Not necessarily," Felix pointed out, pulling one leg up as he leaned against the headrest of his bed. "We found out more about these creatures because of that. Now, not only do we know that Kieran is able to sense and interact with them… we also know we can be hurt by them. As scary as that sounds, that means we have to be more careful. Plus, it seems they can talk just fine and do have ways of interacting through sound. Not to mention…" He glanced over to me and narrowed his eyes. "Kieran noticed something that he didn't want to mention that might also be pretty important."

Mira let out a sigh before perking up. "That's true. Can you still call them ghosts though? I mean, I thought ghosts can move through walls and stuff, yet that one couldn't, or maybe it was just my imagination."

Felix went to open his mouth before pausing, a frown forming on his lips. I found my attention drifting to outside the window, watching as the water trailed delicately down the glass. "I don't think they're ghosts."

"Huh?" Felix blinked.

I turned to him, and, noticing Mira's confusion, clarified, "For a while now, I haven't thought of them as ghosts. There's just something about them that, while otherworldly, doesn't seem dead and, well… can a ghost die?"

Mira stiffened as Felix's eyes snapped wide.

"Ki, what do you mean?" Mira cut in, voice trembling.

I hesitated, chewing on my lip as Felix managed to put two and two together. "You don't mean—" His breath cut short and he slowly glanced over to the shoes, stuffed into one corner of the room. "What we smelled and your expression. That really was…"

"Blood." I finally spoke, voice soft. "But that wasn't the worst part." I centered myself, drawing in a long breath and slowly letting it out before catching both of their gazes. "I'm sorry I couldn't say, but I didn't want to make the situation worse for you two."

"Come on, Ki, just spit it out," Mira coaxed, voice surprisingly gentle, compared to the words.

Opening and closing my mouth seemed to be the only thing I could do for a minute before I finally just let it out in one burst. "There were ten of them. Ten of those figures—" The other two stiffened, curling into each other. "They were lying on the floor, twisted, broken, bleeding out." I found my arms hugging me close, my body trembling at the image seared into my brain. "They were piled on top of each other, thrown to either side like some twisted art. All white, wispy and faded. One of them… one of them was one of the two figures, running through the hall when we first arrived." I caught their shock filled gazes. "That figure, it was still ALIVE and then… it was de…" I put a hand to my mouth, shuddering, unable to continue.

But it seemed I didn't need to. I felt arms circling around my neck, a warmth pressing into me. "I'm so sorry," Mira muttered, voice hoarse. "I figured it was something, but…"

I felt a hand on my shoulder and glanced over toward Felix. He lightly tightened his grasp, an encouraging smile falling across his features. I could tell he was still off about what I said, but…

I took a deep breath, slowly pulling away. "Right. Thanks." I shook my head as Mira sat back, but still stayed close. "But that's just it, ghosts can't DIE, so I want to know what they are. After all, you can't kill something that's already dead, which means…"

"They're not dead," Mira breathed as Felix stared down at his hands. "How is that possible? Someone who's not dead, yet can't be seen and can't interact for the most part?"

"What could cause that?" Felix mumbled, his brow furrowed in contemplation. "There's no scientific data on something like that, even with our new technology. Is it a new discovery? Or… if that's the case, who was that girl?"

"Don't go conspiracy theorist on us," Mira cut in before downing the last of her cooled hot chocolate. "However, that does bring up a good question. How is it that someone who looks like you is one of those figures, but not dead? I would assume she was an ancestor; but if they aren't ghosts, then what could she be?"

"Then who is she is the question I would like to know," I murmured, hiding my mouth behind my cup as my thoughts whirled, grateful for the change in topic. I pushed the bloody image from my mind, instead focusing on the girl in question.

Mira sighed and leaned back, staring at the ceiling. Her fingers twisted around Felix's. "But, amongst all that? What I'm worried about is, if we got away that thing saw us, what if it follows and tries to hurt us or our families?"

That sent a chill down my spine and seemed to quiet even Felix, leaving us all in contemplation. It was a worrying thought, and something I didn't really want to think about.

"Well..." I perked up, deciding to interrupt the silence, "we can cross that place off the list. We know, in general, that these creatures are ethereal to most people. For some reason, I can interact with them and start picking out details of what they probably look like. They can talk and I can sometimes hear what they are saying and they can also interact with everyday objects such as paper or knives. On top of that, a few of them seem to be able to interact with people like you two even though you can't sense them, which means they're probably more powerful." I let out a sigh, my head falling into my hands with a groan. "And that just leaves me with more questions about this entire mess."

I heard shuffling and movement, but neither Felix or Mira responded for a moment. I eventually felt a hand on my shoulder and glanced up toward Felix. "Come on, let's worry about that in the morning. It's been a long day. Let's get some rest for tonight."

"The three of us?" I felt a faint smile trail onto my lips. "It's been a little while. I'll take downstairs then. Don't want to get between you two."

Bright red shone on both Felix's and Mira's faces and I felt my expression shift into a smirk. After a moment, and some spluttering, Mira muttered something under her breath, so faint, none of us could hear. I leaned closer to her and she glared at me. "I said we can sleep together. I would rather know you two are okay."

The smirk dropped back into a grateful expression.

Meanwhile, Felix resembled a very lively flame, bright red as he jerked his hand away from hers. "I'll... I'll get us something to eat." He hurried out the door and downstairs.

I threw my hands up. "You two..."

Mira pouted, but didn't argue.

I stood and patted my clothes down before turning toward her. "Speaking of, did you call your father yet?"

Mira promptly jerked away, twiddling her thumbs and I frowned. She glanced toward me out of the corner of her eyes. "I'm not sure I want to. He might make me go home, and I don't think... I don't want to go home or else I'll have nightmares."

I grimaced, conceding that was very much possible. That was part of the reason I was grateful Mom said it was fine, as hesitant as she was. I didn't think I could deal with being in a room by myself when I knew those things were around and dangerous. Still... "I get that, but your father is probably still worried."

She stared at the sheets, her fingers curling into them. Eventually, she sighed, slumping. "All right."

I smiled and nodded. "I think I'm going to help Felix. I'll see you in a few." I turned and headed downstairs, giving her a few minutes. I walked into the kitchen, hearing the clattering of pans. I meandered over, peering down into the already bubbling bowl of noodles. "You work quickly as usual."

Felix barely gave me a glance, stirring the pot. "Yeah."

I pulled back, taking a seat. I knew if he needed anything, he would ask.

I sat for a while before he asked me to keep watch on the pot while he grabbed things. I slowly stirred the noodles as he cut up some meat and cheese.

"I TOLD YOU I CAN TAKE CARE OF MYSELF! IT'S NOT LIKE IT'S THE FIRST TIME I'VE STAYED OVER WITH THEM, FATHER. I'M NOT A KID ANYMORE! I'M STAYING HERE AND THAT'S FINAL!"

I jumped along with Felix as we heard a slam, followed by pounding footsteps. Mira pushed herself into the room, expression livid. I was not so stupid as to ask, but Felix seemed to have no qualms.

"So, what happened?"

"What happened? Father is being a jerk and telling me to come home anyway! He doesn't want me staying with you two because we're 'of age' and he doesn't want me sleeping in the same room with boys! Even though we've slept in the same room together on and off for the last four or so years!" She huffed, taking a seat as we exchanged hesitant looks. "Like you two would even do anything. But no, he doesn't trust any of us. It's BS."

"Yikes," Felix muttered, focusing back on the pot.

I waited as recognition slowly dawned. "Wait, does that mean…" He turned to give us a horrified expression. "Does that mean your father is coming? Now?"

"If he is, just say that I'm over at another friend's house or something." Mira rolled her eyes.

I shook my head. "Not going to work, your bike is still outside, remember?"

She pursed her lips, glaring at me, and I kind of wished I'd stayed silent. I mean, I understand her father's decision. I didn't see her in that way, but she and Felix did have a thing and, well, I'm not a kid. I'm well aware of the implications. "We'll just stay here and rest for the evening until your dad comes. We'll deal with things then, all right?" I asked cautiously.

I could almost feel her twitch before letting out a breath, arms flopping to her side. "Fine. But I'm right, aren't I? I trust you two not to do anything and vice versa, right?"

I chuckled. "You don't have to worry about me. I wouldn't dare touch you with Felix in a five-mile radius of you."

My laughter increased as Mira blushed and Felix whipped around, pointing the spatula at me. "You're damn right. I would kick your ass, friend or not." He blinked before promptly turning back toward the mac and cheese. He was suddenly very quiet, considering even his ears seemed red, I could probably assume why.

I let my chuckles die and leaned back to relax. No point in worrying about Mira's father, after all, he wasn't going to be angry with me, I was just the third party.

A sharp pain slid through my skull and I winced, quickly sitting upright and grabbing my head in one hand. A moment later, it faded. I quickly shook my head and stood. "I need to go the bathroom." They didn't say a word as I stood and left, walking into the front hallway. I hesitated, glancing over toward the crooked phone and grimaced. Should I actually put it back on the hanger? I winced as another shot of pain pierced through me and I stumbled.

I felt my shoulder hit into the wall and bit back a yelp as pain flared from my wound. I blinked and stilled. Through the glass panes on the side of Felix's front door, there was a girl... a familiar girl.

Without much thought, I flung myself toward the door, pushing it open and hurried outside, ignoring the rain soaking my new clothes. I slid to a halt in front of the girl. She examined me, relief shining over her delicate features as she placed one hand to her chest. Her black hair was drenched, obscuring one vibrant green iris as damp hair curled over her cheek.

"Who are you?" I managed to get out. She opened her mouth and frowned before shaking her head. She examined her hands for a moment before nodding and taking a hesitant step forward.

I blinked, confused, only to find myself letting out a loud yelp as she tackled me. Thin arms wrapped around me, trembling. I overbalanced and splashed to the ground, wincing as pain shot up my back. Still, I felt the arms around me and the girl buried her head in my chest.

What. The. Actual. Hell?

I felt that sharp pain in my head once more before a surprised shout sounded behind me. I tilted my head up as Felix hurried to my side with Mira standing in the doorway. "Are you okay, man? I thought you were going to the bathroom, not outside!"

I glanced toward the girl who tilted her head up toward Felix. A moment later, pure worry shone on her soft features. Her lips formed into a word as she pulled herself away, fingers lightly touching my bandaged shoulder. Her eyes were red, but it was hard to tell whether she was crying or whether it was the rain. She shook her head and sat a little straighter, suddenly seeming a little older. She seemed to be speaking firmly, pointing at me with a stern look, made worse with the fact that she was practically on top of me.

She glanced between Felix and myself before turning toward the doorway. Relief shone once more and she pushed herself up to her feet. She hesitated for one second before reaching down and grasping my wrist. With a strength I wasn't expecting, she pulled me up and onto my feet, startling Felix into taking a step back and surveying the area wildly, a hand moving up to his ear, as if he could hear something.

"Ki..." Her voice was a quiet whisper that I somehow still managed to hear. How did this girl know my name? I heard movement and, following her line of sight, I noticed two white figures standing off to one side. They were the two from the amusement park the other day. One was the person with the gun: a petite figure, but why a gun? The other was a burly man. He resembled a signature bodyguard, all muscle, power and, like the girl, familiarity. That was all I could gather as the girl who I was searching for let go of my wrist. She was probably about the same height as me, if not a bit shorter, but it didn't seem to affect her as she glanced at her bodyguards, if that's what they were, before turning back toward me.

She scrutinized me for a moment, nodding to herself before giving me a faint smile. Her hands reached up, palms warm against my cheeks in a gentle gesture, pulling my head forward to meet hers. Words that, even if I couldn't hear, I could almost guess flitted from her lips. "Stay safe."

I found myself nodding, though I wasn't sure why. She pulled away, turning to her comrades and gestured. They set themselves on either side, following behind her as she disappeared into the rain. I stared after her before letting out a quiet curse.

I never did get her name or figure out who she was!

Damn it.

"Kieran." I turned toward Felix, who was giving me a strange expression, arm dropping to his side. "Dude, why don't we get inside?" I glanced down at my now soaked second set of clothes and sighed, tramping after Felix as he occasionally glanced back at me. Mira was standing near the doorway, watching with trepidation. I slipped inside and closed the door, only to find myself bombarded with questions from

Mira.

"Are you all right? What happened? He wasn't out there, right?" The questions came in rapid succession and I quickly threw my arms up, withholding a wince as I stretched my wound.

"Guys! I'm fine!" I interjected, pushing Mira away to give myself some space. "It was the girl we were looking for."

"She came to check on you, didn't she?" Felix questioned, voice quiet. "I thought..." He paused for a moment with a deep frown. "I thought I heard something as you stood up earlier."

I spared Felix a glance, unsure what to make of what he just said, before turning back to Mira.

"I think so. She had two people with her and one of them held a gun." I stepped past, hurrying to the kitchen where I smelled food.

Felix and Mira followed after me, lost in thought. I took a seat, ignoring the squelch of my clothes as I let out a breath. Mira stepped around me, grabbing the food which must have been basically done when I left, while Felix took a seat to my left, gaze firmly on mine. "Ki, what do you mean? Did it have anything to do with the window? Why—"

"Oh, so you did notice." His features twisted into a strange, worried expression as I continued, "You're right." I leaned back, staring at the ceiling. "Right before you got the door open, that man was about to stab me, and I highly doubt I would have been able to walk after. However, at the same time that you opened the door, something broke the glass and caused the man to drop his knife. Do you know anything with enough force to do that besides a gun?"

"But a gun? Only cops hold those, and it is more of a nostalgia thing. None of them use them due to the lack of crime," Mira pointed out as she took a seat, placing two other bowls of mac and cheese in front of us. It was a pretty simple meal, but Felix was pretty good at least with the easy stuff. Plus it was something warm, which I would take. I quickly dug in as I thought over what she said.

What she said didn't sound right.

"Maybe they also know about these things? The things Kieran sees?" Felix stated, startling us. I glanced over, confusion probably clear on my face, for he continued, turning toward me. "We have seen a lot more police around lately and your vision has been acting up for a little over a week. Could it be that something happened? Could it be the police knew about that thing?"

"But how would that relate to the girl Kieran saw?" Mira pointed out around her spoonful of cheese. "They're obviously not police, so then—"

"How would they get a gun?" I muttered, thoughts going a mile a minute. "Why would they even need one?"

"You mentioned you didn't think they were ghosts. What do you think they are?" Felix leaned forward, placing his now empty food bowl down.

I followed suit, humming in thought. I honestly didn't know. They seemed human in so many ways, the girl that kept approaching me was very much human, yet I knew for a fact that neither Felix nor Mira could sense her. "They're human, I want to say, but they are not."

"They're not aliens or something, right?" Mira's voice hitched up. "Maybe it's an alien invasion?"

Felix rolled his eyes, but I didn't throw the idea away; after all, what exactly could it be?

"Our technology is advanced. Maybe someone stole something. Maybe it's another country. I wouldn't jump to aliens," Felix pointed out, leaning back in his seat.

"Yet you believed they might have been ghosts?" I deadpanned and he shrugged. "Still, the idea that it might be technology isn't that far-fetched, I suppose."

We sat in silence as the rain dully thrummed overhead, slowly draining into a gentle drizzle. I let out a yawn and Felix chuckled. "Why don't we get some sleep? We've had one hell of a day."

"Don't need to tell me twice," I muttered as Mira nodded. We headed upstairs and I changed, yet again, after taking a nice shower. The warm water felt great after all that running around and the cold that soaked into my skin from the wet clothes. After quickly checking and resetting the bandages, we spread out three sleeping bags and lay down, myself in the middle with Felix and Mira on opposite sides. I peered toward the door, making sure it was locked before I curled up into the warmth.

"Hey, Ki?"

"Hm?" I hummed, letting Mira know I was awake. I could hear the soft snores signaling Felix was asleep. I didn't try to roll over to face her, too tired.

"Thanks for saving us. If you hadn't been there…"

I furrowed my brow, confused. "I agreed to go and, well, it is partially my fault since we were looking for something that would only really benefit me."

"Yeah, but we were planning to go there even if you said no."

I shot up straight, head whipping toward her in shock. I heard Felix grunt before he rolled over. Mira sat up, hair falling messily around her, hands to her chest, nervous.

"What do you mean?" I tried hard to keep my voice quiet, but I could feel anger and worry hum through my veins.

"We're worried about you. We thought we would try to help you find her. Felix was the one who came up with it. I mean, we've been doing research together, but he found something that seemed to worry him and didn't, well, he didn't want to scare you. So, we've met up for the last week while you've been home to learn more about hauntings. That's how we knew of the hole in the wall."

"Oh," I muttered, feeling a bitter taste flood my mouth. "What were you thinking? You know you can't really sense them. What did he find that scared him? Do you remember?"

Mira winced and turned away. I felt anger and hurt sing through me and I forced myself to lay back down, rolling over so I didn't have to face her. "You know? Never mind. Obviously, whatever it is, you couldn't share with me. Still, I can't believe you. To do something so stupid." Something about those words.

I was stupid. So, so stupid. I'm sorry, Ki.

Pain, worse than anything I felt up till now, shot through me and I couldn't cut off the scream as my hand slammed to my head and I thrashed.

Why did you do it? Why did...

That was my voice, I knew that. Who was I speaking to? What were we talking about? That other voice, the one who spoke first, I should know it. I should recognize it.

Kieran! They're coming. Can't... me. Please! You've got to... member me!

Save me.

I felt something cool on my head and the pain started to fade. Why did I remember that? Those words... Who was that?

"Kieran? Kieran!"

I groaned and blinked tiredly. Mira was hovering above me, tears on her cheeks. I heard water and then Felix leaned over, draping a cloth over my forehead again. He placed it down, concern clear on his face. "Dude," was all he said, but the strangled tone was enough to indicate I definitely worried them.

The cloth felt nice on my face. Darkness grasped at the edge of my vision and I found myself falling to sleep, even as the distant sound of a ringing doorbell sounded in my ear. I wondered who it was. I finally slipped away into a restful sleep instead of one due to unconsciousness.

Chapter Eleven

When I awoke, it was to a dull throbbing and my own bedroom ceiling. Mother's attention snapped to me, a seat pulled up to the side of my bed. She surged to her feet and hurried over, brushing the hair out of my face. "Oh, Ki, dear, how do you feel? Any better?"

"How?" My throat felt scratchy. Did I scream? I didn't know.

"Felix and Mira were worried sick. Mira's father went to pick her up. They convinced him to bring you here. He left a few minutes ago after Mira said she would go home once she was sure you were awake. Both Felix and Mira are downstairs. I'll let them know you are up." She scanned me, hands drifting over my face before she pulled back and stepped out of my line of sight. I heard the door creak and her shouting about me being awake. She returned only a moment later with a glass of water. The headache was gone. Though the words still rang in my head, the last bit staticky at best.

"Thanks, Mom, I feel a bit better already." I sat up, startling her and downed the water before attempting to swing my legs over the side of my bed.

I barely got a foot down when I heard the door open and I spotted Felix and Mira. They must have noticed my attempt to get up and I knew instantly that it was going to be futile. They hurried over as Mother berated me on trying to move so soon.

"Ki! You scared us! Are you okay? You're not hurt, right?" Mira's voice pitched up as she hovered around me while Felix stood back a bit, watching me with a careful gaze.

I let out a sigh and moved back under the covers, though I still stayed sitting up so I could talk to them easier. "I'm fine. I'm already feeling a lot better."

"That's good." Felix's voice was surprisingly soft. "We weren't sure what to do. I guess it was a good thing Mira's father came. Do you know how eerie it is to hear you whimpering not to go to the hospital whenever we bring it up? I could have sworn you were listening to us. It took a heck of a lot of convincing to get Mira's dad to bring you here instead."

"Really?" My attention drifted over to Mira, who nodded, tears on her face which she quickly wiped away.

"That's why they brought you home." Mother spoke and she stood. "Let me get your father, he can help." I watched her go, wondering how Dad would be able to help me with this, before letting my attention drift over to the other two. Mira moved to where Mom was and Felix took over Mira's spot.

"Ki, I'm sorry. I didn't mean…" Mira hiccupped and it was then I realized why she was crying. She honestly believed it was because of her that I lapsed into that episode. I let out a sigh, before finding an unenthusiastic chuckle slip out.

"It's fine. I was upset that neither of you told me, but I'm glad everything worked out the way it did. I don't know how I would react if I lost two of my closest friends." The last part I whispered, realizing as I spoke how awkward my words were. However, they heard anyway. Mira choked for a moment before sobbing anew. Felix draped an arm around her shoulder, pulling her head into his side even as he turned away. Man, this was awkward. "I am still pissed though. You were going to go there without me?"

"So, she did tell you." Felix sighed and waved it off. "Dude, you wouldn't believe some of the stuff I've found on your symptoms, some crazy shit." He faced me, eyes glowing in a way that spoke volumes. "Mira and I didn't think we should worry you. I guess it was a good thing we decided to have you come with us."

"What did you find?" I found myself curious.

Felix scanned the room before lowering his voice. "You know, after you mentioned the danger? I found some old news articles, hidden in old archives of the computer. Yet, if you actually calculate the dates, they were from a little over a year and a half ago."

I almost choked as I realized. "That's around the time I started noticing these things."

Felix nodded as Mira pulled back, wiping her cheeks of the remaining tears. Felix cut himself off, giving her a once over. She him a faint smile. She then turned to me. "Yeah, Felix and I both started finding these strange things, like I told you last night. I tried to check any books on the subject while he went through computer archives. There is something wrong."

Which was something I felt since a year and a half ago, everything felt wrong since then.

"So, you know the pandemic? There are some sites that say it never happened." Felix's voice was so quiet and he seemed almost agitated. "I didn't believe it, but when we were talking yesterday about technology, stolen technology at that?"

"You think someone's trying to cover something up? I highly doubt that has anything to do with my symptoms. Last time I checked, I was fairly normal, ignoring that little fact."

Mira and Felix exchanged worried expressions. "That's why we're not sure what to believe."

My attention drifted toward the window in thought. It made sense, it couldn't be coincidence that they found sites mentioning that there was no pandemic, that things stopped happening a year and a half ago. I let out a sigh and returned my attention to them. "Come on, we'll think about it later, you two probably stayed up all night worrying, didn't you?" Blushes formed on their cheeks as they both glanced away and I let out a short laugh. "Thanks though, I mean it."

"Anytime." Mira spoke quickly, scrambling to her feet as Felix gave a short nod.

"Well, I think Mom should be home from work now, I'll let her know you're fine." Felix let out a quiet cough, as if to hide the blush as his gaze drifted toward Mira.

"Sounds good, I guess I should head home myself." Mira nodded and they both slipped out the door, waving good-bye.

I watched them go, both amused and worried. Everything they mentioned, sent a stabbing pain through my head, as if a part of me was shouting at myself, pointing to pay attention. But, considering how much happened today, or, er, yesterday. I wasn't sure where my attention was even supposed to go.

"Kieran? Son, you up?"

The door opened with a faint squeak and Father stepped inside, hair frizzed and glasses slipping. A strange apparatus sat in his hands. He noticed my staring and peered down at the box-like thing before shrugging. "I heard from Rebecca that you were up. I happened to be working on this." He cringed before shaking his head and stuffed it in his pocket. I stared at him, curious. Rebecca? Why would he just use Mom's name? That seemed strange. Father stepped forward and took a seat on the only chair in the room. "So, want to explain how this happened?"

I stared at my father as he waited patiently, wondering if he even noticed the slip before I pursed my lips, uncertain. Yet he always listened before.

No, don't. Not this time.

That voice spoke in my head, warm, yet distant. Why?

"My head hurt, that's all. I guess it was just a lot worse than normal." I found myself muttering.

Father examined me quietly, a strange expression in his gaze, before he sighed. He leaned back, hand lightly tapping at his pocket, where the box was. "Son, I was wondering, have you seen more of them lately?" I started, hesitating. His attention firmly settled onto me, a knowing expression sitting there. "So you have. Don't worry, I won't tell your mother, it would worry her sick if I did."

"Thanks," I muttered, earning a quiet chuckle from my dad, who did a quick pat of my leg through the sheets as he stood.

"Ah, I might have something for you, a way to help you with that headache, it won't do much, but for short term, it should help." He reached into another pocket, which admittedly, since he was wearing a lab coat, included more pockets than I could count, and pulled out a device that appeared to be a pair of headphones. He gently placed them over my ears before flicking something on the right-hand side. A quiet gentle tone filled my head and I suddenly felt sleepy. The headache that resided behind my temples faded.

He gave me a warm smile. "Sleep tight, all right? I'll check in on you later, okay?" His words were gentle and I only really figured them out by somewhat reading his lips, so it was more just me assuming. He carefully helped me back down into a laying position, pulling the covers up. "I'm sorry, Kieran. I'll fix this. I promise." Those last few words, did he really say them? I wasn't sure because at that point, I felt a small smile cross my face as I slumped downwards, falling back into a pleasant sleep.

Chapter Twelve

When I woke up for a third time, it was to the headphones being gone, the sun being up, and feeling something was terribly wrong. I squinted through the sunlight and slowly sat up, rubbing my eyes with the palm of my hand. Why was I wearing headphones to sleep? Oh, right, I was getting those headaches because Mira had... Mira had...

Wasn't Mira just a classmate? Why would Mira know me, the loser? No, that wasn't right. Or maybe it was. Wasn't I missing something? Gah, something was definitely off, my head felt fuzzy and my mind felt like it was trying to copy the wingbeats of a hummingbird. In other words, hella fast.

"Kieran! It's time to get up!"

I groaned and pulled myself out of bed. I didn't remember having anything today. But I did recall promising to go out with Mom and Dad to the amusement park, but didn't I already do that? When did I say I would go out with them? Didn't I already go a few weeks ago with... who was it again?

What the hell was I missing! My thoughts and memory were completely scrambled. I heard pounding and pulled myself out of bed, I peered down from my window in time to spot another one of those figures, racing to my house. The white hair, all scruffed up as if the figure just woke in that state, startled me awake and I shivered as something I knew I should remember flung itself at me. Something familiar happened recently.

Boards, rain, a haunted house, and two people.

But never in my life had I been to a haunted house before. I knew this. I was more of a family person than a go-getter.

Right?

Please tell me I'm right. I feel like I'm going insane.

I found myself slipping out of bed and hurrying downstairs. Part of me wanted to just hide under the sheets, another part of me was curious. Why was this thing so desperate to come here? I passed by Mom, who was humming a small ditty while she sat on the couch, doing needlework. Wait, huh? Needlework? Father was at the kitchen table, fiddling with the black box from yesterday. He peered up and grinned. "How are you feeling, son? Sleep well?"

"Uh, yeah. Thanks, Dad."

"It's fine, it's good to see you are finally up. Your mother and I were starting to wonder if we would have to wake you. We'll be leaving in about a half hour, you know."

"Leaving?" Why was Father saying leaving? Where were we going? Usually, they would be a bit worried, right? About my headache? I knew everything felt a little out of whack, but...

Father gave me a strange expression, curiosity glinting behind his glasses. "Yes, to go to the amusement park. We've been planning this for a few weeks."

"Oh, right. Um, I'm going to go outside for a bit, I need some fresh air."

"All right, just not too long, you'll get plenty when we leave later."

I nodded and walked out the door, my limbs locked into a robotic movement. I opened the door and peeked outside, to find that no one was there, but a police car, trundling down the street. I wondered why so many police were out and about. I frowned, realizing the figure was gone, and shook my head before heading back inside. Mom was starting to get ready as Dad finished up the last of his gadgets, screwing in one more bolt before letting out a whoosh of air, a satisfied grin on his face.

"Ki? Ready to head out?" Mom asked from across the room. She was in a light summer dress with her hair tied back. I nodded, glancing down at myself before racing upstairs to get changed. I threw on a tank top... which, didn't it have cheese on it at some point? I shook my head. Of course it did. I was addicted to those cheese-fries, after all. I almost skipped down the stairs, finding myself excited to go out, a bag draped over my shoulder with the bare basics, suntan lotion, swimsuit, you know, the usual.

Shouldn't I be scared of something? Shouldn't I be hurting? I winced, attention drifting to my shoulder. There was a faint scrape on my shoulder that Mom must have bandaged for me last night, right? How did I get it? I haven't been out of the house...

Nope, don't remember.

We hurried to the car and headed out, passing by houses without a word. I leaned into the seat in the back, staring out the window with boredom, chin rested in my hand. We passed nondescript houses and the school.

I wondered how Mira was doing.

Wait, why was I wondering about Mira again? Wasn't her house around here?

I thought so. Didn't I bring her an assignment one time? Or... I felt lancing pain through my head and quickly got onto another line of thought. The weather was beautiful, the sun shining brightly, unlike the day before.

Okay, that's it.

I closed my eyes and quickly shuffled through my scattered memory. I KNEW something was wrong. I remembered different things conflicting with each other. I remembered a boy that I'm almost certain I should know. Shouldn't I know him? I wasn't sure. Yet he talked with Mira like it was nothing. I blushed as I remembered them kissing. Whoever that person was must have really liked her. Then there was Mira, her crying about causing me pain and her stoic face as she ignored me in class as I asked if she had any time this weekend. I mean, the girl sat in front of me. Couldn't I at least attempt to make one friend?

But I was already her friend.

Yet I was never her friend.

What. The. Hell. "Mom, I'm not feeling so good. Can we

postpone this trip?" I peered toward the rearview mirror, pleading.

Mom's gaze flicked my way and her brow furrowed. "Honey, are you sure? We've been planning this for a while now. You were the most excited about it. Did something happen?"

I opened my mouth and closed it. She just gave me an out. I had an out. Why couldn't I convince myself to use it?

"I think he needs some rest, the two of us can go. Is that right, Ki?" Father spoke up and I quickly nodded.

"Yeah, you've been planning to go out for a while. Enjoy yourselves. I must have just got too much sun yesterday or something."

Mother gave me a strange expression that seemed a mix between conflicted, understanding and downright confused. Finally, she let out a breath and nodded. "All right, sweetie. We'll do that. Call us if you need anything..."

I blinked, confused as she gnawed on her lip, murmuring to herself under her breath before turning back to face me. "Sorry, must be thinking of how things must have been like in the old days." The way she said it seemed a mix of nostalgia and worried. "If you need anything, contact the amusement park, they'll contact us, all right?"

I nodded, relieved that they were still deciding to go to the amusement park. Briefly, I wondered why they weren't more worried, but then I found myself wondering why SHOULD they be? Deciding it was better to not dwell on that confusing topic, I decided on the things I could do with my parents gone, because I didn't want to just stay home. A part of me, a large part, wanted to check something out.

And having my parents hovering over me would not work. I would have to thank Dad later.

Mother didn't seem happy as we pulled back into the driveway. "We'll be back around five, all right? I'll see you soon." She dropped me off, kissing my cheek before hurrying back into the car and down the road. I blushed, feeling awkward before slipping into the house.

I wanted to gather some things.

As I stepped outside, I scanned the area, feeling a frown cover my face. The streets seemed the same, the sun was the same, everything seemed the same, but…

Another headache pulsed through my brain and I stopped in my tracks. This would be when an arm would descend around my shoulders, right? But, why an arm? That thought sent another jolt through my head and I cried out, finding myself crouching. My head hurts! My hands clasped tightly to the sides of my head, as if trying to push in the brain that seemed to be trying to barge on out. Finally, after a few agonizing minutes, it faded to the back of my mind and I shakily pushed myself to my feet. I turned and walked past the house, past the school.

It was a little while later when I found myself staring at a familiar, yet not familiar, two-story home. A man stood outside with his last name written on the back of his shirt. Mr. Kenworth. That was his name.

The man glanced up and scrutinized me with a strange expression. "What are you doing here, boy? Didn't my daughter already tell you to stay away from her?"

Huh? What the hell?

"I'm sorry, sir, I don't know what you mean?"

He must have seen the honesty on my face because he blinked. Absolutely confused was an understatement as he stared at me. His expression shifted, flashing between a couple different emotions, almost clouding over at one point as if in a daze, before it disappeared. The genuine smile on the man's face disconcerted the hell out of me. Did I want to know the reasoning behind all of that? Was he recognizing ME? Or thinking of someone else? But the latter didn't make sense, so… "Oh, right. I was thinking of the wrong boy, it must have been the other Kieran. You came over near the end of school to bring those assignments, didn't you?"

The other Kieran? Who was he talking about? Another version of me or someone else? Unable to really do much about the confusing statement, I nodded and he stood, quickly clapping his hands to rub the dirt away before stepping over. "It's a pleasure to meet you again. The name's Mr. Kenworth to ya."

I felt I had this conversation before, but didn't he ask me to call him something else? "It's a pleasure to meet you too. I was just wondering if your daughter was around. I wanted to ask her about summer work." I had summer work, right?

Mr. Kenworth laughed and slammed his hand into my back, causing me to almost stumble. "Man, it's rare for you young ones to start so early. But I guess that just shows how good our education system is. Sure, she's up in her room. Just knock." His expression hardened and I gulped. "But don't you dare try anything funny, you got that?"

Didn't I laugh at this comment once? But I believed it was directed toward someone else, right?

I said that a lot today.

I quickly nodded and hurried inside. I moved through the halls with surprising ease, like I did this before. Within no time, I found Mira's room and knocked on her door without really thinking about it.

"Coming!" a voice called from inside before the door opened, exposing my classmate. Her brown hair was tied up and brown eyes sparkled with curiosity, before she frowned and groaned. "You again? How did Dad even let you into our house?"

Why WAS I here? I didn't know her. Yet... "I wanted to talk about the summer assignments. I was thinking about writing about ghosts for my English one and—"

She seemed to stiffen for a second, just like her father, before her expression lit up as she nodded her head wildly. "Ah! I forgot, we're in the same English class." A frown graced her face as she mumbled something that sounded suspiciously like, "Weren't we always in the same classes?" before she shook her head and gestured. "Come in. I didn't know you liked ghosts."

"Only recently." I shrugged. For once, I felt like I wasn't lying. Do you know how strange it is to feel like you're lying when you're telling the truth? Or at least, you think you are? Gosh, this was making my head hurt for a totally different reason. This made no sense.

"I see. So, was there anything in particular that you want to know?" Mira took a seat on the only chair in the room, a black swivel, which meant I only had two options.

I figured I would be safest with the floor. That rug appeared to be very comfortable. "I was wondering. Can you explain to me your interpretation of how a ghost could exist?"

Where were these questions freaking coming from? Hell. I would say they were out from left field if I didn't feel like I'd legit had this conversation before.

"Hm." Mira tapped her lip, definitely deep in thought. Something flashed across her face for a second, as if she was stumbling over some memory or something, before it smoothed out. Were Mira and her father having the same problem as me? That would explain the strange occurrence earlier.

No, they didn't seem to remember me, at least not at first, but I knew. I knew Mira for a different reason. I just couldn't quite pinpoint why that was. I heard a creak from downstairs and stiffened. Panic surged through me and I didn't know why. Mira flinched and then blinked, confused. "Huh? I wonder why I did that?" She glanced at me. "Oh, I never answered your question. Well, I think it is more to do with before the pandemic, they're lingering spirits from before the new technology that are unable to pass on. The reason why we have new hauntings is probably because they finally managed to move from their place to accommodate the changing of society, or following their killer or whatever." Even as she spoke, a strange frown crossed her face.

Both of us stiffened as a long, drawn-out creak sounded from the door. I glanced over at the opening door, along with Mira. I noticed Mira's eyes glaze for a moment before she looked back at me. I, however, kept finding myself staring at the white figure who seemed to be struggling, hands on his knees and chest rising and falling quite visibly as the door slipped closed behind him.

The white figure tilted his head up and spotted me. Within seconds, he raced forward and gripped my arms tightly.

I almost let out a scream, but I quickly clapped my mouth shut, instead creating a choking sound as the boy, for that was what it looked like, gripped my forearms tightly. Wait, how the hell was a figure holding me? He shouldn't be able to! Mira seemed to jump, noticing my stiffness in worry. However, I only gave that a brief glance as I heard wind whisper over me, even though the windows were firmly shut and it wasn't even breezy outside.

Thrum. Thrum. Thrum. My heart pounded, my skull aching with each aching beat. Thrum. Thrum— "Kieran."

That name. This thing knew my name. Could I scream now?

I bet Mira thought I was crazy, or having a spaz attack. Actually, she probably did because she just raced out of the room, screaming her father's name as the door slipped shut. The boy's gaze snapped to her as she ran out before he shook his head and turned back to me.

I had seen this before.

Didn't something like this happen, a year and a half ago?

Please don't for… Save me!

"Ki."

When did I close my eyes? I quickly opened them to see a boy with choppy blonde hair and piercings. He seemed a mix of relieved and downright terrified. I stared at him and slowly tilted my head. "Who?" Was I an owl now? Probably.

The person jerked, staring at me with a mixture of shock and despair. "Hey, it's me…. Don't you recognize me?"

A part of that sentence, it was scrambled and even the boy appeared frustrated. He opened his mouth, as if trying to say something, but each time, it just kind of came out empty. Finally, he shut his mouth and stared at me, almost pleading.

Should I know him? I wasn't sure.

I shook my head and he growled before snapping his head up. He glanced over his shoulder before turning to me. "I'm sorry I startled you. But you have to tell Mira." His expression shifted as a frown gathered on his face before his entire face lit up and he stared at me. "Ask her if she's had a crush on someone, anyone."

"Whoever you are, I can't ask that, I don't even know Mira—"

"Yes, you do!" the boy cut in, voice going into hysterics. "We both do. Just promise me. All right? That's it."

I opened my mouth when the door was flung open, both Mira and her father hurrying inside. Mira's father moved up to me and the boy quickly jumped out of the way, releasing me. It was only then when I found myself slumping down, as if no longer supported.

"Lad, are you okay?"

I nodded, catching my breath before grinning weakly. "Yeah, I'm fine. I'm used to it." Not a lie. Huh…

Mr. Kenworth pursed his lips. "All right, but you should go home. Will you be able to get home yourself or—"

"Thank you, sir, but I'll be fine." I pushed myself to my feet, stumbling only slightly. I could see the boy watching me worriedly, he almost seemed like he wanted to support me, only to pull away.

"I can take him home if you want," Mira piped up, startling all of us. She grinned. "I want to ask him a few more things on the assignment anyway, so I'll do that on the way. Is that okay, Father?"

Mr. Kenworth hesitated before he ruffled Mira's hair. "If you're okay with it, then it's fine by me." He glared at me. "But if I hear a single peep that you did something—"

"Dad!" Mira cut in, glaring at him. "I'll be fine. He's just a classmate, that's all."

"I know." Mr. Kenworth chuckled before turning his attention fully onto me. "Well, I do hope you are feeling better. Take care of yourself."

"Thank you, sir." I nodded as I tried to keep track of the boy out of the corner of my periphery. Now that I had moment to think, wasn't he a white figure earlier? Why could I see him? And so clearly? Was he going to hurt me? Scare me?

I didn't think so, after all, even though I knew he was one of those figures and that no one else could sense him, I didn't feel nervous. I bet everyone was shouting at me, telling me I should know this person. Believe me, I understood. But you try remembering when there was nothing there to remember. All right, now I was definitely going crazy, I was talking to someone else in my own head.

I shook my head and sent Mira a grateful smile. "Thanks."

"No problem, Ki." The words fell from her tongue with obvious ease, but her expression showed something different entirely. Mr.

Kenworth didn't bat an eye, he just nodded to me and slipped out the door.

"Why did I call you Ki?" Mira muttered, soft enough where I barely heard. Why did she call me that?

The boy practically lit up in curiosity and he shuffled next to me, peering at Mira in a mix of loss and hope.

I sent him a look and he quickly raised his hands and backed off. Mira shook her head. "Come on, let's get you home."

I followed her as we stepped out of the house and down the street. It felt comfortable, walking beside her as the other boy stuck to her side, keeping pace. His hand would occasionally reach up, suspended an inch from her shoulder before dropping back to his side.

As we walked, I realized I did feel better, in truth my head wasn't pounding, it was more a dull ache at the back of my mind. The boy was giving me a long, complicated look, as if debating something. A small part of me gave a worried start. I recognized that expression. How?

Finally, a mischievous grin crossed the boy's face and he suddenly walked over and slung his arm around my shoulder. "I never fully believed you before, but you really can sense them. Sense me."

Really can... My eyes widened as it finally clicked, or at least, finally made a bit more sense from my earlier ramblings. This person was one of those ghost-like apparitions I'd been seeing.

Why wasn't he ghost-like, similar to the others? No, he was, then he wasn't. So, why wasn't he now? Why could I hear him? Speak with him?

Fear jolted through me and I pulled away, causing him to stumble. He turned to me, cautious. "Ki?"

Mira turned to me worriedly and I waved it off. "Sorry, thought I saw something. The heat is probably getting to me."

She rolled her eyes. "It's not that hot out."

I shrugged and she raised an eyebrow, amused, before staring ahead. "You know, I don't think I've come down this way. Your house is around here, right?"

"Yep." I popped the p and she let out an amused sound.

Frustration flashed across the boy's face and he frowned. Part of me wanted to know who he was, but another part of me was scared. And I didn't know why.

I shook the feeling off and turned to fully face Mira. "Hey, Mira, this may seem like an odd question, but…" Mira glanced at me, listening quietly. Part of me felt flustered; I was asking a girl I didn't know if she had a crush on someone. That was like asking her out. Yet another part was groaning, thinking, we're going through this again?

Ugh. Would you two sides shut up already?

"Do you have a crush on anyone?" There, I said it, happy?

Mira's face flamed up and she stuttered, anger overcoming her embarrassment. "Why the hell would you ask me that? You creep!"

Well, I saw that coming a mile away.

I quickly raised my palms up towards her to reduce the damage. "No, it's not me. Someone I know was curious and was too scared to ask himself. Don't hurt the messenger!" Again, not wrong. Though the boy's glare indicated he was not amused by my words.

She paused and then turned away, backing down. "Sorry, didn't realize." She peered over to me. "If you're wondering, I don… do…" Her face contorted into the semblance of a frown, mumbling under her breath. The boy's expression was hopeful, he hurried up to her, fingers reaching towards her. They passed right through when she shook her head and grinned. "Nope! I'm quite single."

Something cracked in the boy as he stilled. I felt a part of me cringe at those words and again, I didn't know why. "Ah, I see." I felt my lips twitch upward into a semblance of a happy expression, though I didn't feel it. I didn't have to say more.

"Ki, you idiot, why would you ask that?" A frustrated expression flitted over her face. "That was strange."

I shrugged. "I don't mind." Really, I didn't. At least it made me feel a little better. Maybe I wasn't going completely delusional, crazy, whatever it was.

"Great!" She paused before her attention shifted sidelong toward me. "By the way, you've been looking to your right for a while now. You spotted something, didn't you? Is that why you asked about ghosts?"

I swore I had this conversation before. I nodded. Let's go with that. How else could I describe the situation?

"Oh, I thought you were going to be one of those pretenders, I wasn't sure what to think when you decided to talk with me."

I shrugged before drawing to a stop. "Anyway, this is my place. Thanks for bringing me home. I appreciate it, you didn't have to."

Mira waved it off, examining me quietly before a faint blush fell on her face. "It's no problem. You are surprisingly polite."

How do I respond to that? "Thanks?"

Mira must have realized what she said, because the blush deepened and she quickly waved it away. "If you ever want to talk about ghosts, just let me know, okay? Bye!" She raced down the road and out of sight in no time. I blinked slowly before turning to the boy who was with me the whole time. He was slumped on the ground, gaze toward the cement of the sidewalk. I knelt down and reached forward, shaking his shoulder.

"They told me, when they found me, after I ended up like this, not to get her involved. Not to try to force either of you to remember. It wasn't hard, I've been with you all this time, I've known. So, why didn't I listen?"

"Hey, you okay?" I asked, not understanding a lick of what he was saying.

The boy tilted his head up, seeming a bit more whitish than before, more vaporous. His eyes pleaded with me. "Ki, do you remember?"

Ki, why won't you remember!

I shook my head, pushing that voice out of my thoughts as I stood up and reached towards him, startling him. "I might not remember, but you seem like someone I wouldn't mind getting to know, plus, you're one of the few figures I can actually talk to."

The warm expression that flashed on the boy's face startled me as I pulled him up. "Thanks, Ki."

I nodded, not sure what to say, and headed inside. I wanted to talk with this boy, even if I didn't know him, he was still one of those creatures. Maybe he could tell me what the hell was going on, who they were.

I took a seat on the couch as he scanned the room, hesitant, before taking a seat. He seemed to stumble for a minute before getting himself coordinated and seated correctly, how odd.

I shook my head, but before I could say anything, he spoke. He just kept speaking, as if, if he didn't say it, he wouldn't be able to. He spoke about how we went to the arcade, how he had a crush on Mira, though I felt like that was an understatement for some reason. How he and Mira researched my symptoms and how we thus ended up at a haunted house that had one of the things he turned into inside, intent to kill us.

I was kind of glad I didn't remember that.

He told me about how he was supposedly adopted, but now he wasn't sure.

Those words, they all FELT familiar, but...

How he was warned that something was wrong, but was too late to realize.

Something about what he said, the whole situation, wasn't quite falling into place. As if I needed one more puzzle piece that was supposed to fit right in the center of a picture. Yet, I had no idea how I lost it.

The boy's frustration grew as the day continued, along with his fear. As if he was desperately afraid of something, or someone. He kept peering over his shoulder and shivering.

Something about that felt familiar.

"I was your best friend. Please, Ki, remember me."

Remember me. Didn't someone else say that?

Was I...

The boy examined me before draping his arm over my shoulder once more. His arm was shaking and he seemed on the verge of breaking down entirely, as if my lack of remembrance physically hurt him as much as Mira's denial mentally hurt him. Yet, a warm grin slid onto his lips. "Come on, Ki, let's go to the arcade, then grab something to eat. I do have to meet up with Mira." He blushed, but met my gaze.

I couldn't help but sigh. "Felix." Delight shone in the boy's eyes and he let out a cry of relief.

"So, you do remember me."

What could I say to him? That name was... His face twisted and suddenly he was on his feet, seeing something I couldn't. "Hey!" I yelped before shaking fingers landed over my mouth. How the heck was he touching me when he couldn't touch Mira earlier? I would have been more creeped out if not for how careful he was being.

"Sh..." The boy's voice trembled along with his hand as he held my mouth, almost on top of me. I listened and could hear the distant sound of tires, footsteps, and a siren? I could pull away fairly easily, but something in his voice and posture stopped me. I heard footsteps and then a sharp knock on the door. The boy and I stiffened as we waited. He was hovering over me, attention rapped on the doorway as terror shone from his face.

"I've run out of time, but..." He glanced down at me, voice low, only then realizing how he had me almost completely pinned to the chair. He quickly pulled back and scrambled to his feet. "I'm sorry, Ki!" His attention swiveled between the door and me. "I'll have to tell Sylvia, she'll be delighted to know you remember me, at least. You can see us clearly now, can't you?"

I furrowed my brow before I nodded. No point in denying that.

He peered over his shoulder. "Don't be reckless, and be careful. If you think you sense someone like us, ignore it. Try to pretend you don't sense us, just like everyone else, okay?"

I went to respond, but he was already darting away, through the back door as the knock sounded again. I stared after him before I scrambled to my feet, hoping to avoid getting our door busted in. I hurried over and opened the door, letting off a cough at the same time. The police officer, for that was who it was, took a step back, with an apologetic expression. "My apologies, we heard there were some problems in the area. Is everything all right?"

I nodded. "Sorry, officer. I wasn't feeling well." I winced as that reoccurring feeling in my skull came back. The officer gave me a sympathetic look before he furrowed his brow. "Are you Doctor Harris's son?"

I blinked, surprised at the use of my father's name. "Yes, why?"

"Oh, you looked familiar." Lie. I could tell he was lying as he gave me a too happy expression and quickly bowed his head. "Well, I best be going." He turned and headed back to his cruiser as I watched with a frown. Why did the police officer know my father? Through my father's work? No. Father was an inventor, a scientist of sorts. Why would the police know him? I shook my head and closed the door, locking it before heading to the back door. It seemed fine, I quickly locked it after taking a look around and found no one.

This was so aggravating, that almost there, but not quite feeling. I couldn't stand it. My thoughts flickered back to what that boy said. Felix, that was his name, right? I said the name so casually, as if the word regularly slipped out. Yet, I had no idea who he was or why he knew Mira. Heck, I didn't know why I knew Mira. Did we used to go to the arcade together or something? How would that be possible?

I felt a headache pierce through my skull and I winced. My fingers glided over my ears, as if trying to feel for something that was no longer there as I tried hard to push the headache away, deciding to switch my thought process in hope of letting it die down. I could try thinking of it later, but as I massaged my temples, I found myself thinking about the night before. Dad came in because of my headache, I knew that. He gave me a set of headphones. Where were they? Did he take them back? Were they the reason? The reason why everything was... wow, I was going crazy. My dad? Setting me up for something as crazy as this? I must be delusional.

Speaking of my dad, I heard the sound of tires and peeked out the window. It seemed Mom and Dad was returning home already. Had it really been so long? Well, I had been listening to that boy for a while. I stepped up to the door and opened it as they walked up the steps. Mother's expression was warm and happy as Father nodded to me.

"You feeling better, Ki?" Mother asked as she slipped inside.

Father closed the door, waiting quietly for my answer.

"Yeah, thanks. How was your day?" I took their bags, much to Mother's protest and Father's amusement and exasperation.

"It went fine. Everything all right, son? You seem a little pale." Father scrutinized me with a worried gleam, clear through his glasses. Was I still pale? Well, it was a crazy—I already used that word, drat—how else would you describe it though? Insane? Yeah, let's go with that. It was quite the insane day.

"Darling, did you get any food or sleep?"

I paused and shook my head. Mother gave me this expression that spoke of her dissatisfaction before bustling me into the kitchen and sitting me down at the table. She quickly put together a snack as Dad watched, just giving me a sympathetic gaze. He wasn't about to stop my worried mother. Geez, thanks, Dad.

Within no time, I found myself with a full stomach and under the covers of my bed, the lights off. I blinked, staring at the ceiling, lost in thought. Well, I guess I could just get some sleep. Wouldn't hurt, right?

Oh, who was I kidding.

I wasn't going to get any sleep at all, not with all these thoughts running through my head.

Chapter Thirteen

I stared at the ceiling of my room, unable to comprehend the reason behind the bumps and swirls I could see in my mind's eye, aka: what the hell was going on. The house was quiet as it was the dead of night and I couldn't seem to get any sleep as I guessed. I let out another long sigh and sat up, peering out the windows. The moon sat low in the sky, hanging over the world like a hovering bat or something.

I didn't know, my brain was kind of fried at the moment.

I pushed myself out of bed and headed downstairs, toward the kitchen, maybe some water would help. Before I got a chance to rummage in the fridge, the phone went off with a jarring ring and I stumbled, quickly grabbing it up so that it didn't wake my parents.

Panted breaths sounded from the other end before a voice, shaking with something like fear, spoke. "Ki, I don't know what to do. Something's here and it's trying to get in and Papa's hurt and help!"

Wait, Mira? "Where are you?" I demanded, quickly bending down to tug my shoes on.

"At home. I'm barricaded in the living room, but…"

"I'm coming, just hold tight." I hung up and raced out the door, not caring that my shoes weren't on all the way, or that I was dressed in an old pair of pajamas. Something about her voice and about what that boy said about the haunted house. I hoped I was wrong, but wasn't Mira's house closest to that place?

I jumped on my bike, which appeared to have already taken some damage, or no, it didn't. Yes, there were the familiar mud stains on the side. I pushed on the pedals, part of me wondering why Mira called me.

After all, for part of me, today was the first time we really talked, but…

My breath came in shorter and shorter gasps as I quickly made it to her place and skidded to a halt. The lights were on and the front door open—bashed. Dammit! Stop it, brain!

I jumped off, not caring as the bike fell over and ran into the house, scanning the place wildly. The first thing I noticed was the blood: it was on the walls and floor and it jolted me into panic. Were Mira and her parents all right? I heard bangs and jerked my head to the stairwell. I raced up the stairs and stopped short when white flickered in my vision. A moment later, that white morphed, and though almost see-through, a gaunt figure with wild eyes, sharp knives and a too wide grin appeared in my sight. He was scraping at a door on the verge of collapsing, giggling the whole time. That was Mira's room! I thought she said she was in the living room. For a split second, I wondered what I could do. That thing was a figure, just like Felix. My body decided to move before my brain fully connected the dots, slamming into the man, causing the both of us to topple. The knives flew out of his grip as his head smacked into the floor with a thwack.

Blood trailed down in gruesome streaks and he seemed to be on the verge of death, which I didn't think was possible. His skin was stretched so thin over bone, it was more bone than flesh; eyes sunken in so deep as to be hidden stared back at me as clawed fingernails scrambled for the knives, his pockmarked face barely hiding the deathly paleness.

I moved before I could think again of how this should be impossible. I quickly knocked the knives away, ignoring the nick that caught on my skin before slamming my fist into his nose. He twitched, reaching up for me. I jerked my head back as a clawed finger came close to slashing me. I quickly threw another punch. I heard a crack and then he went limp under me. I gulped, heart pounding out of my chest.

"Ki?" The weak voice caught my attention and I whipped around as Mira peeked out of the door. There were cuts on her arms and cheek, rips were visible on her frilled nightdress as tears trailed down her cheeks. She stared at the floor, utter confusion on her face. "What is… who was it? Did you chase them away? Was it a ghost like I thought?"

I gave her a confused look before staring down at the crumpled and bloody figure. She didn't see him, just as I suspected, so…

I quickly scrambled off him and hurried over to her. "Are you all right? He won't hurt you—"

"I'm fine, but Papa." Her voice shot up and her lower lip trembled. "He…"

I didn't have to hear any more.

I heard her gasp and almost jumped, whipping around only to notice that the blood was starting to pool over the ground behind me. He was thoroughly unconscious, I knew that.

"Is that blood? Are you hurt?" She could see the blood?

"I'm fine." I shook my head and turned back to her. "Where are your parents? What happened?"

She sniffed and just pointed behind her. I peered through the doorway. Her father was not in a good state, a vicious gash cut across his head. She must have dragged him in there.

"Mother was out. She hasn't come home yet. I don't know why I called you, it was the first thing that came to mind when Father was suddenly slashed and the door broken in. When I didn't see anything, well…"

"You said you were in the living room."

She peered at me before she nodded. "I was, but then he got in and Dad and I ran upstairs. For some reason, I kept listening for footsteps and hearing those creaking sounds. That's the only reason why I'm…"

"Well, let's check on your father and call the ambulance. The perpetrator is down now."

"All right." Her words were soft spoken, which startled me. Somehow part of me equated her with being talkative? Admittedly, the situation didn't really lend itself to that, but you catch my drift.

I shook my head and found myself once more examining the felled body. He definitely was not getting up anytime soon. I could hear Mira talking over the phone from down the hall as I walked into the room to check on her father. I winced, quickly checking for a pulse and, to my relief, I found one. But the blood, no wonder Mira was worried. It didn't take long till the first sirens sang near the building. My attention drifted toward outside the window, spotting the red and blue flashes lighting up the dark streets. I wondered what Mom and Dad were thinking. Did they realize I was out now? It was kind of a rash, spur-of-the-moment decision, so who knows.

I heard Mira open the door as I kept my attention on both her father and the guy. Would the police find him? Since they couldn't really, well, sense him? Actually, could they touch him for that matter? I mean, I did, but Mira couldn't so… but he could touch Mira, at least the knives could. Argh, my head hurt for a completely different reason.

My worry was answered when one of the officers came near the doorway and peered inside, spotting me and Mira's father, but completely overlooking the body on the ground. That was, until a loud beeping sound rang out. I almost jumped out of my skin, but the officer reacted very differently, as if expecting an attack. The officer whipped around, arms up and scanning the area. I tried not to stare, I really did, but my eyes still flickered downwards. After all, he was facing the completely wrong way.

I would have found it hilarious, actually, but Felix's warning rang in my head, so I kept quiet. When the officer finally noticed the blood stains, I could just about spot the frown, even turned at the angle that he was. I bet they didn't see that every day.

But then, how did they sense it in the first place? What was that beep? An alarm? I shook myself out of my thoughts as the guy reached to his waist and rapidly spoke into the intercom before turning to us. "The ambulance will be here shortly, for your father." His gaze flicked to Mira before he continued, "Are you two all right?"

I nodded, not sure what else to do. I couldn't convince myself to say anything. After all, what could I say? I was the one who barged in and defeated that guy, yep. Yeah, that would go over real well. I didn't have much time to think about it because, the next moment was a blur of movement. One second, I was next to Mira's father, the next, he was being bustled into the ambulance while the police officer turned to the two of us. "Why don't you two get changed and we'll follow—"

Mira cut in, shaking her head as she watched her father's ambulance. "I don't care. Let me go with my father, I'll get changed later."

"That's—"

His words were cut off as Mira stepped passed him, heading toward the cruiser with an anger and frustration in her step. I quietly followed after her, not arguing, especially since I would have no way of explaining why I DIDN'T have a change of clothes. Mira briefly peered back at me, confirming my thoughts that she realized as well as I did how problematic that could be before she turned to the officer. The officer sighed and gestured to the back seat. He let us in which, by the way felt REALLY weird. I didn't know what happened to the other guy. He was just dragged away? Maybe? I couldn't really tell with all the men blocking my sight and all.

My attention drifted to the outside of the window, staring at the late-night lights as we left the area. For some reason, as we moved along, I found my thoughts drifting to that other figure. Felix? Right. Where was he? Did he know what happened or was he somewhere else at the time. I had no means of knowing or finding out and I wasn't sure if I wanted to.

I tilted my head back slightly, watching the moon hanging low over the horizon as if it wasn't quite sure what it wanted to do. Mira was off to one side, staring out the window in thought as she picked at her torn nightdress, not that I blamed her.

The police officer was just as quiet, especially after Mira's earlier comments. He was a plain older man without any distinguishing features. Mira blinked, pulling away from her staring, and leaned forward. "Hey, where are we going? I thought we were heading for the hospital!"

"You will, but we have to file some reports first, which was why I was advising you to get changed. But what's done is done. You understand." The officer kept his voice neutral as he spoke, not turning our way once. I furrowed my brow as Mira pursed her lips. She seemed like she wanted to argue, but held off. Probably a good idea too, because I didn't think it would change anything at the moment.

Eventually, he led us to a back entrance of the police compound.

Honestly, that's the only way I could describe the large place. He gestured us through the door into a back waiting room. Why the back? I almost wanted to ask, but held my tongue. I had a feeling that it probably wouldn't be a good idea to ask. I didn't know why, but I was not going to question the feeling at this point. The officer gave both of us one last look, gaze lingering on me before he turned and slipped out the door. The room was quiet. The air had an almost sterile quality to it and the stone of the walls made it feel colder than it was. Only two doors led to the room, one to the outside and one to probably the rest of the police station.

"I wonder what they want with us. I thought he said to fill out some paperwork, but I'm worried about Papa. And, I mean, I'm not sure they'll believe me," Mira muttered and I glanced sidelong toward her.

"I'm not sure." I leaned back, staring at the ceiling as I let my head rock back and forth, a song playing slowly through my mind. "They had a machine, to detect that thing." That's all I could call it at this point, I felt like I should call it something else, but my mind was so rattled right now, I was going to get another headache and, no thank you, I was not in the mood for another migraine right now.

"Really? They can detect ghosts?" Her entire being seemed to sparkle for a moment before she grew solemn. "But why would they never mention it?"

"Maybe because it would sound insane?" I muttered, finding myself agitated. I was feeling a huge sense of déjà vu.

"Maybe…" She didn't seem convinced, though I didn't get a chance to ask as the door to the rest of the police compound opened to reveal the police chief. I blinked, eyeing the insignia on his chest. A police chief? What did a police chief want with us?

The police chief took a seat across from us and I let my arms drop on to the table, leaning forward in a mix of curiosity and worry. Mira seemed to follow my example, though she was a little more forceful when she did it, palms on the table. "Why are we here? My father's on his way to the hospital. I have to know if he is all right!"

The police chief, a balding man in his forties with a protruding chin and sharp muscles, let out a sigh and smiled. "Don't worry. Your father is stable and in good hands. We will bring you to him in a little while, but first—" he cut himself off, shaking his head. "It is good to know that you two are all right, if in slight disarray." He briefly took in the state of both of our clothes before continuing, "May I ask about the specifics of what happened to you?" His eyes flickered to Mira and then back to me, as if sizing me up. I shivered, but let Mira speak, after all, it was her tale.

"Only if you promise this will be quick." She spoke up with a clipped tone.

"Do not worry. We've already contacted your mother and the nurses we have are the best of the best. There is no need to worry."

She hesitated and, honestly, I felt a little weirded out right now. The man just kept smiling as he spoke. He was trying to calm her, but at the same time, it was so easy to tell that it wasn't his main focus. It was disconcerting. "Well, there really isn't much to tell. Father heard a knock on the door, but when he went to open it, there was no one there. Well, no one we saw. Not until he was… not until something cut him. We fled to the living room and I cal—" she stopped, a deep frown gracing her lips before she nodded and smiled weakly. "I called up to Kieran to let him know. He was staying over to study with me."

I felt a warmth in my stomach at her words as the officer shifted his attention to me and I nodded. I was worried about what Mira might say. Yes, I knew she covered for me earlier, but the situation was more tense now than before and we were talking to the police chief of all people. It would be suspicious if they found out she called me and I literally ran over, and that she didn't call the police first. She definitely realized as well, because she continued, "I happened to hear footsteps and realized the door was on the verge of breaking down and so with Ki's help, we managed to get upstairs, but then that thing attacked us." She trailed off, obviously not sure how to continue.

I quickly took over, grimacing. "I felt something, like wind? Maybe whatever it was slashed at me." I was totally making this up as I went, I couldn't just say I tackled him, right? "I heard footsteps and felt the wind, so I just figured, what the hell, and tried to grab at it. Somehow, my hand grabbed something." I pretended to stare at my palm in false confusion. "It was really strange, but the next thing I knew, I'm holding something and I just… punched?" I shrugged and left it at that.

The police chief stared at me in silence, a strange confused glint in his gaze as he examined me quietly. "It was good you two were able to survive."

"What was that? That thing that attacked us?" Mira burst in and the rest of us winced as her voice echoed around the room.

The police chief brought up a hand, as if trying to get his ears back in working order before he spoke. "That is what we call a 'specter'."

"A ghost, I knew it!" Mira almost jumped, but I couldn't help but feel unsettled, staring at him quietly. The police chief noticed and his lips twitched up just the tiniest bit, which worried me more.

"I wouldn't say it's a ghost. I would say it is more a fragment." This quieted Mira down as confusion shone on her features. "They are beings that no longer exist with us, but still have some influence on our world, such as being able to attack other living creatures such as yourselves. They can be incredibly dangerous, but are usually pretty harmless." His expression hardened as he crossed his hands over each other on the desk. "However, lately, there have been more and more instances of them showing up and causing havoc, which leads me to a question." He hesitated, eyes flicking once more to me.

Okay, now I was just getting annoyed. It must have shown in my posture because he quickly returned his attention to Mira and reached to his side. Had he been carrying anything when he entered? I don't remember. But either way, he promptly placed a manila folder down on the table, open before us.

I could feel Mira twitch in shock beside me as I stared at the picture. It was a strange thing. Almost sci-fi in its creation. A thin piece of metal that led to a monocle-like apparatus and a pair of gloves with strange ridges sat on the paper. There were other papers behind it, including what I could barely make out to be a gun.

"These are anti-specter creations. If you are willing, we are putting together a small group to seek out these things and bring them in."

Mira's eyes narrowed. "What do you mean?"

The police chief reached forward, lightly laying his fingers on the folder. "It would mean you could avenge your father and protect your classmates and friends from an upcoming threat."

"And why us?" I couldn't help but feel suspicious. This seemed incredibly sudden, after all. "And how would you detect them anyway?"

The police chief hesitated before he spoke. "Well, to answer your second question, we have means of analyzing the electric waves those things leave off, allowing us to generally locate their whereabouts, as you have probably seen. As for the first question, the choice is yours. People who have associated with these creatures understand the danger and we can't just let others find out, so it's either this or..." he shook his head. "The other option isn't really an option. Or at least, not one we have to worry about."

I frowned, what did that mean? I wanted to ask him, to bring up why it wouldn't be an option, but my throat jammed into my mouth as Mira interrupted, expression deadly serious. "I'll do it."

I jumped and turned to Mira who was staring at the man with a strange sternness. "That thing hurt my father, almost hurt Kieran and there was nothing I could do, plus..." her expression widened, her posture shifting to one of anticipation as she leaned forward. "Even though they aren't ghosts, I've always wanted to see a thing like that! Close enough, right?"

Was she serious?

Yes, a part of me supplied, she was completely serious.

My thoughts flickered to that boy. Felix? That's what his name was and what was the other name he used? Sylvia? That name FELT so familiar.

Truth be told, I had two options. I could say no. It would be fairly easy, actually. What could they possibly do to me if I said it? Make me write a pact that I'll never speak of it? Kind of pointless since I was already doing that anyway. But, at the same time, maybe they knew more about these things than what he was saying now. I mean, they did somewhat explain that machine that let out the beep to show the fig—no, specter was near. If I said yes, I could maybe find out why I kept getting these headaches and what those things were.

It was a gamble, a tough gamble, either way.

Before I could say anything, however, the door opened and a person came inside. He was tall with blond hair cut short and somewhat handsome features. "I'm sorry to intrude, but—" he cut himself off, noticing the manila folders before his gaze darted towards me. His posture seemed to stiffen for a moment before he walked, purposefully, over to the police chief. He bent down, hand covering his mouth. He must have said something because the police chief stilled, smile dropping. A moment later, he snapped forward, closing the manila envelope with a startling BANG. "Sorry, it's come to my attention that my officers are in need of my assistance." He turned toward me, a strange expression on his features before he spoke. "My cohort here will take you home."

"But—" Mira's voice cut in, only to stop short as the chief continued.

"Don't worry, I'll have one of my men take you to the hospital so you can check on your father."

Mira pursed her lips, but nodded. The man who came in so suddenly walked around the table toward me. "Sorry about that, you must be Kieran. I've heard a lot about you from your father."

"You know my father?" I hesitantly asked, noting as the police chief gestured for Mira to follow him. She turned with worry as she caught my attention.

I waved as she stood up. "I'll talk with you soon, call the house when you can, all right?"

"I will." She nodded before hurrying after the police chief.

I shook my head as I felt something on my back. My gaze snapped to the blond-haired man, noticing a strange expression cross his features. "Let's go."

I found myself stumbling to my feet, as he guided—or tugged, it was hard to tell—me toward the exit. "Come on, it's been a long day. Let's get you home."

I felt a little uncomfortable about the suddenness of the situation, but this guy knew my father, so who knows? I followed as we stepped back outside, heading toward the car park. Plus, he was working with the police chief, so he probably wasn't someone to worry about, right?

"How do you know my father?"

"We work together." He glanced back at me. "He's a genius, I could only HOPE to match his abilities."

I peered back toward the police station. I hadn't gotten a chance to give my answer.

My attention was pulled away as the man started humming as we walked towards the car park. Part of me wanted to ask what they worked together on, but another part was hesitant and I wasn't sure why. He was keeping his arms to his sides, almost hiding in the billowing pockets of his clothes.

I wasn't sure how to feel about that until we arrived at the car. I whistled, impressed, before frowning. Didn't this car seem familiar? I thought for a moment before shaking my head. I would have remembered seeing a Mercedes 550. I slipped into the car and watched as he closed the door for me. He stepped around to his side and slid in.

I found it a little strange that one hand still sat in his coat pocket as we drove out of the parking lot. "Why did you want to bring me home? It seemed like you had business with the chief."

"Oh, I'll get back in time, but I would be remiss not to bring my colleague's son home first."

I pursed my lips in discomfort, but didn't argue, staring out the window as we went. The night lights flickered, as I realized, with dawning horror, that neither of my parents were aware I had left. When we came to a halt, I quickly thanked the man and raced toward the door. I heard the car turn off and, as I reached the door, I heard footsteps and felt something press into my back.

"I do need to talk to your father about work. I know it's late, but it's important. You don't mind, right?"

I did mind actually, but I didn't say anything. My adrenaline was fading and I was getting incredibly tired. I gestured and he gave a nod, not moving his palm from the crook of my back. He was pressed a little too close for comfort as he rang the doorbell. I would have just walked in, but I forgot my keys in my mad dash earlier and Mom had a habit of locking all the doors when she went to bed, which made me wonder how those things kept getting in the house.

I saw the lights turn on and, after a few minutes, the door opened. Mom stood in the doorway in her normal sleepwear, pants and a t-shirt. She must have just rolled out of bed, yet she was as alert as ever. She noticed me and, I almost had to cover my ears as she yelled, "Ki! What in the world are you doing out so—" only for her to suddenly cut off, her entire posture freezing in place. I peeked up toward her, surprised at the sudden cut off, only to notice her gaze was no longer on me, but on the man beside me. For a split second, she had a strange, almost glower directed toward the man.

"Oh, hello, ma'am. It's good to see you again. Is your husband home?"

"Yes. I'll get him, now Kieran—"

"Mind if the boy stays for a moment?"

I thought Mom would say no, but her face suddenly smoothed out, expression dazed before she turned and hollered up to Father. It was a little disconcerting, briefly reminding me of the time in class where everyone believed the air conditioner malfunctioned. Thinking about it, how would that cause the glass to break anyway?

I stepped away, now very much wanting to leave and just go to bed. I felt fingers curl around my shoulder and jerked, turning my head just enough to notice the man smiling at me. He didn't say a word.

Before I could say anything or try to move away again, Father came down the stairs. His hair was a mess, gaze half-lidded and letting out a jaw-cracking yawn as he reached us. He froze, still as a statue, just as his gaze met the man's. His sleepiness seemed to vanish in an instant, a cold anger replacing it. The man squeezed my shoulder before letting go. "Just checking in on how your end of the project is going. After all, the due date is coming very soon."

"You don't have to remind me." Father's gaze flitted to me. "I'm well aware."

"Oh? I wasn't sure. After all, it would be terrible if things weren't completed in time. You remember what happened last time, right?"

Father's smile was stiff when he replied, "Yes, of course."

The man nodded, waving with the hand NOT sitting in his pocket before turning to leave. He paused and peered back toward me. "Just to confirm, you are all right, correct? You weren't hurt?"

My gaze shifted to Dad as he watched the exchange before returning my attention to the man and nodding.

The man smiled. "All right, I'll let Mira know you are all right. Take care." He waved before leaving.

We watched him go and I couldn't help but frown. Wait, how did he know Mira's name? Did we say her name during the meeting or something? I tilted my head in thought before letting out a sigh. I was too tired for this. "What project?" I couldn't help but ask, turning to my father.

Father jerked, startled. "Oh, just a time-sensitive one. There should be no need for you to worry about it. Speaking of, what happened? Where were you? What are you doing up at this hour?"

The barrage of sudden questions made me dizzy as I tried to piece together what he'd asked me. My tired brain caused me to hesitate longer than I wanted, unable to actually figure out what to answer first. My father seemed to realize because he let out a sigh and gestured, "I'm going to assume you sensed one of those things again, right? Here, wear these tonight." He stepped into the other room for a second, returning with a pair of headphones that seemed really familiar. Oh, those were the ones. I wondered what happened to them. So, Dad took them back? Why? Deciding not to worry about that, I hesitantly took them, wondering what they had to do with seeing those figures.

I mean, those figures weren't the easiest things to understand. While some seemed dangerous, like the police chief said, and from what I noticed earlier with the crazed maniac, some seemed nice if not outright friendly. I mean, Felix never hurt me and I wasn't scared of him in the slightest and then there was that girl, Sylvia. I vaguely remembered meeting her in my muddled memories, just like Felix. The moments where I laid in bed from one of my migraines and she was there to check on me. I remembered that happening recently, though I can't remember what caused it. Though, how did I know that was Sylvia?

Of course, this just made me more confused. How could some be so dangerous and deranged while others were kind and gentle? What were—I cut off my thought process as a burgeoning headache started to threaten. I winced, taking and shoving the headphones on my head in hopes that they would help. They did before. My father seemed startled by the sudden action, but didn't resist.

I heard a gentle hum as my father reached forward, patting my head lightly. The gentle gesture and the soft hum were enough to not only dull the headache, but once I was upstairs and back in bed, I found myself falling into a quiet, dreamless sleep.

Chapter Fourteen

I awoke, staring up at the ceiling of my room, disconcerted. I quickly riffled through my thoughts and frowned. How did I end up in my room? I'd just gotten home from... I winced, head pounding. I slowly sat up, headphones slipping off, landing on the pillow with a thump.

I stared at them, confused. I was wearing them? When did I get them back? Picking them up, I scrutinized the design. They were light, lighter than I expected. On either earpiece was a rectangular contraption and the piece that went over the head seemed adjustable and fit behind the head. However, there was no wire attached. How was I supposed to listen to music with these?

Shouldn't I be worrying about something else?

Placing the headphones down, I stood.

Now that I thought about it, didn't Dad give me headphones the last time this happened? I thought I had fallen unconscious last time too. Gah, everything hurt. I should remember something: I knew I should. I rubbed my temples, trying to figure out what I was supposed to be thinking as I stumbled forward to get changed, only to freeze.

White.

A white figu—no, a figure with black hair and cute, familiar features stared at me with horror. I stiffened, taking a step back, noting how the door to my room was wide open. The back of my leg bumped into the bed and I almost fell backward.

I yelped as she raced forward, palms lightly pressing into either side of my head.

Then, I remembered.

I'd gone over to Mira's house to help because she called me and then I attacked that thing the police chief called a specter. After, I was brought home by that man and I got another of those headaches. Dad gave me the headphones, or, well, I snatched them from him as he held them toward me. I stared down at them, uncertain. Did they make my mind go fuzzy? No, I didn't think so.

I slowly reached up, pulling her arms away from my head. Her skin felt surprisingly warm to the touch, shocking me for a moment. She stiffened, as if uncertain, before slowly pulling back, slipping her fingers out of my loose grasp.

She blinked and opened her mouth, only to hesitate and take a seat. Hope practically vibrated from her, her posture shifting forward as a heart-warming smile slide across her lips and yet, it made my heart clench painfully for some reason. I took a seat, no longer precariously falling backward. "All right, who are you?"

She opened her mouth and then closed it, shaking her head. She seemed to debate for a moment before giving a sharp nod, catching my gaze. "Sylvia."

Her voice was soft, but not in the whisper like way of most of these creatures, no, it was much more. It was clear and light, but uncertain.

Sylvia, that was the name Felix gave and the name of the girl I spotted a few times lately, right? So, how did I know that before this moment?

She stiffened before suddenly lurching forward until she was right in front of me, almost on top of me. I couldn't help but let out a yelp as that hope grew stronger and a wide happy grin crossed her face. "You can hear me, everything I say, can't you? You can not only see me, but I can say my name. You know I'm here!"

"Yes, and can you get off!" I couldn't help but strangle out. Her elbow was digging into my ribcage and her knee was someplace I'd rather it NOT be.

She blinked and examined what she was doing before letting out a shrug. She did move away, but not much else as she suddenly gave me a tight hug. Well, that was counterproductive.

"I'm so glad. So glad. You have no idea."

I blinked as something wet dripped onto my shirt. I could feel the girl shaking and glanced down, confused. She was buried in my chest, fingers curling into my now very much ragged shirt tightly as quiet sobs echoed from her small frame.

My hand seemed to move of its own accord, patting her head as a song, one I hadn't heard since I was young, hummed from my lips. The girl stilled at the song, though my shirt grew more wet. I was definitely going to need to change.

"You remember?"

"Remember?" I muttered, cutting off the words.

The girl pulled back, quickly trying and failing to wipe away the tears. She didn't do a very good job: her cheeks were blotchy and her eyes were red-rimmed. A part of me, a distant part of me, wanted to pinch her cheek and chuckle. I could not figure out where that part came from, so I quickly shoved it away.

"Yeah." Her expression shifted, that happy glow slowly fading. "You do remember who I am, right?"

I stared at her in silence. What could I say?

"I am—"

Pain.

Her words were instantly blurred out as that pain returned almost tenfold through my head. I felt myself collapse, and I probably would have hit the floor if not for a surprisingly strong, but thin pair of arms grabbing me. "I'm sorry! Don't! You're fine, stop it!"

Who was she speaking to? Whether it was to me or someone else was completely lost. I grimaced, trying hard to push away the migraine that seared through my skull. I found myself sitting on the bed once more, gentle movements causing the pain to subside enough for me to return my focus back on the girl. She bit her lip, peering straight at me. "I'll leave, but please. Be careful. They are getting close to finishing… Mira."

I felt myself waver, the gentle pressure pulling away as the girl slowly moved back. "Watch for Mira."

I went to open my mouth, to ask what she meant, but I felt unconsciousness grip me and, the next thing I knew, it was morning.

Did I faint? I shifted, my attention drifting upward as the faint bleeding light of the rising sun danced over the ceiling. It must have been only an hour, but there was no one there.

Was it a dream?

Considering I was half on and half off the bed with a stained shirt, I would have to believe otherwise. So, she had been there after all.

What happened?

Deciding the best course of action was to simply not worry about it, I got changed and descended the stairs, headphones draped around my neck. What? They were actually pretty comfy, all right? Sue me. Actually, you know what? Don't. I don't have the money for that.

I shook my head as I entered the kitchen. Mom seemed to be in a trance, her gaze distant as she slowly stirred a pan in front of her. A pot that was burning. I yelped and hurried over, turning the stove off, startling Mom badly. She jumped, whipping around with her fingers almost grasping my throat. She stopped and pulled back, staring down at her palm in uncertainty and horror, as I blinked, utterly confused. What was that all about?

"Oh, Ki. I didn't sense you there." She slowly pulled away, dropping her arm to her side as she turned her attention toward the now burned scrambled eggs and sighed. "I guess I'm really out of it this morning. Thanks, dear." She picked up the pan, scraping what she could into the garbage as I watched her worriedly. She seemed to notice. "I think I might need help this morning. Can you grab the bacon for me please?"

I nodded, heading toward the fridge as I carefully watched out for her. Thankfully, the earlier trance was gone and she was starting to return to her normal self. Part of me wondered why she didn't ask about last night, another part of me was grateful because I had no idea or excuse. We worked in silence, for the most part. Finally, breakfast was ready.

Not going to lie, it was kind of fun to spend time with Mother. I almost never had time to spend with her which seemed odd, considering she was always at home. She seemed to appreciate it too, a soft expression on her features, so different from the cold one from earlier.

"So, dear, what are your plans for today?"

I swallowed, placing the fork back down on the plate. "Not much. I don't really have anyone to visit." I trailed off, frowning. "Well, except maybe Mira. I do want to check up on her. I want to know how she is."

"Mira?" Mother debated for a few moments, emotions flickering faster than I can keep track of before she nodded. "Ah, that girl in your class, right? You finally made friends with her?"

"Yes, Mom." I barely hid the sarcasm as she chuckled.

"Sorry, dear, but it's good to hear you finally made a friend. I was getting worried."

"I'm not that bad," I muttered before frowning. Why did this conversation feel so awkward? "What about you?"

She blinked before placing a hand to her chin, deep in thought. "Well, I was planning on grocery shopping and maybe making sure your father actually gets to work on time. Speaking of—" she turned and seemed to be about to yell when the doorbell rang, causing both of us to jump.

"Who could that be?" she murmured, shaking her head as she walked toward the front room. I shrugged, taking a bite to eat. I almost choked when I heard, "Oh! Mira, dear, how are you today? Come in, we're just finishing up. Ki was just telling me about you."

I quickly swallowed, hitting my chest before placing my fork down once more. I turned and stopped. Mira was grinning. She was decked in some fancy items, a visor that covered one eye, reminiscent of the picture I saw yesterday and a holster with a gun? She also seemed to have a thin something or other under her clothes.

Mother didn't bat an eye at her ensemble.

Shouldn't she be worried about the fact that Mira had a gun? At least?

"Oh! Ki, what do you think?" Mira spread her arms, doing a quick twirl. "Cool, huh?"

"Er…" Mother, of all people, sent me a questioning expression at my hesitant stutter and I quickly continued, "it looks good on you." Whether we were talking about the new additions, or the blouse and skirt she had on which helped accentuate her figure, I wasn't sure, but... "What brings you over today?" Mother seemed surprised at my question and I mentally slapped myself. I'd said I was going to meet her and now I'm asking why she's here. Smooth.

"Oh, I was supposed to meet with your father. They told me this morning when they gave this to me, so I came racing over. Dad's out of the hospital, by the way, he decided to meet up with Mom," she trailed off, her grin dropping for a moment before she shrugged. "So, where's your father?"

Nothing. None of that conversation made any sense, but I shook it off as Mother clapped her hands. "Right! I was about to wake him when you came in. Hold on, dear, and let me get him." She turned and walked up the stairwell.

She didn't question what Mira meant about her father being in the hospital. Was Mom okay? I turned back to Mira, only to realize that I was left alone with her. Damnit, Mom.

"So, what do you think of the specter gear?" Oh, so they had been separate questions. Awkward. "I guess your mom didn't really notice, which I remember reading about—" she frowned, mouthing out the words before shrugging. "I figured you would notice, though, since there is a certain aura about you. Do you want to check them out?"

Before I could say one way or another, or think of what she meant by aura, she reached behind her ear and unclipped the visor. She walked over, clipping it behind my ear. I yelped, feeling a slight prick.

"Hey! What was that for?" I snarled and she shrugged.

"It shouldn't hurt that much, and anyway, it's only for a second, try it."

I grumbled obscenities under my breath that I would rather not repeat before letting out a sigh. I reached up, pulling the visor forward and down. I blinked, staring through the visor with confusion. Everything appeared so vibrant through the visor, as if in sharp relief. Not going to lie, part of me wondered what one of those figures would look like in this, speaking of… "I'm guessing you wore this on the way here. Did you notice anything?"

She was staring at me, causing me to start. She must have realized because she jerked, seeming to find the floor more interesting. "Oh. Uh… no, not really. If I did, I only caught a brief glimpse of something wh— gray."

Gray? Huh, that's strange. I heard footsteps and turned just as Father descended the stairs. He appeared to be utterly exhausted. I frowned, as I noticed something odd. Now I understood what she meant by aura. The area around Father seemed strange, almost a little warped. I wasn't sure what to think of it as he spotted me.

He froze, his gaze darting from Mira to me before he harshly bit his lip. So, unlike Mom, it seemed Father was able to notice the strange technology. But why? The movement quickly turned into a smile. "Hello, Mira, morning, son. So, Mira, what brings you here so early?"

What was with the strange reaction?

Mira must not have noticed because she replied with a warm, "Morning! I was just here to show Ki something and—" She tilted her head, brow furrowed before nodding. "I was told… read… something that I was supposed to speak with you to get some adjustments done on my new gear?"

Father stared for the longest time before letting out a deep sigh. "Is that why my son has one of my visors on?"

One of? "You made this?" I asked incredulously. Part of me figured since it vaguely reminded me of what he'd worked on in the past, but another part of me kind of hoped I was imagining things.

"Well, I helped develop it, yes." He seemed like he wanted to say anything but that, a sour lemon probably more edible than those words. "But Mira, how did you come across that? It's still in its prototype stage."

"Really?" She hummed before shrugging. "I was given a chance to hunt specters and they gave me this last night, I think."

Realization flashed over Father's face and he kneaded the bridge of his nose. "Right. Of course." He paused before turning to me and I realized I had no idea of what to make about Dad's reactions. I know he knew about these figures, but it seemed that he was perfectly all right with Mira as well. Did he remember Mira like I did? Or like Mother did? "Ki, do you mind giving Mira and me some time?"

I hesitated, peering between them. I reached up, trying and failing to feel for the clasp that Mira put on. Only to frown in annoyance. How did you take this thing off?

"Here, let me do it." Mira reached up, feeling behind my head before pressing something. I yelped, feeling a sharp sting once more before the visor retracted. I massaged my ear, glaring as Mira pulled away. "Geez, didn't know you were such a baby."

"I'm usually not, thank you very much, but that thing hurts!" I growled. It felt like someone was inserting giant needles into the most sensitive part of my ear and twisting until it found a place it was most comfortable. Shivering at the thought, I let my hand drop as Father took the device.

"That's strange, it's not supposed to hurt." He stared at me quietly, before placing the device onto the table and walking behind me. "Son, can you show me your ear?"

I grumbled, letting him examine it as I took a bite of my now cold bacon, blech.

I heard muttering that I couldn't quite decipher and Father stepped away with a sigh. "All right, what about you, Mira?"

"I don't really feel it." She shrugged before pulling her hair back enough for Father to examine her. He didn't touch her, just examined the area with a frown.

"It's probably all right." He picked up the device and turned back to me. "Go ahead and finish up, then help your mother pick up the groceries, gosh knows she'll need the help when she decided to ask me what I wanted for the rest of the week." He let out an annoyed sound. "How would I know anyway?" I chuckled as he sent me a warm expression. "Anyway, lunch aside, we'll be done by the time you get back, all right?"

I went to open my mouth in protest, not wanting to go out, but got a sharp look from Father before he headed to his workroom. Oh, right, I never mentioned that he had a workroom, did I? Meh, I don't really think about it that much since the whole house was usually his workroom, but yeah, things like this were usually what he developed in there.

I groaned, quickly swallowing the last of my soggy and cold food with no relish before washing it down. Better than nothing. Now where was Mom? I wasn't in the mood to get yelled at, so might as well help her out.

I could do with getting out of the house for a little while anyway.

Chapter Fifteen

Mother came downstairs not long after and the two of us made our way out the door. I hopped into the passenger seat as Mother drove to the grocery store. The ride there was silent, the sun beating down overhead was warm, even with the air-conditioning on. "Ki, are you all right?"

I blinked, peering over toward Mother. My elbow was against the windowsill, cheek pushing into my fist. "Yeah, why?"

"You seem different lately. But then, I guess that could be me as well." She shook her head. "Things have felt strange. But I can't figure out why." She smiled. "But I'm probably just getting old and it's nothing for you to worry about. Now, about those groceries, do you want anything special?"

I paused, getting a little whiplash from the change in mood and topic, but decided to follow along, shrugging. "Not really. Maybe just some homemade pot pie?"

Mother chuckled. "All right, we can do that. Maybe I'll pick up a cake as well. Your father did get a hefty paycheck recently, so we'll be good for some time."

Hefty paycheck from the company? I frowned. If they were getting so much money, then why did Dad always seem so upset and tired?

As if he just wanted to quit everything, but he couldn't.

I couldn't fathom being in that sort of situation. Mother's smile dropped and worry took its place and I wasn't surprised. Both of us were worried about what Dad was dealing with lately and if those prototypes, as he called them, that Mira brought were any indication, then he knew about the specters and not just from me.

The realization hit me like a stone wall to the chest. He knew about those creatures from someone else. Someone else out there knew what these things were. I frowned, trying hard to think. I should have known this already. Something about last night. A conversation…

I didn't… I didn't remember!

Someone knew about these things, I remember seeing pictures like what Mira was wearing, but I couldn't remember why I knew or who had them. Mira, at this point, knew more than me. Father too, or so it seemed. But then, why did Father never tell me? Could it have something to do with who he worked with? But then, why did he always seem to wear that pained expression?

Did it have to do with me?

I was jerked from my thoughts when the car suddenly stopped, the engine turning off with a sputter. I turned toward Mother, who was watching me with a sad expression. She reached forward, pulling my head toward her chest. "It's okay, sweetie. Whatever it is, you'll figure it out, okay? Don't cry."

I… I wasn't crying, was I? Deciding not to bother thinking about it, I let myself be hugged by Mother, shaking. Too much was happening at once, my thoughts shattered and broken and being torn apart with each new piece of information.

I felt like my mind was going to break.

~ * ~

Slowly, I gathered my thoughts, pulling away from Mother. She laid her hands on my shoulders, watching me with a soft and worried expression, one also filled with determination. "Son, if anything happens, if anyone hurts you, just tell me, okay? And if you can't…" she smiled and gently ruffled my hair. "Contrary to how I might present myself, I trust you'll know what to do if something happens."

"Mother? Do you know what's going on?" I left it purposefully vague, unsure how else to really ask.

She hesitated, actually thinking long and hard about it, before letting out a sigh. "I wish I did. Part of me knows I should know, but the other part of me denies that knowledge." She let out a breath and pulled back. "But I believe you will find your answers. You're a smart boy. Your father and… raised you well." She trailed off, her brow furrowing. "Wait. Why did I say it like that? Who…" she shook her head, returning her attention to me. "Sorry. I guess I'm just as tired as your father." She turned to open the door, her expression soothing out from its earlier confusion to a gentle smile. "We can't worry about that now. Let's get our heads in the game and grab some food. Your father is going to be starving by the time we get back."

I chuckled at the thought and nodded. I slipped out of the car, racing around it to catch up with Mother. "Mother? Thank you."

She stiffened, eyes watery for a second. The moment passed into a flicker of confusion, before a gentle warmth crossed her features. She pulled me close once more, startling me, before quickly letting go. "Of course, Kieran. It's my pleasure."

I chuckled, deciding to ignore the strange reaction. If Mom wanted to tell me, she would, though it seemed she might be in the same state as me, not remembering. I wasn't keen on that, but it was good to know I wasn't alone in my uncertainty. I turned toward the store, deciding to worry about the what and the whys later. For now, as much as I disliked shopping, I guessed I could spend a few moments with my mother.

 ~ * ~

The rest of the day was pretty quiet, I didn't sense any of those figures around all day. Though, it did make me wonder. Now that I had time to think, what were those figures? I mean, that guy from the other day attacked Mira and myself, I remember that much, but that boy, Felix, and the girl, Sylvia both of them didn't seem to want to harm me. If anything, they both seemed relieved when I showed I was okay. Heck,

Sylvia outright hugged me without a care. What did that mean though? Did that mean some of them were kind and some not? Didn't I ask myself this before? If that was the case, what were they? They couldn't be humans because humans couldn't pass through things, but those things sometimes could. Yet, I could touch them. So, what did that mean for me? Why could I touch and see and talk with these things? Yet Mira needed a special tool to do it? Am I supposed to be worried, trying to attack these things when I find them? Or am I supposed to know them? Are they supposed to be peaceful? What made them so different from each other?

Those questions, no matter how hard I thought about them, or how much, I just couldn't come up with an answer. My memories of what I knew and didn't know made no sense to me. Thankfully, after a few hours, Mira had a chance to get away from Father. The visor now fit her snugly, the clothes less noticeable under her blouse. "Yay! No more headaches!" she chirped as she practically skipped into the room.

I started, attention darting up from where I was sitting on the couch. "Uh…"

"So, Ki, I was wondering," she trailed off, fidgeting slightly before smiling. "Do you mind going to the diner with me?"

I blinked and frowned. "I thought—"

She promptly shook her head, a desperate tension curling over her shoulders for a second before it returned to normal. "Nope! I'm free for the rest of the day and you said I looked cute!"

What. The. Hell. I put a hand to my head and groaned. She hesitated and I stood. "Look, whatever you're doing—"

"Ki, this isn't a date. I just want to spend time out with someone else who can spot them, all right?" She said, her expression neutral. "Please?"

I debated for a few moments, briefly remembering the boy from the other day and sighed. "Fine, friends."

She hesitated and smiled before heading for the door. Part of me felt terrible as I followed after her. For a moment, in my periphery I could have sworn I spotted something. I jerked, trying to catch it, but there was nothing.

On our way to the diner, Mira was almost snooping into every corner, acting like some sort of secret agent or spy. It would have been funny if it wasn't so ridiculous. Eventually I sighed, caught her elbow as she was passing by, and practically dragged her the rest of the way to the diner. She didn't resist, but she did pout.

"Hey, I was searching for specters! They could be anywhere."

"They weren't." I cut in as the door opened and we stepped inside. Just like last time, I found myself pulling the two of us into a corner booth, away from the doorway. I guess it was a habit at this point, though I'm not sure from what.

Mira took a seat across from me with a huff, elbows on the table and chin in her palm. "Okay, fair. You were able to sense them even before I got this." She pointed to her eye-piece, frowning slightly. "Right?"

I only hesitated for a second before nodding. "That's why I stopped you from making a complete fool of yourself." I leaned against the table as she crossed her arms over her chest, unamused. "I find that, if they are aware we can sense them, then they will be less likely to appear and with you ducking and weaving as if trying to be a ninja or spy, it makes it more suspicious." As I said the words, I noticed the tension ease from Mira's shoulders, a thoughtful expression shifting over her features. However, I felt a little unsettled at my own words, that seemed correct, but also only partially.

That thought was reinforced as I found myself scanning the room. I noticed an older man I've seen before sitting in the corner, sipping something that was probably coffee, but the old woman usually at his side was gone. A waitress, no, the waitress from a few days ago came over to take our orders, a gentle smile on her lips and no figure at her side.

I put in my order, trying and failing to find the little boy that always seemed to cling to her skirt. She sent me a strange expression before briskly walking away. Mira stared at me for a bit before leaning back in her seat. "Man, it's been ages since I've been here. I mean, you don't have to ogle the waitress that's—" She frowned. "Someone else's job... Wait, why did I say that?"

"I wasn't ogling." I leaned back with an annoyed breath. "I was searching for something." I decided to be truthful, briefly wondering what Mira meant before shrugging it off. She was acting weird almost all day, I wasn't going to press it.

Mira perked up, gaze snapping to me. "Oh! One of those specters?"

"Yeah. He appeared like a little boy. It was the last time you, Felix and I—" I cut myself off as I realized what I said. Mira stared at me, a strange expression twisting her features.

She opened and closed her mouth before finally saying, "I'm sorry, can you say that again?"

Huh? That was different. "About the little boy?" She shook her head. "You, Felix and I? I mean, I know it's not proper gram—"

"Kieran, shut up."

I slammed my mouth shut as Mira rubbed her temple, a sharp grimace on her lips. "That name... why do I know that name?"

"Felix?" I leaned forward, curiosity and fascination flitting through my stomach. "I barely remember him, but I think he used to sit with us in this diner. He knew about these figures as well. I think all three of us did."

"That's impossible." She broke in, but continued to mass—no, drill into her temple in a sharp grimace of pain. "I didn't know about these things until recently. How could I have..."

Suddenly, her expression evened out and she shook her head. "Sorry, what were we talking about again?" A smile crossed her lips as she leaned forward, pressing closer to me. "You know, you shouldn't be ogling waitresses when I'm right here."

What the hell? "Mira, we weren't talking about that." I gestured, pausing only long enough to receive our food from the waitress, who sent me a parting glance before quickly retreating behind the counter. I brushed it off before continuing, "We were talking about—" I stopped as I noticed Mira's whole body seem to tense like a coiled spring. I quickly dropped the subject and let out a long breath. "—how I wasn't ogling anyone."

Her whole body seemed to loosen, her shoulder relaxing down as she leaned forward over the table. "Damn right you weren't." She chuckled, reaching forward and pushing a finger into my forehead before pulling back. "Anyway, let's finish eating. I need to head home soon."

I nodded, letting her take lead on the conversation, only jumping in whenever she seemed to want a response. She mostly talked about what she needed to get done for school vacation and what her plans were in regards to patrolling the town for those figures. I probably should have been paying more attention, but my mind was racing with what just happened. Mira seemed to have been on the verge of remembering Felix, then, well, that happened. I wasn't sure what to make of it and I wasn't about to try to ask her again in case she suddenly blanked like that again. It was creepy and just plain unsettling.

Meanwhile, it seemed Mira completely forgot about that part of the exchange as we finished up, preparing to head out. For a brief moment, I thought I spotted one of those figures pressing up to the glass of the diner, but they were gone as soon as Mira followed my gaze. I guess having only the one visor could be quite detrimental.

"Hey, why do you only have a visor that covers one eye? Did Dad explain that?"

Mira paused, placing the last of the money down for the bill. Mira, for some reason, decided to pay for the bill, saying something about how she asked me out and all that. I didn't argue.

She scanned the room, hesitant, before gesturing outside. "Come on, we'll walk and talk." Once we left the diner and walked for a little while she continued, "From what your father said, it's so we don't get confused. One can see, I guess you can say our world, while the other is able to sense that other plane."

Were they really separate planes of existence though? "Doesn't it give you a headache?"

She hesitated before nodding. "It does, but not nearly as bad as before. Your father helped a lot. Before it was mostly migraines, now it's more of a pressure." She trailed off before turning her attention fully to me. "But Ki." She seemed to sparkle as she clasped her hands in front of her chest. "I'm finally getting a chance to sense ghosts! Er, well, specters, but still! I've always dreamed of this since I was a little kid. And now it's finally happening! I don't care how much it might hurt, if I can help people with this sight and continue my passion for ghost sightings, then I'm going to!"

I watched her quietly before letting my shoulders slump. "All right, but what if one of those ghosts is someone you should know?" Like Felix? But I wasn't about to bring that name up again.

She blinked, tilting her head in innocent confusion. "Ki? What are you talking about? Those ghosts are just that. Specters. They can't be people." She grinned. "If they are, then they've become twisted by something, so I might as well free them, right?"

Free them, eh? I thought over that girl I kept meeting, Sylvia? Maybe that was her name and the boy, Felix. What of them?

Mira's words. They rang true, but they also dripped of falsehoods and I couldn't figure out why. "If you say so."

She nodded, ignoring my hesitance as she peered around. "It's only too bad none of them could show up. If they did, I can use this lovely piece." She patted her waist where that gun was.

My brain was already confused enough, so I decided not to ask. She mentioned it briefly earlier, but it seemed she was really hyped up now. I was hoping to keep some semblance of understanding in the craziness.

Unfortunately for my sanity, she explained anyway. "So, you know this thing? It shoots out a particular particle wave that can disrupt those things. Your father tried to change it, but it seems like someone above him set the 'lethality' so he told me to only use it if I was in danger." She air-quoted before continuing, "Those things are already dead, or basically almost dead." She paused, hesitant, before she shook her head. "How could a particle wave be lethal anyway?"

I slowly turned my gaze to that gun, my insides literally freezing up. That thing could kill those figures.

And I knew I should know some of those figures. That they weren't...

That Mira's definition was dead wrong.

"Please, Mira." She turned to me as I spoke, voice shaking. "Promise me you won't use it without a very good reason?"

She blinked and frowned. "You sound just like your father right now."

I did? Deciding to worry about that another time. I stopped in my tracks, startling her. "That thing. It's dangerous. Just promise me you won't use it unless you have to, unless one of those things is literally trying to—"

"Ki!" She cut in. "I understand your concer—"

"Do you?" I snarled. "Are you completely positive those things are already dead? Can you tell me, to my face, that if someone tells you it's lethal that you don't question it? That the idea of killing—"

"I'm not killing, I'm saving!" she shouted, cutting me off. I found myself startled at the tears on the verge of curling down her cheeks. "You know there is no such thing as death anymore! I thought you of all people would understand! Those figures need to be saved! I'm just trying to help them. That's all this is, a means to separate them from this plane so they can move on! How can you not understand that?"

"Easy." I toned down my voice, watching her sadly. "Because I've sensed them a lot longer than you have and I know they aren't ghosts, they aren't dead." Those last words. I wasn't sure why I thought or said them, but they FELT like they were the truth.

Mira stared at me, mouth open to argue some more before snapping shut. "If they aren't dead, then what are they? Answer me, Ki." I stared at her, unable to answer and she turned away. "If you can't tell me, then why should I believe you?" She looked over her shoulder with a strange expression. "Why am I talking to you like this? I shouldn't even know you as anything but a classmate. I shouldn't be feeling—we should have just kept things the way they were." She shook her head and rushed off. I reached up to try to stop her, but found no words creeping up my throat. Nothing but a sigh as my arm dropped back down to my side. Her footsteps faded as she curved down the street, away from me.

What did I do now?

Why…

I bit my lip hard before turning back toward my house. This had been a long exhausting day. I just wanted to sleep and maybe not deal with waking up. It was too tiring.

Chapter Sixteen

The next few days were quiet. I kept attempting to convince myself to go over to Mira and apologize, only to chicken out. Mother and Father both seemed to notice, but didn't push me. Though, I didn't think Dad had the energy even if he wanted to. He seemed to be working non-stop lately, which was starting to worry Mom and me.

Finally, a week later, I convinced myself to actually check up on Mira. When I walked into the kitchen that morning, mother was silent, stirring something in a pot while sending observant looks between me and dad, an overly watchful presence. Dad was busy tinkering with some device that appeared to be some sort of remote, his face screwed up in a way that just screamed of frustration. I could guess why. I never got a chance to ask him anything and now, as he sat there, I couldn't convince myself to ask anything. Was it because I didn't want to worry him more? Or because I was scared of what he might say?

I sighed, letting the fork clatter back onto the plate as I adjusted the headphones I'd now decided to keep on me, garnering both of my parents' attention.

"What's wrong, Kieran, are you okay?" Mother asked, stepping up to me, her fingers drifted to my head and I stopped, blinking, confused.

Something didn't feel right. Why?

"Kieran?"

I turned toward Dad with a frown as he examined me quietly. "Is there something…" he trailed off, a glint of emotion I couldn't identify contorting his expression.

I shrugged, unsure what to tell either of them. I kept getting flickers, whether they were memories or dreams, I'm not sure, and after a week of it, I was downright sick of it. I gritted my teeth, massaging my temple. When I returned my attention back to my parents, I swear something flashed across my mom's features, causing me to briefly remember our conversation from the other day, before she finished reaching forward. I jerked back, but she didn't bother following, letting out a sigh. "Well, you don't have a fever or anything." She pulled back with a faint smile. "What are you planning on doing today?"

I opened my mouth before closing it with a frown. What WAS I planning on doing today? "I think I'm going to go over to Mira's. I want to check on her." I'd argued with her a few days ago, but maybe I could make things up to her? I didn't want to lose my only... another friend. I sent my parents a weak smile. "I just have something bothering me that I want to ask her. I'll probably be back for lunch."

Mom nodded before returning to her pot of what was probably the beginning of the pot pie I asked her to make. She did like to slow cook it, after all. We decided to wait until the end of the week to make it so we could eat as a family. What with Dad being busy lately and all.

"Be careful out there." Dad waved, giving me a strange worried expression before returning his attention to the remote. I didn't need to respond, pushing myself away from the table as I finished the last piece of toast. I walked out the door, thoughts swinging back and forth, confused. I could feel different memories, thoughts, bombarding me. I could picture myself sitting behind Mira at school as we chatted, followed by another, remarkably similar, but different scene where she was just sitting there, writing quietly in her notebook. What was right? Why was I seeing this?

Then there was that boy. Felix. I remembered him, and, for a moment, so did Mira, but then I didn't. It was like trying to peer through fog. What the hell was going on?

"Kieran?"

I jumped, startled out of my thoughts before whipping around to come face-to-face with Mira. She was standing in front of a, no, Felix's house? Why was I over here? Either way, I hesitated, noting she was in the same gear as the other day, her clothes a simple shirt and pants, nothing fancy like before. I grimaced. It didn't help that she appeared a little see-through. By god, talk about terrifying to think about. She practically seemed like a ghost, and not the ones I constantly dealt with.

"Mira, what are you doing here?"

"I should ask you the same thing." Her voice was quiet, hints of shadows on her cheeks.

I frowned, taking a step forward. "Mira. About the other day..."

She sighed and shook her head. "I know... I know why you were telling me that and warning me." She smiled faintly. "I'm sorry, Ki, while I understand what you were trying to say, I can't agree."

I turned away, shoulders slumping. "That's fine, but can we—"

"Friends? Ki. I don't... I don't KNOW you." I tilted my head up as a conflicted expression curled over her face. "Damnit, Ki, I don't know you, but I feel like I should. That I've known you for a long time, ever since..." She growled before catching my gaze. "Ever since our argument, I've been thinking, wondering..." She pulled back, squeezing one arm close to her side. "Why do I remember you and someone else?"

I froze, staring at her in shock. So, she did remember! I thought she forgot after that last conversation. She smiled wanly as I stepped forward. "Mira, what—"

She shook her head once more before turning back to me. "You know what I said the other day? Well, I remembered and I asked." She gave me a hard look.

"Asked?" I had a bad feeling about this.

"My father. He wasn't with Mother. He was in the hospital." She spat the words out, a frown marring her features. "Those specters did it. I remember that now, how you came over and took one down. How Father... but my mind is also telling me Father is all right and I'm not sure which to believe. I know what I WANT to believe, but..."

"Mira." What could I say to her? That I had similar memories that were just as jumbled? That I almost felt like letting out a breath of relief when she mentioned remembering? As terrible as the memory might have been?

"They could have hurt Papa even worse, or me, or even you." She shook her head. "I'm not going to take that chance." She turned toward me, spreading her arms out to better show off her uniform as we moved away from the house. "So, this is the uniform they developed for this task, it is the uniform your father upgraded. After my argument with you, I talked with them, the people who gave this uniform to me, and they clarified that the reason it works is because I've come in contact with those specters before. As such, I'm able to utilize the energy they give off. This suit amplifies those abilities with electrical stimulation which also allows me to be translucent." She swayed forward and backward, arms clasped behind her back. "Of course, the eye piece lets me spot those freaks of nature as well, so it's a win-win."

I stopped in my tracks, staring at the back of her head as she continued forward. After a couple more steps, she seemed to realize and turned. Her words terrified me. What happened? In just one week? She sounded off, not like the Mira I did remember.

She tilted her head to one side, seeming confused. "Ki? What's with the strange expression? Nothing's changed. I told you this the other... day..." She frowned before shrugging. "I guess I didn't mention everything then. We kind of got cut off during the argument."

An argument that she seemed to be ignoring. I frowned. It was almost like she didn't care what happened. What we talked about. Maybe my words got through to her, but then... I grimaced. Of course, she then remembered what actually happened.

I blinked and choked. Her father... I remembered her father and the state he was in. "Did you go to your father?"

Mira hesitated, expression shifting before dropping. "No. They wouldn't let me check on him. They said he was in urgent care, but he would be all right. Ki, why is it that part of me desperately wants to go check on him, while another part of me desperately wants to hunt down those THINGS and hurt them?"

This conversation, it was almost as if she could remember times when we talked regularly as friends. If so, did that ever actually happen?

If it did, what happened? And why did I not remember anything other than bits and pieces, as if having to drag it through molasses from here to Tokyo? Was she dealing with the same thing?

Conflict crept over her face as she examined me. "You know, you aren't supposed to see or hear me when I'm in this gear, didn't you know that?"

I pursed my lips, fully turning toward her. "What are you saying? I mean, sure you're a little see-through, but, I mean, Dad and Mom talked with you only last week."

"Yeah." She reached up to her head piece, touching it lightly. "I played around a bit more with it after your father's adjustments, so I didn't stand out in crowds as much and found a way to make myself basically invisible. In other words, what I'm saying is that something isn't right about this situation. You shouldn't sense me. I shouldn't be able to talk to you, my memory isn't supposed to be this jumbled and yet..." She furrowed her brow, tapping her head before wincing. Her fingers spasmed and, for a split second, it seemed like her entire body seized up. I felt something, a wave washing over me. I shivered as pain slashed through my skull, my palms flush against the sides of my head as shooting agony shot through every synapse in my damn brain. Thankfully, it passed as quickly as it came and I found myself trembling, barely keeping myself standing.

I must have stumbled backward at some point, because I was farther from Mira. Mira? It was Mira, right? For a moment, only fog covered my brain, before, like a hurricane of wind, it was whipped away and I grimaced. How the hell did I manage to forget the conversation we were JUST having?

I shook my head, making eye contact with her just as she shifted her attention back to me.

She blinked once, twice before glaring at me. "You can sense me." Her voice was monotone. "I don't know why, but you should not be able to sense me."

What the hell? Okay, I could understand the whole confusion thing. But this was almost like she didn't...

Didn't remember our conversation. Okay, was it just me, or did what I said sound really weird? Please tell me it was just my imagination.

No? Okay, fine.

I grimaced as I took a step back, hands up defensively. "Um, Mira?"

"How do you know my name?"

Oh shit…

"It's me. Kieran? We're friends. We were just talking about your—" I was going to say father, but something in her expression caused me to stop.

That conflict was back again, but it seemed to almost be physically hurting her. I shook my head and smiled shakily. "Never mind." I took another step back. "Let's just forget anything happened here, all right? I didn't mean to bother you."

This did answer some of my questions. And did an excellent job of adding a shit ton more. Great.

She shook her head before reaching down to one of the guns at her waist. "No, I need to bring you in…" she trailed off, appearing confused for a second before shaking her head once more and glaring at me. "I need to bring you in so that the director can meet you. After all, you're not supposed to be able to tell I'm here. Only specters can spot me."

"Have you ever encountered a specter?" I asked, taking another step back as she stepped forward, a strange grin slowly curling her lips upward.

"No. But I've been told they appear very similar to humans."

Well, she isn't far off, for the most part. "Okay, so…"

"Which means I have no way to know if you are a specter or not and, though I think you are a classmate of mine, that doesn't mean much." She pulled out the gun, and I found myself recoiling.

"He… hey!" I cut in, attention drifting toward her visor, which seemed to be a little clouded. "You're only able to sense specters through the visor, correct? Yet you can tell I'm here, in front of you, can't you? So—"

Her expression was very strange, contorted in such a way that I wasn't sure if she was excited or scared as I spoke. Excitement, I could guess, with how the gun was trembling and that GRIN was NOT going away. But the scared? The worried?

That, I couldn't figure out.

"You... how do you know that?" She growled. Outright GROWLED at me. Shit!

I took another step back and yelped as I found myself backed into a wall. Where the hell did this come from? I glanced behind me and realized, with surprise, that I was near the school. I must have wandered this way while chatting with Mira, lost in our conversation. But either way, that didn't help me much now that she practically had me pinned to the wall with a gun in my chest and—

By gosh, was she scary! "Mira!" I managed to cut in, voice only trembling marginally, "You JUST told me! Come on, you're smart. You know I'm telling the tru—" I yelped as she leaned forward, manic grin increasing.

"Maybe you are, maybe you aren't. The fact of the matter doesn't concern me. I haven't had a reading yet, but who knows. I am still new to this." I winced as the gun pushed into my ribcage, digging into my side. Yikes, that hurt. "But that's fine. I'm still going to enjoy myself, after all. No one besides you can tell I'm here." She leaned forward. "No one at all."

I felt a chill run down my spine as another shot of pain screeched through me. What was WRONG with her? This wasn't the Mira I knew. She didn't resemble the Mira I knew from either memory.

No. This was a Mira that, right now, my brain was telling me didn't exist. Throwing caution to the wind, since it was already long gone anyway, I coughed, catching her full attention, if I didn't already have it. "So cool and all, but why don't you turn off the suit?" I choked as the gun dug in deeper. "I mean, you literally have me up against the wall. Can you at least check to make sure I'm not a specter? Please?" I tacked on the ending when her grin disappeared into a scowl. She examined me for the longest time before shrugging and pulling away just enough for me to breathe, but not much else. I felt a spasm and then, as if something in my brain clicked, I could tell she was there, that she existed.

Sort of...

I frowned at the thought as I filtered through the crowded and messy memories. What was I supposed to be remembering? Mira... right. She did exist. She'd almost lost her father in an... no... she DID lose her father in an atta—

GAH! I felt like screaming at all the conflicting thoughts. No! I know he isn't dead because I remembered saving both of them. I remembered just having this conversation, but was that not the case?

"Wha..." I hesitated before shifting my attention onto her. "What happened to your father?"

Hitting her with her gun would have done less damage. We just talked about this. I remembered that now, but... her mouth dropped open. A moment later, it snapped shut and she went to respond, only to freeze, a strangled "How?" slipping from her throat.

"I was there. I helped you and your father. Don't you remember?" Those words... they were repeated so many times lately and I still felt like I was missing something with them. She seemed lost, pulling the gun close to her as she trembled. I noticed her start to sway and yelped, quickly steadying her as she went to collapse.

"You did help, but you didn't help. You were there, but no one was there. No one helped but the police, but..." the buts were starting to bug me. Still, I let her continue as she stared at the ground.

Honestly, it made sense. If my brain was in shambles, hers probably wasn't much better.

"They were right to have me follow."

I jerked as something pushed into my back. Why had I moved away from the wall again? Oh right, to catch Mira. I didn't dare peer behind me, gulping.

"And, uh, who might you be?" As much as I wished to say otherwise, my voice ended up shooting up a few octaves by the end when I felt something digging into my back, a faint sound echoing behind me that sounded almost like sizzling. Not a pleasant thought.

"No one major."

"Uh-huh," I muttered, sort of, but not really recognizing the voice. That voice was from that guy, right? The one who talked with Father? But then, I didn't exactly trust my thoughts at the moment. "Then why do you have a weapon to my back?" I managed to squeak out as Mira slowly came to her senses in my arms. I was just praying that it wasn't that deranged girl from before because, by gosh, this was already terrifying enough.

"Because you are remembering when you shouldn't. I know we have a promise, but this is going too far. We're not allowed to wipe you, but we can make sure you don't interact with anyone else. Maybe we can figure out WHY you remember something you shouldn't."

I gulped, very loudly. What did they mean? Wipe? Remembering things I shouldn't? "I don't kno—"

My words were cut off when whatever was in my back pushed deeper. I let out an indignant, half-pained cry. Mira shook her head before she stood up, conflict showing in her tense posture as she steadied herself once more.

"Don't, El—"

"Oh-ho. So, you do remember this boy." El, or whoever it was, spoke up, sounding amused and a little confused. "Strange. So he can remind others. Very interesting. Sorry, my dear colleague, but we REALLY need him now."

Wait! What the hell?

I noticed something glimmer in Mira's gaze, could feel my heart pounding almost out of my chest. My mouth tasted dry as fear plummeted through me. I just knew, knew if this person was allowed to do this, I didn't want to think about it.

Time stood still, I could hear the faint crackle, a shift of fabric, like a glove, just as Mira's attention shifted, her shoulders tensing.

Yet, she wasn't watching either of us.

"Kieran!" A shout echoed around the area as something slammed into me, pushing me out of the way as something else went off. A loud popping crackle sounded out, the air sizzling for a moment. I felt something scramble off me before that same thing tugged me upward. I wasn't sure what happened next, everything was more of a blur than anything as I raced away. Mira was tugging the weapon from the other person's arms, while the person, the man I recognized from the police compound, snarled at her before tugging it out of her grasp.

Thankfully, by that point, we were around the corner and out of sight. That didn't mean we stopped. We raced down the street as my breath caught in my throat. Why did this feel familiar?

A ghostly image. Rain. Wooden boards. I grimaced; my free hand darted to my temple as I stumbled. I was so lost and confused right now, I wanted to scream and demand to know what the hell was going on. Unfortunately, I knew I couldn't do that. I finally turned my attention on my savior, only for my jaw to drop. I knew I should have expected it, but the golden hair and piercings were a dead giveaway. It was Felix. He observed me before sighing in relief and finally slowing. He seemed just as tired as me, panting for breath as we leaned against an alley wall.

"So, having fun yet, Ki?" he asked, throwing an arm over my shoulder. I sent him a glare and he chuckled weakly. "I think it's not exactly safe for you to stay here anymore." He hesitated, lost in thought before catching my attention. "You remember me, at least somewhat. Don't you?"

I frowned before hesitantly nodding because he was right, I did remember him. Bits and pieces. A joke here. A laugh there. Simple moments like playing the newest game at the arcade or searching through books for an assignment. Or, him introducing me to someone I should, no, did know.

I knew I should know him beyond that. That I was only remembering the basics, the bare bones, but it seemed to be enough for him because his grin widened as he leaned forward, pulling me down with him, as if to talk to me in a conspiratorial whisper, only to let out a relieved breath, a wide smile on his face. "Good. Then let's go to Sylvia."

Chapter Seventeen

I wasn't sure what to expect when he said we were heading to meet Sylvia. But one thing was certain, I didn't expect to be taking a bus to the next town over, quite a ways from the amusement park my parents went to the other day, or the one—I grimaced, deciding I wasn't sure on that memory. Either way, passing through the town where I could just barely spot the amusement park I was at not that long ago, we continued on our way. The towns weren't exactly next to each other, there was a lot of woodland and farmland in between. Plus, the bus couldn't exactly go at high speeds so it was going to take around thirty to forty minutes. I kept my head down, feeling worried. Felix was scanning the bus with a nervous air, finger tapping on his leg as it jittered against the seat in front. A few other people sat on the bus around us, but no one right nearby. Though, I'll admit, it was hard to tell who was who. Before, it was easy. If they were white, they were ghosts, but now...

"Is there anyone here I shouldn't be sensing?" I asked Felix quietly. He quirked a brow in amusement before he scrutinized the interior of the bus. He pointed out a young woman who was trying, and now that I was watching, failing to hold onto a young man's arm. The young man noticed my gaze and raised his brow. I quickly shifted my attention. I followed as Felix gestured behind us to show a young girl hopping up and down, waving her arms.

I grimaced, guessing from there I should have figured it out easy enough, but I guess I was so used to them being beings of white that, well, seeing them as actual people was terrifying, especially after memories of my conversation and arguments with Mira kept cropping

154

up. Were they people? Or were they specters like Mira said? Who was that man that was following Mira and almost shot me? Was he watching us that whole time? And why did he seem familiar?

I knew I should relax. It wasn't going to be any LESS stressful than now, but my heart was still thumping in my chest, though for probably a very different reason. Saliva caught in my throat, liquid fire on my tongue. I swallowed, forcing myself to take deep breaths before turning my attention to Felix. "So, where are we going?"

He leaned back, arms behind his head and a subtle grin on his lips. "Oh, just someplace that I know Mira would have loved." He grimaced. "Well, at least when you two—" Static shot through my head and I winced. He stopped, frowning before letting out a sigh. He kicked himself forward, leaning at an angle to peer up at me. "To answer your question, though? Remember when Mira talked about an old amusement park in the next town over?"

He seemed hesitant in his words, but no stab of pain or static invaded my head and, contrary to what I thought, I DID in fact remember that conversation. She said something about it and I thought Felix was there too. I gave him a weak smile. "Sorta?"

"Good enough." He shrugged as he got comfortable once more. He hesitated before tilting his head just enough to peer over to me. "And, it wasn't just my imagination earlier, right?"

"Hm?" I leaned back, letting myself try and relax into the seat.

He followed suit, tension still singing through his body. "Mira. When we fled, it seemed like she was trying to grapple the gun from that man's grasp. Does that mean she remembered? Or..."

I paused, thinking over what Felix just said along with the memory in question. I had noticed, but I hadn't thought much about it until Felix brought it up. But he was right, she put her neck on the line to stop him from shooting us, though only a few minutes before she had a similar gun shoved into my ribcage. "I guess." I hesitated before peering out to the passing scenery. "Maybe it was just instinct or something, or maybe she did remember and wanted to help. I can't say for sure."

Silence was the only response I got for the longest time before

Felix let out a sigh. "I guess. I was just really hoping I wasn't imagining things. That she really did remember us. Me..."

I could almost feel the frustration emanating from my companion. I wasn't completely sure what he meant, but from what I could remember, Mira and Felix were close. I let out a sigh, leaning against the cool glass of the window. Somehow, the conversation made me think of my parents. Were they all right? Was I going to be able to go home soon? I had a feeling I probably couldn't. I mean, that man, I thought, knew my father and Mira knew where I lived as well. There was no safe way to return home at this point. I curled my fingers into the leather of the seat, trying to calm my thoughts. They would be all right. That man, El, never mentioned anything about them and Dad was smart.

Of course, that didn't stop me from already missing them. I wondered how worried they would be about me. I found myself stewing in that thought for the rest of the trip. We continued our journey in silence with me occasionally scanning the surroundings as we blurred past, through the woods. The young man from before moved to a seat farther up and away from me, the young woman sending me a glare before hurrying after him. I huffed, turning away. Okay, so I might have seemed strange, talking to thin air. No wonder.

I might have fallen asleep at one point because, when I awoke, I noticed that off in the distance, was a Ferris wheel without lights on. The spokes gleamed in the sunlight, the edges dulled from what was probably rust.

"There it is."

I jumped, startled by the sudden interjection. Felix chuckled as he stood. The bus slowly came to a halt and I found myself hurrying after him, down the steps. I definitely appeared like a weirdo, now that I thought about it, but it seemed like everyone else ignored me, which worked perfectly. The streets were crowded, much to my surprise, people came and went, heading inside stores and trailing behind others. My head swam as I realized that, once again, I was struggling to figure out who was human and who was a specter. I hung close to Felix, who didn't seem too upset by the notion. He led me through the crowd and I winced as, every so often, I would breeze through a person. I could tell they were there, but I still couldn't really touch them.

At least, not most of them. I was so confused on this, power? Eh, I didn't know what to call it. We wandered through the streets, moving past a shopping area into a more desolate part of town. A long road led to what appeared to be a gated parking lot. Weeds and grass clung to the sides, breaking through the pavement as wind blew like a faint howl through the links. Felix stepped up to an area where the links were broken, gesturing for me to follow before ducking underneath. I couldn't help but feel a strange sense of déjà vu. I shook my head and followed. My fingers lightly touched the cold of the metal as I dipped my head down enough to not scrape the jagged edges. The other side didn't appear much better. A building was placed off to one side, desolate ticket booths with yawning mouths of broken glass. I shook my head and turned away, hurrying after Felix as he slipped past the broken turnstiles and into the park proper. There were rides and buildings set up everywhere, the Ferris wheel dead center. I could hear the faint creaking, seeing the spokes shudder as a wind whipped through the area, tussling leaves and litter about with ease.

Felix turned to the left and I followed, examining the place. Was someone out there? I felt a chill and glanced over my shoulder: nothing. Just open doorways leading to different buildings and shops. I shuddered and returned my focus on Felix. He hesitated at one of the doorways before knocking. It echoed, loud and obnoxious in the silence of the abandoned park. I was so glad it was not night time or raining. It was already creepy enough as it was with the sun filtering through everything. I heard another knock and realized Felix knocked once more before pulling back, stepping slightly in front of me. I blinked, confused before the door suddenly swung open and I found a gun in Felix's face.

I let out a yelp that definitely did NOT sound like a high-pitched shriek. Felix only flinched. "Well, usual greeting aside. I'm here for Sylvia. I have someone with me that she would like to meet."

The man, now that I actually had a chance to observe him, was a thinner boy with reddish hair and narrowed eyes. He was thin to the point of emaciated and… my shoulders tensed. "You're the figure I ran into a while ago." I pointed out, garnering the attention of both of them. "You're the first one I ever ran into!" The boy dropped his weapon, scanning me almost calculatingly.

He grunted, before pulling back and gesturing inside. With his gun, of course, couldn't forget THAT little detail. Dammit, Felix, what did you get me into?

The hallway was dimly lit, even worse when the door clanged shut behind us. The boy stayed at his post as Felix led me farther inside. Ha, ha, going into the jaws of the beast. Right?

Oh god. Bad thoughts.

I shook my head as we descended, farther and farther. Wait, were we going underground? What the… how was this here? I highly doubted that this was part of the original building at this point, and this was proven true when I found a makeshift opening, cut haphazardly into the earth with something like a drape being the only means of separation. I could hear conversation inside, but I couldn't quite tell what it was. Felix sent me a grin, finger to his lips before pushing inside.

Deciding to wait, I hung back, not in the mood to be in the center of attention that I KNEW was coming. I heard a fluttering and then the drape was simultaneously knocked aside as something ran into me. I yelped, backpedaling. I just barely avoided falling, though I wasn't sure how. I shook my head as the person who smacked into me caught me from falling over. She grimaced. "Sorry, didn't realize you were right outside."

"It's fine." I croaked out as my brain caught up with who was in front of me. It was that girl I kept seeing, though this time, she was dressed, not in common clothes, but in something more fitting for an action scene. Trousers tucked into sturdy boots with… was that a FLAK jacket? What the heck?

She seemed to notice where my attention was because she suddenly grew serious as she helped steady me. "You're here." Her tone demanded no argument and was more fact than a question. Startled at her sudden change in mood, completely different from her usually casual affection, I found myself only slightly surprised as she grabbed my wrist and tugged me past the curtain. I found myself stumbling, arm up to push away the curtain so it didn't smack me.

When I lowered it, I found myself frozen, for an entirely different reason.

The other side looked like someone took a pick axe and kept getting it stuck THROUGH the rock. The room was jagged and cluttered, with makeshift desks set up to one side and a table, the only thing that actually seemed well put together, in the middle. An older woman that I recognized as usually following Sylvia around with a gun was off to one side, watching me warily, while a heavyset man, who also seemed familiar, with muscles that could throw me all the way back home, was talking animatedly with Felix. Felix was watching him with both confusion and excitement, as if he wasn't sure which emotion to feel or have.

There were other people, sprawled around the room, but before I could really examine anyone else, the girl from before dragged me toward the table, garnering the room's attention and making me gulp. I caught gazes with, I think, half a dozen people before an uproar suddenly filled the room.

"Another one?"

"Sylvia, we can't—"

"Shut it," the woman with the gun said. She was lithe and held a stern expression, one I think she probably always wore. She definitely appeared like someone who knew what she was doing. "I know this boy."

That seemed to shut everyone up. Sylvia let out a faint sigh, something I only heard because I was standing right next to her, before she squared her shoulders. "This is Kieran, the boy I talked about before and—" I winced, fingers grasping at my head. Dammit, not again.

"What? Can he actually sense us then, even though—"

"Yes." Felix spoke up, stepping away from the heavyset man and standing next to me. "He's been able to 'sense' us." He definitely had quotes around that word. "And has been able to for about a year and a half now."

Silence, utter silence filled the hall.

I felt a shift and suddenly everyone was bounding forward. Felix and Sylvia stood in front of me, as if they were guards.

"Everyone, stand down!" Sylvia spoke, her voice cold and worn. Yet, everyone seemed to hear, because they backed off, fidgeting in their respective locations. Whether from excitement or something else, I couldn't tell. "Now I can get why you are all agitated, but he is not to blame."

"How though? He's been able to spot us since you—"

Whatever else one of the people said was drowned out by static, a loud, erratic, buzzing noise filled my head and I must have stumbled back, because cold rock was digging into my side and my palms were pushed tightly to my skull. I must have pulled up my headphones at one point, because they were pushed taut against my ears, finally drowning out the buzzing.

I shook my head, only to feel soft fingers touch my hairline. I blinked, too tired to really jerk, and spotted Sylvia, examining me in concern. I smiled weakly and she nodded before stepping back and turning around. "He's affected, in a way, just like the rest of us. While he can see and hear us," she trailed off, simply gesturing to me. Oh yeah, like that DEFINITELY explained it. Well, it did in some ways, I guess?

Ergh! I couldn't think straight right now.

"If he can sense us, can he, like the others used to, interact with both us and them?" one person asked, anxiety and hope shining in her voice.

Sylvia hesitated, observing me for a moment before slowly nodding. "He can interact with both sides, but please, don't push him. He's only recently been able to fully sense us."

"What do you mean?"

I let out a sigh, feeling bad at having Felix and Sylvia explain everything. Taking in a breath, I decided to leave the headphones on because, for some reason, I could still hear everyone even with them. "For the last year and a half, I've only been able to see wisps, white beings that appear very similar to ghosts. A few days ago, I started actually seeing them, you all." I gestured toward Felix and Sylvia.

"So you can hurt us," one woman spoke up, angered. "You would be able to—"

"No," I cut in, shaking my head, catching the woman before either Felix or Sylvia. "I can hurt you as much as you can hurt me. No, if anything, I just want to know what is going on…" I trailed off, centering my thoughts. Thankfully, while it seemed others had questions, my vehement response was enough to make them hesitate, so I continued where I left off. "I think it really solidified…" I trailed off once more, head hurting. Was it a few days ago? A week ago? When was it?

"When I was turned." Felix spoke up and I blinked.

Wait, what? "Turned?" I asked, garnering Felix's attention. Sylvia's eyes narrowed before she clapped her hands.

"All right, enough of that. I need to speak with Kieran for a bit. Will all personnel please leave until otherwise specified? Margaret, Harold, with me."

I watched, with a hint of awe, as most of the people filed out, unhappy, but listening to her as they left. Only the woman with the gun and the heavyset man that was talking with Felix earlier remained. Sylvia gestured toward the curtain and Felix nodded, heading out.

If I paid attention, I could still spot his feet under the tendrils, so I guess he was acting as a guard or something. Sylvia gestured me over to the table. "So, from what you said earlier, I can gather some things, but what do you know about us?"

"Not much," I admitted, grimacing. "Just that most people can't sense you. I think I should know you. I definitely think I should know Felix and that my brain is a mess right now with different thoughts."

"Yeah, sounds about right." Sylvia shook her head, shooting a strange expression toward her two compatriots, "What do you two think? Should we get his help?"

Harold shrugged as Margaret analyzed me quietly. "He's survived this long with the sight, could be handy. However, most of the people will be hesitant to get his help. If he gets turned, he could end up as one of them. And even if he doesn't, he brings attention to this place, more so than before."

"That's what makes me curious. Obviously, he's seen us for a while, but everyone else was turned or captured. So why wasn't he?" Harold grunted out.

Turned? There was that phrase again. What did it mean?

Sylvia shook her head, incredibly hesitant before turning toward me. "All right, why ARE you here anyway? I never got to ask because everyone was still around, but..."

"I met with Mira when she was out and about. She was acting strange. She mentioned something about my being able to see her when I shouldn't, which is probably similar to why I could sense you all." I noticed flashes of fear cross everyone's face, but continued on anyway, "I talked to her for a bit and she seemed to remember something? Maybe? Who knows, because right after that, some man held a gun to my back and mentioned something about not being able to wipe me and..." I stilled as the rest of the words trailed through my thoughts. Oh god. I could feel myself pale and shuddered. "I think that man planned to capture me and..." I didn't think I could continue. I was around for enough of my dad's experiments to warrant a guess and it sent a shudder through my very soul, as cliche as that sounds.

"I guess they are getting desperate." Margaret spoke up after a moment of silence enveloped the room.

Sylvia nodded, deep in thought before whipping around. "So, obviously, we can't let them take Kieran. Unfortunately, it doesn't seem like we can explain what has happened to us without him almost blacking out."

"We can experiment to find out what we can say so he can at least get an idea," Harold pointed out. "It's worth a shot, especially since the others will be a little fractured on what to do with him. Some might be eager to meet him, but..."

Sylvia hesitated, gnawing at her lip before nodding and turning toward me. "All right. Kieran, tell me if you start feeling off, all right?"

I nodded, gearing myself up for what was probably going to be another round of shooting agony, decidedly NOT thinking over what

Harold just said.

"All right, so, for starters. We're not ghosts."

I nodded, letting out a breath of relief in the process. I'd figured that, but it was nice to have the verification.

"Secondly, we are still alive."

Okay, that made sense, usually the two would mean the same thing, but then, we were speaking of the same beings who were literally just white figures over a week ago. Of course, that meant—

"Third, we are human."

I stilled, blinking. Okay, I know, rationally, I should have realized that, but, well, look at my previous point.

"Fourth, we reme—"

"Stop!" I yelped out as I felt the beginning of a headache, that buzzing creeping back in. Sylvia jammed her mouth shut with a burgeoning frown before nodding.

"All right, seems we can't explain what happened to us, but is that good enough for you?"

"I…" I wasn't sure what to tell her. No. It wasn't enough, but… "Ergh, I think?" I wasn't sure what to say to her as I rubbed my temples. Most of the things she said were, in actuality, pretty common sense and, I think, she was trying to say something about memory? The tingling I could feel as a warning was indication enough that I was right. Though I was frustrated that it was all I knew. Okay. So these beings, humans, I had to remind myself, had something to do with memory?

Okay, okay, shooting pain, got it. Don't think about that anymore. I shook my head and returned my focus onto the trio, which, ironically enough, reminded me. "Hey, did you guys know anything about an anti-specter group?"

The group stiffened as Sylvia turned to me. "What do you mean?" she demanded.

I frowned. "Mira, someone I should know, joined up a week ago, the one I was telling you about earlier? She now has a visor that can see you and a weapon—"

"We've seen a few of those around the last few days," Margaret said, her voice mostly neutral, if a little angered. "You say she joined up a week ago?" They exchanged somber expressions as Sylvia grimaced.

"Ki, you said she was acting strange?"

I nodded, feeling worried. "Yeah, she said it was a prototype. I meant to speak with her, but I ended up not seeing her for the whole week."

I frowned as Sylvia sighed. "Ah..."

That... That's it?

"So, what now?" Margaret pointed out with a frown, arms crossed. "There is no doubt that the information has already spread to the others about his arrival and I do not believe the reactions will be friendly."

Sylvia grimaced and let out a longer sigh as I jerked up, annoyed at the change in topic. What about Mira! But nope, Sylvia, without my say, decided a change of topic was in order. Thanks, person I don't know. "That's true, their reactions certainly could go either way." She shook her head. "I'll worry about that in a bit. For now, Harold can you get Ki a room?"

Harold grinned, doing a quick salute before turning to me. "Come on, lad, I'll bring you to where Felix is staying, you two can share the room. Not the nicest of abodes, but we do what we can."

"Actually, I was wondering about that," I admitted, deciding to just say screw it on the previous conversation and move on. "How is this all here anyway? I mean, it doesn't seem like you should be able to interact with, well, anything."

The trio reacted with varying levels of bemusement before Sylvia stepped forward. "Well, it's a bit of touch and go. While you are not wrong in us being unable to interact with the environment, we can interact with some things. Things that we might have had with us or things that hold a sentimental value to it. There were a few people, such as yourself, who were able to see us that came to help, but..." She shook her head. "It's best not to ask about that. Also, some of us are better able to interact with your world than others. For instance, Felix and I can actually touch things and move objects. Margaret's gun can cut through glass, though getting ammunition is not easy. Things like that."

I frowned as she finished her statement. There were others that could sense them? I think one of the people mentioned that earlier. So why were none of them here? Or were they? It made my head spin and I decided to follow her advice and not think about it, other things pulling at my attention instead.

Wait, most of the people she listed were… "Okay, can anyone who DOESN'T know me do that?"

Sylvia's lips quirked up as if I said something that both amused and satisfied her. "What do you think?"

I glared at her before letting out a sigh, rubbing my temples. "I'm going to go out on a limb and say no."

"Bingo." She snapped her fingers before her smile dropped. "And that's why we can't let them take you. You are our last link to that world, or what we have left of it. From what we've gathered, because of… circumstances…" the way she flinched spoke volumes without answering any of my multitude of questions, "you may be our ONLY link left between becoming completely lost like some of the outliers have."

Outliers? "Like that guy in the haunted house?" I found myself asking.

Sylvia nodded, a sad expression contorting her familiar features. "Exactly like that. The more lost, the less human you are. That's the other reason why people like your friend are brought in to go against what they call specters and what we call the lost, and why I understood what you meant about Mira and didn't go into detail."

Oh. My head was spinning, trying to take this all in. My thoughts stilled. "Wait, when did I tell you about the haunted house?" I whispered, facing her.

She turned away, walking over to what appeared to be a desk. "Just believe me when I say I know what happened there." She turned to me, papers in hand. "However, I think we've already given you a lot to think about and it's been a long day. Get something to eat and then some rest, got it?"

I winced. "All right. I think…" I trailed off as panic shot through me as I was once more reminded of the time and my earlier thoughts on the bus. "Mom! Dad! I never told them where I was going! I was supposed to be back by lunch and, considering how hungry I am, it is definitely past that." I groaned and slumped to the floor, leaning against the wall. I wasn't sure why I panicked in such a way. I'd already deduced I wouldn't be with them for lunch, but I guess it didn't fully hit me until now. "Damn."

Sylvia shook her head, that sad expression still very much in place. "Sorry, but there isn't much we can do for that. It's hard enough getting chances to see you without them spotting us, getting a note to… your parents are another matter entirely. They'll be watching for you or one of us and we can't risk sending any of our own out."

I bit my lip, realizing the truth to her words. Mom was probably in a frenzy and Dad… I shook my head and pushed myself to my feet. "All right. I got it."

Sylvia smiled, a broad genuine smile that was missing during most of this conversation and she gestured to Harold. "Well then? You heard him. Food and then rest."

Harold nodded, and headed outside. I peered back at Sylvia for a moment, noting her expression shift to a mix of anger and a strange fierceness before she turned to talk to her other bodyguard. I wasn't sure what to make of it, or of her. The more I thought about it, the more I desperately wanted to know who she was and why she seemed to know me. Hopefully I'd be able to learn that information here and soon.

Chapter Eighteen

I pushed through the curtains with ease, following Harold into the small hallway. Felix caught my gaze before turning toward Harold. "So, where to?"

"Cafeteria, and then I'm going to have you bring him to your room. You'll have to share since it's the only one we have left."

"Got it!" Felix saluted, grinning widely. "Just like the sleepover we had before..." He trailed off before shaking his head. "Anyway, food!"

I chuckled, following after them. The hallways led back up to the surface, bringing us back outside and, this time, I was certain people were watching. I scanned my surroundings, spotting people peeking out around corners, their gazes following me as I passed. I could feel myself curl inward. I didn't know how celebrities did it because, by gosh, was it intimidating, being seen and observed by so many. Thankfully, it didn't last long before we ended up in another building that was, probably, at one point, an indoor pool. The pipes were definitely no longer functioning and the remains of mildew coated one far wall, making me cringe. Ignoring the safety hazards of that...

"I know, I'm not fond of it either, but this is the only place that has a bar that is still operational, since we were able to manipulate the pipes enough to create a weak flow of electricity through water."

I nodded, grimacing as we walked to one side. It made me wonder how they got food in the first place, but that just brought me back around to wondering why it was that only Sylvia and Felix were able to interact with anything, which did NOT help my ensuing headache. So, pushing that to the side, we walked to the cafeteria. Whatever noise I'd been hearing from the other room disappeared as we stepped inside and I sighed. I did NOT like all this attention.

The room was large, obviously having been a place to eat and relax when this was still a park. A long table with a door behind it was set up to one side with two people stationed there, one next to the door and one at the counter, passing out food. For some, it seemed that they could easily hold the bowls. Others were being fed, their fingers passing through the ceramic. How did they swallow? Where did the food go? I felt sick to my stomach at the sight, noticing the emaciated appearance of most of the people here.

"Scary, isn't it?" Felix whispered to me. "Most people outside this place barely survive for more than a week, tops, before they either become lost or die."

"What is this place though? Who created it?"

Felix shrugged. "I've only heard bits and pieces. Supposedly, it was Sylvia, but how or why? Well, the why is obvious, but how, I'm not sure. I really don't know anything about the girl besides what I just told you."

I frowned, taking that information in with everything else as we stepped up to the counter. The woman turned to me with a genuine expression, only to freeze, doing a double take. "You are—"

"We need three bowls please." Harold spoke up, drawing the woman's attention away from me.

"But he doesn't need our food. I barely have enough to feed—"

"He is an escapee like the rest of us right now, Sylvia's orders."

The woman clammed up, nodding before piling three bowls with what seemed like a thick stew. I guess it makes sense for people to believe Sylvia made this place if everyone was following her orders, but that just brought around the questions Felix brought up. How and why? Yes, it seemed obvious, but I couldn't help but shake the feeling that the description and reasoning weren't quite right. Plus, she was a girl my age and a lot of people here seemed older and more experienced in surviving in these harsh conditions, so...

Speaking of… while I understood the hesitance from the woman, I still felt uncomfortable. I thought she would be happy to give me some food. I was a link to the real world for them. Then again, both Harold and Margaret mentioned people might not be fond of me being here. I wondered why? I shook my head and took a seat in one of the chairs, letting out a sigh as I chowed down on the food. It wasn't exactly anything. It was very bland, but it did the job of filling my stomach which was really all I needed at the moment. I finished up, my appetite dying a little each time I tilted my head up to examine the others, the ones who couldn't be seen, watching us with wariness. Thankfully, to my limited sanity, Felix and Harold, who didn't seem to have that problem, finished up, and all three of us retreated from the cafeteria.

I definitely did not feel welcome here and I wasn't sure why. To anyone else, I would be the sole person living here. I shuddered at the thought. But then why did they seem to watch me so warily? Why did they seem…

"They're jealous."

I jerked, peering over toward Harold. I opened my mouth to respond, before hesitating, he watched quietly as I debated. "But why? I mean, I'm their link as Sylvia called it. Why wouldn't they be appreciative?" I knew I sounded a bit whiny, or almost selfish, but it kind of hurt. My thoughts flickered to the guy on the bus who moved away from me, to my parents, and now the side that I was hoping to help was shying away.

Harold sighed as Felix pursed his lips. "I don't get it either. Why would they be jealous of Kieran?"

"Right. You were just recently turned." Harold surveyed the area before gesturing us through the doorway. The red-haired boy from earlier gave me an uncertain expression, features cold, before turning away. We descended the stairwell as he continued, "I won't lie, there are a few people who are happy that you are here besides Sylvia. They are the more optimistic of the group. However, many people here have been suffering under these conditions for months, if not longer and many are on the verge of giving up. This place was created only a year ago after all, and

I believe people have been turned since long before that. The few who have been able to sense us have come before, only to be turned or captured by the police. Most people here are wary, fearful and…" Harold turned to me with a wistful gaze. "Many have lost much in this time, including their very names, and then there's you, who comes waltzing in. You, who their founder and protector remembers and cherishes. You, the boy who, even after so long, still has everything that they lost. If I didn't already know you and Felix as well as I do, I could only imagine how I would be feeling as well. I don't think I would be one of the optimistic ones."

"But that's…" Felix trailed off as I thought over what Harold said.

"So, they're not only jealous of the fact that I still seem to be amongst the 'real people'," there had to be a better way to say that, "but also because Sylvia seems to like me and because I've been like this for a full year and a half when others haven't…" I trailed off. Now would be the perfect time to ask my earlier question. "Wait, others were able to sense you?"

Harold nodded, staring off into space as we stopped in front of a doorway with nothing but a rug covering the entrance. "When it first happened, there were quite a few who could sense us, but as time passed and every single one of the ones who could were turned or…" He shook his head. "If you are curious, only a few people knew about you before today. The guard, Phillip, you met earlier, the one with the red hair? Myself, Sylvia and Margaret. That's it. Everyone else suspected or wondered if they happened to spot you while in town, but due to Sylvia's request, your situation was kept a secret."

"Oh." What could I say to that? My head swam with thoughts. To think, I wasn't welcome on either side. Yet I was supposedly the only link both sides still had. I did NOT miss the irony in the situation.

I peered back the way we came, examining the line of electric lights precariously set up along the floor. I understood why they were laid out on the floor and I was surprised I hadn't tripped over any. Guess these guys wouldn't exactly have to worry about that little dilemma. At least it was something.

I pursed my lips, feeling my shoulders slump. Of course they would be angry. Now that I thought about it. Jealousy made sense. How many of these people had been able to sense like me and then were turned? How many were forced to live like this, only for someone to coming waltzing in, as Harold called it? Sylvia was seen as the founder, their protector. For her to want to watch out for me and protect me, it must anger so many…

I almost wanted to apologize to everyone here. I didn't know why I was like this, or how I'd 'survived' when others hadn't. It made me feel sick.

"I've given you a lot to think about. I do apologize and I hope you do realize not everyone thinks this way. As I stated, there are actually people here that are grateful for your arrival, all right?"

I jerked, head snapping to face Harold. He nodded, before changing his attention to Felix, a faint good-bye whispered between them before he turned and left. I watched him go before Felix lightly pulled me past the curtain that acted as the doorway to his room. It was gently lit with a lamp set up on one side and a twin-sized mattress that DEFINITELY had better days and could barely fit a single person. Plus, was that trash sticking out of the side?

"Hey, at least I have a bed, I am much better off than most here," Felix teased, spotting my expression which was probably screwed up in distaste, though the hint of sadness spoke just as much volume as his teasing tone.

"Sure, but still…"

"I know what you mean, man." He let out a sigh, finally dropping his grin. "It's hard here. Ever since IT happened, it's been damn near impossible. I'm lucky because, well, you know me?" He questioned hesitantly, sparing me a glance. Whether he was being wary, knowing I might curl up in pain if he worded it wrong or if he was just uncomfortable saying it, it was hard to tell. Still, it brought up an interesting point.

I scanned the room and paused before slowly turning to Felix.

"Okay, that's great and all, but there's only one mattress."

His grin reappeared and I glared. He just chuckled. "Well, it's either A, one of us goes out and grabs a mattress or blanket and brings it back, or B, we share."

"And you can't pick up anything worth a damn, can you?" I realized with a twitch that would not go away.

He shrugged, humming in a way that was definitely supposed to CONVEY innocence. I let out a sigh. "And, of course, from what I've seen and what Harold said, I step one foot out of here without someone else and I will be bombarded with everyone's attention, which doesn't sound like it will be a good thing."

Felix winced. "That's... really true, man." He let out a sigh. "I didn't really think of that. I'll be honest. I thought people would be happy that you are here. After all, you could help us, but I didn't realize just what state everyone here was in. I never thought of what Harold mentioned. To think, so many people have lived like this for so long. They just watch someone with something they don't have, something they want, crave..." He trailed off before sighing. "I won't deny it. I've felt the same way—and not like that, you jackass!"

Did he notice my smirk at his language? Oops. "But you made it sound so cheesy."

Felix rolled his eyes. "I'm supposed to be the sarcastic one. Not you."

"Don't worry, you can have it back." I let out a breath, taking a seat on the floor, or at least, attempting to. Felix grabbed my arm before I could sit and shoved me toward the bed. I stumbled, falling onto it with an oomph before glaring across at the boy who decided to sit where I'd been not two seconds earlier.

"Hey, don't go glaring at me. I just figured you would need the sleep more than me, plus at this point, I'm more used to the ground since it took me goddamn ages to get that thing down here."

I frowned, mouthing out the words. Had he been like this that long? Felix seemed to realize what he said and noticed my expression because he sighed. "Look, it's not as bad as I made it out to be. It only took about three days to find the mattress and get it down here. All right?"

"Right…" My brain was definitely too tired and confused to figure it out so, letting out a sigh, I lay back down. "Fine. I'll take the mattress."

"Thank you." Felix spoke up, a hint of sincerity slipping into his voice. I let out a huff before rolling onto my side, trying to get comfortable. It smelled bad and there were some springs that were definitely digging into my side, but it was more comfortable than the rocky floor and, while a little cold, it was thankfully summer, so I wasn't too worried.

"You didn't have to push me though," I muttered as I got comfortable.

Felix snorted. "Didn't have many choices."

"Uh huh. Good thing Mira wasn't here…" The words trailed off as I frowned.

"You do remember." The words were faint, hopeful.

"Sort of. I remember you having a thing for Mira and I think she reciprocated?" That would explain why I felt so uncomfortable the other day.

"Well, considering the amount of times you berated me when I couldn't make a move when we started dating, then yes, very much so."

I frowned. Dating… wait. They had been dating. For a while now. Or, for a while before he became whatever this is. I pursed my lips, my thoughts fluctuating like water through my head. Felix's quiet stare caught my attention, how distant it seemed. I will admit, I felt almost a little uncomfortable because, something told me, that expression didn't seem right on him.

My thoughts flickered and I couldn't help but ask. "Felix?"

"Hm?"

"Where were you?" He seemed confused and I quickly elaborated. "You were gone for a long time, over a week. I never saw you. Were you here that whole time? Or…"

Felix let out a faint snort and shook his head. "No, I wasn't here the whole time." He paused, a sadness almost pulling him downward.

"I... I went to check on my mom."

Oh, right. Felix's mother. I never did check on her, though I didn't necessarily have a reason, now that I think about it. "And?"

A morose smile slowly curled over his features. "She has no idea who I am." The words were blunt, to the point, and filled with despair. "Can you imagine, Ki? What it's like to stare into someone's face that doesn't know you are there? That has no idea you exist? Do you know what it's like to..." He shook his head, letting out a long breath. "Mother has completely forgotten about me. She doesn't check my room, she doesn't talk about me. She acts as if she's always been a single woman living a comfortable life on her own. It—" He cut himself off before turning toward me. "Hey, Ki?"

"Huh?" I found myself a little startled by the sudden change in tone, leaning up slightly so my chin was settling into my palm.

Felix fidgeted for a moment, nail scratching at the stone, deep in thought before he pulled away and returned his attention to me. "Do you know what happened to me? The day that I—" Once more, he cut himself off, wincing.

I blinked, tilting my head slightly to the side in bewilderment. Seeing my expression, he let out a snort and rephrased, "What I meant was, and this may sound odd, do you remember? The day you———me?"

Urk. massive headache. Ouch! I forcibly pushed it away, trying hard to return my attention back toward my friend. He just waited, pursing his lips. I had no doubt that he was aware how much I was hurting right now, and he stayed quiet, but I could tell he had something he still wanted to say.

I took a deep breath, trying to center myself as I backtracked. I might not have known what words caused my headache, but I could infer. It wasn't hard to guess he was trying to find out what I know regarding this whole situation. I wish I could tell him, but to be frank, I wasn't sure how much I DID know.

So I tried to remember, as far back as I could.

I frowned in frustration as I realized how much I was struggling to actually keep track of how things were, when things were, anything.

"Kieran." The name wrenched me out of my thoughts, causing me to jerk up, as Felix sighed. "I'm just going to get straight to the point, since it seems you aren't sure what I was talking about." He paused, hesitation curling over him before he straightened his shoulders, as if preparing himself, continuing where he left off, "I wanted to tell you what I remember… of the day I no longer fully remember."

I'm sorry. What?

He noticed my confusion and faintly chuckled. "Yeah, I know, but I really have no other way of saying it."

I shook my head, gesturing for him to continue, watching him quietly.

He nodded, taking in a deep breath. "All right, so, I was just heading home from your house after you caused a huge panic between me and Mira. We just got back from the haunted house and you just started seizing up or something. We got you home, but it nearly gave us both a heart attack." He shook his head, a faint smile flickering on his lips for only a moment before it faded. "Anyway, I'd gotten home and, to my surprise, Mom wasn't home yet. Usually, she's there in the mornings, but…" He trailed off, almost curling into himself, something that deeply unsettled me. "It was eerie, being alone. There was a faint humming sound, and I heard cars pull up outside and…" He frowned, placing a fist to his head. "Why? Why can't I… It was always so clear." He turned to me with clear desperation. "Ki, I don't remember. I could have sworn I did. I could have sworn… no, I KNOW I remember. The emotions, the fear, that momentary flash of absolute pain, as if every part of my body was being ripped apart and electrified all at once." He shuddered as I found myself sitting up. "But the next thing I really remember is being here. I was staring up at this very same ceiling, Harold watching me. Of course, I had no clue who the dude was and promptly freaked. I ran, finding my way home, but Ki… it was all so different." His gaze met mine with a haunted expression. "There really is no way to describe it, the feeling of being here and yet not. Of knowing who I am, but also having no clue." He let out a breath and shook his head. "Oh geez, look at me, being all distraught—"

"Felix…"

"Really? Dude, you know me better—" Felix cut out, his words coming to a screeching halt.

I watched him, before letting out a breath. "Do you really think just sitting there, avoiding the situation, is going to help?"

"It's what you do." Those words were not supposed to hurt as much as they did, but his solemn voice pierced me and I found myself grimacing because, well, he wasn't wrong.

"I know." I finally convinced myself to speak, fingers curling into the mattress, pulling at the weakening threads. "But isn't that why I can say it? Because I've done just that and found out how badly it all went…" I found myself unable to figure out the proper word to use, but it seemed I didn't need to.

Felix grinned. "Horribly wrong?"

"That works."

He chuckled before leaning back, staring at the ceiling. "Sorry about that, I just wanted to get that off my chest and figured now was as good a time as any."

"Don't worry about it." I yawned, finding myself falling back down on the mattress, feeling sleep drag at me.

"Right, I'll try not to."

I snorted, but didn't respond, hearing a faint chuckle from Felix before the sound of shifting clothes reached my ears, showing he probably settled down. My attention drifted to the stone wall without really taking it in. My memory was messed up as all hell, but at least I wasn't completely alone.

That just made me wonder. I winced as pain hummed through my skull and pulled away from the thought. Trying to parse through what Felix said, what supposedly happened to him. There would be no way for me to figure out what was going on with occasionally remembering bits and pieces. It was going to take more than an afternoon at this rate. I let out a long breath and I let myself slip into a fitful sleep.

Chapter Nineteen

Waking up the next morning when I could not feel the sun was in no way fun, by any stretch of the imagination. I groaned, curling in more, only to regret the action a second later. Everything was stiff and aching. I mentally cursed, the words more half groggy rambling than anything. I shook my head, slowly sitting up.

"Oh! Sleeping Beauty's up."

"Felix, shut it," I grumbled, wincing.

"Ha-ha, yeah, that's how I felt the first time I woke up down here as well, really throws you for a loop, doesn't it?"

Understatement, I thought, shaking my head a little more, finally getting my bearings enough to scrutinize the room. It was just like the night before, the only change being that Felix was already standing, waiting for me to get up.

I slowly sat up and cringed as I noticed my dirty and ragged clothes. I could feel them sticking to me and I couldn't help but wish I had another change of clothes or something. Though, considering the situation I was in and where I was, I was just going to forgo thinking about it. I stood up and followed as Felix gestured us outside. We arrived at the cafeteria in time for the smell of lunch to start to fill the room. The lady from before was just finishing preparing when we stepped in, and though she was hesitant, she still gave me some food. I really had to thank Sylvia when I next spoke with her.

Of course, as soon as I thought that, I heard footsteps coming from the pool area. Go figure, she was a mind reader. Sue me, I was tired.

She stepped in, Margaret and Harold right on her heels. She

spotted me almost right away before smiling. She hesitated, almost as if she wanted to run over to join us. She instead grabbed some food and took a seat beside me, sitting close. Felix was trying hard not to laugh sitting next to me as the other two just shook their heads and took seats a bit more away, giving me breathing room. "So, what do you think? This place is pretty straightforward, isn't it?"

"Yeah, just a bit." I wasn't sure what to say to that. I hadn't really explored much of the place, if I recalled correctly. Heck, I hadn't gotten to the Ferris wheel yet.

"Don't worry, I would usually say you'll figure it out, but..." she trailed off, glancing over toward Felix, who nodded, as if in encouragement. "Okay. Felix and I both are able to interact with you and that world much better than anyone else, and because of that you're in danger, so why not get rid of the danger?"

"What?" I think I dropped my spoon there, because I definitely heard a loud clatter as it fell back into the bowl.

"We've been planning on setting up an attack on the... whoever made us this way and so we've been stock-piling as much as we can for the last year or so. With you arriving and with you being the only person left who can sense us and all, now would be as good a time as any to launch an attack. What do you say? You in?"

I stared blankly at her. Huh? What did she mean? 'An assault?' As in, actual fighting? I knew I was being stupid with that question, but I couldn't seem to wrap my head around the idea. Sure, I had to do something similar when we were stuck in the haunted house... wait, wasn't I mostly running for my life? When did I fight? Was it when I was saving Mira? Wait, who?

Why was the floor so close? Oh. I thought someone was holding me and calling my name. Geez, did I faint?

"I'm fine," I muttered, pushing myself slowly back up. My head swam with so many different thoughts, even more than yesterday. It was like memories from almost different versions of me were invading my head. Considering I was not in some strange future story or something, that didn't really make sense. I shook my head and returned my attention to…

As soon as my gaze met Felix's and Sylvia's, it almost seemed like there was a tear. A snap that couldn't be heard, just felt.

This time, I was somewhat expecting it, the shooting agony. I was not expecting to be joined by two other voices.

"What was that?" Sylvia groaned once it passed, heavily leaning against the table.

Felix knocked his palm against the side of his head with a faint moan. "Dude, is this what you've been feeling lately? Because, by God, am I sorry."

I winced and shrugged. "Not the worst one, though I'm wondering why you two were affected."

Sylvia went to open her mouth, only to freeze alongside Felix before they exchanged incredulous expressions.

"Is it possible?" Sylvia murmured.

"I didn't think so." Felix shrugged, sending me a quick questioning raised brow.

"English please?" I groaned, slumping onto the table. I was still exhausted by my half sleep last night and this didn't help.

"Right," Sylvia said, deep in thought. "Let's just say, thank you for the pain, because I remembered something I didn't expect to remember. Speaking of, have you ever been to the police headquarters?"

Blinking at the non sequitur, I shook my head. "I've been to the police department, but…"

"Close enough." Sylvia shifted closer to me… she was REALLY close. I noticed other people start to file into the room, giving us a wide berth. "There's a building not that far from that which houses what we're searching for. A…" She hesitated, grimacing before leaning close enough that I wished I could lean back… if Felix wasn't right behind me, chuckling. "A machine."

I blinked, confusion foremost on my mind. "Okay, and?"

Sylvia appeared like she wanted to slap me for a second, letting out a quiet groan, pulling away. "And so…" She emphasized the words, indicative of her annoyance. "There is a machine that we're searching for that MAY, in fact, be the CAUSE of all this."

I stared, realization slowly dawning on me, along with horror. "Wait, a machine from our hometown?" I yelped, managing to keep my voice down, but just barely.

A spark of curiosity shone before she grimaced, flickering over toward Felix. Felix and she exchanged a despondent expression before returning their focus to me. "Yes, that."

Huh? Did I say something wrong? Eh, I'm not going to worry about it, other matters are a bit more important, thank you. "Okay, so why is there a machine that is creating, well…" I gestured. "Sitting right in the middle of a suburban neighborhood?"

"If we knew, we would tell you, but this is all the information we've managed to gather while in this state."

"Ki, do you know why we call some of us 'The Lost'?" Felix cut in, causing me to start. I shook my head and he continued, after getting a nod of affirmation from Sylvia, who seemed to be deep in thought about something. "We call some of us that because, unlike myself and Sylvia, many of the people here barely remember their own names. The ones who struggle the most with daily things such as eating and opening doors? They maybe remember bits and pieces of what they should. Those who've gone mad from this… curse, are called 'The Lost'." He hesitated before turning away. "Harold mentioned that many of the ones who did have contact on both sides became The Lost. For instance, the man we met in the haunted house. He and his victims were all Lost."

I frowned, thoughts briefly flickering to what I remembered from that, before suddenly freezing as twisted faces and sticky blood shot into my thoughts. I barely managed to hold back my gag reflex, fingers digging into my jaw. That memory… of the twisted corpse of… "Those were humans," I murmured, turning toward Felix, who grimaced. "Those were humans and… one of those figures killed them."

"Yes." Sylvia spoke up with a sigh. "We'd heard rumors about the place and sent someone to investigate. They did not make it back, so I sent Margaret." She waved toward the woman, who was eating quietly, watching the exchange. "She told me what happened."

I observed the woman before my shoulders tensed. "You were the one who saved me when that man was about to stab me."

Margaret surveyed me carefully. "Yes. That is correct." Her voice was soft, but harsh. "However, he then chased you into the forest where I lost his trail."

I thought over her words before giving her a faint smile. "Doesn't matter, he was taken care of..." I pursed my lips. "Still, thank you. I never thought I would be able to thank the one who saved me then."

She quickly turned away as Sylvia smiled brightly. "I told you!"

"Told her?" I tilted my head and she quickly waved it away, expression once more turning somber. "Oh, that makes me wonder..." I peered around the cafeteria. "You said the Lost are those who completely, well, lost it. If that's the case, then wouldn't they have the least amount of effect on the world? Similar to the people here who can't even hold a bowl to eat?"

Sylvia paused and the four of them exchanged looks as I waited for their response. "That is a good question." Sylvia finally turned back toward me. "We aren't exactly certain. My theory is that, when you become Lost, you no longer have your humanity to hold onto, so you hold onto something else, whether that be physical or psychological. My guess, in the case of that man from the haunted house, was that, while he no longer remembered who he was or why he was there, he held onto the belief that the place was his. He was probably holding on to what was left by convincing himself he couldn't move through objects, and, as a result, he was unable to." She grimaced. "It's a bit convoluted and something we haven't thought much on. After all, once you're a Lost, it's only a matter of time before you..." She pursed her lips, gaze flickering to the surrounding group. "The people here are able to avoid becoming lost because they have each other alongside me, who still has a strong link to the other side." Her gaze flicked to me. "But those who are alone..."

I pursed my lips, fingers curling into the table. So, if I understood what she was saying, the only way that a person could hold on to humanity, to not fade away, was to make others aware he was still 'alive' by killing and by convincing himself he was a regular killer, not some ghost or shadow. It was scary to think that he could have very easily given up that idea, walked through a wall, and slaughtered all of us. I shivered violently at the thought.

I heard a quiet cough and jerked, attention shifting to Felix. He turned to me and said, "Unfortunately, there's not much we can say about that. I'm glad things worked out the way they did at the haunted house, but I think we have other things to talk about." I couldn't help but agree, wanting to get off the topic. "Needless to say, Sylvia and her group have managed to maintain a balance within this place, but we want to do more than retain balance, or at least, she definitely does."

"We want to stop whatever is causing the people to turn and revert ourselves back to normal... whatever normal really is for us." Sylvia finished, garnering my attention once more. "That machine, from what we've gathered, should be able to do that for us."

I pursed my lips, taking another spoonful of the soup as I thought over what she said. "Can you give me a bit to think about it?"

Sylvia blinked before nodding. "Of course, I don't mean to push you, but..." She scanned the cafeteria as it slowly began to fill, a quiet chatter in the air. "Please decide quickly, we don't know how fast we need to move."

"Right." I stood, finding my appetite gone. "Anyway, I haven't gotten a chance to explore this place."

"I'll join you." Felix stood, bringing up his tray as he headed around the table.

"Actually, Felix, I need to talk with you. Margaret, can you watch Ki for me?"

Margaret simply stood and brought her bowl over to be washed before waiting by the door.

"She's as talkative as ever," Felix muttered before turning to me. "Sorry, dude, seems like I'll be needing to talk for a bit. Meet up with you later?"

"Sure." I waved as Sylvia, Felix and Harold finished up and left, leaving me alone with just Margaret in an entire room of Specters. I quickly returned my bowl and bolted out of there. At least, with this, I knew most of them were probably eating lunch, so I'd be able to explore in peace. Maybe I'd take a look at the Ferris wheel. I highly doubted there were any operational rides, but I wondered if there were old game places or a mirror house. Shaking off the idea, I walked down the lane, Margaret a few paces behind. The sun beat overhead, clouds occasionally blocking it before swiftly disappearing. I wondered if a storm was coming. I guess I might have to cut my exploration short if it started raining.

I wandered through the old park, quietly observing the deteriorating remains. It definitely appeared as if it hadn't been touched in a while. Now that I could examine it up close, I could spot vegetation creeping over some of the rides and locations, graffiti decorated bits and pieces of the cement walls and signs that were, somehow, still standing, covering up the name of the park. Some steps descended into another part of the park, cracked and crumbling. I carefully moved down them. Off to one side, having been hidden by trees and buildings and vegetation, I spotted a roller coaster. It appeared twisted and broken as the clouds once more covered the sun. Creepy, but actually somewhat cool.

I mean, it still was utterly creepy, but I didn't think I would really have to worry too much. The only ghosts around were the Specters anyway, and I could sense them. I shivered as a wind whipped past, causing the nearby metal to creak. I shook my head and kept moving, only to pause, something near the edge of the park catching my attention. I surveyed the area, spotting Margaret not that far behind, arms crossed, yet at attention. I walked over to the edge, peering into the surrounding concrete woods. There was no other way to describe it, the vegetation thoroughly took over this part of the park. Cracked roofs collapsed under thick branches, the brick tumbling down the side, caught by roots and vines. It was really fascinating and eerily beautiful.

It was amazing, what happened when things were forgotten and yet, as I stared over the landscape, I couldn't help but feel a sense of sadness. Shaking my head, I went to turn, when, once more, I spotted the movement and whipped around. Behind me, hidden by the vegetation and crumbling remains, was a man, dressed the same as Mira, his features somewhat hidden by shadow. Behind him, I caught a few others and found myself taking a step back.

Thankfully, it seemed they weren't observing me, but Margaret. Why?

Or was it because…

They slipped from tree to tree, staying in the shadows, which was made easier as the sky slowly clouded overhead. I quickly turned away, not sure whether to get closer to find out what was going on, or stay away.

My decision was basically made for me when I heard a soft beep and noticed one of the people turn my way, their eye piece slightly obscured by something. This seemed to catch the others' attention.

I heard whispering and, curiosity getting the better of me, I leaned against the tree as if resting, but trying hard to listen. I didn't catch much, but what I did catch was enough to worry me.

"Human child… abandoned? Maybe an orphan or runaway? Not a Specter." The words were cut off and muddled, but I got the gist of it. "Protect and extract. This place is dangerous. Is that Specter observing the boy?"

I pulled away from the tree, purposefully walking away from them, trying not to make it seem like I noticed them. As I thought, these people were just like Mira. I needed to let Sylvia know.

Deciding to take advantage of their distraction and run with it, I hurried away, catching Margaret somewhat off guard. As I passed, I said in a hushed whisper, "Hurry," and kept moving.

She seemed to understand and followed after me as I headed back to the base, only glancing over my shoulder once. They were following, but at a good distance. I quickly turned away so they didn't think I was observing them. Soon, we arrived at the underground base I still knew almost nothing about. I knocked, vaguely remembering how Felix did it before and grimaced as I once more found the gun way too close to my face. The red-head spotted me before lowering the gun and gesturing, expression still as straight as ever. I passed him and hurried down the steps, Margaret not saying a word, but surprisingly following behind. I wasn't sure if I could remember my way to the conference room, but it seemed like I could as I found myself standing, once more, in front of the rug blocking the door.

Not hearing any major conversation, I slipped inside. To my relief, I spotted Sylvia sitting off to one side with Harold, scanning over what seemed to be paperwork—how the heck would they have that? Now that I thought about it, didn't she have some earlier? And would they really need to worry about paperwork anyway? Felix was chilling at the other end of the room, leaning back in a chair that seemed like it was about to collapse at any moment. Sylvia's attention shifted away from her work as I hurried over, wanting to warn her while I had the chance.

"You're back earlier than I expected. Is everything all right?" she asked, as she placed the papers down, passing some over to Harold.

"About that…" I hesitated, actually taking a moment to think through what I was going to say. "While I was out and about, I happened to spot some strangers wandering around the overgrown area of the park. They were in the same gear as Mira. I'm not sure what they want, or why they were here, but they were following me and I'm not sure if it's because they recognized me or if it was something else to do with me not being a Specter," I mumbled the end as I noticed everyone now had their full attention on me, and it made me sound almost ridiculous. Almost selfish, or was I just paranoid?

Sylvia's expression was grave, a sadness permeating through the room as she stood. "I guess we overstayed our welcome."

I heard the clack of wood on stone. Felix stood and frowned. "Now I get what you meant. I'm not surprised they've sent people here, especially if they suspect Ki came this way." He walked over, placing an arm around my shoulder as I almost stumbled forward. "Don't worry, dude. Sylvia here expected as much. You're not crazy."

"Sure," I muttered, but decided not to argue as Sylvia turned to Harold.

"Harold, get everyone out. We'll have to leave this place. This may be our last chance, but if it fails, you know what to do."

"Geez, you've got the A team here. We won't fail." Felix brought a fist up, grinning, causing her to smile.

I was totally lost. What the hell were they talking about? Did they actually believe someone was coming? That they would be here already? Shoot, it was literally a day since I arrived, if that. Unless… "They were planning to attack before I arrived," I found myself voicing out loud, drawing everyone's attention. I stilled, realizing I'd accidentally spoke and felt my face heating up. Sylvia let out a quiet chuckle as Felix let go, slapping a palm over his grinning mouth. I just sent him a glare as Sylvia settled down, once more showing a neutral expression.

"You're not wrong. We've been expecting an attack for a while now." She gestured to Harold. He nodded, hurrying out the door as she continued, "However, we needed to change our plans a little when you arrived. Felix here was willing to help us. Margaret and I were designated to leave and head toward the base that holds the machine we need to destroy, but…"

"Now that I'm here, that makes it difficult." My attention shifted toward Margaret who appeared to be a little upset for some reason, which must have meant something since I rarely ever saw an expression on her stoic features. "So, what now? Are we still going to that base?" I turned back to Sylvia.

Sylvia nodded, gesturing for us to follow, Felix pushed me forward as Margaret trailed behind. I sent him a glare, but followed suit as Sylvia wound her way through a different area of this underground location, eventually opening into what seemed to be an old deserted parking garage. "We've been thinking over the different ways we would get there without being detected and eventually managed to figure out a route. Unfortunately, the four of us are probably going to have to go together since Felix and I are the only ones who can operate a vehicle due to our unique condition. Margaret is one of the only ones here who can defend against those who would want to attack us. You, well, are obvious."

"Thanks," I muttered as I examined the crumpled garage.

Where the hell was this when I was exploring earlier? The only thing I could assume was it was underground, proven by the steep ramp I spotted off to one side. Empty spots and debris littered the room, along with the decaying remains of one or two cars that had been mostly stripped of their parts. Most of them appeared as if they hadn't run in years, but… we passed all of them, getting to a little car off to one side. I think it was the only one in the place that was at all 'operational,' though I used the term lightly. I wouldn't be caught dead in it. The doors were gone and the roof was almost ripped off, but Sylvia had no qualms jumping into the front seat. I stared at it as Felix hopped in, observing the place with amusement as Margaret pulled herself into the back, crossing one leg over the other and crossing her arms, without a care in the world.

I felt like there was a joke in their somewhere, but I was too lost to figure out what it was. I shook my head as Sylvia turned a key, that seemed to already be in the vehicle, and it sputtered to life. I slunk forward. "You know, this seems rather sudden. Aren't you—"

"You said they were right outside the park, correct? And that they followed you?"

I nodded, but before I could say more, I heard sounds echoing above us, loud through the cement of the ceiling. I tilted my head back, focusing on the ceiling as I tried to figure out what that sound was before paling. It was the ricochet of gunshots.

Chapter Twenty

"The squad he saw, they must have been discovered." Margaret spoke, voice neutral. "Those escaping may not be able to distract them for long. We should move."

Distract? But there were only a few of them. Could just a few people—my thoughts cut off as I remembered Mira's expression, felt the gun dig into my stomach and shivered. Right. Only a few people here could defend themselves. Though the squad was probably few in numbers; if they kept to the shadows, which would have been easy with the cloudy skies, then they would have put up a fight.

I heard another round of gunshots from above and gritted my teeth before hurrying into the vehicle. I promptly regretted it when I didn't spot any seatbelts and heard a "Hang on" echo from Sylvia as she jammed the car into drive and shot forward.

Oh... oh shit.

"Do you know how to drive?" I found myself asking as we swerved toward the ramp and shot up it.

"No. We couldn't waste the gas for any of us to learn," she responded as she punched through the undergrowth hiding the entrance and landed on the ground, the tires catching for a moment before we pelted forward. I grabbed onto the nearest thing that felt sturdy. Holding onto the rusted-out piece of the car for dear life, I would have closed my eyes, if I didn't think I would be flung out at the slightest bump. Felix was cheering, having a blast as Sylvia had all her concentration on the wheel. Margaret...

Really? How the hell was she so calm? I almost did a double take when I spotted her just sitting there serenely, palms resting on her thighs. I would have laughed at the ludicrousness of the situation, if I didn't feel overwhelmed. I jumped into the car because of the gunshots and because everyone seemed to know what they were doing, but...

I still hadn't a clue! Did they expect me to spot someone when I left? Or did they not want me involved? But that didn't make sense either. I would have pulled away from the safety guard out of aggravation, but I didn't dare loosen my death grip as we almost left the ground on another bump.

Then I heard a sound and twisted just enough to peer behind us, the sound of rustling clothes indicating I wasn't the only one. One moment, I was spotting a car behind us, another moment, what was probably a bullet, slammed next to the tires of the car behind us as it swerved out of the way. I jerked, hair blowing past me, obscuring my vision slightly as Margaret kept the gun raised, peering down the sights. She turned in the seat, one leg up on the seat itself while the other was using the side piece at the bottom that was still intact as a stabilizer, or so it seemed. Her hair whipped past as another gunshot rang out and the car behind swerved.

"So they had backup, figured they would assume we would try to leave. I guess the distraction wasn't enough." Sylvia's voice floated backward as she clicked her tongue and rumbling sounded above. Darkening clouds obscured the sky, almost turning a deep black. Great, that was all we needed.

Why wasn't I panicking more on the freaking car chase gun match? My priorities were so freaking messed up right now.

Felix was staying surprisingly quiet and Sylvia seemed to be focusing heavily on the road and the other car as it swerved up next to us. I almost felt my breath catch in my throat as I spotted Mira in the passenger seat, gun raised. She noticed me, but, to my surprise, she didn't hesitate. I felt our car jerk as a wave echoed past the car, a mix of a gunshot and a legit sound-wave. I heard a yelp and cry from the two up front and noticed Margaret grimace as the car weaved. What the hell just happened?

Another rumble sounded as wetness splattered on my hand, which was now cramped from where I was gripping. Another gunshot rang out from Margaret, but it was hard to tell from my angle as I tried to focus through the rain that seemed to hammer down around us. I felt the car jerk and almost felt myself get flung forward as we collided sidelong into the other vehicle, or maybe they collided into us, it was hard to say.

One more gunshot from Margaret, I think, and then a cry before we shot ahead. I shook my head and peered back to see the car chasing us swerve off to one side, tire finally shredded, before slamming into a tree. The door opened and Mira stumbled out of it. Blood trailed down the left side of her face. As we whipped around the corner, I caught her expression. I shivered at the dead, hate-filled gaze that followed me as she slowly lowered her gun with a small smirk.

"That was way too close. Holy shit," Felix voiced out, more high-pitched than usual. Though I didn't blame him.

I slowly uncurled from my position, turning enough to spot the two up front. Sylvia nodded as wind blew through the remains of the car. Rain pelted us, soaking into my skin. Thank the heavens it was summer and warm because this would be even worse otherwise.

Sylvia trembled, jerking the wheel as if… as if her arms…

I leaned forward just as the other two seemed to realize what was going on.

"Shit!" Felix shouted, grasping the wheel as Sylvia slipped through it. I lunged forward, trying to help, only to slam into Felix as he grabbed the wheel, causing it to twist just a bit, his fingers falling through a moment later.

I felt it more than saw it. The car jerked, the road slipping away from the tires as we careened to one side, off the beaten path. Shouts echoed in my ears as my free hand slowly drifted up to cover my head, or maybe quickly, it was so hard to tell as the others tumbled, the smell of the rain barely overpowering the burning smell. I heard cries, and felt as the car tipped. It slammed into the ground. I felt myself let go of the handle at the impact as I was flung forward, skidding across the ground, coming to a standstill by the tree, water trailing down my face.

Silence.

All I could hear was oppressive silence, the once overpowering pound of the rain, the harsh breaths, all of it. It was as if I'd gone deaf. Something dripped down my skin that felt thicker than the rain. My ears rang as sound slowly came back, shouts and scrambling. I felt the water dissipate and a shadow cover me. Who?

"Ki! Ki, are you all right? Hey!" The voice hurt my ears and all I could do was groan quietly.

That's when I felt it and I almost cried out. Pain flared up my side, almost as bad as the headaches that slammed through my head so frequently of late.

"Shit, seems like he got badly banged up in that crash. What the hell happened back there?"

Who? Ah, right, Felix. I tried to sit up, only to crumble, my hand slipping out in the ground rapidly turning to mud.

"Hold still, we'll take care of you." The first voice, right, Sylvia, that's who it was, spoke up. I could only nod as she gently slid her fingers under my side. I didn't resist as she helped me sit up, Felix on my other side. I shook my head, trying to clear the last of the fog from the crash. One eye seemed red and I quickly closed it, bringing an arm up to wipe at it before pulling away. I was injured, as I thought.

"We can't stay here." I gritted my teeth, thoughts flickering to Mira. "She did something, didn't she?"

"You're probably right. I feel like I am less connected than before." Sylvia's voice was faint, almost panicked. But that didn't sound right. Sylvia was never panicked. Worried, sure, but... I went to stand, only to yelp as my legs crumbled beneath me, pain shooting up my leg. Did I twist it?

I shook my head, examining the car before shooting a look at the others. "Wait, what happened to everyone?" Felix and Sylvia exchanged worried expressions before turning back to me.

"The rest of us, we slipped out of the car before the crash. None of us are injured, a little bruised from falling, but... You were the only one." I wasn't sure whether to feel frustrated or relieved. Though, if that was the case then, how was Sylvia holding me?

I must have voiced the question out loud, because silence suddenly met my ears and I turned my good eye toward Sylvia, who was staring down at where she was holding me, surprised.

"It's probably because it's you, Ki." Felix spoke up, checking me over quietly.

Ugh, I suppose that makes sense, as much as anything else in this moment.

"We can't really move like this. Not with him injured." Margaret's voice caught my attention and caused Sylvia to stiffen.

"We can't just stay here or leave him here," Sylvia snapped toward Margaret as she loomed out of the rain-filled forest.

"That was not my intent. We almost made it to the town during our chase. I know someplace we can stay that won't ask any questions."

I could almost sense the hesitant air as I grunted and, using Felix as support, turned to her. "Lead the way."

Margaret stared at me before nodding and walking down the road. Maybe it was stupid, what with my body hurting like hell, but I followed after, getting the occasional observant worry sent my way by the others as I stumbled forward.

Thankfully, she was right, it wasn't much farther until we reached what seemed to be a little inn on the outskirts of a small town. It appeared run-down, but useable. Ignoring the beer cans thrown into the shadowed corner and the dilapidated state of the entrance hall.

However, she was right. The clerk barely looked up, just taking some money she plopped on the table before pushing over a set of keys. Did he notice Margaret? Or did he just personally not care? Maybe he just thought it was better to keep his head down? Whatever the case, it wasn't long until I found myself sitting in the only chair in the room, my body screaming at me for stupidly walking what felt like miles, though it was barely a half-mile. I heard movement and tilted my head up enough to spot Sylvia walk past and stare out the window, the rain clouding the pane. I heard the sound of a shower running and noticed Margaret leaning in the corner next to the doorway. The room had seen better days, but it was out of the rain, so I couldn't complain and it had two decent-sized beds, so there was that too.

"How are you feeling?"

I found my expression shift to deadpan, deciding not to say a word, and Sylvia winced. "Right, stupid question." She hesitated before sighing. "We need to get you checked out, is that all right?"

I frowned, before slowly nodding. "Yeah."

There was a large moment of hesitation before she turned to me with a devastated expression. "I'm sorry. I have no idea what happened. There should have been no reason for me to lose control—"

"It's fine." I grunted, trying to sit up and lean forward, catching her gaze. "Look, whatever happened, it's probably because of whatever is happening to you and Felix, right?" I was able to gather that much in my confused state at least.

She stared at me before nodding. "Right. And, well, I guess it could have also been that gun. I felt it earlier, when Mira fired. I know it missed us, but there must have been something else. I felt almost disconnected. Like the world just slipped away for a brief moment before snapping back into place. I have no other way to describe it. Maybe it messed with me…" Sylvia trailed off before she clenched her fists tight enough to shake. "If that's the case, then I can only hope Harold got everyone out in time. I wish we could move, keep going, but…" She slowly uncurled her fingers, slumping. "You need to rest. We'll figure out what we're doing tomorrow." She reached forward, fingers slipping through my hair, only some of it moving as she delicately touched my scalp. Thankfully, as her fingers traced over what was probably a wound, I found her smiling faintly. "Thank gosh it's only a shallow cut and you didn't pass out."

"If you're wondering, I don't have a concussion," I said, smiling faintly to alleviate her worry. Now that time passed, I was able to take stock of myself and, thankfully, I was only banged up. I would be black and blue tomorrow, but… just sitting here I already felt a lot better.

I just needed a good shower.

"By the way, you keep mentioning this plan, but what are the details of it?" I asked, causing her to pause in her ministrations before continuing unabated.

"I suppose that's a valid question." She finally pulled back. "I'll be frank, it wasn't much of a plan, but it was the only option we had." She peered out the windows for a moment before continuing, "It's honestly very simple. There are three groups: those who can't fight who are to flee to a specified location, those who have some means of interaction who can distract any attackers and then Margaret, myself and, eventually Felix, who were to head toward the location I mentioned earlier." She turned back to me, a heavy sadness in her gaze. "There was no rendezvous, no second chances. Once the plan started, either we would see it through to fruition or..." she trailed off, but I could understand what she meant. After all, if Sylvia failed, the only one with a large amount of interaction with the world and the leader of the group, then there was really nothing left for those she protected.

"So, it's all or nothing." I voiced out, feeling more than a little nervous at the prospect.

She smiled, her lips turning up just the slightest bit with a tired warmth. "There really wasn't any other choice. I need to protect as many as I can but..."

I examined her quietly, noting the way she scratched at her arm before quickly pulling away, trying and failing to straighten her back. It was a stark reminder to the fact that she wasn't much older than myself. If anything, she was probably around my age. I wasn't going to dare ask, but it was weird to think someone my age carried so much weight on her shoulders.

For some reason, I felt a pang shoot through my chest, one of anger and sadness, but I quickly pushed it away, it wasn't going to help to pity her.

All the sudden, I felt arms wrap around me. I was startled out of my thoughts noting it was Sylvia hugging me tightly, letting out a long, jittery breath.

"I'm so glad to have you by my side. I really am. Thank you, Ki."

I let out my own breath, feeling a faint smile tugging at my lips. I couldn't help but hug her back. I was still soaked through, but it seemed she didn't much care, being pretty soaked herself.

"You know, you should probably change into drier clothes when you get the chance." I voiced out and she stiffened.

"I'll get right on that when I have a change of clothes," she mumbled, but didn't let go.

I pursed my lips, letting out a sigh. Right, I forgot about that… Still, it wasn't long before I found my head resting against her shoulder, feeling surprisingly relaxed.

I didn't know her, but a small part of me couldn't help but feel very comfortable around her. In the moment, I wasn't going to argue with the thought.

Eventually, she pulled away as the sound of water switched off from the bathroom and after a few moments, Felix slipped out, drying his hair. He was already dressed in the same clothes from before and I realized, with a groan, that I would have to do much the same. I guess my earlier comment was pointless. None of us really had a change of clothes. I guess I would just have to hope for mine to dry out, or check if I could use a blow drier. There should be one here, right? I pulled up my shredded shirt and jeans and slumped. Well, at least they didn't get too bloody, due to all the rain.

Oh boy…

Felix turned to me before sighing and pulling his shirt off before tossing it to me, startling me. "Dude, you are a mess and everyone can notice you. We don't want people asking too many questions."

I stared at him before peering down at the shirt. I guess he had done what I was thinking, since it wasn't quite as wet as my own clothes. "Would people be able to notice this?" I muttered. Felix heard it anyway and snorted.

"How the hell should I know? Dude, just… put it on after your shower."

I hesitated for a moment, thinking through what he said before letting out a sigh and nodding thankfully. I walked into the bathroom, almost jumping into the shower in my dash. I quickly stripped and stepped in, grateful for the warm water as it eased tense muscles and helped the ache building up in both my head and body.

I would be so glad when this was all over, whatever the hell this was. I pulled my leg up, slowly twisting it forward and back. Thankfully, it was just that, twisted. If I gave it some rest tonight, I should be fine for tomorrow and the hot water was helping. Other than that, there were a few scratches along my body, but somehow, I came out fairly unscathed. Of course, it was probably a good idea to get a second opinion, and maybe a proper look in the mirror to confirm some things, but... I let out a breath as the water finally stopped shedding brown and red and came out clear, before shutting the shower off and getting dressed. I kept my pants, trying to blow-dry them as best as I could, but threw on Felix's shirt, grimacing on how loose it was on me. Damn.

At least I could wear something that wasn't completely in tatters. I'll just have to hope that people can see it, if not, it would probably lead to a couple awkward questions. At least it wasn't winter. I let out a breath, turning toward the mirror to take stock of myself. I lifted my hair, noting the long thin scar over my left eye that was already healing. I remember reading once that head wounds bleed a lot, so maybe that was where all the blood was from? I wouldn't have been surprised. Small lacerations decorated my arms and I could spot a forming bruise on my cheek. I lightly touched it, wincing. Probably not my best idea. I guess I should make sure to rest on my right side tonight.

Well, at least the shirt showed in the mirror. I wonder if Felix would show? Or one of the others?

"Hey Felix!"

"Dude, I don't have anything else to spare."

"It's not that." I said as the door opened.

Felix peeked in, only letting out a slight breath, whether it was frustration or relief, I wasn't sure, before he stepped closer. "What is it then?"

I turned back toward the mirror and paused. Out of the corner of my gaze I grabbed Felix, pulling him next to me. I heard him yelp in surprise, but found myself unable to pay attention. I was clearly standing there, dressed in Felix's shirt, but that was it. My arms were wrapped around nothing. It was as if the very air itself was missing, just, nothing.

Actually, now that I was paying closer attention, my arm seemed less clear. My head pounded and I quickly turned away. Felix was watching me, his gaze on the mirror and then flicking to me. "Dude, what is it?"

"Felix, the mirror…" I found myself unsure of how to ask.

"What about it?" He turned to it, leaning forward slightly. He reached up, pushing some of his hair out of his face. "It seems normal to me."

He could see himself? How did— I cut off the thought and shook my head, letting go of Felix. "I'll be out in a moment."

Felix blinked, before shrugging and heading out the door. I didn't much care if he thought I was going crazy. I knew I was at this point. I once more leaned over the sink, pushing up close to the mirror. I pulled at the shirt, and the mirror reflected the movement. So, whatever this machine did, it erased all aspects of a person, even their reflection… and yet it didn't erase what was on them. Or, no, as long as it was connected to them, then it was as if it didn't exist, but once they gave it away it was as if that rule no longer applied. So, would Felix be able to take this back? I pulled away, suddenly feeling a little self-conscious. I appeared ridiculous, staring at a mirror like this. I turned, pulling my attention away as I stepped out the door in time to spot Sylvia and Felix arguing. Huh? I blinked as Sylvia turned to me, slumping as Felix outright grinned. "See? There's nothing wrong—"

"Sure there is! How are you so okay with giving up your only piece of clothing? What about winters? Do you have any self-respect or…"

Felix let out a sigh. So, they were wondering about that as well. Have they been arguing since Felix left? "I know what it means." Felix peered down at himself, crossing his arms over his bare chest. "It feels like I lost part of myself, but that won't last long, right? We're going to change back and, well, whatever happened to us earlier is fading, so I'll probably be able to swipe something if I need to."

I groaned, realizing what he meant as I plucked at the shirt. I didn't mind not wearing one, but I could definitely tell how it would make others uncomfortable. I peered down at the remains of my other shirt. It might work, if he could actually hold it, but...

I tossed it to him, curious, and he stumbled, almost catching it before it fell through.

I winced, okay, probably shouldn't have done that.

A strange expression crossed his features before quickly being wiped away. "Dude, seriously? At least some warning next time." He turned to me with amusement. Sylvia just sighed.

No one tried to pick up the shirt.

And to be honest, if I was the only one visible, it wouldn't be good if everyone pointed out the already forming bruises and picked me up to go to the hospital or something. I groaned as I meandered over to the bed and collapsed, too tired to really think about it or respond because that really was an impromptu thing for me to do. I was done with today. No more. I wasn't dealing with this right now.

Sylvia and Felix watched me, seeming, ironically enough, fondly sarcastic. I spotted Sylvia smiling as Felix chuckled faintly. "See? He doesn't care."

"I'm just saying..." Sylvia turned, heading toward the doorway as I let myself drift off to sleep. Just because the aches were fading, it didn't mean they disappeared.

Chapter Twenty-one

When I awoke, it was to the sound of, grunting? I blinked, noting how the sky was still dark and stormy. So I hadn't been sleeping long. Then why was I awake? I glanced over to the doorway in time to notice the way Felix was gripping the knob his fingers slipping through occasionally, aggravated. He seemed to be holding it? I wasn't sure why though.

"You push outward," I mumbled, causing him to jerk and glare at me. That's when I noticed Sylvia was gone, maybe out with Margaret or something? I wouldn't be surprised if they were gathering information or whatever they normally do.

"That's not the problem, Ki." He hissed and that's when I noticed the door shake slightly. "These doors don't lock properly and I already checked, it isn't Sylvia or Margaret."

It took me all of two seconds to realize what he meant before I heard a curse from the other side of the door and stiffened. I jolted out of bed and raced over, holding the door closed alongside Felix just as a sharp tug pulled on it. "Who is it!" I shouted. I heard a stumbling sound before running footsteps faded away, down the hall. I stayed there for another moment, heart pounding, before I blinked, realizing what just happened and almost let out a laugh. Felix only sent me an unamused expression before both of us peeked our heads out the door. There was no one there and from the beer bottle slowly rolling to a stop down the hall, it was probably a drunk or something.

Thankfully, for my sanity, I just backed away and took a seat on the bed as Felix closed and attempted to once more lock the door. Really, who uses locks that flimsy? It seems partially rusted and is barely more than a strip of metal.

I noticed him slump into the only chair in the room, letting out a grunt. "I'm doing that way too often lately."

"You make it sound like you're constantly holding doors closed," I muttered, observing him as he frowned.

"You don't get much privacy when you are in this state. It's only been a little over a week, but, Ki, be thankful that you don't have to deal with this. I don't know how someone like Sylvia survived for a whole year and a half." He walked over and took a seat on the bed. "Thankfully, it seems that whatever that thing was that happened earlier is fading. I don't want to know what would happen if my fingers slipped through like in the car." He stared down toward his hands and I grimaced. Yeah, I didn't want to know either.

I pursed my lips, shrugging. "I don't know what you've had to deal with, but I know it must have been difficult." I let a small smile cross over my lips as I continued, "Still, thank you for watching my back, Felix."

"Dude, of course. We weren't going to leave you alone in a place like this. I might not be able to do much in this state, but…"

"You kept that door closed long enough for me to wake up and come over. Just like I helped you escape…" I trailed off before letting out a sigh. "Right, the haunted house. That's what this reminded me of."

Felix chuckled. "Only this time, it was reversed, wasn't it?"

I smiled and nodded. "Yeah, it was."

Felix watched me, his gaze almost piercing before he smiled brilliantly. "Ki, did I ever tell you how glad I am that you know me? That you remembered my name?"

"I kind of figured," I deadpanned and he laughed. I shook my head. "So, where are Sylvia and Margaret?" I stretched out my legs, feeling much better from earlier. Either I took a really good short nap or… I glanced out the window, rain still trailing down the panes, but hard to notice even with the faint lights decorating the edge of the hotel.

"From the sounds of it, they are out gathering intel." Felix shrugged. "I didn't really get a chance to ask anything else before they left."

I only partially heard his response as my thoughts shifted back to what happened earlier. I didn't want to imagine what would have happened if that person made it inside because Felix was unable to hold the door closed. But how was that possible?

"Actually, what was that person doing? Was it an accident? After all, there is no such thing as crime, right? So, why…" I muttered, wincing as a faint headache echoed in the back of my mind.

Felix just watched me quietly, a sad expression on his face as I turned to him, utterly bewildered. "Felix, I don't… I don't get this. Why is… I REMEMBER knowing that crime doesn't exist anymore, but then… the haunted house, the bodies, the person who just tried to come in? Those are all…" I was glad I was sitting down as my fingers jerked to my head. "Why is this happening? I don't get it. Is that why Mom still locks the doors? But it's never happened, but it has happened and—"

"Kieran!" I jerked as Felix gripped my shoulders tightly, locking his gaze with my own. "Calm down, all right?"

I bit my lip, feeling myself shaking as he pulled away.

"I don't know." He shook his head before throwing his hands in the air. "Screw it! Ki, we'll figure everything out later, all right? Once we take down that machine Sylvia keeps mentioning and return back to normal, like Sylvia said, that should solve everything."

"When did Sylvia say that?" I couldn't help but weakly joke back.

I got a deadpan look for my troubles and a sharp, "Dude, really?" in response.

But I didn't mind, letting out a laugh as I relaxed, deciding not to think about it. "Thanks, seriously."

"No problem." Felix put his fist forward, lightly bumping with my own, just as the key jingled and the door opened.

Sylvia and Margaret walked in before Sylvia blinked, watching me in confusion. "What are you doing up? You should be resting. We have a long day tomorrow."

I chuckled, pushing myself to my feet, only cringing slightly before slipping back into bed. "And I'm guessing I'll find out what's left of this plan of action in the morning."

"You guessed right, now get some sleep."

"Yes, ma'am." I chuckled as she glared at me before hurrying over to the other bed, causing Felix and me to chuckle and Margaret, of all people, to smile faintly as she turned, locking the door as best as she could.

I let out a yawn before pausing, peering toward the door.

"Dude, don't worry," Felix voiced out, grinning as he leaned back in the chair. I stared at him before laughing and laying down, curling into the sheets.

Right, I would be fine. Things would be fine.

After all, it was probably just my imagination.

Crime doesn't exist and hasn't for over a year.

Chapter Twenty-two

This time, I awoke with the sun beaming down onto me, shedding in gentle oranges and purples, causing me to moan. I was not dealing with this. I was NOT a morning person. I slowly sat up, feeling a slight twinge as I stretched. Thankfully, it seemed that I was correct. I'd somehow come out of that accident without any lasting damage. I would be a little stiff today and might have a slight limp, but, other than that, it seemed I would be all right. I let out a breath of relief before scanning the room. The others were in varying states of wakefulness, including, to my surprise, Sylvia. I peeked over to her, as she rolled over toward me. We stared at each other for a brief moment before she... smiled warmly? Wait, why was she giving me that warm smile?

And why did it feel familiar? "Morning, Ki-ki."

"Uh... morning?"

She rubbed her cheek before, freezing in place as if realizing something. The room was surprisingly quiet and, as I found myself observing everything, including the other two who quickly turned away, I noted the somber air.

Wait what? Why was—before I could continue my thoughts, where I could already feel a headache coming, Sylvia jerked and slipped out of bed, roughly grabbing the door to the bathroom and slamming it shut. I didn't know she could do that... what with the whole slipping through areas issue.

"Yikes," Felix muttered. "That was strange." He frowned for a moment before shaking his head and returning his attention to me. "Anyway, dude, I'm surprised that you are up."

"Gee, thanks," I deadpanned, keeping half of my attention on the closed door. Why did she act like that? Almost as if one moment she was thinking of something, the next... not only that but, she called me Ki-ki. I can't remember anyone calling me that and yet I know someone once did.

Felix quickly waved his hands. "Oh, come on, man, you know what I was talking about. You already woke up once and you seemed pretty injured yesterday, so I figured you would probably need the rest." He rolled out of bed, standing up to move away from me as Margaret shook her head with an amused expression.

I sighed and pulled myself out of bed, grimacing as I stood. Thankfully, the door to the bathroom opened and Sylvia walked out, once more her normal self, standing straight and tall. "Get ready. After that, I'll tell you our next plan of action."

"Uh... sure." I shook my head and hurried to the bathroom to get cleaned up. Not long after, I found myself sitting on the bed with Felix on the other and Sylvia in the chair. Margaret was leaning against the wall behind Sylvia. The room was lit with the bright morning sunlight, faint creaking sounding from the wood.

"So, what are we doing now?" Felix leaned forward, chin sitting in his palm. "Last time I checked, we still had a ways to go and on foot, we're not exactly safe."

"A ways to go... where?" I spoke up, realizing I still didn't really know where we were going. "I mean, I know we need to go find that machine and all that, but I'm not sure we talked about where that actually is."

Sylvia exchanged equal expressions with the others before turning to me. "Okay, do you know the police station that you and Mira were taken to about a week ago? Give or take?"

"Sorta?" I spoke up, trying hard to think back. I honestly didn't remember much from my time with Mira and the Specter.

"Close enough. That building is where we need to go, it's right outside of o—your hometown, only a mile or so from the library. That building acts as both a police department on the surface, and a lab. We're going to infiltrate and find the main lab center and destroy whatever devices are in there that might be causing this. Since we don't know what it looks like, we'll just have to make sure we do a thorough job."

"Gotcha," I said, letting out a breath as Sylvia leaned against the arm of her chair, once more deep in thought.

"However, like I said, it's in your hometown, which is still a couple miles away." Sylvia frowned. "We only have a few options and unfortunately one of them, we discovered, is no longer an option."

"Want to explain that a little?" Felix gestured, cocking his head slightly.

Sylvia sighed. "We were thinking of taking a bus, since it is the easiest means of transportation for people like us." She gestured to herself and Margaret. "However, when we were gathering information yesterday, we learned that the bus stations are being watched and anyone found getting on or off the buses are…" She trailed off, but I don't think she needed to say more. I winced. I felt terrible, but there wasn't much we could DO about that. "So, we'll have to go with the other method. But first, we need to grab something to eat. None of us ate last night and I, for one, am hungry."

I guess my stomach didn't argue, grumbling softly. I pressed my palm into it, wanting to just shush the darn thing for now. Unfortunately, the others noticed anyway.

"Yeah. That's definitely a priority…" Felix trailed off before turning back to her. "Speaking of, why didn't you pick anything up yesterday during your gathering of information, if that was the case? I kind of had my hands full myself, so I couldn't exactly leave."

Sylvia blinked, only to blush brightly, fidgeting. "I kinda forgot?"

All of us could only stare before Felix and I let out simultaneous sighs. Margaret smiled faintly, only to wipe the smile off her face when Sylvia glared at her. "And SOMEONE didn't remind me."

Margaret only shrugged.

"Anyway, that aside, what are we doing after we eat?" Felix brought up, quickly switching topics, which was fine by me. I was pretty hungry, now that they mentioned it, and the sooner we got food, the better, in my opinion.

Sylvia's expression caused him to jerk and he quickly turned away. I raised an eyebrow before turning toward her. She shook her head, continuing her train of thought, "Okay, to be honest, what we need to do is to procure a vehicle of some sort." I frowned, debating about that, only for her to drag my attention back. "Margaret..." She trailed off before turning to the woman. "With what happened yesterday, after we procure a vehicle, can I have you return to check on Harold and the others?"

Margaret actually appeared outright hesitant, showing this was probably a last-minute idea by Sylvia, or so I had to assume, considering I almost saw a flash of disapproval from Margaret.

"Wait, then why did she come with us if you are just going to send her away?" I pursed my lips. "That seems—"

"Ki, this is none of your bus—"

"Actually, it is," Felix broke in, surprisingly neutral-toned, pulling his chin off his palm. His arms dangled between his legs. He leaned forward, giving her a sharp look. "If you keep changing the situation and who he can rely on every moment, what do you expect from him? Everything is already confusing enough. Do you really think sending any of us away is a good idea? Plus, a gunner can be handy to invade a base, or at least, cause a distraction. There is no point in going back. After all, as you said, this is our only chance. So why are you cutting our odds?"

Sylvia pursed her lips, almost on the verge of biting clean through. "What do you want me to do?" She kept her voice low, as she glared at him. "Yes, I keep insisting that this is our only chance, but those people, I care for them. If any of them—"

"If any of them die, it's not your fault." Surprisingly, the words trailed from my mouth, causing everyone to jerk, turning to me.

"What?" Sylvia stared at me quietly.

I hesitated before letting out a sigh. Well, in for pound or whatever the phrase was. "I was only there a day at most, but while I was there, I saw how you were leading them, how much they all seem to respect you."

"But that's why—"

I sent her a glare, causing her to snap her mouth shut. "That's why I think they were aware of the situation. They may not have liked me, but they trust you. Which means that they want you to succeed." I turned toward Margaret, who was watching quietly. "If you really think it would be better for their survival to send Margaret back, then go ahead. However, if you think, for a moment, that we might need the help to make sure they return to NORMAL, then..." I trailed off, rubbing my hair. "I don't know why I'm saying all this, you've dealt with this situation far longer than me, but I guess, if I were them, I would rather know I have someone who knows how to fight protecting someone I respect, or love, than them worrying if I'm safe, especially if I believed there were no other ways to escape this." I gestured to all of them. "But hey, what would I know?"

Silence invaded the room as my words finally trailed to a stop. Sylvia's head was bent downward, hair obscuring her expression. Margaret was tense, fingers covering her face as Felix outright turned away, attention on the window.

Well, I definitely just made this situation awkward.

Eventually, Sylvia let out a long breath. "I almost want to tell you she ran out of bullets, but she does have a magazine left after yesterday's incident."

I blinked, only to feel my face heat up at the insinuation before shaking my head. "A magazine? That's better than nothing, right?" At Margaret's nod and faint smile, I finished my question. "Do you mind staying with us?"

"I am okay with that idea." She spoke up, surprisingly soft.

I smiled. "Thanks."

"It's my job," she pointed out.

"If you say so." Felix leaned back, grinning, hands behind his head. "Now about that food."

"You're skipping something pretty important," Sylvia huffed before chuckling quietly. "Anyway, don't worry, we'll grab food soon, but first..." She glanced over to me. "While I won't argue any more regarding that topic, I have to ask." She hesitated, brushing her fingers over her thigh for a moment before she continued, "How do you feel about the idea of procuring a vehicle?"

"What do you mean?" I returned my attention to her, curious about what she meant.

"Well, we need to get to the base, and the only way we've set up to get through is with a car. After all, we can't take the buses now and no other routes will work since security is fairly tight. But we've managed to make adjustments to the car route to help us bypass any security."

"And I'm guessing those don't work if we're walking that same route?"

"No." She shook her head. "It's using the metal of the car, it makes it more difficult to detect things like us, usually. We don't know why or how it works, but it works."

"Gotcha." I stretched before leaning forward, chin laying on my palm. "So, how do we get a car?"

Everyone turned to me and I stilled as a strange expression crossed Sylvia's features. She began to fidget slightly. "About that... Well, there's only one of us who is actually visible and none of us know how to hack into a car, or, well, steal a car, for that matter."

I stared at the three of them before massaging the bridge of my nose, feeling an entirely different headache coming along. "Does that mean..."

"Hitchhiking," Margaret stated simply with a slight smirk. I felt myself twitch and I pursed my lips.

Felix was on the verge of cracking up as I turned to him before returning my attention to Sylvia, an apologetic expression explaining it all.

"You got the other one working," I questioned, and no, I was NOT pleading, thank you! "I don't know the first THING about hitchhiking."

"Do you know how long we worked to get that one working?" Sylvia deadpanned. "Half the parts came from people who were turned. A new car or even a stolen car would not be as easily changed."

Ah... okay, fair. That still didn't answer the second part though.

Sylvia, seeming to notice my hesitance, grinned encouragingly. "I don't know why you are so worried. It's not that difficult. You get a driver's attention, open the door, hesitate as if unsure, allowing us time to get in and then get in yourself. After which we'll find a way to take care of the driver. Once that's done, you can drive and we'll be on our way."

"Take care of the driver?" I asked uneasily.

Sylvia paused. "Let me rephrase that." She winced. "We'll make sure the driver doesn't get injured, we might just knock them out or something. That's all."

I let out a breath of relief before frowning. "You make it sound so easy. Plus, it'll make me more of a criminal than I already am," I pointed out, disgruntled, frowning at my words before continuing. "Can't we come up with something else? Like renting a car or something?"

"With what money?" Sylvia said, much to my chagrin. "This is the easiest way I can think of to get us anywhere and, considering how many miles we have left to go, it's possibly our only way. Plus, I already mentioned the situation with the base."

I groaned. "Fine, fine. I'll get an innocent driver's attention."

"Well, when you put it that way."

I huffed. Great, just what I needed. I really didn't want to be dealing with any of this, but I also wanted this just to be over and done with so I guessed my options were somewhat limited, as they say.

"Well, he matches the appearance of a runaway anyway, with the scrapes, bruises and clothes." Felix, of all people, mumbled out, surprisingly not too keen on the idea either. I thought he would jump at it. Speaking of... I plucked at my friend's shirt. It felt great to take a shower yesterday, but I could tell the shirt stank and my pants definitely appeared a little worse for wear.

"I look homeless." I frowned before realizing what I said. I slowly tilted my head up in time to see the somber and conflicted expressions on everyone. "Right, sorry, that was insensitive."

Sylvia shook her head. "It's fine, as you said, this should be over soon and then… then we can all return to our homes."

"So, you know where you're supposed to live?" I asked, standing up and patting my clothes down, since it seemed like we would be leaving soon.

"Mostly. People like the three of us and Harold know, but anyone with less of a connection? It's lucky if they remember their names."

I winced at the thought. That sounded like a certain type of hell and, as I thought back over what I saw at the park. I guess in a way, it was. Especially now that I knew that all of them were human at one point. It almost made me sick to think about it. "Anyway, why don't we grab some breakfast, we have another long day ahead, don't we?"

The others seemed to agree as we all did one more clean-up and got ready, well, mostly me, before heading out. We left, and I couldn't help but notice marks on the door and winced at the reminder of what happened last night. Had that actually been a drunk? Or was it something worse? Did they figure it was just me alone in there? What would… Felix turned my way, expression filled with curiosity, but I shook my head. "It's fine," I mouthed and he shrugged before turning back ahead. I frowned, deciding not to think about it as we wandered outside, turning in the keys before heading to the nearest restaurant, a fast-food joint, it seemed. It wasn't anything exciting. Actually, the only 'exciting' part was when they realized some of the food was missing from the back after Sylvia slipped behind the counter to nab some. We didn't stick around to eat, I'll just say that.

I observed the little town, munching down on my breakfast, noting the occasional attention sent my way. A few people stepped away with disgust at my bedraggled state. Gee, thanks. Thankfully, none of the others talked to me so I was only made to appear bedraggled, not crazy.

That was all I needed, to add crazy to the list of what people saw, even if I fully well knew I was already crazy for thinking any of this would work. Also, the idea of committing a crime when they weren't supposed to exist partly confused the hell out of me. I mean, I SAW Sylvia 'steal' some food earlier, so… crime existed, it explained the haunted house, last night and what we were going to do in only a few hours and yet it didn't. Crime was gone, the police only needed to go around to help keep the peace, but that wasn't right either. I grumbled, deciding not to continue this train of thought, feeling the headache incoming. At least it won't be too difficult, after all, with the lack of crime, people are a lot more willing to help strangers and interact with others. I couldn't deny, part of me wanted to go back to the time before all of this, where I didn't have to worry about crime and machines and specters, when life seemed so peaceful.

I massaged the bridge of my nose as I turned toward the road. Unfortunately, that wasn't an option. For now... I tilted my head up, surveying the area. We were on a main street and, contrary to how little I pointed it out, it was actually fairly busy, one or two cars almost always passing by either direction. I scanned my clothes and worked on straightening them a little, finally giving up when both Sylvia and Felix gave me a look. Even Margaret had an eyebrow raised in amusement as she shifted her gun on her shoulder. Gee, thanks, guys.

I huffed and turned, only to stop, frowning slightly as I stared ahead. Off to one side was a school, empty due to the summer break, but outside were still a few cars parked. Maybe there was a game happening in the nearby school yard? It sometimes happened. As I walked farther down, I felt myself feeling a little unsettled as, up ahead, a four-way intersection caught my attention, a truck passing nonchalantly through. I shook my head, walking up to the intersection and observing the area quietly. This would probably be my best bet to get someone's attention. I spun to take in the full view of the place before shrugging and raising one arm like I was in school.

The others stared at me before Sylvia tilted her eyebrow up so incredulously, I couldn't help but shift uncomfortably, and I wasn't sure why.

"Why are you raising your hand like that?"

"Isn't this how you get someone's attention?" I dropped my arm to my side, feeling more than a little embarrassed as a few people scooted away from me.

"Dude," Felix chuckled. "Then again, I guess we shouldn't really blame you, it isn't exactly common, I've really…" He frowned, his expression twisting for the briefest of moments before he focused back on me. "Anyway, it's just something from a long time ago that I learned. You stick out your hand and put up your thumb, like so." He showed me, doing exactly as he said and I followed suit.

To my surprise, not that much later, someone pulled up to one side, parking just next to the curb and rolling down the window. For a moment, I wasn't sure if they were just parking at the red light, or because I was trying to get their attention.

"Hey! Are you okay?" The voice from the car was rather energetic, if a little curious. I hesitated before walking over, arm once more at my side.

"Yeah? I was just hoping to get home?" Yeah, that was definitely more of a question than a statement. As I stepped up to the car, I peered inside.

It was a small car with enough seating for all of us, if the others were willing to squish past the driver, over the middle console and into the back. Oh, that would be entertaining to watch. The girl herself was petite, probably a little shorter than me with honey brown hair and curious blue irises. She peered over me, a split second of hesitation crossing her features and I noticed her knuckles clench over the steering-wheel before she smiled. "Are you by yourself? How far is your home?"

"Yeah, I am." I tried hard not to turn toward my companions as I continued, "And not that far, only really the next town over, but I hurt myself and, well…" I was suddenly thankful for the indication of my slight limp, because I just realized the advantage it gave me for sympathy. Though that only made me feel worse when she blinked, probably spotting the bruises on my arms and the way I was holding myself, a bit more exaggerated, but not by much, and let out a little gasp.

"You need to go to the hospital!" she spoke up, her gaze on the cut on my head, which I honestly forgot about.

"No, it's fine. I already got it checked out, but…" I trailed off, unsure of what else to say regarding the 'supposed' situation. I was making this up on the fly and I could definitely tell. Thankfully, it seemed as if she didn't notice.

"Ah, right. Here—" With that, I heard a click and took a step back, startled, as she reached across the center console and pushed at the door-handle. I hesitantly opened the door, feeling a sharp wind as Sylvia dashed past me, scurrying over the middle console before taking a seat in the back. I noticed the girl wince, confused for a moment as the other two followed suit. Felix gestured before diving into the back like the other two.

"You coming?"

"Er... yeah." I pursed my lips, feeling a bit sheepish and outright bad about the situation as I slowly sat down, closing the door. I heard it lock, seeing the red disappear to indicate as such. The engine revved before we pulled away, back into traffic and taking a turn.

"So, where am I dropping you off? Oh, the name's Kelly, by the way, what's yours?"

Kelly, huh? I turned enough to face her, occasionally receiving a moment of attention before she focused back on the road. "Ki..." Deciding to just leave it at that, I continued, "Can you drop me off in the town just north of here? My house is a couple blocks away from the school, so—"

"What's your address? I'll just drop you off right at your place."

I hesitated and for a split second, I saw a frown cross her lips. "Er... well, I don't really want to go home just yet, but—"

"But what?" she cut in. "You're completely in tatters. I could have sworn you were homeless and I'm not going to ask what you are doing all the way out here like this. But I'm not one to leave someone where they're not going to be safe. If that means your home isn't safe, the—"

"No!" I cut in with a glare, surprised at my own vehemence before quickly backing off. "No, that's not it." I let out a breath. "I'm worried, but there's something I need to do first."

The girl tapped her fingers against the steering wheel as we pulled out of town, a silence enveloping the car for all of two seconds.

"Smooth," Felix deadpanned. It took all my effort NOT to turn around and send him a sharp glare to shut up. Though one finger did shift slightly with my disapproval, trying to stay out of the girl's line of sight. She didn't notice, but I did hear a quiet snort of amusement from Sylvia.

"We're in the car, as terrible as his acting skills are, at least we've made it this far." Sylvia shrugged, causing my eye to twitch. Gee, thanks.

I couldn't rebuke them without Kelly thinking I was psychotic or something… and they fully well knew it.

Oh boy, I wasn't sure what was worse. Not knowing they were there or knowing they were there and being unable to do anything. I quickly returned my attention back to the road as the trees passed on by.

"So, Ki, was it? How old are you anyway? You look pretty young to be out and about by yourself. What about your friends?"

Did she assume everyone had friends? "I can turn that question right back on you, you know," I pointed out before turning to her. "But I'm old enough to drive. I just haven't gotten my license yet." That felt both completely true and partially false, stupid inconsistencies.

"Yeah. I know that feeling. I got my license as soon as I came of age." Kelly chuckled as she turned down another street. I was starting to recognize the area, but we still had a good twenty minutes to go, which meant I had a little less than that to come up with some way to hijack this car. Great.

I do hope those guys in the back are thinking of something as well, because I couldn't come up with anything. Then again, I doubt I was really trying that hard. I spared a glance to the back to spot Sylvia and Felix watching the exchange, talking between themselves and occasionally reaching out to see if they could interact with her or anything. Margaret just seemed content with relaxing and letting them work. Sylvia seemed to be able to touch the buttons and switches on the dash, though it involved her practically leaning over the entire middle console. Thankfully, the thing was small, with enough room for me to practically fit myself in front of it. Felix mostly just tried the doors and seats. I wasn't sure how helpful they would actually be… "So, what were you doing out?" I decided to attempt to make small talk, unsure what else to really do and not wanting it to be completely awkward, even though it already was for me.

"Hm?" She hummed, swaying side to side for a moment before shrugging. "I needed to be out for a bit, since it's summer break and I'm going to be starting college soon. I was heading toward the haunted amusement park, because I heard about it from a friend, but the road there had been cordoned off by police and everyone was forced to turn around. Something about danger regarding collapsing buildings?"

I could almost hear the three in the back stiffen, the air almost suffocating for everyone exce—

Kelly scrunched her brow, wiping her head around to stare behind her before quickly returning her attention to the road, shivering. "Man, that felt WEIRD."

Okay. Nope. Not going to ask. "Did the officers tell you anything else?" I asked, trying to keep my voice neutral as I could practically feel Sylvia wrench forward, gripping my shoulder in what was probably a white-knuckled grip, if the pain was any indication.

"Hm? Were you looking into it yourself?" The girl mused and I quickly shook my head, thinking fast.

"No, I just have a friend who's really into that stuff, old buildings and haunted locations, so…"

"Ah, gotcha." She chuckled. "Unfortunately, no. I couldn't get anything else and so I had to turn back. I wasn't about to leave this town without some photos though, so I stuck around for a few hours and then spotted you. Oh yeah, I was a part of the photography club, which is why I wanted some photos." She grinned, and that's when I spotted the little camera resting on her chest, a thin cord around her neck.

"Oh right, thanks for that, by the way." I murmured, realizing I never thanked her. "And photography? I didn't know there—wait… what school did you go to?"

She chuckled. "It's fine, most people don't realize there's a photography club. And anyway, you don't have to thank me, it's fine. You almost look like my younger bro—" She cut herself off, brow furrowing, gaze distant for a moment before she shook her head. "So, you want me to drop you off in front of the school?"

I almost felt the whiplash in the change in conversation. Yikes. "Or close to."

"Sure, though..." Her attention drifted to her dash and she huffed. "First, I gotta get gas. I'm absolutely on fumes. Which sucks. I could have sworn I just filled it."

"I wouldn't know." Well, that was pointless to say, but she got a quiet chuckle out of it.

"Right, you mentioned that, sorry." She peered over to me before turning forward once more. "Anyway, there's a gas station up ahead. Let me pick up some gas and then we'll get going. That should be fine, right?"

"Yeah." I couldn't help but shift my attention to the three in the back. Sylvia and Felix were deep in conversation with Margaret observing. She spotted me watching.

"That will buy us more time." Margaret smiled faintly as I returned my attention to Kelly.

"Great! And, you know, my house isn't too far from here either, which makes this much better." She said, her attention briefly shifting toward me before returning to the road. "That way, I can drop you off and head home myself. Say, how have I not seen you around school before? I would assume I'm only about a year or two above you?"

I blinked, staring at her for a long time, unable to answer for MULTIPLE reasons.

One of which being… how the hell would I know? "I usually stick on the ground or second floor."

"Oh! Okay, the senior classes are all on the top floor. Those stairs are TIRING, but I guess I can't complain too much since there is always a nice cross-breeze with the windows open." She shook her head as we turned into a nearby gas station. "Anyway, here we are. Just give me a bit and I'll be right back. If you need to go the bathroom, you can. I need to grab some stuff anyway." She turned the key, slipping it into the pocket of her sleeveless sweater. It was cute, I noted, and loose enough that Sylvia was able to quickly grab it as Kelly was getting out of the car with her purse over her shoulder.

Which I hadn't seen. Where the heck did she have it? I saw her pull open the gas cap and decided I might as well follow her advice, slipping out to head to the bathroom as she recommended, but mostly to get away from the suffocating feeling of a too packed car. Plus, I was just done with being near the others at the moment, not including Margaret, ironically, and so needed a few minutes to myself. I headed into the bathroom to relieve myself and think over my options. There weren't many and it made me sick. What was I going to do?

Chapter Twenty-three

As I washed my hands, I found myself staring into the mirror. I appeared incredibly tired with circles almost to my cheeks and an almost permanent crease in my forehead, lovingly slashed on one side with a healing cut. No wonder it drew her gaze. I let out a quiet breath as I realized my time was almost up and I was going to commit a crime. Though crime shouldn't exist and here I was getting another damn headache at the situation. At this point, I just wanted all of this to be over and done with. Was that so much to ask?

Obviously, yes, as I walked out to see both Felix and Sylvia glaring at me in annoyance. I only rolled my eyes and headed back over, thoughts flitting through my mind of what options I had. I frowned, stopping halfway to the car. I could see Kelly in the store, had she finished filling up already? Margaret was still in the car, gently feeling over the fabric as if in a trance, a surprisingly gentle smile on her face. Though it was gone as soon as she spotted me watching. I shook my head, turning my attention to the two standing before me.

"Earth to Ki. Glad to know we've finally gotten through to you." Sylvia frowned, hands on her hips. "I have the key, this could be our only chance, got it?" She waved the key in front of my face before grasping it tightly. "I would try to drive myself, but that would do no good with my state at the moment, and all we need is another accident..." She shivered, crossing her arms over her chest.

I didn't feel much better, a splitting headache slamming through me, causing me to stumble. I felt hands gripping my shoulders tightly and heard a quiet cry of pain. Why the hell was I getting a headache NOW, of all times?

I took harsh breaths, trying to center myself. I managed to force myself to pay attention.

"Sylvia? Kieran? What's—are you two all right?"

Sylvia? Was Sylvia feeling this too? Just like before?

I heard a large exhale and felt the headache fade. Sylvia's attention was on the keys held in her trembling palm and she now seemed much more hesitant from before. Felix glanced between us, worried. "Here. Get in…" Her voice was neutral. She shoved the key into my hands and practically dove back inside when I opened the passenger side door. Felix stared for a bit, watching me quietly.

"Thanks." I spoke under my breath, noting that, thankfully, no one really noticed my little episode. Though, I wondered why Sylvia was affected this time and not Felix.

"It's fine." The fact that he didn't add anything else to the sentence spoke volumes. However, before I could say more, he slipped into the car as well, leaving me with no option but to follow suit.

I didn't like this idea. I would be stealing a car and couldn't even blame it on anything. Maybe if Sylvia and Felix had some control, they could drive the car away and it would look like a supernatural force was involved, but considering they both seemed to be deeply lost in thought and well past listening to, or trying to work with me, it wasn't happening.

I stared at the key in my palm, clenching and unclenching around it.

"She's coming, hurry up." Margaret's tone was calm, but quick.

Why? This was BS on so many levels. I turned my head up. Kelly was at the cash register, obviously getting ready to leave.

If I didn't leave now, I don't think I would be able to convince myself to leave otherwise. "I'm sorry," I couldn't help but whisper.

I flung myself over the middle console into the driver's seat, jammed the key in and, remembering at the last minute to shift gears as I watched people do in the past, I slammed on the gas. A screech of tires echoed and rang in the air as shouts of surprise sounded around us. I whipped the wheel around and aimed for the exit of the gas station, barely clipping the siding of the cement paving before taking off down the road. Heart pounding way too many miles per hour and foot flat to the floor in a way it probably should NOT be.

"Slow down!" Sylvia's voice cut through my thoughts and I quickly pulled my foot away, and pressed down on the brake.

I'm so glad I'd at least had a few practices in arcades, even if the games were nothing like actually driving.

I slowly let out a breath as we drew to a halt, though my heart still pounded out of my chest and I felt absolutely sick to my stomach… and not because of my reckless driving. So much so that I jammed the door open and stumbled out, holding my mouth. What did I just do? Commit a crime? But that shouldn't be possible and I felt that that wasn't the reason I was nauseous. No, it was something else that was not only affecting me.

Sylvia almost fell out of the car, shaking. "Why? I wasn't this nervous when I drove." I could faintly hear her whispered words as I held my mouth, my thoughts and stomach roiling.

"Dude! Kieran!" Felix's attention drifted to behind us, nervous. "We really need to go, now. I don't think we're nearly far enough away."

I knew that was right. Even in my blind panic, I could tell we were still pretty close to the gas station.

Slowly, much to slowly for Felix and even Margaret now, I calmed down and took a seat back in the driver's seat in the car. Just sitting there, not doing a thing as the car hummed.

Somehow, that didn't help my panicky feeling. Soon enough, all of us seemed to come down from whatever high we'd gotten from that little escapade and I got myself situated, Sylvia in the front seat, and we pulled away from the side of the road once more. Margaret and Felix let out a breath of relief once we were on the move, though Sylvia and I still seemed a little uncertain.

Deciding, like usual, not to think about it, I pulled the stick down to drive and carefully allowed the car to roll forward.

I could go straight and that was all I really needed to do.

~ * ~

I continued forward, Sylvia occasionally giving me directions, though her voice was much lower than before and she seemed quite out of sorts, though I guess I couldn't blame her.

I was feeling out of sorts as well as we traveled, feeling more and more so as we got closer to our destination, my head pounding in an increasing rhythm that I was somehow keeping at bay, with no idea how I was doing it.

Learning to drive, on the fly, also didn't help. I probably would have had fun, if not for that strange nagging feeling in the back of my mind. After that initial spurt, I took it fairly slow, getting a feel for the wheel and the gas and brake before speeding up a little to get moving. At least this wouldn't take long, though I was starting to get quite fearful of the repercussions.

Then again, what would the repercussions be of literally a hundred-plus people suddenly appearing out of nowhere in similar or worse states from myself? It was a really strange thought, now that I was actually thinking about it.

I shook my head, drawing my attention back on the road as we passed by the school. I felt strange, passing by it so quickly on a day like this.

It felt like ages ago when I was just here, talking with Mira and… and Felix.

Then just Mira…

Then…

I swallowed thickly, pulling myself away. I didn't even want to imagine what would happen if we had to pass my home like this. I wasn't sure if I could handle it.

Thankfully, it seemed we didn't have to; instead driving back roads to avoid prying eyes. We passed the library and continued on. I stared back, startled. The library was at the edge of town, I knew that. I remembered Sylvia mentioning it, but where, exactly, were we going?

Not only that, but the police…

Wait... Where was that police department again? I remembered arriving there with Mira and leaving with that guy, but... Why couldn't I remember where it was?

I gritted my teeth in frustration at the missing piece. I remembered we traveled a while to get there after Mira was attacked, but...

"We're almost there. Is everyone ready?" Sylvia's voice cut into my thoughts and I jerked, returning my attention to her. She was staring at me, quietly, a strange expression on her face as the vehicle continued forward. The rattling wheels, the vibrating of the steering wheel, the hum of the engine, it all seemed to remind me of the situation we were in and how little I knew about what we were even doing.

I didn't like it. I didn't like it because I wasn't sure if I would actually come out of this one unscathed, or...

Or if I would be in the same hell as them, without a chance of escape.

I couldn't stand the thought.

"Slow down, we're getting close." Sylvia's voice cut off my thoughts as I lightly tapped the brake, pulling to one side of the road. Houses decorated either side, spaced out perfectly. I could see people out and about, a set of kids walked past the car, laughing to each other. I wondered how I appeared right now. Could they tell this wasn't my car? Could they tell I wasn't supposed to be driving?

Was I just starting to succumb to paranoia? Most likely and it was not a pleasant thought. I shook my head and peered up ahead. The first gates appeared to lead toward a winding driveway. I thought I remembered coming this way with Mira, but it was a distant memory, and a jumbled mess I was not about to try to piece through to find. I took a deep breath before facing Sylvia. "So..." I let the one word trail off, not sure what to say.

Thankfully, Felix had my back, or so it seemed. "This is great and all, but sitting here isn't going to help us get in there, you know." Felix pointed ahead, gesturing toward the gates. "I hope you know how to get through, because you sure as heck never told me."

Oh, I honestly thought he knew, but then, Felix always did roll with the punches, normally.

"I'm getting to it!" Sylvia cut in, glaring, though the slight trembling in her hands indicated otherwise. Was she scared? If so, I definitely didn't blame her, part of me was outright trembling in fear for what we were about to do, which I thought was to invade an enemy location and…

Then what? Hope we find the machine and shut it down?

It would be great if they would tell me these things so I wasn't panicking as much, or at least so I could FOCUS my panicking.

"Sylvia, now is your only time to talk, you know that." Margaret, to my surprise, spoke up, her voice even and quiet. Maybe it was my imagination, but I swear I caught a moment of warmth in her features. I returned my attention back to Sylvia.

She was shaking, badly. I felt a sharp stab of pain, this time in my chest instead of my head and I reached a hand to her shoulder. "Hey, you okay?" I whispered quietly.

She froze before letting out a long sigh, deflating under my hand. "Yeah, sorry…" She focused on the three of us, shifting sideways in the seat and pulling one knee up on the cushion. "All right, so here's how it's going to go. From what intel we have managed to gather we know there are a total of two gates that we will have to pass through. The first one is simply a gate to check for people like us while the surrounding fence is electrically charged, weak enough not to cause damage to normal people, but dangerous for us. Don't ask me why, neither myself or the scouts knew, maybe our bodies are more susceptible because of this." She gestured to herself, her gaze locked on mine. "That's why I decided we would have to use the gates. However, it shouldn't be an issue, simply because they don't expect our people to be able to drive." She let out a breath, centering her thoughts. "The scouts said that the gate opens automatically whenever it senses a car pulling up. Don't ask how we figured it out." She shivered before continuing. "The next gate is a little trickier. They will want an ID, something to use as proof for entrance." She hesitated. Margaret, reaching into her pocket, pulled out an ID card, of all things. She handed it over and I carefully took it, spotting the name.

Some Charles guy, he was pretty plain. "We have, under good authority, found out that he will not be available to work at all today, or for the next while."

I decided not to ask what she meant by that.

"So, your plan is to have Ki use an ID of another person, even though he's completely recognizable as himself?" Felix's voice couldn't have been any more dead if he tried. I couldn't help but agree. Also, how the hell did they GET an ID?

"Idiot, we know that." Sylvia cut in, just giving him a look before continuing, "That's why I wanted us to stop here—"

"Before that…" I turned to Margaret. "How did you get an ID, of all things?"

Margaret stared at me for a bit before smiling in a way that sent a shiver down my spine. "We've been scoping out this place for almost a year. We all know who works here and a LOT of houses are surprisingly easy to get into, if you know the tricks of the trade."

Okay…

Not going to ask any more.

"Back to what I was saying." Sylvia cleared her throat, "Ki, wait here, all right?"

"Do I have a say in the matter?" I couldn't help but ask. Sylvia's only response was to smile before slipping out the door of the car.

And take that however you want because I couldn't tell if she opened the door or literally just walked through.

Felix let out a cackle, leaning back in the seat, hands behind his head.

I let out a sigh, switching the car off as Margaret hummed gently and followed after Sylvia.

"You were helpful."

"Wasn't I?" Felix chuckled before letting out a quiet huff. "Look, I'm not sure what's going on either…" His voice trailed down, nervousness taking over. "We're literally walking into enemy territory and it almost feels… no…" he smiled morosely. "It's ridiculous. What are we supposed to be able to do? No offense, Ki, but you aren't exactly…"

"I couldn't punch someone properly even if they stood still and spread their arms out." I spread my arms out before letting them drape over the back of the seat, facing him. "I know, believe me." I pulled up a shaking fist, deciding to just show him. "Hell, I can't even steady my hands, not exactly saving material, am I?"

Felix's attention drifted to my fingers and he smiled faintly. "Well, hey, at least I'm not the only one." He pulled a hand up, clapping it into mine. I pulled back as he tilted his head back, attention on the ceiling. "Still, I think you get my concern, and it's frustrating, because once again, there is nothing I can do." He slammed a fist into the fabric of the seat, startling me. "Every single time… every single damn time, I couldn't do a thing and this happened and now, I can almost feel myself slipping away, every moment that we sit here, waiting. It's…" his voice trailed off before he let his head drop, expression sad, as a weak facsimile of a smile flickered over his face. "Ah, this isn't like me, right?" He coughed, seeming a little embarrassed. "Anyway, just know, Kieran, I have your back, okay? Whatever happens in there, I won't let you get hurt—"

"Ah, how sweet!" I grinned as he glared at me.

"Dude, you know what I meant."

"I know, I know." I couldn't help but let him notice my expression. "Believe me, I know and I appreciate it. It's nice to know someone's got my back, and same for you."

He quickly turned away, causing me to chuckle.

"What's the laughter all about?" Sylvia's voice, once more, caused me to jump. She slipped inside, a ratty sweatshirt in her hands with a hood. She held a few other odds and ends too, including a ragged shirt that she threw toward Felix.

"What, did you have to go into your secret stash or something?" Felix snorted, as he caught the shirt, tugging it on.

"Yes." Sylvia rolled her eyes. "No, actually, there was a secondhand store right around the corner." She handed the hoodie over as Felix choked at the straightforward answer.

I took the hoodie, examining it before pulling it on, figuring that was what she wanted. It smelled as bad as everything else, but at least it wasn't falling apart.

"Wait, seriously? I didn't notice a store or anything."

"No surprise, it's a small store around the corner, I'm surprised it's still in business, to be honest." Sylvia barely turned toward Felix, tossing him a... was that a knife? Good thing it was sheathed because he fumbled the catch. "Thankfully, it always has a lot of goods and the caretaker never seems to notice when we nab something, either that or he doesn't care..." She trailed off before shaking her head and handing a knife to me as well.

Though I wasn't sure what I could do with it. I strapped it to my waist, letting the hoodie cover it. Thankfully, it strapped onto my pants just fine, though it felt surprisingly heavy.

"Now that we are all at least somewhat armed..." she winced. Clearly, while somewhat armed was the best we could do, THAT didn't mean it was good enough.

"All right, so we get through the second gate and then what?" I decided to skip over that since it seemed they thought an ID and a hoodie would be more than enough. Yeah, I highly doubted it, but I wasn't about to say that out loud.

Sylvia hesitated. "Next, we're going to park near the back entrance. It's a short trip, from what we've gathered from the few of my scouts who managed to slip through. Once you enter, you can either go right or left, the left more obviously leading to the front overhanging entrance, the right leads to the back with what I can only infer is probably a parking garage."

Huh... that does sound a little familiar.

"If we go to the parking garage and slip in there, we should be able to walk to the back door. There shouldn't be anyone in the conference room, at least, from what the scouts who managed to get that far have mentioned. So, if we pass through that, we'll be in the building proper." She sighed, stilling her fidgeting hand. "Beyond that, we have no knowledge of the place. Those taken or having gone in that far have never returned, so we don't know what to expect. So, we… no, I was thinking of splitting up into two groups."

I winced. Wasn't splitting up a bad idea? I remember hearing that once.

"While it's not the best course of action, staying all together in one group, lost, is worse."

"So how do you propose we split? Basically, who would be going with Kieran?"

Sylvia hesitated, exchanging looks with Margaret. "The other point that I haven't mentioned is that while one group will be searching for the machine, the other group is going to be on the lookout for the person behind the machine." Sylvia's expression twisted into a mix of hatred and… loneliness? No, that couldn't be right. "There's a certain person I need to ask… I don't remember much, but I remember his face." She smiled weakly. "It's frustrating, isn't it? To only remember a face, with some strangely attached emotions, but nothing else. No name, no voice, no actions, nothing at all to tell me who he was or why…"

He? Who was she talking about? She noticed my expression before quickly waving it off. "Don't worry, that's for me to deal with. I'll be also searching for the machine, but my main priority is to speak with that man. While I might not have been able to do it outside here, I have a feeling I'll be able to talk with him once I get inside, especially if the machine is broken."

"Do we know what this machine looks like?" Felix pointed out, leaning back in his seat.

"No. We don't. But I have a feeling it should be obvious, something this big wouldn't be secluded in a little room off to the side." She shook her head. "To answer your earlier question, Margaret will be coming with me, and Felix, you go with Ki—"

"Why?" Felix cut in, frowning. "Margaret is the main fighter in our group, why would—"

"Just… trust me. I have my reasons, okay?" Sylvia spoke up, her voice suddenly pleading.

"It's because a gun bullet can pierce through things that otherwise couldn't be touched." I said, attention drifting toward Margaret. "As much as Felix or Sylvia might be able to interact, only the two of us can actually HIT things."

Margaret's expression was surprisingly impressed as she shifted in her seat.

"Right in one." Sylvia snapped her fingers. "For some reason, I'm not surprised." She shook her head. "Anyway, so that's the reason she's coming with me. I think we've been squatted here for long enough, it's time to get a move on." She clapped her hands. I rolled my eyes, but got the car running once more, trundling down the road with the speed of a snail.

Honestly, I did not want to do this, and considering no one spoke up for me to move faster, I wasn't the only one feeling this way.

We rolled up to the first gate and I waited. It was a basic gate, nothing special, two cameras stood on swivels in the upper two corners of the gate, shifting to face us briefly. A click sounded from the gate before it swung open. I started through, noting a guard post off to one side, but I couldn't spot anyone inside. The road wound ahead a bit more, curving around some trees before we reached a second gate, where I was suddenly glad I'd already put up the hood. Two police officers… er, no, security guards stood to either side of the gate, weapons slung over their shoulders.

If there was no crime, why the heck did security guards need automatic weapons? And why the heck did they not question it?

I kept my slower speed, coming up to the gate as one of the guards stepped forward. I rolled down the window and smiled. "Lovely day, isn't it?"

Okay, brain, I know you're fried, but come on!

I could almost feel the incredulous expressions from behind me as I handed out the ID. The guard, surprisingly enough, just smiled. "Yes, it is, it's been peaceful." He scanned the ID. "Oh, you finally found it, good for you." He handed it back and I nodded, pocketing the ID.

"Yeah, took forever. Anyway, I need to get going, I'm already late as it is."

The guard shivered, and I noted he was a younger fellow, probably only a little older than me... why was someone that young in the security force? Did he know of the situation? "Yeah, El—I mean, Commander is not going to be happy."

El... that name. "I know, it's going to suck." I moved toward the gates as the guard waved me through.

They clanged open as he returned his attention back to me with a wink. "You need a new picture though, that picture does not do you justice."

I blinked, as I found myself pushing lightly on the gas. Okay, so he did notice it was different. Then why—

His gaze flickered to the inside of the car as if searching for something before he returned his attention back toward me and grinned, waving good-bye. "Have fun in there. I know you will do great! Maybe convince that diehard to make some changes in there, so glad I'm not an officer."

Okay, what? Why the hell wasn't he raising the alarm?

I found myself going through the open gates, almost automatically taking a right as my thoughts flew a mile a minute. What did that mean?

"He still remembers?"

I jerked, peering over toward Sylvia, who was... watching Margaret sadly? I briefly allowed myself a chance to peer back, only to freeze as I noticed the woman facing the window, hand up to the glass as an expression I never saw before crossed her face.

Why was she looking like that? "Margaret?"

"I know that boy." She whispered. "I know him, and I know he knows me."

"I'm not so sure." Felix spoke up as I found myself pulling into a parking garage that I definitely remembered seeing before, a familiar black car set off to one side. I parked before focusing on the other three, car off.

"What do you mean?"

Felix turned toward me before shrugging. "Maybe he does, but if so, then why didn't he say a bit more? Why didn't he look us in the eye? If anything, it seemed like he only gave us a cursory scan, to check the back. I'm not sure what was up with him, or what he was saying, but I don't think he remembers. It might be something else."

"Right. I forgot about that." Sylvia's voice chimed in and I glared. "Forgot?"

"Right, Yeah. Sorry?" She gave a sheepish grin before shaking her head, expression once more even. "I remember hearing about this from Harold." She hesitated. "He was once a part of the police force, you know."

Really? That... actually would explain a LOT. "So..."

"So, he was only changed into a Specter a few months ago, and during that time, he and others in the force learned of the existence of Specters, even if they couldn't sense them. You could almost say, two factions appeared in the force between those who wanted to help the Specters and those who wanted to get rid of them. Needless to say, you could probably guess which side won out. It was thought that all those who disagreed were..." She stopped, shaking her head. "But I guess it isn't far-fetched to assume a few managed to slip away and join as guards or in other positions."

"Is it possible that you were able to slip in and out so often BECAUSE of these people?" Felix pointed out. "Also, I have a feeling he probably recognized Ki, so—"

"So let's just assume he did. The police have probably been told he's a dangerous criminal to be apprehended. But this guy was just a security guard. Would he associate Ki to Specters?" Sylvia mumbled. I shrugged, slipping out of the car.

"We don't know, but staying around here is just screaming to get caught," I voiced out, quietly shutting the door before heading toward the entrance of the garage. The others scrambled after me in their own ways as we headed toward the gate. The sunlight was bright after the shade of the garage and I quickly covered my eyes. The road was quiet, no one coming in or out. I frowned. It seemed wrong somehow.

What the hell was going on?

"Do you think the police force is out looking for a stolen car?" I turned to Felix, who was watching me in curiosity. "It's so empty here, I'm just wondering if our little 'crime,'" that was definitely air-quoted, "might have gotten most of the police out of this place." He shrugged. "I mean, this thing looks like a police compound and yet we haven't come across anyone yet."

"It's possible." Sylvia's words were hesitant, and worried. "But assumptions won't do us any good. Let's just get a move on." Sylvia pointed out, hurrying over to the back door. I followed suit, frowning as a thought flickered to my mind.

Wasn't this where my father worked? Could it be—

Almost without thought, I reached toward the handle. I stilled, surprised to note how it was unlocked.

"Okay, that's very strange." Sylvia outright gulped, Felix just seemed nervous beyond belief. I couldn't blame them as my heart pounded in my chest at the now OPENED doorway.

Why, in a police compound, as Felix called it, would the back door not be locked? Even without crime…

At this point, my entire being was screaming that this was a trap.

But why go through such an elaborate measure in order to set up a trap? They would have been able to get us in the garage, or at the gates or… Shaking my head, I stepped inside the dimly lit room, thoughts flickering to the last time I was here. Mira and I were sitting in those chairs to the right, the chief of police sitting on the left and then El coming through that doorway. I stared at the simple door before squaring my shoulders. Well, when in Rome or whatever.

I stepped up to the door, carefully pushing it open. It led into a long hallway lit by fluorescent lights. Doorways decorated either side and it seemed like the room we were in was at the corner, one hallway going right, the other going straight. I glanced back toward Sylvia who hesitated before she stepped up to me—

What the—why was she hugging me? I felt her grip tighten on me for a second before she pulled away, heading toward the right without turning back. I stared after her in shock as Margaret followed behind. "Be careful," Margaret said, voice wavering just a little bit.

"You too." I whispered, voice low, but it seemed to carry to the two of them, if the slight hesitation from Sylvia was any indication. I watched them go before turning toward Felix. "So, you ready?"

"Are you really asking?" He shook his head, walking past as I closed the door. "Anyway, I'll scout ahead and warn you if anything's coming, got it?"

I nodded, okay with that idea as we started going straight. High windows let in the sunlight as doors decorated the right side of the hall. My footsteps sounded loud to my ears over the ceramic flooring. Quiet chatter echoed from one or two rooms as we passed, but nothing jumped out at us. Only once did Felix have to shout to tell me to hide. Thankfully, a conveniently placed janitor's closet was right there. Let's just hope it wasn't the janitor though.

Considering the footsteps walked right on by, that didn't seem to be an issue. Too bad there weren't any uniforms just sitting around that I could throw on, but I highly doubted that would have worked either. I held my breath, as one of the nearby doors opened and an exchange of hello's echoed down the way. I wondered what Felix was doing. I could hear him near the two as they talked, but I couldn't quite make out what they were saying as the conversation faded away.

"You can come out now." Felix's voice was soft as I slowly opened the janitor closet and peeked out. He was staring down the hallway, gnawing at his lip.

"What did you hear?"

"Oh, only that they are searching for you, no surprise." He hesitated before catching my gaze. "They also mentioned that you can't be wiped."

"What?" I asked, utterly confused.

"I… I don't know, Ki. I thought everyone—" He cut himself off. "This isn't getting us anywhere, let's get moving, all right?"

I nodded, gently closing the door and continuing on as my thoughts raced. I couldn't be wiped? But why? El said something similar to that.

Still, it made absolutely no sense.

Unable to do much else, I shook my head and carefully continued down the path as I frowned in thought. I needed to figure out where I was going. Walking around at random like this wasn't getting us anywhere. I tiptoed my way down, following after Felix. Honestly, I was a bit surprised how easy it was so far.

Then again, maybe I was speaking too soon.

Chapter Twenty-four

It was a few minutes later when Felix called over, "Ki, there's a map over here. Take a look." His voice was surprisingly subdued, and I had no idea why. I observed the area, noting it was as empty as ever, still strange, and walked over.

Part of me wondered how Sylvia and Margaret were doing, but that was quickly wiped away as I curved around the corner and spotted a doorway that seemed to lead toward a stairwell. A map was set on the left-hand side of the door, which Felix was scrutinizing heavily. "What are you looking at?" I muttered, stepping over. He didn't turn to face me, finger tracing the path we were on for a bit before landing toward the center of the building.

"This…"

I followed his directions, briefly reading over the words, before freezing.

I jerked forward, hearing Felix yelp as I stared at the words. They finally connected as I voiced it out loud, "Memory Erasure Room."

Memory Erasure?

Memory…

I took one step back, then another, my heart pounding. I hadn't really thought it was memory! I knew my mind was a mess, but—

Why? What? How?

Searing pain thrashed through my head and it was all I could do not to scream as I collapsed onto my knees, palms pushing into my skull. The stabbing, twisting agony was worse than ever before, my head felt like it was going to split right in half.

Julie Boglisch

I could feel something on my shoulders, but it was fleeting. I slammed a hand over my mouth, just stopping whatever screams I knew I was going to let loose. I stumbled to my feet, not sure why I was moving, but knowing I needed to. I needed to be somewhere, there, why? I stumbled forward, pushing through the doorway before almost falling down the stairs, mind and gaze blurry. I felt something grasp my arm, pulling me back as the door clacked shut behind me.

"Kieran! Come on! Mom's here!"

"Sylvia! Mom!" Crash!

"Why? Kieran, why? Why is she..."

"Sylvia! Please, stop... Sylvia!"

"I'm sorry..."

"It's for the best... don't worry, I'll make the pain go away... You won't have to re..."

I felt my legs crumble and knew I would have hit the ground this time, if not for the steadying hand. Who?

I was trembling, my legs barely supporting my weight. Someone was kneeling in front of me, I could tell, but... hands sat on my shoulders as a voice echoed through the stairwell.

I slowly pulled my hand away from my mouth, unsure whether I'd kept it there to stop me screaming or throwing up. The pain faded as vague images clouded my mind. A young woman with deep black hair, humming a tune. A loud high-pitched screech. Blood. Lots of blood. But I couldn't remember what it was from, it just seemed to be everywhere.

"Kieran!" The voice cut through the fog, causing me to tilt my head up, gaze still blurry from tears before I locked eyes with Felix.

He seemed outright terrified, concern clear on his face. He was on one knee in front of me, hands on my shoulders. He noticed my attention was on him and slowly pulled back, letting out the heaviest sigh I'd heard from him. "I'm... what..." he trailed off, as if unsure what to say.

I pushed myself against the wall, staring at my hands. Huh? One of them got cut somehow, maybe from forcing the door open? I'm not sure. The brightly lit stairwell hurt my eyes and I closed them, pulling in long and slow breaths to calm my racing heart.

It was only then when I realized why my head was still hurting, and I blinked. Sirens. Sirens were peeling out, ringing over the metal stairwell.

"Emergency in reactor core. Overheating occurring, all employees, please retreat to safe distance. I repeat, all employees, please retreat to safe distance." The words echoed over the stairwell, clear from some intercom speakers.

Oh, they hadn't noticed us. This was somewhat of a relief, but why was a reactor core overheating? What was a reactor core? The memor—THAT machine?

"I'm fine now. Thanks, Felix." I spoke up, slowly pushing myself to my feet, using the wall as support.

"No, you aren't." His words were blunt, but I couldn't disregard them. "Something happened." He glanced toward his hands before peering back at me. "For a brief moment, I felt…" He trailed off before shaking his head. "Come on, we need to get moving." He grinned. "After all, this isn't going to keep you down, is it?"

I chuckled weakly, pushing away from the wall. Well, he wasn't wrong. I could already feel the migraine, because that's honestly what it was, fading. Though the nausea was definitely still there as I took the steps carefully one at a time. I heard pounding footsteps, and quickly surveyed the area, but there was nowhere for me to go. I thrust my hood up just as a few workers raced up the stairwell. They barely seemed to notice, racing away from something.

The core.

I exchanged looks with Felix before we hurried down the stairs, now more determined to get there. Reaching the bottom of the stairwell, we peeked through the window of the doorway. Red lights flared, whirling near the ceiling. But the hallway was quiet, everyone probably having already left. The only thing was the echoing sirens that I was starting to tune out. We glanced at each other before nodding and slipping out the door.

"This way." Felix gestured, pointing to the right. I nodded, following after him. I was thankful that he'd been able to memorize the map, because I definitely hadn't.

We walked down the hall, our footsteps ringing up and down the empty hallway.

Yet, we weren't running. It was almost as if both of us were too nervous and anxious to run.

Finally, we came across a well-secured door. Metal plates crisscrossed the door, a number pad to the right. Felix stared at it for a moment, before grinning. "I knew learning that would be helpful," he muttered. I let him work, realizing he was now in tech mode.

I hadn't seen this side of him in a while. Not since...

Since...

He was researching my symptoms with Mira and delving into the under-web.

I peered behind me, wondering what was happening with the others, was there anyone inside? Was there anyone we had to worry about?

"There, got it." A click sounded as Felix gestured for me to open the door. You know what? I'm not going to question how he managed to trick a computer program when he couldn't touch half the things. I opened the door, slowly peering around the doorway as I opened it. Only to freeze as I actually caught sight of what was on the other side.

Through the window, I hadn't been able to spot much, mostly just a console, but...

I stepped inside, followed by Felix as the door clanged shut behind us, clicking into place.

The reactor core, because that honestly was the only way to describe it, was a giant machine easily two stories tall. Thick wires coiled around the machine, connecting to different sections of walls. A loud humming filled the air, pulsing out in uneven waves. Wires snaked over the ground and, in the middle, surrounded in glass, was a box.

A box just like what my dad had been tinkering with for as long as I could remember.

I slowly stepped forward, walking over the wires as Felix

scrambled behind me. I reached up, fingers just brushing the bottom of the glass, feeling it vibrate. Electric waves pulsed from the machine, interconnecting with the wires and panels placed around it.

"This is…" Felix spoke up as I pulled back. I could hear the sirens fade as the hum died down, the pulsing more a steady heartbeat instead of the frantic pounding.

"Will all employees please return to their duties? The reactor core is fixed. I repeat, will all employees please return to their duties." The voice over the intercom spoke once more, sounding weary. Had they been trying to fix it this entire time?

But, what could they have used to fix this thing outside of this room? Was there a central computer station that someone was sitting at? Did they know we were here?

They could probably tell it was me. So why were there no sirens going off?

"It seems the sirens were cut," Felix spoke up, frowning. "But why? Who—"

"I was right." A voice echoed from the other end of the room, on the left-hand side of the machine. I jerked, feeling Felix stiffen beside me.

Stepping around the cords, right hand hidden behind the wall of thick wires, was Mira.

Well, I thought it was Mira.

"Mira? Is that really you?" Felix's voice cracked as his attention shifted to her.

I didn't blame his hesitation as I took in the condition of the girl in front of me. I just saw her yesterday. I KNOW that, and yet, for some reason, she was dressed in a white hospital gown which trailed to her ankles, her feet bare. Her hair was tousled, and not in a cute way.

Why a hospital gown? I briefly remembered Sylvia mentioning a lab. I noted bandages around her wrists and one at her elbow, lightly spattered in blood. It was more than a little worrying.

The main issue, however, was her eyes. One was covered in that glass-like piece I saw her wear the last few times I met her, and her other… her other was piercing into me with a cold precision that made me shiver.

"The Specter, what did it say?" She stared at me evenly, stopping in her place as she met my gaze, voice monotone.

"Mira! I know you know I'm here! Can't you hear me?" Felix stepped forward, voice spiking upward in an unusual moment of vulnerability.

She spotted him before returning her attention to me. "You know what? I don't care. I just want to talk with you, only you." She took a step forward, a strange sound echoing beside her. "You'll be able to explain it, right?"

She smiled and I found myself taking a step back.

"Alert to all officers! We have an escaped patient on the loose, I repeat, we have an escaped patient on the loose! Any available units—"

Anything else the speaker said was lost to me as I stumbled backward, watching as Mira finished walking around the corner, sword dragging across the metal floor, sparking as it trailed just inches from plastic wires. How the hell did she get a SWORD! I could only assume it was a specter-type item, considering the way it seemed to hum, faintly pulsing from a core set along the middle of the blade. "Mi—" Felix's voice cut off as Mira brought the sword up, lips twitched up in just the right way to send a chill down my spine.

"That boy beside you, he is familiar and yet not, but you are more so." She took another step forward, sword at her side, not dragging like before, but not pointed toward my gut. "Can you explain? Ki? Why I remember you and yet don't?" She took another step forward, only about four steps in front of me. Felix was paralyzed at my side, seemingly wanting to move forward, yet unable to.

"Do you know?" She took another step forward that sword trailing over on the ground once more, as if too heavy for her to keep up for long. "What happened after you escaped from me? What those Specters did?"

I recoiled as she grinned.

"Some ran, yes, but some of those things fought." She leaned forward and I almost tripped over the coil of wires inconveniently under my foot. I stumbled back, only to freeze as, with lightning speed, Mira darted forward and gripped my shirt with her free hand. "Because you escaped, because we couldn't find you, because those THINGS escaped, do you want to know what happened? Hm?" She hummed, as I reached my hand up to my neck, grasping at my shirt. I didn't want to hurt her, but-

"Mira, please stop!" Felix reached forward, trying and failing to grasp her shoulder. She slowly tilted her head toward him.

"Felix—" I tried to get out, only to feel her push me back and spin, sword barely avoiding cutting through me. I crashed to the ground, peering up in horror as Mira twisted, the blunt part of the sword slamming into Felix's side.

"Mi—" Felix was cut off as the sword stilled, vibrating in Mira's hand. Felix crumbled forward, curling up on the ground. I dragged myself forward, scurrying past Mira.

Relief seared through me as I noticed the distinct lack of blood.

I felt something at my neck and stilled. "He was annoying me." Mira's voice was quiet. "Yet, I couldn't... Ki? Why couldn't I kill him?" She giggled, and that was probably the creepiest sound I heard yet. "Those things killed everyone, everything. My father, my friends, my comrades. Everyone." Her chuckling shifted into outright laughter as the sword bit into my skin. "And yet, another part of me screams that they are alive! And yet I've seen their bodies, and yet I haven't—" I just peered up at her, hearing Felix gasping for air beside me. She pulled back, spreading her arms. "And I'm not dead! Isn't it hilarious? Am I alive? Am I really living or just convincing myself so? After all, I can see these Specters too. These foul creatures who should not exist and yet I can't harm even one of them?"

I heard pounding and jerked, glancing toward the metal doorways. Mira's arms dropped. "You know? I did remember someone. I remember learning how to work a computer from someone." She stepped back, giving me a moment to breathe. "You want to know? Don't worry, no one will bother us in here, not after the overheating core, not with the doors locked."

"You locked the doors?" Felix coughed, tilting his head up. I'm not sure why he tried, but-

"Of course."

I stilled, had she heard him? I pushed the thought away as the implications of what she said finally hit me. The doors were locked. She'd locked us in. Fear flared up my spine as I realized we were all alone with this... this twisted Mira. What about Sylvia or Margaret?

My thoughts were cut off as Mira started to hum faintly, a distorted tune. "You know? Somehow, I knew you would be here. I just knew it. After all, Ki wouldn't leave me, but he would. But he didn't, he's here to save me, to hurt me, to remember me, to forget me—" Her words started to spin together before she suddenly stopped, expression flat.

Her sword was once more against the ground, fingers limp. "Ki, please tell me. Am I—what am I supposed to—who am I?" Mira's voice broke, finally shifting away from the frenzied monotone from before. For a brief moment, it made me think of the Mira I knew, the Mira Felix and I both remembered.

I heard shifting and jerked, as Felix pushed himself up onto his hands and knees, before quickly grasping his side, letting out a quiet grunt. Just because he hadn't been cut, didn't mean he came out unscathed, I wouldn't doubt something was cracked. But he seemed to push it aside, glaring up at Mira. "You are our friend and my..." Felix bit his lip as Mira stilled. Could she hear him? Or was it just my imagination.

She glanced at him. "I know you," she whispered, voice strangled. "I know you and yet..." She slowly crumbled to the ground, sword clattering at her side. Yet, her grip remained firm. "Who are you?"

I closed my eyes, a quiet choked sound from beside me. Scrambling echoed in my ears as Felix moved past me. "I'm... I'm your... Felix. I'm Felix. You gotta—"

"I'm your what! Just spit it out!" Mira shouted, causing me to snap my eyes open, turning to Mira whose attention was firmly trapped

on Felix. She heard him, but why this time? Why was Felix hesitating? Was it because he didn't believe she was listening? Or couldn't hear him?

Felix held his rib as he struggled the rest of the way to his feet. He lurched forward, determination clear on his face, even through the pain. "I love you, Mira. Please... please remember me."

Mira stilled as the words rang through the room, almost echoing off the metal. I found myself startled and it seemed I wasn't the only one.

"Love?" Mira asked quietly, hesitation and hope slipping into her voice. She pushed herself to her feet and took a step forward, hand reaching toward Felix. "Felix?" A tear slipped down her cheek as she took another step—

"Intruder alert, intruders in the reactor core, immediate removal is necessary, I repeat, immediate—" The voice echoed, jerking us all out of whatever spell we were in. Why? Why did it take so long? Wouldn't they have realized earlier?

My attention snapped back toward Mira who let out a scream, stumbling backward as her hands reached for her head. The machine seemed to pulse for a moment before stilling.

"Mira!" Felix stepped forward, only to let out a pained yelp as, faster than I thought possible, Mira grabbed the sword off the ground and swung it upward.

"Leave me alone! It hurts!" Her other hand grabbed the sword as her gaze snapped to me as she slowly started to straighten, face clouding once more into a cruel grin. "You know? I don't know what I was doing there. What's the point of remembering when my memory isn't reliable?" she asked before whipping around. Felix barely pushed himself backward enough to avoid the foot to the face. This time, he didn't quite manage to stay upright, collapsing as he held his side.

Mira' s expression was calm before splitting into one of utmost despair.

"End it, please," she whispered softly, for a brief moment, her expression twisted into anguish. "Please, end it. I don't want this. I don't... I don't want to hurt him."

My throat caught in my mouth, as Felix groaned out a pain-filled and anguished, "No."

A memory flashed through my mind, pulling itself to the forefront. Black hair trailed down, eyes wild and desperately sad. "*Ki-ki,*" a faint whisper. "*Please, I don't want to remember. It hurts to remember.*"

"Sylvia?" I found myself whispering, only to freeze. Why was I thinking of Sylvia? Why was I remembering Sylvia?

"Agh!" Mira's cry jolted me out of my thoughts. She stumbled backwards as the machine pulsed beside us once more. This time, it was more erratic, as if struggling more with each pulse.

"Don't worry, there is still time. I'm not the only one in this state," Mira said, a heartbroken expression on her face as her arms dropped to her sides. "Part of me wanted to kill you. Part of me still sees you as a cherished friend."

"Mira?" I whispered, noting it was really Mira I was talking to… and that she was no longer paying attention to Felix, as if he no longer existed to her.

She smiled, a genuine soft smile. "I'm not going to be me for long." She turned to the machine. "This is the cause, isn't it?"

I could only nod as she turned back to me, the tears from before once more trailing down her cheeks.

"My memory is practically gone, it's all in shambles." Her smile pierced me, stabbing into my chest. "Ki, forgive me."

The light seemed to die before that original smile returned, along with a spine-chilling laugh. I barely had time before I saw silver thrust forward. I yelped, dodging out of the way as the sword pierced through where my stomach had been not a moment earlier. It clanged against the wire behind me, causing the thing to ring and tremble, but she didn't stop, pulling back and slashing in the same movement. I ducked, stumbling over one of the wires as I scrambled away.

"Mira! Please! Stop!" Felix was reaching a hand forward, before crumbling once more, trembling. I barely had time to notice before I found myself circling around the machine. This time, Felix's voice didn't seem to reach her.

What was I going to do now? Felix was hurt, Mira was deranged and I had a knife at my waist as my only defense. Great! What now? How did I stop this machine? Not only that, but my time was almost up. It was only going to be another few minutes before this place was stormed and that would be it.

I had to destroy the machine before then.

Chapter Twenty-five

I heard a swish of air and yelped, backpedaling, and almost tripped over the wires as I avoided Mira's swing. Her hair flowed around her, the manic grin back on her face as the metal bit into a piece of the plastic coating the wires. The hilt was probably insulated, since I could spot a hint of sparking along the metal as she tugged it out, but I barely paid it more than a minute of thought as I darted to the far side of the room, fully circling around the machine. It appeared the same, no matter what angle I was at. A cylinder in the middle of the room, a staircase on either end against the wall which led to a balcony on the second floor and two paths that seemed to stretch from the balcony to the machine. I hesitated for a moment, unsure of what to do, only to hear Felix shout, "Move!"

I didn't think twice, jumping forward toward the nearest staircase as something clattered behind me. My ringing footsteps echoed off the metal of the stairs, barely covering up the sounds of my pounding heart. I glanced over my shoulder briefly as Mira watched me from the bottom of the stairwell. She placed one foot on the corrugated metal of the stair. That would hurt, to walk barefoot, but she barely gave it any mind.

"Ki, come here. You still haven't answered my questions." Her voice held an almost sing-song quality to it.

"I don't know what to tell you!" I responded, gaze flitting between her and the upper floor. Just as on the bottom floor, there were about three doors around the edge of the room, embedded into the wall at uneven intervals. Windows shone to the other side, but unlike the pounding from downstairs, there was nothing from up here. I wondered why, but pushed the thought off.

"Of course you do." She giggled. "You've known for a while, after all! That's what started this, isn't it?"

What was she talking about? I hurried around the edge of the building as she bounded up the last of the stairs with a sort of ease that did not bode well for me at all. How the hell was she so agile right now? Was it because she simply didn't care?

I briefly glanced down, spotting Felix through the open slats of the flooring. He'd managed to get himself over to one of the consoles and seemed to be typing into it, occasionally glancing up toward us. I caught his eye just as he smiled and returned to work.

What was—No, I didn't have time for that, as evidenced by the sudden sound of clanging and the screech of metal. I dodged to the side, pushing myself up against one of the doorways as Mira's blade slashed through where I stood only a moment before.

Shit! That was way too close!

Not taking another moment to think, I darted away from the door and continued my circumvention of the second floor.

"KI! Take the next path to the center!" Felix shouted from below and, without much hesitation, I followed his orders, darting onto one of the two paths I spotted earlier that extended from the edge of the room to the machine. A console was set up in front of it, just like the one Felix was frantically working on below.

"There, got it!" he called up, just as a hum echoed from the machine. The strange box-like contraption hovering in the middle of the glass chamber seemed to be pulled to one side, closer to my console, as if...

As if to be able to observe for abnormalities or...

"Thanks, Felix," I said under my breath as I slid around the console, ignoring it altogether and heading right up to the glass. If I could just get to that machine, if I could just break it somehow, that's what I needed to break. That box.

I slowly turned to face Mira as she drew to a stop, having stepped around the console as well. We were only a few paces away from each other. The sword sat at her side, humming slightly. Her head was tilted, as she observed me with a quietly chilling expression.

She didn't say anything as the doors below shook and a hissing sound filled the air. I didn't want to imagine what they were doing below. My palm pushed into the cool glass, thrumming against my skin almost like a heartbeat.

"Mira, I'm sorry that this happened," I found myself saying, softly. "Hopefully, when this is all over, we can help you…" I trailed off. She stopped for a split second, a faint expression of anguish on her face.

"I want that too." Her words flowed out before her gaze hardened and she darted forward, removing the last few inches between the two of us.

"I'm sorry, Felix… Mira…"

I pushed myself to the side, my body slamming into the railing of the podium and almost toppling over the edge as the blade whizzed by where I just stood. A sharp clang and shatter echoed in the air. I turned just in time to watch the blade slide through the black box. Time stood still, for one fleeting moment.

A shockwave slammed into me. Mira was tossed into the console behind, head slamming hard as she crumbled. I felt myself tumble over the side, barely catching on the metal as sirens screamed.

Pain slammed through my head and it took everything I had not to lose my grip, my hand aching as I swung a full story above the ground. I might not die from this height, but I was not going to be walking. My free hand scrambled for purchase as my head throbbed and spun.

Thoughts surged, threatening to pull me away, divert my attention. I could feel my head splitting in half, my fingers slipping.

"Kieran! Come on! Mom's coming soon!" Sylvia danced in front of me, arms spread wide as a bright smile curled over her face. The sun shone down as we waited near the intersection about a block from the school. Traffic was hectic, as usual, with cars swerving in and out of parking spaces.

The four-way intersection was bustling. A few of my classmates raced across the lines as cars moved along with them, barely stopping to hit the walking meter before going. Pretty typical, to be honest. My backpack sat heavily on my back, pulling at my shoulders. I just shook my head, watching as Sylvia hummed, rocking back and forth as we waited at the corner, where Mom usually picked us up. I was excited for today, to be honest. Mom found time to get away from work for a while and we decided it was time to go out to celebrate our birthday, which was tomorrow. I was fine, however, with going early. I could always celebrate the day itself with Sylvia and Dad, if we had the chance. I heard the sound of tires and returned my attention to the road. Pulling up to the sidewalk a little in front of the lights was Mom's car, a little sedan that honestly fit Mom to a tee. She pulled to a halt, blinkers on. I stood up from my seat on the cement wall that surrounded the little park behind us, as Sylvia raced over to the car.

The window was rolled down and Sylvia was chatting happily, arms sitting over the window as she leaned forward.

Honestly, why doesn't she just go in? I chuckled, walking over as Mom reminded her to use the door, or so I could assume as she pulled back, blushing brightly.

"Forget again?" I called as I walked up behind her. She turned and glared at me.

"Ki, leave it," she muttered, earning a laugh from Mom. She was vibrant today, with a warm smile crossing her pretty face as long black hair, so similar to Sylvia's, curled around her chin. She was dressed casual today; a blouse and skirt combo that was nice on her. Sylvia always joked we would look like Mother when we grew up. She might, but not me. Pretty wasn't exactly what I was aiming for.

"Kieran!" Felix's voice echoed from behind and I turned, spotting my friend. I chuckled and walked over, exchanging a quick fist-bump. "Oh! Your mother's here. I won't bother you for too long, but do me a favor, okay?"

"Sure." I said, "Wha—"

"Ki! Hurry up!" Sylvia's voice caused me to roll my eyes and turn.

No. Something… I don't want this.

Sylvia stood next to the car, door open. She was leaning against the door, annoyed. Mother was peeking forward, arm over the steering wheel as she watched in bemusement.

A screech filled the air. My gaze turned, as if in slow motion, as a car whirled around the corner, coming from the school. A young driver sat inside, glee and panic on his face as he barely dodged the traffic, zigging left, right, lef—

"Sylvia! Mom!" I shouted, only managing to take one step forward. Sylvia pushed away from the door as Mother whipped around in her seat.

The out-of-control car clipped the parked car behind Mother's before slamming, full speed, into the back of hers. The screech of metal against metal, the screams, they were nothing as I raced forward, barely catching Sylvia as she was flung backward. The car door slammed into her side, barely pushing her out of the way of the vehicle as it plowed forward, pushing Mom's car into the intersection... I slammed to the ground, Sylvia in my arms as I turned just in time to hear a long screeching of tires, the acrid smell of burning rubber and—

CRASH!

I ducked my head as debris from the cars slammed into the sidewalk.

I slowly tilted my head up. Smoke rose in the air as sirens and screams wailed.

"Kieran! Are you okay!" Felix's voice shook as he knelt beside us.

I shoved Sylvia, her shaking form, into his hands as I stumbled to my feet, giving her a brief once-over. She was injured, but alive. But Mother! Everything in me was screaming that there was no point, but— I stumbled over toward the remains of the accident. The two cars were nothing but crumbled heaps. A truck, having probably been coming through the intersection normally, was at an angle, the driver barely crawling out. But that wasn't my focus, no, my focus was on the sedan, the little car I stood next to only a minute earlier.

I stared at the ruined remains of Mother's car, feeling myself collapse to the ground. It didn't resemble a car anymore. Crushed and mangled and utterly destroyed. I turned my head, wanting to scream at the driver that slammed into her, but one glance at the car was all I needed to know he wasn't doing anything ever again.

He couldn't do much when his head was on the ground a few feet from the shattered remains of the car… with the rest of the body still in the car.

A part of me thought it was fitting karma, yet another part of me wanted to throw up, sickened at the sight, but my whole body was shut down, my mind grinding to a halt. Mom… she still hadn't gotten out. She wasn't getting out, was she?

My fingers slipped on the metal of the railing, tears tracking down my cheeks, unbidden. Someone…

"Kieran," Sylvia's voice was weak, hands wrapped and head bowed in despair. We'd just come back from the funeral, and I felt dead. Father was barely holding himself together, but Sylvia?

Sylvia was close to Mother, even during the accident. She'd been right there and I knew it hurt her, more than I could ever imagine.

"I don't want to remember," she whispered, turning to me with a tear-filled expression. "Why can't I forget? Mother's expression when it happened? The crunching sound? I don't want to remember Mother like that. So why do I have to? WHY! Kieran, please, tell me why!"

"I—"

"I just want to forget it all. Even now as I try to remember Mother, I keep seeing her face right as the car hit, fear. She was scared, so scared."

I pulled her close, arms wrapping around Sylvia as I forced myself not to cry. I wanted to, so badly. But how could I? One of us needed to remain strong.

But I guess I wasn't strong enough for both of us.

My arms had no strength left in them, I could feel them shaking, weakening, but if I let go… Sylvia…

I peered down at my homework, having no inclination to do it. It was about two or three weeks since the accident. Sylvia was mostly recovered physically, but Mother's sudden death had been tearing at the family and I could feel it. I felt my head slump and hit the desk with a jarring bang. I let myself rest, not wanting to deal with anything.

I felt a tug, an uncomfortable feeling in my stomach, and frowned. Deciding to listen, I stood up and slipped out of my room over to the bathroom. I knocked on the door, curious. "Sylvia? You in there?"

I didn't hear a response, but frowned as the feeling continued, I pushed my ear to the door, a faint hissing sound reaching my ears.

A distant smell wafted through the edges and alarm bells rang in my head. I didn't know why, but I definitely knew something was wrong. "Sylvia! Answer me! Sylvia!"

Still nothing.

I twisted the handle, slamming my fist into the door once more as it didn't move. Why the hell did she lock it? "Sylvia!"

I pulled back, foot slamming into the door, kicking at it with as much strength as I could. It buckled a little, but these were strong doors. I knew Dad was out, so it was just the two of us. Deciding to hell with it, I wound back and got myself ready, curling inward and aiming my shoulder as much as I could. I slammed forward, feeling the wood give under my assault. I pulled back once more before shooting forward, almost falling on my face as the door smashed open, falling to the ground with a crash!

Immediately, a smell wafted to my nose, so strong, it stung. My hand slammed over my nose and mouth as I noted two bottles placed side by side, a strange concoction swirling in a bowl next to them. However, my attention was quickly drawn to Sylvia, who was slumped over the tub, arms dangling inside and lips turning a pale blue.

Horror filled me as I took a deep breath of fresh air before pushing into the bathroom. I grabbed Sylvia, shaking her desperately. Her head lolled to one side, but she didn't move.

Thinking fast, I put my hands under her arms and tugged her out of the bathroom, away from the smell. Once I knew we were in the fresher air, I pulled out my cellphone—

That… that's not right, Sylvia… why?

My fingers trembled as I dialed 911 as fast as my shaking hands could. My eyes glued to my sister as I spoke rapidly into the phone as soon as it connected. The operator spoke, trying to calm me, giving me directions.

The next ten minutes was absolutely nerve-wracking as I did everything I could, waiting for the ambulance to arrive and hoping it wasn't too late.

I couldn't... I didn't want to lose anyone else! Not now.

My hand slipped and, for once, I found myself unable to attempt to reach for safety, I was just so tired.

"Kieran!" Felix's voice jerked me out of my stupor as his hand grasped my wrist. My gaze snapped up toward him, startled. How did he get up here? He was holding his side with his free hand, kneeling heavily on one leg.

"Felix, wha—you're hurt!" I shouted, staring up in shock.

"Yeah, thanks for the reminder. Now get up here!" He growled, tugging. I gritted my teeth, indecision flashing through my mind for a brief second, more memories, just at the edge of my consciousness, threatening to overwhelm me again.

"Right." I reached up, clasping my fingers around the edge of the platform, pulling myself up with Felix's help. We fell onto our back and side, breathing heavily. Though Felix didn't stay down long, he slowly pulled himself over to Mira, literally dragging himself to her side before checking her head. Meanwhile, my thoughts were running wild as I parsed through the surge of memories. Mom was DEAD. So, then who was the woman who took care of me this last year? Was it just— no, it couldn't be a figment of my imagination. My mind might be scrambled as all hell, but that didn't seem right either. As for Sylvia, who—how— was she—

OUR mother?

Sylvia always joked we would look like Mother when we grew up.

We... Was Sylvia?

I was jerked out of my thoughts as the sounds of hissing and banging from before returned.

"Code red! I repeat! We are in code red! All employees, please evacuate the premises, I repeat. All employees, please evacu—" The intercom system cut out and I shivered. That was not a good sign.

Felix hovered by Mira as I slowly pulled myself up, shaking my head to clear my thoughts, I would figure all this out later, not when we were in the exact middle of the police compound, or whatever the hell this place was. Felix barely gave me a glance before saying, "Well, you heard him. Let's get out of here."

I frowned, peering over my shoulder. Was that all we really needed to do? I observed the machine, noting the way it was now completely dormant. The glass was shattered, sword still stuck clean through the black box, which must have plummeted at some point, for it was now amongst the wires near the bottom of the glass chamber it used to hover in. I frowned. Well, the sword was useless now.

I stood up, hurrying over to Felix as he let out a faint breath. "She's still breathing, but Ki, we need to get her to a hospital and I don't think this place is anything like a hospital. We need someplace I can trust to take care of her." He tilted his head up to me and then froze.

For a long time, he observed me before turning away. "And, hey, I'm... I'm sorry."

I wasn't quite sure what he was talking about until my thoughts flickered to my most recent memory and I sighed. "We'll worry about that later, come on." I leaned down, getting Mira over my shoulders, thanks to Felix's help.

Thanks? Wait...

"Felix?"

"Hm?"

"Are you..." I trailed off, hurrying back over the metal path and to the edge of the room.

"I'm me." He said, voice absolutely distant. "I'm ME."

I smiled, unable to erase the hint of happiness at his words. Did that mean everyone was—I cut off that train of thought, stumbling. My thoughts were threatening to overwhelm me again and my whole body hurt as I tried to repress them. Now was NOT the time.

I heard a click and stilled just as a door on our level swung open. Felix froze beside me, hand holding his side and squatted slightly.

Nothing happened. The door hung open with no one charging through. I slowly stepped forward to peer inside and noted the hallway was only lit by faint fluorescent lights and red blaring. Ah, right, I'd tuned out the sirens.

We hurried down the hallway, the door closing behind us with an automatic click. So, it was remote controlled. I was not sure I liked that idea.

However, I could hear shouts coming from the room we'd left so I guess I couldn't be too upset.

Mira was thankfully pretty light, but she was still taxing on my strained shoulders as we hurried down the walkway. Felix was absolutely silent, but I didn't blame him. If he was dealing with the same thing as me, it was going to take a lot to figure things out.

I wondered where Sylvia and Margaret—

The faint sound of gunfire was enough to give me a general idea. I exchanged glances with Felix before upping our pace down the hall, hurrying to the right where I spotted Margaret, gun at her side as she raced forward. Behind her was Sylvia and… Dad.

My eyes widened as I slid to a halt, barely avoiding running into the group as we converged at the corner of a three-way intersection. Sylvia stilled, spotting me.

Emotions whirled in my mind and questions burned, but I just grit my teeth. Dad appeared worse for wear. He was exhausted, deep circles under his eyes and skin sickly pale. He smiled weakly upon noticing me, stumbling forward and giving me a quick, if scarily tired hug. So, Dad was who Sylvia was talking about earlier. Part of me should have guessed, but—

"Took you long enough," Sylvia joked, hurrying alongside me as we guided Father forward. "We opened that door as soon as we noticed you were stuck in there. We barely had time to close it and come meet with you before the police were on us."

"That was you?" Felix spluttered, asking for me as I examined the girl beside me quietly. She remembered, didn't she?

Sylvia nodded, expression serious as we stayed equal with Margaret's pace. Mira shifted on my back, groaning, and I let out a breath, slowing to a halt, causing the others to stop. I squatted down, letting her off my shoulders as Felix knelt down beside her. She blearily blinked, peering around at the small gathering. "Where—"

"Mira!" Felix's quiet cry of relief startled everyone as he suddenly hugged her tightly. "You're okay! Oh, thank whoever," he muttered.

"Fe... Felix?" Her voice broke. "Wha—where—how?" Tears trailed down her cheeks. "Who?"

My heart stilled at that last word, as did all of us, I think. Felix slowly pulled away, devastation clear on his face. "Mira? What... what do you—"

"We don't have time for this," Margaret cut in, tugging them to their feet. Mira seemed to let her as Felix let out a yelp. I was startled by her sudden movement. "We are in enemy territory. We need to get out of here." Her voice was shaking, but a strange firmness was in it.

"Yes." Father said, glancing at me and Sylvia. We exchanged looks and, for a moment, I could have sworn a faint sad expression crossed her face before she turned ahead.

"Come on, let's hurry out of here."

We continued on our way. Margaret pulling Mira along as Felix followed behind, gaze drilling into Mira's back with so many emotions, I could feel it from where I ran.

"Where is everyone?" I found myself asking, noticing the empty hallways as we took another turn, light shining through the high bar windows.

"Already outside or in the reactor room. Other than that, your guess is as good as mine." Sylvia said, keeping her gaze straight ahead.

Hm... something wasn't adding up in my memory. The last thing I remembered was her trying to kill herself and now she was next to me, as if nothing happened, but no... that couldn't be right. Was I just missing something?

"There aren't any more of those devices, correct?" Margaret asked, question directed toward Father, who shook his head.

"Not that type, no, I was in the middle of developing the next one, but never finished. The only other thing they have is…" he trailed off.

Well, whatever it was, hopefully we wouldn't have to worry about it. We slowed to a halt as we approached a doorway that was awfully familiar. Wait, was this the way we came in? I must have taken a huge loop around the place then. Sylvia cautiously opened the door, peering inside before gesturing for us to follow. We hurried after her through the back room and pushed open the second door. The sun beamed brightly down at us, along with the shine of metal and the loud click of safeties sounding off. I peered out, freezing. Sylvia, who peeked through, quickly pulled back inside, trying to close the door. It was wrenched from her grasp as the door was caught and swung open. Police officers barged into the room, guns up and at the ready, surrounding us before we could blink. I pushed my back against Sylvia, Felix pressing into my side. From what I could tell, we were in a circle, backs pressed against each other.

As for the officers… Headphones sat over their ears and their expressions were glazed. Wait, glazed? I thought Dad said there were no other machines? I quickly thought through our conversation and stilled, right, he said no more like that one.

"No." Father breathed, spotting the contraptions. "That thing shouldn't—"

"Shouldn't be able to control so many people?" A familiar voice spoke up, standing near the doorway. My head snapped to the side. It was the man from before. The man who brought me home, and who almost shot me in front of Mira.

"El." I said quietly, drawing a bit too much attention toward me.

"I'm glad you remember, though I'm not happy that you CAN remember," El said, hands in his pockets.

"What did you do to them?" Felix called out, holding Mira close to him. She didn't seem to be resisting.

El briefly peered at him before turning to Father. "Now, why don't you get back to work. We need to fix the system—"

"Hell no!" Sylvia stepped forward, fist up and getting right into the man's face. "I'm not forgetting again! I don't care how much it hurts! You aren't making me forget either of them again!"

El peered down at her before a spark lit in his eyes. "Could you be?" He hummed, before glancing over toward me. "Ah, we do still have a way to correct this, don't we?"

"You will NOT touch my children!" Father shouted, stepping in front of Sylvia. "You will kill me before you lay a hand on them!"

"Oh, you have no right to say that, considering—"

"That means nothing! The machine is gone! Just give up and let it go!"

"I can't," El said, voice flat. "I may not agree with the utopia that my sponsor was striving for, but I know the power of that thing you created. Just watch." He gestured to the men around us with one hand, the other tightly clasped around something in his pocket, if the bulge at his side was any indication. "Such a small piece of technology developed as an add-on has this much control. Why would we give up on something like this? Now, hurry. The government will be on us soon unless we get the main system back up."

What the hell was he talking about? Main system? Government? Utopia? There was someone above him?

I heard movement and a gasp and glanced back. Some of the controlled officers drew closer, guns raised, except for in front of Sylvia and myself. I briefly noticed some of the guns dip a little, aiming toward our legs to cripple us, not kill us.

Unlike with the others.

Kill, right. Death really was possible.

Utopia…

What utopia?

Crackling sounded through the radio on one of the men's jacket. Maybe he was a higher-level officer?

"Help requested in district C! I repeat! Help requested in district

C!"

"Rioting in district A! It's mayhem!"

"We need an officer over here right away! People are going cra— Guh—"

"Dammit," Father cursed, breathless. "I thought destroying it would be enough."

"You were wrong," El's voice was even. "Look at what your son caused. Everyone is like that girl behind you." His gaze flicked to Mira. "Lost, confused, enraged. What do humans do in that state? When they are not controlled? When they are not told what to do and how to think? They riot. They attack." El smiled. "And this is proving my point, but you know how to stop it, how to return to a nice peaceful life, right?"

Peaceful? Could I call the last year and a half peaceful? Because whatever it was, that thing had to have been created then, didn't it? I heard a shift and then gunfire cut off our conversation as Margaret, of all people, let loose, cutting down the men beside her before pulling Sylvia along with her. I'm not sure what the hell happened. One moment, we were still, the next, gunshots and shouts were ringing out as we raced into the sunlight, pain slashed past my leg, but I ignored it as I dived to one side, Felix and Mira going the other way. Dad, Sylvia and Margaret leapt forward, Sylvia slamming the door in the officers' faces, leaving just El outside, stumbling backward in shock at the sudden movement. I glanced toward Margaret, gaze widening as I noticed the multiple wounds crisscrossing her body. It seemed she avoided anything major, but she needed to go to a hospital, or at least get bandaged, and soon.

"Come on!" Sylvia shouted, pulling us with her as we raced toward the garage.

"Get back here!" El shouted, tugging a thin computer-like chip out of his pocket and quickly thumbing over it.

We disappeared into the garage, jumping into the car. It obviously wasn't set up to hold so many people, but we made do, Mira sitting on Felix's lap, with Margaret and Sylvia in the back, Dad and I in the front, with me somehow in the driver's seat.

Don't ask me, we all just rushed in. I turned the key and whipped out, my thoughts flicking to that boy in my memory who caused Mother's death, the one who… No! I was not going to let that happen to any of us, I spun the wheel, gaze determined as we flew out of the garage and headed toward the gates.

"We need to destroy that device." Father spoke up, coughing. "I can disrupt it, but…"

"What was that thing?" Felix choked out, though he didn't seem too upset about the situation. Smooth.

"A device I made to help make sure the waves would be received properly. An enhancer and a slight modifier. However, it was also developed to manipulate remaining memory," Father spoke up faintly.

My gaze met Sylvia's and—

I remembered—

"Sylvia, why?"

"Because I was scared," she admitted, staring up at me from where she lay, prone on the bed, her arms strapped down for her own protection.

"But you didn't…" I trailed off, biting my lip.

"You know? You are very strong," she whispered. "Even Father… did you know? He was working on a way to forget. To forget the pain of losing Mother and just retaining the good times."

"But that's…"

"A lie, isn't it?" Sylvia interrupted, facing me. "But, isn't what he's doing the same as what I tried? A way to forget? That's why I envy you. You can still be you. You aren't trying to forget, are you?"

"I…" What could I tell her? Though the whole situation was heart-wrenching, I didn't want to forget Mother's final moments. I'd always be wondering. What happened? Why forget the bad times and only keep the good? It was painful, I wouldn't deny it, but… "I'm not as strong as you think," I finally admitted. "I'm just as scared of forgetting. If anything, I'm holding on more than you."

She smiled faintly before closing her eyes.

Chapter Twenty-six

I could hear Father talking, but my attention was on the road and my thoughts. We passed by the first gates, which were wide open. Not a single guard was visible, and if I really thought about it, I should have been wondering what El was doing with the device earlier. Honestly, there was so much I should have been worried about, but at the moment I couldn't focus on any of it.

I was sitting in the kitchen, head in my hands as my father's tinkering sounded in my ears from the other room. I knew what he was working on. A memory erasure machine. I knew he was a genius inventor, but...

I heard a sound and sat up, turning my attention to Father as he stepped in, beaming smile on his worn face and black device in his shaking hand. "It's done, son."

"Father?"

"Your sister won't be in pain anymore. We can start over with the good times pushing us forward."

I was hesitant. Admittedly, scared at the thought, but, as I thought over Sylvia's words, Father's ecstatic smile, I couldn't help but find myself nodding.

He smiled brightly before tinkering with it a little and pressing a button.

A button which caused all of this.

So, that's what happened. I peered up as we passed the second gate. This time, I was well aware of how open the gate was and how worrying that was. It seemed the others noticed as well, because the car was eerily silent as we passed down the street.

Then, I saw them. People scrabbled at their heads, holding them tightly, children sat at the corner, crying.

As we drove down the street, the town all around us, a strange air of heaviness, nervousness and anger filled the place.

"Everyone's memories returned." Father spoke quietly, "And it must have been too much."

I watched as an old man, an old man I watched so long ago, sitting in a diner alongside Felix and Mira, keeled over, the old woman from before at his side. I shivered as I spotted an accident off to one side, a car having swerved into a building, as if jerked to the side. Screams and cries filled the air and smoke curled toward the sky in the distance, from where, I wasn't sure.

"It's not just Specters, it's everyone!" Sylvia choked, pressing her face to the window. "Everyone's falling apart!"

"Well, are you surprised?" Felix's voice was dull. "A year and a half we've lived a lie. A year and a half of altered memories, repressed feelings, forgotten times. If it all comes back at once."

I shuddered. Everyone here, well, almost everyone in this car, was lucky to have been recovering their memories when it happened, but I found myself suddenly thinking of the Specters who could barely eat and stilled.

Wait, if it was memory manipulation, then why was it that Specters existed? How was it that a simple erasure of memory, discounting how complicated that SHOULD be, would cause people to not be able to hold things? Or interact with people?

The questions, even as my memory returned to me, only seemed to be adding up. I thought we would be ending things! Not making them worse!

It wasn't far-fetched to think that everyone was in the same mindset, an eerie quietness filling us.

I'm not sure what happened, but I found myself stopping near my— our— home. That was the only way I could think. We all needed some rest and time to think and Father seemed to be on the verge of keeling over. While the house probably wasn't the safest, I had a feeling the police were going to be busy dealing with the people going insane. Or who already were insane and could now actually affect things.

I shivered. If some of the Lost, as Felix and Sylvia called them, were around, then…

I was starting to worry about this little town.

I stepped forward, ahead of Sylvia and grabbed the key that was always hidden behind the house number, barely cringing at the feel of a spider web breaking under my fingers. I pulled out the key and opened the door, walking inside. The house was empty and tired. The door was closed and lights off. It just appeared abandoned. The others hesitantly followed. We all stepped inside and I closed the door, locking it. I guess some habits don't die even if memory disappears.

The house was different. While some areas were clean, others seemed like they hadn't been touched in over a year. Dust covered certain items, as if they had been left to rot… forgotten. Including a picture frame, on the wall to one side.

I found myself walking up to it, Sylvia at my side, Father was slumped over on the couch, fast asleep already. Mother… no, the woman who pretended to be Mother was nowhere in sight.

Part of me wondered where she was, but another part pushed it off, exhausted. We had other things to deal with, and worry about. I saw Sylvia reach up to the dust-covered frame, fingers trailing over the glass. It was hard to believe we forgot such a thing, or more so, that in forgetting my sister I also forgot everything tied to her. It was a picture of the four of us, before the accident. Mother's smile was bright as she hugged the two of us, Father at her side. To have not remembered this, to have left it to rot, it hurt to think about.

'Why don't we get ourselves some rest?" Felix's voice was faint, his attention definitely on Mira, as I realized when I turned. He was observing Mira with a gentleness he rarely showed, as Mira leaned against him, tired.

"Yes, for now," Margaret said, so quiet, I barely heard her. I glanced toward her as she winced.

"Will you be okay?" I asked quietly.

She nodded. "It appears worse than it is." She hesitated. "Though, if you have any bandages on hand, I would prefer some."

"I'll get them." Sylvia spoke up, moving away and returning surprisingly quickly. Well, not that surprising I supposed, it was her house after all.

Margaret took it, a weak but grateful expression on her face before she started tending to her wounds. Examining her now that we had a moment, it seemed my earlier assessment was wrong. Most of the wounds were superficial, there were just a lot criss-crossing, making it appear worse.

Once I was sure she was all right, I let my mind wander, noticing Sylvia was already gone.

I wasn't sure I could sleep, my mind racing as it was, but I let everyone do what they wanted. I found myself meandering up the stairs, only to stop as a door I should never have forgotten caught my attention. It was partially open. I hesitated for only a moment before carefully pushing it open some more. The door creaked and groaned as it twisted on unused hinges. I winced, but peered inside anyway. The light was on, flickering dully in the late evening glow. Dust covered everything, a bed, sheets tangled as if someone rolled out of them at one point and no one got around to cleaning them up, lay limply over the bed. In the middle of the room, staring at different posters that were barely hanging on the wall, was Sylvia. She turned her head, gaze locking with mine before she turned away once more. "We forgot so much," she finally said after a while, tilting her head to the ceiling where a fan sat overhead.

I couldn't argue with the statement. Examining the room quietly, I recognized every part of it, from the dresser that held my sister's books and supplies, to the lava lamp on the side table which very clearly had burnt itself out over the past year and a half. Sylvia finally turned to me and paused, uncertainty clear in her tired features. "Ki?"

"Hm?"

"Can you give me a few minutes?"

I hesitated, briefly, before nodding and pulling away. I closed the door just a bit before heading toward my room.

In an utter contrast to Sylvia's room, nothing was too different in my own. I spotted the lamp, noting the scratches all over it, as if someone inexperienced fixed it. Huh, I wonder if I changed it without remembering? How amusing that would be. The amusement, what little there was, was short-lived.

The door creaked open behind me a few minutes later and a familiar voice spoke up. "Ki? Can I talk to you for a minute?" I turned to Sylvia, surprised she followed me so quickly, but then thought it over and decided it wasn't that strange. I wouldn't want to be alone in a room like that right now. I took a seat on the bed as she closed the door behind her, staring at the door for a moment, as if it was a novelty, before sitting beside me. She stared down at her shaking hands, tightly gripping her knees.

The room was quiet, filled with bits of dust and a strange heaviness. I didn't say anything. I didn't know what to say or how to act. This was my sister, and it certainly explained why I seemed so comfortable around her and yet, I had no idea what to do.

"It's really been almost two years since that accident, hasn't it?"

I nodded, palms resting in my lap as I scanned the bumps and divots in the ceiling. "Yeah." A tightness pulled at my chest and I found myself struggling to breathe. I tried to calm myself as memories flashed through my mind. I wondered if I would have been overwhelmed like the others if my memories hadn't been slowly coming back to me.

It was strange. I felt like someone else, someone who shouldn't be here, but at the same time, I was someone who should be here. I wondered if Sylvia felt that same way.

"I'd always thought it was strange." Sylvia's voice was tight.

I pulled my attention away from the ceiling and spared her a glance. Her hair covered her face before she shook her head, an odd half-smile on her features. I just continued to watch her, feeling a frown cross mine. The smile, thankfully, faded as she seemed to collapse inward. "How are you... how are you so calm?" Her voice cracked slightly and I winced.

Julie Boglisch

"Do I really seem calm?" I found myself saying, and, as I analyzed my own words, they were said in such a flat tone, I found myself wondering. "I could say the same about you," I pointed out bluntly.

She let out a soft laugh. "Maybe you're right." She stood. "It's been a long time since we've talked, but..." she turned to me, unsure.

"Neither of us know what to say," I said when I noticed she didn't continue. It wasn't wrong. It felt, strange. I'd lost my sister, but at the same time, a lingering part of me didn't. Was it remnants of that machine? I wasn't sure and I wasn't sure I wanted to know.

"You're not wrong..." Sylvia trailed off before peering out the window, watching something that I had no interest in. "Everything is a mess."

I stared at her before standing up, arms crossed. "That's true. So then, how are you holding up? Now that your memories are back and you can touch things again."

She grew silent before peering up toward me, unamused. "Do you really need to ask?"

"No, probably not, but I'm asking anyway," I said, not budging.

"Just like I remember," she whispered before letting out a quiet chuckle. "You know? I always kind of remembered that I knew you. Even while I was in that state, I remembered you. Not much, just bits and pieces, but I don't think I ever truly forgot. It, well, I remembered quite a bit more in the last few weeks."

"Which is why you were always checking up on me, worried about me." I let my arms drop as I parsed through what she said.

"I wonder, is it because, somehow, you still held some memory of me?" Her attention drifted up toward the ceiling, the afternoon light lazily drifting over it.

"I don't know." And I really didn't. I knew nothing about this entire situation and it annoyed me to no end. When I thought everything would be cleared up, I was happy. But now, I was only more confused and lost, overwhelmed as I tried to parse through my thoughts, memories, emotions... everything.

I turned to the window, away from my sister as I stared down at the eerily quiet street. Orange and yellow dappled the trees. What was usually a beautiful glow seemed so harsh today.

"Ki, I..."

I hesitated before turning to her, noting the shake of her frame, the clench of her fist, the sharp bite of her lip. "Sylv?" The nickname came out of my mouth out of nowhere, causing her to still.

It was only for a second, a brief moment before she suddenly threw herself at me, holding me tightly. I felt tears on my shirt as a choked sob sounded from her throat. "I was scared. So scared."

I found my arms holding her, pulling her close. The warm embrace. It felt so familiar.

It was just like after Mom died.

I felt my throat clench as I bent down, leaning against her shoulder.

I didn't want to cry, I didn't want to. But I couldn't help it as everything that happened, everything that was happening, finally hit me. Mother was dead, Father was sick, I'd almost lost my sister twice and we were still no closer to getting out of this whole mess than before.

I was tired, just so tired.

Couldn't someone else deal with this? I didn't want to deal with this anymore. I wasn't that strong.

I just—I stilled, as part of me realized.

Strangely enough, I just wanted to forget.

That realization, it froze me to the core. That's what started all of this, that desire to forget, to not want to deal with anything anymore.

I guess I understood, but... I opened my eyes, not realizing I'd closed them, and stared at the doorway as my sister continue to sob into my shoulder. I remembered thinking that I didn't want to forget.

And now, as I thought over the past few months, no, years, I found myself still thinking the same.

I didn't want to forget. As much as it hurt, as much as it felt like I was breaking from the inside, I'd rather remember. I found myself holding tighter.

I could also understand, why anyone would want to forget.

And I didn't blame them. I couldn't blame him.

I needed to talk to Dad… but later. For now…

I just let myself relax. There was no point in holding anything in right now, why did I need to be strong? A moment of weakness…

There was no crime in that.

Chapter Twenty-seven

It was a while later when we finally broke apart, Sylvia wiping at her cheeks as a smile crossed her face. "Thanks, Ki. I needed that."

I chuckled briefly, shrugging. "Yeah, well, let's get downstairs."

She stared at me before nodding. "Yeah, but first, let's wash our faces. We look like a mess and yes, that means you too."

I rolled my eyes, but didn't argue, grateful for a chance to splash some water on my face to freshen up. I wasn't completely fine, but the cry helped.

Thank gosh no one else was there though. If I didn't have my memories back, that would have been awkward, but I couldn't say I minded being able to be near my sister, now that I did remember everything.

We descended the stairs to find everyone scattered around the house. Dad was fast asleep on the couch. Mira and Felix were on the other. Mira's gaze was distant and Felix seemed absolutely heartbroken. I would ask, but right now, I honestly didn't feel like dealing with anything else.

Did that make me callous? I wasn't sure.

Margaret was in the kitchen, poking through all our groceries. I wondered where the woman I called Mom went. I had a lot to ask her. But right now was probably not the time.

I felt my stomach twist as a loud growl echoed around the room. Margaret jumped before peering back toward me. Sylvia chuckled. "Why don't we get something to eat for everyone? I bet we're all hungry after that."

That was an understatement. Margaret nodded and the three of us got to cooking. It wasn't long before the rich smell of soup wafted through the air. We decided on a simple chicken noodle, since everyone was probably still a little out of it and or not feeling well. I toasted some of the bread we had, buttering it while my sister worked on making up a salad.

A simple meal, but it was kind of nice, just being able to work in peace. Margaret stayed quiet, which didn't really surprise me, but she was also much more distant, which I didn't think was possible.

Within no time, we were gathering around the dining room table, or at least, most of us. I glanced over to the couch, squatting down next to it to wake Dad. I could tell he was exhausted, there was no doubt, but it worried me that he hadn't gotten up yet.

After a few minutes of me shaking, or at least what felt like minutes, he finally let out a groan. He stared at me for a long time before letting out a breath of relief. "Kieran, you're okay," he whispered.

I nodded, helping him sit up. "Can you stand?"

He hesitated and I could tell he was really thinking his answer through, which worried me more than I wished to admit. "I'm still quite tired. I think I'll need your help for now," he finally relinquished, which only spiked my worry more, but I didn't say anything, just hooked one arm under his, wrapping around his back as he leaned heavily against me.

We made it to the kitchen, where he plopped down in the closest seat. I took a seat beside him, Sylvia right next to me. On the other side of the table sat Margaret, Mira and Felix. We were all quiet as we ate, hunger seemingly first and foremost on our minds, or so it seemed, with how we devoured everything.

Finishing up dinner, Felix agreed to clean up, Mira trailing after him. She gripped his sleeve, but still seemed quite out of it. I wondered if something was still wrong, but I pushed away the thought.

First, I needed some answers and I wasn't the only one.

"Dad," Sylvia hesitated, causing Father to jerk. The word sounded so strange, but Sylvia pushed on. "What's going on?"

He stared at us for a long time before letting out a long sigh. He seemed to deflate in his seat, his usually always moving hands limp.

It was so strange to see how much of a toll all of this took on Father.

"Let's wait until those two get back from doing the dishes, shall we?"

Sylvia pursed her lips, but didn't argue. Thankfully, it wasn't long before the two returned. "Oh? You waited for us?" The somber tone of Felix's voice spoke volumes. I nodded as he took a seat, helping Mira.

"All right," Father said, getting all of our attention. "I guess all of you certainly have a right to know." He stared at the two of us and I found myself turning away. I knew why this started. I just didn't know why it was HAPPENING.

"Two years ago, I lost my wife in a car crash," Father started. "A few other things came up, and it was tearing our family apart." Pain twisted over his features. "I truly just wanted to help; it was nothing more than that. I found a way to create a device that, I thought, would be able to erase certain memories. I won't get into the long and complicated details, but you can see it as sending out specific wave patterns to mess with the synapses in the brain that include memory, a simple pulse through those synapses and memory is erased."

"You..." Felix's voice jerked me out of my thoughts as anger flashed on his face. "You created that... thing?"

"That THING was not my intention. I only wished for us to be able to move on, having only the happy memories. I wanted to do that for—"

"For us," Sylvia said with a hardened gaze toward Felix. "He did it for us, for me."

Felix frowned, but backed off so that Father could continue. "Unfortunately, the technology was stronger than expected. It completely blocked the receptors in the brain from anything relating to the memories in question."

I frowned, trying to parse through it. Sylvia had no qualms. "Would those receptors also cause—" she cut herself off, a mix of anger, hurt and resignation on her face.

Father nodded. "With all receptors blocked, the brain tries to adapt, but there is no information there to adapt to." He pursed his lips. "If I'd known what it would do if I turned it on, I never would have. The electronic waves messed with not only the synapses in the brain, but also in the atoms associated with those synapses."

Okay, we were starting to get really technical here, but I was able to gather the gist of it. "Because of those waves, Sylvia and the others..."

"They became Specters." Father's gaze was absolutely heartbreaking as he stared at Sylvia. "My own daughter, I made into such a cruel existence. A human who couldn't interact with the human world. Whose body was moving out of sync with the rest of the world because of my device, and because I had no memory. I had no means of fixing it."

Sylvia stared down at her clenched fists, shaking.

"But then, why were some more affected than others?" I asked, thinking of all the Specters I met.

"I think I could maybe answer that," Felix muttered, deep in thought. Everyone turned our attention on him as he scrutinized each of us. "If it's electronic waves and the increased shaking of atoms, well, I guess you can basically say it would amplify any characteristics of a human. If they were healthy, they wouldn't be affected as much by the waves, but if they were already a little unstable, dying..."

"Then it would have created the Lost," Sylvia continued, realization dawning on her. "Those with no reason to live or to try to remember, and if it was a more powerful wave, something that had an increased output, that would explain all those who were forced to change after they remembered us. They would have needed a higher output to change those who somehow didn't forget."

"But how would that be possible?" I asked, annoyed. "How was—if it was brain waves, why would certain people avoid it?" I was, sort of, avoiding myself, to be honest, but they all seemed to get it anyway.

"Why would..." Felix muttered as Father turned to me.

"I can't be certain. But those with a connection, if the main memory is gone, muscle memory still exists. It wouldn't be farfetched to assume that those with close relationships, or tight families might not forget everything." He hesitated. "I guess a better way to phrase it is that, while we might forget names and faces, we never truly forget the feelings associated with a person, that memory, practically engrained in our psyche, would be unaffected by the wave."

"Which would explain why so many people remembered at the beginning." Sylvia hummed, deep in thought. "Then, why was Ki... why was he the only one who survived that long?"

Father hesitated. A deep anguish crossing his face. "That's..."

"It's something you don't want to talk about." Margaret's voice startled us, her words soft, yet firm. That's, however, when I noticed how much she was shaking, fingers twitching in her lap. My gaze snapped to Sylvia and Felix and I noticed that, as calm as they were portraying themselves, they all seemed to be affected by Father's words. Felix was holding tightly to Mira, occasionally checking her, fingers lightly touching her hair. Sylvia kept turning her gaze down to her lap and then briefly outside before returning attention back to Father.

I have no doubt they were worried, not only about their own situation, but about those they once cared for as well.

"You're not wrong." Father sat up, pulling my attention back to him. "But that's not the issue right now. Right now, we have some things we need to fix."

I wasn't sure I liked the idea of brushing off what he meant, why he didn't want to talk about it.

I'll be honest, while most of my memories were back, I was struggling to remember the time after that thing was turned on. Those few months after were a blur.

Was it because the waves messed with my mind?

"Wait, so how do we remember now?" Felix blinked, speaking up.

Father chuckled weakly. "It's because I didn't DAMAGE the receptors, only coated them."

Realization dawned on me. "The waves from that machine. They were blocking our thoughts. Could that be why…"

I exchanged looks with Sylvia as she seemed to realize as well. "So that's why Ki's memory kept fluctuating, it's because a new wave would need to be sent out to replace the old, and in that time, the previous wave was degrading enough that—"

"Memories were able to slip through!" Felix realized with a grin. "And because of that, it also meant anyone associated with Kieran would also be less affected."

"Correct, or so I can assume," Father interrupted. "Because my son remembered you and wasn't completely wiped like most others, his memory, while scrambled, was able to maintain something of a balance. Forgetting, but not completely. This, as a result, allowed him to be between the two, spectrums, I guess you could call it."

This was starting to make my brain hurt. And it seemed I wasn't the only one. Felix groaned as Sylvia frowned.

"So, what now?" Mira asked, voice soft. "I… you talk about memory, but…"

"Right, right," Father said, getting our attention once more. "I never finished my story." He let out a sigh. "See, a month or so afterward, someone came by, a science 'friend' of mine. I'd told a few people about the device and, after confirming it worked—"

"Huh?" I cut in, confused. "How do you confirm you forgot your memory?"

"I wrote down specifics." Father left it at that as he continued. I wondered what those specifics were… "It was supposed to be an achievement, a great scientific discovery. At the time, I had no idea that Sylvia ended up like she did. I knew something happened, but…" he smiled weakly. "I was foolish, foolish, but excited. I had something that I thought could help people. I could see Kieran was happy. I was happy." His smile dropped. "But I trusted the wrong person. We talked and he mentioned how we should create a way for the device to work over distances. I didn't think much of it, after all, it wasn't exactly easy to make or mass produce, so I was fine with that. We worked until we created that machine you saw and then…" his expression was so hard and angry, I found myself jerking backward in surprise. I never saw Father that upset before. "That's when I realized what he intended to do. He already set the machine in motion, saying it was to create a utopia, a place without pain or fear. Maybe at one point, I believed him, but after that month, after realizing how strange things were, I wanted nothing to do with it. I told him I was going to back out. That I wasn't going to work on it anymore."

His fists clenched and I felt a shiver run down my back. "Needless to say, he did not like that one bit." His whole posture seemed to slump, what little energy he had once more draining out of him. "There was nothing I could do. I wasn't about to allow him to... so I continued working on the project. After a few months, he allowed a little more freedom, but by that point, there was nothing I could do besides work."

"So that's why," I muttered, staring at the table. That's why he always seemed so sad and tired. Why he was always seemed to be fiddling with something and why he was so exhausted right now. "Then, who was that woman?" I asked, getting Father's attention.

Father stared at me before shaking his head. "I'll be honest, I do not know."

I shuddered at the realization that Father didn't know either, but I let him continue, "Once that device was operational, I was designated on another project, a corresponding one." He gritted his teeth. "A mind manipulation device. While the main device was just to erase memories, this one was created to tamper with those memories, an add-on, if you will. That device, after working so long on the first, took almost no time at all to create."

"But why?" Sylvia spoke up, voice soft. "Why would—"

"They ask me to create something like that?" Father's expression was faint, a tiredness that I doubted was going away any time soon. "Because, while the memory loss was having an effect, too many people were questioning their memories. The device was created to make sure... to make sure no questions were asked. You could say, it was used as a way to curtail the population. After all, if no one asked, no one cared and that one was, unfortunately, easier to produce."

I winced, realizing what he said.

"So that's why we were told death didn't exist and believed it. Why we didn't question the lack of cell phones, or the idea of crime not existing." Felix frowned. "Scary."

More like terrifying. I thought back through just the past few weeks. "Is that why I kept getting headaches?"

"That's the other reason, yes, because the main machine did not completely block your memories, you noticed all the changes, but your mind was unable to cope with it." Father sighed. "I knew that, but there was nothing I could do about it. At least, not at first..." His gaze flipped to the headphones still sitting around my neck. "Those headphones, they are the only pair I was able to create that can block out those waves and that isn't connected to the main network."

My hand darted up to the headphones as realization dawned on me. So that's why... that's why I could still hear, but my memories were less fogged. So Dad had protected me in some way.

"So, what now?" Felix asked, arms crossed. "The machine is destroyed, so why is everything still in chaos?"

Father winced. "I mentioned electronic waves and atoms, right? The process for turning is a slow one, so it's not as damaging to the body, however, when the machine was destroyed, you could say a pulse went out, destroying all previous waves and forcing the atoms and synapses back into place. For some people, that shift would drive them insane, but for others, they wouldn't be able to handle it if they were frail or sickly. It would be worse for those who were turned into Specters. Their whole body would try to suddenly reconstitute to the natural world. It's a blessing that all of you are fine."

I shivered at the thought and I didn't think I was the only one. The earlier hesitation, worry and fidgeting grew worse. Sylvia, Felix and Margaret were definitely not calm at this point, but they didn't push.

"That doesn't explain the mind device though," Felix pointed out, voice shaking, but continuing the conversation. I was grateful that he was, because I sure as hell wasn't going to be much help here, not with how my mind was spinning.

"Right." Father leaned back. "I'm not sure on the specifics, but my guess is that my coworker—" The way he said it was answer enough to his opinion on the matter, if the growl was any indication. "—was able to tweak it so that it works in a short radius without the help of another device. It probably wouldn't be as effective, but if they can get the right wave lengths…"

"Or if they can convince you to go back, like they convinced you to continue," Felix muttered, causing Father to stiffen and… me to wince?

Strange.

"I don't think we want that happening," Sylvia muttered. "So, what we need to do is destroy that device and find your coworker. Of course, with El still out there and the population going somewhat insane, that's not necessarily going to be easy." She groaned.

"Well, the insanity should only last a day or so, right?" Felix's questioning voice was filled with desperate hope. "I mean, if they snap to automatically…"

"We don't know," Father said, eyes drifting closed. "We've never tried reversing the process before. I don't know what damage it would do, besides what I assumed and told you previously. But I do know that it's probably starting to hit other towns. From what I remember, we were able to create a one-hundred-mile radius where our influence with the machine was active. The shockwave could still be reaching the outer edges."

I winced. Oh, good.

"So then the faster we move, the better," Margaret said, standing. "I'm getting some sleep. You all should rest as well." She left, disappearing down the hallway. I wasn't sure where she was going, but we all let her. Father seemed like he was falling asleep in the chair anyway and Mira was dead to the world, leaning on Felix's shoulder.

The fact that Felix didn't really notice showed just how much thought he was putting into this, and I didn't blame him. It was a lot to take in. I sighed. So, we now knew what happened, mostly. So, we needed to get that machine away from El and find the coworker Dad talked about, but why didn't he say a name? The way he spoke indicated that it was probably someone else besides El, who mentioned a sponsor, so...

I frowned as just more questions continued to pile up. Though, we finally did get some answers. Either way, it made my head spin and I decided sleep was, indeed, a very good idea.

~ * ~

When I awoke, it was to the first signs of dawn seeping through the windows. The sky was still dark, but hints of light were peeking over the horizon. It would have been pretty if it wasn't a morbid blood red. I usually loved red skies in the morning, but today, it just seemed eerie and unnatural.

Of course, that matched with everything I remembered from the days before. I slowly got up, slipping out of bed. I blinked, noticing Sylvia sleeping on the floor, curled up in a bunch of blankets and pillows. I briefly wondered why she didn't use her room, only to remember the state of it. Plus, I doubted she wanted to be alone right now, especially since she probably had more on her mind than I did right now.

To be honest? I didn't mind her staying with me.

I headed downstairs, feeling tired, but pushing it aside. Felix was already downstairs, cooking quietly in the kitchen. He seemed distant, lost in thought. I came up beside him, flipping into the fridge to grab something to drink.

"Oh, you're awake." His voice was faint, his attention focused solely on the pan.

I leaned against the counter, chugging some water before letting out a sigh. "How are you feeling?"

"I've been better." He finally turned his attention away from the food and over toward me. "That was a lot to take in yesterday, wasn't it?"

I nodded, taking another swig of water. "How's Mira?"

Felix's expression twisted. "Not good."

I let out a breath, placing the bottle down on the counter as I stared out the kitchen doorway, noting as people started to move around the house, probably waking up now that the smell of food was spreading. "Well, now I know why I didn't want to know about my symptoms."

"You're never going to let that rest, are you?" Felix joked back and I grinned.

"Hey, I did warn you."

He huffed, flipping the pancakes onto a plate before starting on the next set. It smelled good. "Yeah, you did, but I don't regret it."

I stilled, my back digging into the counter as I leaned heavily against it. "Really?" I muttered, thinking over the past few days.

Felix hesitated for a split second before scoffing. "I mean, I don't like what's happening, but…" he frowned. "I hate the idea of forgetting even more, forgetting you, my mom and dad." He winced, fists clenched, knuckles white. "I would hate to forget Mira. I mean, I get it, but…" he slumped, letting the pancakes cook up in silence.

"Believe me, I know." I pushed away from the counter, swiping up the bottle of water.

"Ki, how are you dealing with this?"

I stopped, bottle suspended a few inches from my lips. Honestly? I wasn't. I was ignoring it. Trying not to think about it. I laughed softly to myself at the irony. "I could ask the same thing of you."

Felix remained silent for a while as I quenched my thirst, not leaving, but not standing right next to him either. "Do you think, when this is all over, we might be able to find a way to fix this? To restart?"

I stared down at the floor. "I don't know."

"Heh, yeah. I guess that makes sense." Sizzling and flipping sounded in my ears. "Anyway, I need to give those bastards a piece of my mind. I'm sick of being a puppet on a string, something that can be controlled at the snap of a finger or, well, the push of a button." He turned to me, burning in anger. "I'm sick of what they've put everyone I care for through. So, Ki? I don't care what you say or do, but I am going to make sure those bastards get what they deserve."

I smiled and he seemed to relax, grinning in return. I turned to the doorway, waving. "I'll get the others up, since it seems breakfast is ready."

"You know it."

I chuckled, feeling a little better. I wasn't fantastic, but after the last few conversations, I did feel a little better. The situation was still out of control, but at least I knew what the situation was.

When we sat down for breakfast, it was Margaret who brought up a situation that I, honestly, should have thought up earlier. "We can't stay here much longer. They'll be after your father and it's not going to take long for them to realize we came here. They may be dealing with the upheaval of the population, but they aren't going to take long to rally and send someone over to get him back."

"We can't allow that." Sylvia's glare was answer enough to that as she stuffed a slab of pancake in her mouth, chewing angrily before swallowing.

"We don't have any options on where to go, though." Felix frowned as Mira peered between us, that same confused expression on her face as the other day. It was eerie not hearing her chime in or join on the conversation and, while I didn't really notice last night, it was obvious this morning. Especially now that I was rested and starting to parse through everything.

"I know where my coworker would be." Father spoke up, catching our attention. "Whether El will be there or not, I am not sure."

"He could be, but even if he isn't, we should go there anyway. El said he was working for a sponsor, after all."

"It's worth a shot." Felix stood, picking up the plates and hurrying to the kitchen. I agreed, anything was better than nothing at this point. All of us quickly got cleaned up. Father was still exhausted, slumped in the chair. I hope the exhaustion will go away soon. It was worrying.

I shivered at the memory of Mom and quickly pushed the thought to the side. "But who IS the coworker?" I reached over, gently shaking Father when I noticed his lack of response. He groaned quietly. "Sorry, Dad."

"It's fine, son." Father's voice was faint and it made me wince.

"Where is that coworker you were talking about? Who—"

Father hesitated before slowly sitting up. "Right. His name is Leonard. He lives a few miles out of town, in a lavish mansion he acquired for himself recently." He shook his head and sat up. "I can get you there."

Lavish mansion outside of town? That sounded… blood and rot crashed into my thoughts and I almost backpedaled. Thankfully, I was sitting, but my action caught the others attention. "Do you mean…" My voice wavered, thinking of the haunted house from all those weeks ago.

It seemed I wasn't the only one who realized. "Wait, seriously? That place?" Felix shuddered. "Why would anyone buy that?"

"Ah, so you know of it," Father said, voice low. "Supposedly, he bought it after the hauntings stopped."

I shuddered, only to freeze when I noticed Dad pushing himself to his feet. When I went to stop him, he sent me a look. "Kieran, I'm not so fragile to have this break me down. I'm going to make sure you and Sylvia are safe." He pushed himself up and trudged over to the door. "Where are the keys?" I stilled, hand gently touching my pocket. He gave me a sharp if somewhat pleading expression and I quietly relinquished them, feeling the attention of the others as they came into the room.

"But not everyone is going to fit. It was tight already yesterday."

"That's why you two are staying here—"

"No!" Sylvia walked up, almost wrenching the keys from Father's hands. "I don't care what you're thinking right now, I'm going to go and I'm going to take care of that… that person." She growled. "I'm tired of this and I'm going to make sure this ends, one way or another."

I stared at Sylvia, wondering if someone was still using the mind manipulation. She was so different from my memories, that fragile girl who tried to commit suicide was not who I was seeing right now. She matched the girl I saw over the last year. The fire in her gaze, the way her stance was so rigid, yet the way she kept her voice down, even as it came out in anger. It was both similar and so incredibly different that I wasn't sure what to think about it.

"I don't think anyone wants to be left behind." Felix hesitated, glancing toward Mira. "But…"

I scanned over our ragtag group, because, seriously, there were no other words for the people standing here right now.

Sylvia let out a breath, somewhat deflating before turning to us.

"Sylvia." Margaret's voice was neutral, but I could hear a faint waver as she stepped forward. "Would it be okay if I go and check on a few things?"

"I want Mother." Mira's voice was quiet. I stilled.

Right, they…

My attention drifted toward Felix, who seemed to be deep in indecision. He spotted me watching and smiled. "I want to check on Mother, but I already promised to go with you, and I have a feeling Father will take care of her."

I didn't question it. There were already enough things to worry about, if Felix remembered his father and mother, then…

"All right." Sylvia spoke, her voice was quavering. She was okay with them trying to separate earlier, but I think now, with how overwhelmed she was, the hesitation was a bit more apparent. Still, it seemed she made up her mind, posture straighter. "Then I know I'm probably not a leader or anything anymore, but can I have you, after you do what you need to do, check up on the others? The one's who hopefully escaped? Make sure they are safe." She paused, peering over to Mira before returning her attention to Margaret. "And please bring Mira to her home. We don't know what state her parents are in, so keep an eye on her."

I could see Felix grimace, for a moment tightening his hold on her before slowly letting go. Felix turned to Mira, a sad and hopeful expression on his face, and I could see a moment of hesitance in Mira before she tilted her head up.

I turned away as Sylvia stared behind me, shock clear in her posture. A moment later, Felix was by my side, hand patting my shoulder before he slipped into the car. I followed after him, briefly noting the sadness on his face, as silence rang down the street.

I rested a hand on his shoulder. His whole posture slumped and I didn't blame him as not a word echoed from outside.

Sylvia, after giving Margaret a few more orders, followed, sitting in the front seat as Dad got into the driver's seat. Within moments, we were off.

Felix didn't look back, his fists clenching in his lap as a quiet snarl rang in his throat. The switch was obvious, as the sadness swiftly changed to anger. "I'm going to make them regret trying to mess with us, with people." He was shaking, quite visibly. Sylvia and Father stayed quiet as Felix slammed his hand on the leather of the seat. "I don't... they are not going to hurt anyone else."

I nodded, draping my arm around his shoulder, much as he always did for me. He seemed startled at first, but didn't push me away.

I peered out the window, noting how it seemed the sun was almost directly overhead. How long did we spend talking? I could see smoke off to one side as we stayed close to the side roads. I could see people outside, walking around in a daze. I wondered, would I have been like that as well? If it wasn't for whatever happened that stopped them?

I almost wanted to ask Dad what really stopped them from taking me or turning me, but I was scared. I honestly didn't want to know anything else. I was tired enough as it was of everything I was learning. I was not about to add to this list if I could help it.

Not until everything was said and done. Maybe... maybe then.

I peered out the window, sounds of honking and cries reached my ears, even through the glass. I furrowed my brow, observing the surrounding area closely. The town was growing busier. Off to one side, someone was fleeing his house, a terrified expression on his face. Cars weaved back and forth in front of us as we got closer to the middle of town. I thought it would be a straight-forward shot. Just go there, talk with the guy and...

Actually, what were we going to do?

"Hey? I forgot to ask this, but what are we doing, going to a madman's place anyway?" Felix spoke up, having finally pulled himself from his thoughts.

Father was silent, his knuckles white and grip tight on the steering wheel. Sylvia hummed before glancing over her shoulder at us, slightly turning in the front seat. "Well, we need to make sure they stop trying to force Dad to work, we need to find that memory manipulation machine and destroy it and…" she frowned. "That is a lot easier said than done."

Felix snorted. "Yeah, because El will definitely be at the haunted house where we can have a nice little chat with him and the big boss. Really? What's the likelihood of that happening, and smoothly?"

"It's better than sitting around and twiddling our thumbs," Sylvia said brusquely.

The two glared at each other and I just shook my head, once more diverting my attention to the outside. As we curved around a corner, I paused. The streets were cluttered. This was where I'd heard all the sounds from earlier. Cars honked, trying to swerve around others or even onto the sidewalk. Officers were either helping to funnel the traffic, or checking each car, much to my dismay.

Then again, it didn't seem like I was alone. "What is going on? Why is there so much traffic?" Felix peered out the window, sitting upright.

"Are they trying to flee?" Sylvia muttered, observing the surroundings carefully.

"It's possible." Father spoke up, rubbing his face. "It wouldn't be improbable to assume that everyone here is scared of what happened. They don't understand it, can't figure out why their memory is suddenly back, or all messed up. They might blame the area or…"

"Or they might have suddenly seen a Specter," I said, catching the others' attention as I stared to one side. Down the street, just a little way from the havoc of the intersection and checkpoints, a few officers were dragging out a stretcher. A hand dangled from it, a rotted twisted thing. Sylvia must have noticed as well, for she promptly gritted her teeth, turning away. Felix wasn't much better, covering his mouth as he gagged. "Or, well, the remnants of one."

"Oh, yeah, that would probably terrify some people," Felix choked, "especially if suddenly, they remembered a loved one only to find them…" he shivered and I turned away from the scene, noting the haggard and lost expression on Dad's face.

Sylvia noticed, but didn't say a word. I let out a breath, leaning forward. "Dad?"

"It's fine, son. I should have known better than to assume a prototype like that would... I should have done more tests or never created that THING at all."

"But you did it for a reason, right?" Felix, surprisingly, was the voice of reason this time. "I mean, now that I remember, Ki was absolutely miserable and he was the one dealing with your, well, your wife's death..."

"The best?" Sylvia said softly.

Father was silent as he weaved us around the traffic, pulling into a side road that was less crowded. It led us farther into town, but I think all of us would rather avoid dealing with the police right now. Actually...

"Dad, where are we going?" I thought we were going to the haunted house, but the route we were taking...

Father didn't say anything for a little while, deep in thought. "Your conversation just reminded me of something, that's all."

I frowned, but didn't argue. The others were deep in thought, watching our surroundings, which were much the same.

"Geez, did a zombie apocalypse occur?" Felix joked weakly as we noticed a car accident up ahead; the cars were left abandoned.

"I wouldn't call it that," I muttered, causing Felix to roll his eyes.

"Dad, this is the opposite direction," Sylvia pointed out, pulling our attention away from the cars.

"I know." He briefly glanced back at me before turning forward once more. "I don't know what I was thinking."

"Are you going to do something stupid, like drive us to safety and confront the guy yourself?" Felix huffed, arms crossed over his chest.

But when no sound came out, he loosened up. I jerked forward, leaning between the center console. "What, seriously? Dad, we can help!"

"No, son. There are things... things you still don't remember and I don't want you to remember. I'm not going to let you anywhere near those…"

Don't want me to remember? Surprisingly enough, anger welled up inside me and it took everything I could not to lash out.

Sylvia, however, wasn't so restrained. "What do you mean." The question wasn't a question: a pure statement if I ever heard it. "A memory is a memory, good, bad or indifferent. Forgetting something…"

"Don't you know? The term Dissociative Amnesia?" My father's voice was quiet, worried.

"That…" Sylvia hedged, pulling back a bit. "What does that have to do with Kieran?"

"Dissociative Amnesia is usually caused by a traumatic or highly stressful event. Usually, it has added symptoms, but due to the electronic wave manipulation, those were kept at a minimum. Kieran, do you remember, how scared you were of going to the hospital?"

I stilled, thinking back. I remember talking to Mira and Felix about that a long time ago.

"So that's why you never brought Ki to a hospital? Because of that amnesia?" Felix asked, leaning back in thought. "But what does that have to do with going the opposite direction?"

Father tightened his grip on the steering wheel. "There was a certain incident with my coworker. I was able to get you out, but—"

I shivered, not liking the sound of that.

"But something happened," Sylvia cut in as we pulled to a stop at one of the lights, a few cars in front of us and people hurrying up and down the street on either side.

Father simply nodded, lightly tapping on the gas to move forward. "I'm not putting you in that situation again. I'm not…"

"Dad." I pursed my lips, thinking through everything for a moment. If it was something my mind was forcing me to forget, even with all the stuff that happened recently, then maybe I didn't want to know. But that wasn't the point right now. Maybe I would remember it, maybe I wouldn't, but not knowing, that constant fear that a part of me was missing, that something would always be missing. I think that scared me even more.

Maybe I wouldn't have noticed, if all of this hadn't happened, maybe I would have preferred not remembering some sort of traumatic event. But now, now more than anything I wanted to know, wanted to remember every part of who I was. To reconfirm that I was still me and hadn't changed. Or, well, hadn't changed without my knowledge. Resolve strengthened, I glared at my father, causing him to still for the briefest of moments as I said, "I don't care. We need to fix this, and make sure it doesn't happen again. Whatever traumatized me enough to make me forcefully forget memories…" I trailed off.

"I do, though." Father's voice was soft, but it still dragged me out of my thoughts. "I don't want to see you hurt again. Not anymore. Not because of my mistakes."

"That's not your decision to make," Sylvia said harshly. "That's up to us to decide and Kieran just told you, he doesn't care. So then allow us to help you and take that bastard down. If he really did hurt Ki…" a sharp grin crossed her face, eerily similar to Mira's expression when she wielded the sword earlier. "Well, I have some pent-up anger to get rid of."

Before Dad could respond, the ear-splitting sound of sirens cut off our conversation as a police car swerved around the corner. Dad jerked the wheel. Yelping, I gripped onto the nearest thing, flashes of Mom's accident briefly breaking into my thoughts, before we pulled to a stop on the side of the road. I let out a breath, relaxing slightly.

"Dude, you can let go now."

I blinked, spotting Felix just staring at me. I grinned sheepishly and pulled back from the tight hug I'd given him.

Ah, whoops? He just rolled his eyes, waving it off with a light chuckle before his expression grew serious. I followed his gaze, noting that the police car was off to one side, an officer unsteadily walking out of the car. Whether it crashed, or was just parked haphazardly on the sidewalk was hard to say. The officer seemed dazed, confused.

"Hey, he's that security officer we met on the way into the facility, the one Margaret knew. What is he doing in a police uniform?" Sylvia asked, peering around Father, who was taking in deep breaths to steady himself. "What's going on?"

"I don't know, but I'm going to check it out, it seems almost like he's in a daze." Felix slipped out of the car, keeping the door open. I decided to follow, more curious than anything.

Plus, I wanted to get out of the car for a bit, my mind running a mile a minute.

"Hey! Wait up!" Sylvia's voice carried over to us as I glanced back. I noticed her quickly saying something to Dad, before scrambling out of the car. Dad watched us go, a tired and resigned expression on his face.

As if he'd given up.

I gritted my teeth and followed after Felix. No, Dad, we're not giving up. We just don't want this THING controlling us anymore. I don't want it controlling you anymore.

Felix was beside the officer, helping to steady him as he held his head, headphones dangling around his shoulders; they were probably knocked loose earlier. As I caught up to them, I heard the tail end of the officer's words. "Assigned to patrol, even though I'm just a security officer. I took a different route and… what is going on? What happened?"

A different route? Glancing at the headphones, it finally clicked. "You must have gone just out of range of the field." My voice was soft, but both Sylvia and Felix heard it. "If you were under that…" I trailed off. The man, and now that I was observing him closer, he did look an awful lot like Margaret, turned to me before his expression lit up. "Oh! It's you!" He stared at me for a long time. "I'm going to guess your name wasn't the one on the ID."

I shook my head.

"We shouldn't be talking here. We have to move." Sylvia started hurrying down the street.

"Hey! Wait! What are you doing? You know what's going on, don't you? Why this is happening?"

"Sort of?" I shrugged. "Not much we can tell you, but…"

"Is it that El person?" he asked, reminding me that he mentioned the name earlier. When I nodded, he continued, "You won't be able to speak with him willy-nilly." He hesitated. "I know where he is, but—"

"Oh, no. If you go back into range of that thing, we don't know what will happen to you." Sylvia stomped back. "We don't need an officer suddenly switching..." she trailed off and a thought came to mind.

Switching? "Hey, you said you know where El is, right? Take me there." I gestured to him, leaning on one foot. I could feel Dad's eyes on me as we talked, though I don't think he heard what we were saying. I did, however, feel the need to hurry up our conversation.

"You thought the same thing," Sylvia said, voice faint.

"Would you mind explaining it to me then?" Felix groused.

"Not now." I turned back to the man. "They are searching for me, right? We don't know where they are, or what they are planning."

"We'll be right behind." Sylvia sighed, heading back to Dad's car, pulling Felix along. Was she really okay with what I was about to do? Or was it that we just had too few choices? I briefly wondered if they would be able to convince Dad, especially with how much he argued earlier. I couldn't hear the conversation, but I could see that Sylvia was explaining the idea. I couldn't spot Father's expression, but it was probably a mix of exhausted and pissed.

"That's great and all, but can someone explain what you two are talking about?" The security officer flicked back and forth between me and where Sylvia went off to. I grinned.

"Oh, well, if you were still being manipulated, you would have already captured me right now, right?"

He nodded and then let out an, "Oh."

"So, what do I need to do?"

The man grinned. "Leave it to me, I'll make sure to drive slow enough for your friends to follow." He gestured to the police car, pulling himself back inside and quickly turning it around before I slipped into the front seat, getting comfortable. Thank gosh for small towns. Sometimes they could be a good thing. Now, it was time to see El.

Chapter Twenty-eight

Every so often, as we drove through the streets of town, I would glance back to see if Dad was still following, and was always relieved to see he was. So, Sylvia must have convinced him. Either that, or he was too tired to argue anymore and simply didn't want to leave anyone behind. I did kind of just jump into the officer's car out of nowhere after all.

The plan, as rudimentary as it was, was pretty simple. I was going to go inside, led in by the officer, to be taken to meet El. Sylvia and Felix would follow behind, disguised. At least, that's what I mentioned to the guard, who agreed and said he would grab a couple uniforms for them before bringing me inside. His place was a small one-story home. When I glanced back to see if the others were still following, I noticed Sylvia staring in shock, as if she recognized it. However, when I asked her about it later, she quickly waved it off, mentioning that she saw it before when she first met Margaret. Ah, that would make sense. Felix and Sylvia quickly got changed and, to be honest, while the uniforms seemed a little big on them, they weren't ridiculous. Maybe they might be able to do it? Father, on the other hand...

I glanced toward the car, noting how Dad still hadn't gotten out. From Felix's and Sylvia's tense expressions, it wasn't hard to tell there was an argument involved in some way. They probably were arguing the entire time. I did feel a little bad from them. Though I was also worried to see Dad draping his arms over the steering wheel. Was he going to be all right? Still, I wasn't going to ask how they convinced Dad to do this. Though, again, it was probably more likely they convinced him by pointing out that they were going to do it with or without his help. After all, the idea was pretty simple, and probably not the most effective, but it would do the trick of getting inside wherever we needed to go.

Of course, it didn't take long for me to recognize where we were going and I found myself unamused by the entire thing. After briefly stopping at the guy's residence, we continued to where we needed to go. In the end, we still ended up at the haunted house, much to my dismay. I really was hoping we could avoid this place. Why couldn't it be somewhere else? Like back at the police station? Or just a random new location? Why the haunted house?

I shivered at the memories that bombarded me and, before I could stop myself, I asked, "Did they find all the bodies?" Of course, after I said it, I slammed both hands over my mouth, berating myself harshly.

However, the guy only cringed, rubbing his head. "Bodies? I remember hearing about it, but…" he shook his head and I let out a sigh. "I'm going to guess you've been here before. You don't seem like the type of kid to go killing anyone, or you would have probably done it to me with that knife at your side, so I'm going to assume there were extenuating circumstances to you knowing about that."

Right. I'd completely forgotten I still had my knife. I reached toward my waist, pulling my shirt down enough to hopefully hide it a bit better. The officer didn't say anything, just continued on down the road. As we pulled closer, I could tell work had been done on the building. From the front gate I could tell that the once ankle-high grass was now cut down to normal, a pristine and clinical appearance to it. Vines that once coated the brick walls were gone, though the brick still needed fixing up. I could see the guard, shaking his head, wincing. I reached over, startling him. "Sorry, I just wanted to take those headphones off." I pulled them off, noting how they were very similar to my own, though bulkier in a lot of ways. I wondered what the main difference was.

I put them to one side, causing the guard to watch me quietly. I pulled back, watching as we passed by the gates. I peered back, to see that the others were still following. A flare of worry sang through my veins when I noticed the car suddenly jolt, swerving off to one side before coming to a sudden halt. Had something happened? Was Dad all right? But before I could see more, they disappeared from my sight, hidden behind the curve of a bend. Hopefully, they weren't hurt, but at least they were out of sight, which I was grateful for.

It wasn't long before we were in front of the sprawling mansion. The familiar front doors were no longer chained shut and the windows, those that were broken, were covered in plastic. I could see where workers had been, tools dropped in the grass and machines quietly parked off to the side. I wonder if they fled when this whole thing went up?

We pulled to a stop and the guard stepped out, walking to the back to open the door for me. I pulled myself out, grateful he didn't handcuff me or anything. Actually, did he have handcuffs, being a security guard used as an officer? He put a hand to my back, leading me up the front steps. I won't lie, I was ready to bolt it back out through those gates to Dad's car and never turn back, but I didn't want to do that. I just wanted this to end, and I wouldn't know how it ended unless I finished it myself. So screwing together what was left of my nerves, I walked up the stairs and into the main foyer. With the high noon sun shining through the windows, the place had a surprisingly pleasant air to it. Now that it wasn't covered in shadows and spiderwebs, I could see why someone would want it. It was beautiful in that old-fashioned way. I heard a sound and glanced toward the stairway where…

I took a step back, noting as El spotted me, coming to a halt as he descended the stairs.

"I didn't believe the announcement." He tilted his head, watching me warily. "But you are here."

Watching him quietly as he finished descending the stair, I spoke up when he reached the landing, "Believe me, I would rather not be." I noted he still had his hand in his pocket… that device. "But your officers are everywhere." I crossed my arms over my chest. "I would rather not get anyone else involved."

"I would assume." His expression was even, gaze flickering to the guard. "And yet…" he scoffed as the guard pulled his gun up and out, aimed at him.

Wait, WHAT? I whipped around, staring at the guard in shock. His expression was sharp, gaze cold.

"So you were behind my mother's disappearance and this whole mess."

What. The. Hell?

"Ah, you must have been one of the renegades. I thought we got rid of... ah, you're not actually part of the police force, are you?" El was surprisingly calm as he stared down at the gun pointed at him. Renegades? Right! Sylvia mentioned that. Why didn't I think about that earlier? He let us through earlier, now that I thought about it. Was that why he was so nonchalant about some of the other things I said? Was it why he had so many uniforms? It would explain a few things.

I slowly took a side step, aiming for someplace other than the middle of the room, away from the two people in front of me. Peering around, I found the entrance empty and it made me wonder where were all the people controlled by that device? Were they out? Would they be coming back with me being here?

"I wouldn't move if I were you, Kieran."

I jerked to a stop, spotting El briefly glance toward me. Screw that noise. Noticing I was right next to the stairwell, I did the first thing I could think of.

Honestly, I wasn't sure WHY the first thing I thought was to race up the stairwell, considering I had a perfectly good opportunity to just leave and have the guard deal with El. But I think my curiosity and my want for this to be over was enough to get me up those stairs. After all, where else would a madman be?

I raced up the stairwell, hearing a gunshot ring behind me. I didn't look back, just bolted. Maybe I should have run out, but, well, that wasn't exactly an option anymore.

Ah, this was stupid. What could two people do? And I didn't know where Felix and Sylvia were. Or if Dad was all right after the car swerved off the road. My thoughts cut off as I spotted a familiar doorway, I sprinted inside and quickly closed it, leaning my back against it.

Pressing my ear to the door, I could hear sounds from below, conversation and movement. I wondered what was going on. But as I listened, I didn't hear anyone coming up. I slowly opened the door, peeking out. There was nothing. No one was up here. Trusting that Felix, Sylvia and my father weren't going to abandon me here, I decided to continue moving through the second floor. El was probably still downstairs, though whether he was still engaged with the guard or not was up for debate. I wasn't sure if Dad's coworker was here, but it was worth a shot to check. If he wasn't, at least I would be able to make sure we dealt with El. Briefly observing my surroundings, noting that this room was a lot cleaner than last time, I slipped out and examined the hallway. The second floor, from what I could see, had two wings to it. I was in the left wing, about halfway down before it curved around. I hummed for a moment before deciding to continue along, briefly peeking in each doorway I came across. Most of them were empty of everything, in the midst of remodeling or rearranging. But a few appeared to have been finished. There was a bedroom, splayed out in the finest material; a bathroom, way too large for my taste; and...

"Jackpot," I muttered, spotting what appeared to be an office. A window was open, showing that someone was here not that long ago. I snuck inside, quickly examining everything as I went. There were a couple bookcases off to one side and a doorway leading to another room, firmly shut tight. I headed over to the desk, peering over it in curiosity. It was mostly reports about officer movement, scientific observation and the like. I didn't have time to go over everything before the door I briefly noted upon entering swung open, startling me and causing me to whip around, having no time to hide.

Standing in the doorway, a startled expression on his face, was a man only a few years younger than Dad. He was sharply dressed and... had a cup of tea in hand?

What the heck? Why was he so calm when there was a freaking gunshot downstairs?

"Huh, didn't expect you to be here already." The man walked in, closing the door behind him.

"You knew I was coming?" I took a step back, making sure the desk was firmly between the two of us. This must be Leonard, Dad's coworker.

"Of course." He let out a sigh, seeming tired. He took a seat in one of the chairs, placed around the room. I was still tense as all hell, but he just seemed exhausted.

Almost like he was in the same state Father was.

"If that's the case, why are you so nonchalant? You know why I'm here," I said, gripping the chair back tightly, not sure if I wanted to wield it, or use it as a shield.

"Because I also know that everything I strived for, hoped for, has now become obsolete."

"Huh?"

Leonard chuckled, taking another sip. "If your father managed to get the thing up and running again, or just helped me with the memory device, I wouldn't be so resigned. But let's just say, I've recently received intel saying I don't have the time for that." He shook his head, glancing over to me. "Unfortunate, considering I have the final piece to the puzzle right here, standing in front of me, and I can't do a thing about it."

I narrowed my eyes, but didn't take the bait. He just let out a hollow laugh, placing his cup down on a side table before turning his attention to the ceiling.

"You take after your father... and yet you seem so much like her. Like Rose."

"You knew my mom?" I asked, noting the way he said Mother's name with a sense of fondness.

"Why do you think I was so willing to help your father with these experiments? Did you really think I was such a madman to perpetuate all of this?" I didn't respond and he seemed to realize, returning his attention to mine. "Right, you would believe that. Why wouldn't you? I'm the big bad who caused havoc and pandemonium." The man chuckled. "I could give you a whole spiel of how you're wrong, or how I have my reasons, but do you or anyone else really care?"

I slowly loosened my grip on the chair, staring at him in curiosity.

"El, he was startled when I showed up, and didn't try to do anything this time."

"He wasn't supposed to do anything from the beginning. His job was only as an observer. He decided to take action into his own hands to help me, help me with a dream I had. A dream of a utopia without pain, without fear, without death..." The man chuckled, taking another sip. By this time, my guard was fully dropped and I was just watching, noting the way he was slumped in his seat.

"And you're telling me this, why?"

"Because you of all people deserve to know. After all..." he sat up and, within a flash, he changed from the slumped-over form to standing before me, scanning me critically and causing me to stumble backwards, "an experiment that lasted this long, unlike all the others, is crucial to the continuance of my dream, of the utopia. The fact that you appear so much like Rose—"

"If you were so fond of my mother, why are you treating me like an experiment?" I cursed out, using the desk once more as a shield from the man in front of me. It was then I noted a piece of metal attached to the side of his head, similar to a device I saw Mira use, the eye piece.

"An experiment doesn't leave, doesn't run away, and always stays there as a constant," Leonard responded.

Yeah, no, I'm outta here. Once I was sure the doorway was to my right, I bolted, racing toward the door. This guy was crazier than I thought. What did he mean, experiment? I decided not to think about it, wrenching the door open, only to come face to face with a pissed off El. He was holding his shoulder, blood seeping through his fingers. Behind him was the guard from earlier. Headphones sat over his head once more, his expression once more glazed. How? Why?

Shit.

I took a step back, before quickly moving to one side so I wasn't grabbed from behind. "How did you get those headphones back on him? I took them off earlier!"

"We have spares," El deadpanned. "Plus—" he cut himself off and my gaze flicked to the machine. "Let's just say, this thing does have its uses without the headphones."

Short range, at a shorter range and with only one target… right, it wouldn't be far-fetched to assume that the guard was quickly put under control after that initial gunshot. Well, that's just lovely. "So why don't you use that crap on me?" I pursed my lips, reaching toward my waist. I only had one thing on me, and three people surrounding me.

Not my best odds.

"Can't." El shrugged and I paused.

"What do you mean, can't?"

"What Elliot—" so that was El's full name, "—said. Because of your brainwaves fighting off the electrical waves for over a year and a half, it's less susceptible to manipulation. Of course, it's just a hypothesis, but considering he's using it right now and you're not reacting says a lot."

Using it? He's… "You're trying to manipulate my mind right now?" I growled and then glared at the man. "And how would you know that he's using it?"

Leonard tapped the side of his head, the piece I noticed before. If it was connected to his eye— "That thing lets you see those waves which means, it also should have let you see Specters." I pieced together the pieces. "You knew about those things, but still wanted to continue the project. Are you insane?" Yeah, I don't know why I asked that last question, it was pretty obvious. Speaking of, where were Felix and Sylvia? Where was my father? I hoped they weren't put under the influence of that thing.

I noted the faint headache that I'd not really noticed up until now, hanging in the back. I silently thanked my mind. Now I knew why the headache was there.

"Believe what you will about my sanity. For now, come quietly. While we might not be able to completely restart, we can set things up once more and fix them. This time, we'll be able to set it up as a true utopia. No one will have to remember anything that hurts them, or traumatizes them. They can live in peace, without a care, and there won't be anyone who will be able to remember the initial wave."

"Because, if you used my brain waves, or whatever, you would be able to figure out why it didn't work as well," I realized. "Have you been watching me this whole time?"

"Ah, so you don't remember?" The man hummed, suddenly amused. I glanced toward the doorway, barely stopping myself from reacting when I saw Felix and Sylvia peering inside. I briefly wondered where Dad was, but flickering to the way the car swerved... I quickly shook my head, keeping my movement to a minimum. Sylvia and Felix seemed to be waiting, maybe for a moment to move. Well, I would have to give it to them. Still, it was good to know they were all right.

"I don't know. My brain is a little messed up because of all of those electrical waves. Is there something I'm supposed to remember?" I felt a gun push into my side, noting the guard was beside me, gun raised and El watching carefully, arm tense. Right, be careful.

"I guess I can tell you." Leonard paced to one side, giving me a little room to breathe, at least on that front. Thankfully, Sylvia and Felix, after making sure I was aware they were there, slipped back out of sight into the hallway. I tuned back into what the man was saying. "Your father realized early on that something was amiss and made a deal that as long as you remained untouched, without memory erasure, he would continue to work on the project. I had no doubts that, even if we were to erase you, he would have known." He turned to me. "Both your parents were incredibly smart, after all. So, I decided to do a different experiment. To find out how long a human can survive when the human mind is aware it's being manipulated, but not how or why. A little experiment to learn if constant pulses of electrical charges would weaken the synapses of a patient that still knows, or strengthen them." His words were clinical, said in a matter-of-fact tone, as if describing the stupid weather. "I wanted to observe a way to make sure no one would have to suffer that way once the final product was completed, so you weren't the only experiment. The more recent ones, even in short term, proved less effective, unfortunately. I believe it's because they were under the influence much longer than you, so a radical shift into the electrical stimuli, well..." He let out a sigh as my brain clicked. I heard a movement, and it wasn't hard to assume that Felix had been about to barge inside, demands flying.

I wasn't so restrained. "More recent experiments like Mira?" I glared. I would panic a bit more about being an experiment for the last year and a half, but not right now, not when I had a gun in my gut.

The man smiled. "Yes, she was one of them. I do apologize about that. None of us expected that to happen." He shook his head, peering out the window. "Anyway, we don't have time for this. It won't be long until the government arrives." He turned back to me. "El, bring him to the medical room. We need to get the experiments done quickly."

"What experiments? You already did all your damn experiments for the last—" I was cut off as the gun suddenly jabbed me and I was, quite roughly, reminded of my situation.

"I can't make solid proof through hypothesis and observation," he said, watching me in a way that felt familiar.

A familiarity that I noted I'd been feeling for a while. Since he mentioned Mother. No, even before that. When he first entered, but why? I've never met this man in my li—

A splitting headache slammed into me and I cried out, both hands darting to my head. Damnit! I thought I wouldn't have to deal with these anymore. I stumbled back, briefly noting the gun was no longer anchored into my gut.

Faint words trailed into my ears. "Get him to the medical room."

Medical room? Why—Terror surged through my veins as a sudden wave of memories cut off my thoughts.

"Will this help?"

Where am I? Dad? Sylv... syl... who? Who was it? Who was I trying to remember? I held my head, voices echoing in my ears. "He'll be stable, but he'll have to stay here while we check what's going on."

"No, he can co—"

"I would not advise that he go home with you. Not until we figure out why his brain waves are off. We have the medical equipment here, trust me."

What are they talking about? Who is that? Dad and, who? I could smell chemicals and bleach? A hospital? No, a medical room?

"Fine. I'll be back soon."

"Of course." Footsteps receded and I wanted to call out, yell, 'Wait.' But I could almost feel my brain shaking in my head, vibrating. Why did it hurt so much? It's been hurting since... since something. What was it?

"He's gone." That voice! Why was he still here? "Don't worry, you won't remember a thing." The words scared me enough to force myself to find out what was going on, but everything was blurry, white and- "Don't open your eyes. We have some experiments we have to figure out. After, we need to check if your father would be more willing to expand his work. You will be a good little child." Fingers gently touched my cheek. "Just like your mother, my sister, you will help me fix this world, right?"

Fix? Mother? Sister? The blob covered my face, obscuring my vision and I panicked. Before I could do anything, something slammed onto my wrist, pushing it into the bed. A headache crashed through my head, sending me reeling. A moment later, it faded, but it was enough to feel leather over my wrists and waist. What is this? Where am I? Why is this happening?

I'm scared!

I was going to be sick. That was... Why did I suddenly remember? Remember something like that? The terror from back then still pulsed through me as I snapped back up to the man. His stance was completely different, the once slumped, tired form was straightened. He watched me in a way someone might observe a frog on a slab which was enough to cause warning bells to slam through my head. I know it had only been a second in my thoughts, the startled expression from the guard and El was proof enough as I noted the lowered gun. But that barely registered in my mind as I saw that expression on Leonard's face. It had been there the entire time, I just hadn't noticed. No, I couldn't notice because I'd been trying not to.

Because then it would remind me...

Remind me of a time when Dad wasn't there. When...

I suddenly understood what Dad meant earlier. I was quickly able to suppress the remainder of the memories, but what slipped through was enough to tell me that I didn't want to be within a mile of this... Fear momentarily gripped me, promptly followed by a searing rage.

The knife was in my grasp before I realized and I lunged forward, anger surging through my veins. My throat ached and I heard a faint scream, but I ignored it. This bastard! A startled yelp from El and a clattering sound echoed through the room as all hell broke loose. But my only attention was on that fucking shit of a scientist. His eyes widened as he dodged away from my slice. I quickly followed through, curving the knife so it would swing back in a wide arc, clipping his arm as he spun to get away.

I could hear shouts and movement behind me, but it was mostly tuned out as we weaved around the desk, me lunging whenever I got the chance, getting more pissed off as he dodged again and again. Why wouldn't this fucking bastard stand still so I could hurt him? I wanted to hurt him. I wanted to see his blood spilled! I'd been so terrified and he'd treated me like some old-fashioned asylum patient. Pain flared through my mind. It was only a few hours. A few hours in that room before Dad returned and got me out, but— I stabbed forward, blood splattering over the blade as I scraped past his cheek, right near his eye. I could feel the warmth splatter onto my fingers, but I brushed it off. My other hand reaching, grasping at fabric as the dagger stabbed forward. A howling scream pierced my ears as I noticed the blade dig into his shoulder blade. I ripped it out and, this time, I noticed the once calm features were now bloody and twisted in terror.

Good.

As soon as I thought that, I froze, knife inches from his face, his back to the same bookcase I'd been pushed against earlier. His eyes were crossed, focused on the knife trembling right in front of him as my whole body heaved, chest rising and falling. My hand shook, inches from gouging out his eye.

I'd been about to...

Because of that sudden influx of memories... that pain.

I suddenly understood what happened to everyone else, to Mira, to the Lost.

If I was suddenly forced to remember that I was being controlled, if I suddenly only had the memory of anger or pain...

If I didn't remember anything else, would I have stopped myself?

I shakily stepped back, watching the man slump, wide eyes staring up at me. Sylvia and Felix quickly came over, not saying a word, not trying to catch my gaze as they made sure he was secured, Sylvia wrapping him enough to make sure he couldn't move. I noted that El was secured in much the same fashion, a device smashed into the ground. The guard was out like a light, probably collapsing after being manipulated so often, no headphones on his head. I briefly noted the gun was on the other side of the room, looking like it landed there. When did that happen?

I took another step back, attention drifting to my knife, splattered in blood. I could feel a little slowly dripping down my cheek and I wondered how it got there. That's when I noticed just how much blood there was. I knew I nicked him and got a clear stab into his shoulder, but the amount of blood on both of us was... it was like a madman attacked him. I felt like throwing up.

I let the knife drop. Now that the terror and anger were fading, I felt almost empty. Now that I had all my memories back...

I didn't want them.

I didn't notice until I felt Sylvia pull me into a hug that tears were trailing down my face. Well, at least I knew why I never wanted to go to a hospital. That nonsensical thought pushed to the forefront and I could only let out a hiccupping laugh, wrapping my arms tightly around Sylvia as I buried my head in her shoulder. Was it over? I didn't want to deal with this anymore. I felt a supporting grasp on my shoulder as I stood there, crying.

I could hear something from downstairs, but I didn't care.

I didn't care about anything. Not right now.

Chapter Twenty-nine

I'll admit, it took a bit longer than I would have liked to calm down. Once I finally got myself under control, we hurried downstairs to find out what was going on.

I stared, watching as people raced about. A couple officers noticed us as they came up the stairs. "What are you doing here?" The officer that spoke noticed the blood on my shirt. Sylvia helped me clean up my hands and face, but there wasn't much we could do about the shirt. The officer tensed, but Sylvia quickly moved in front of me.

"The two people involved in the memory manipulation are upstairs, fourth room on the left. You all know about the memory manipulation, correct?" She spoke up, getting exchanged looks from the officers.

"Come on, we should get out of here," Felix pointed out, gently grabbing my wrist and pulling me toward the entrance. I glanced back at Sylvia who continued to talk to the officers, having them follow her. I didn't think about it, how people might not believe the idea of memory manipulation.

Would people do like I did and forcibly forget?

Felix led me outside, letting go of my wrist just as quickly as he grabbed it. I didn't mind, honestly, I was way too distracted right now with everything going on. I had a feeling it would take a while to piece everything together. I could only imagine how others, who hadn't slowly been recovering their memories, were faring. As we headed back to the car, I realized that I hadn't seen things. The car swerved, almost landing in a ditch.

"What—"

"Your father. He collapsed. Sylvia managed to get the car under control, causing us to stop here." Felix walked over to the car as I hurried after him. For a brief, panicked moment, I thought something was wrong with Dad, but as I caught up with Felix, I noted the faint rise and fall of Dad's chest and let out a breath of relief.

"He's probably exhausted." Felix opened the door, noticing my relieved expression. "Sylvia figured he was probably pushing himself." He reached forward to shake Dad's shoulder. When he didn't wake, Felix sighed and glanced toward me. "Want to help me get him in the back seat? I think I can speak for both of us by saying I don't want to be here anymore."

"Right." I helped him pull Dad out so he was laying more comfortably in the back. Felix got into the passenger seat, leaving me the driver. I stared toward the house, not really seeing it with all the trees in the way, but… "What about Sylvia?"

"She had a feeling they were coming. She told me if we got separated to tell you she'll meet you back at your place." Felix shrugged. "I'll leave it up to you, but I think she can take care of herself."

I didn't divert my attention from the distant mansion, but I did shift the car into gear. If she said so, then I had no qualms fleeing this place, and possibly fleeing the memories as well.

I turned the steering wheel, getting us out before glancing over to Felix. "Hey, thanks…"

"I didn't really do much," Felix joked, a somber expression on his face. There was a tension to his jaw. His fingers dug into his palms. "I was kind of useless, actually."

I shook my head as we left the mansion behind, going through the wide-open gates. "You helped knock out El and the guard. Speaking of, how did you two do that?"

Felix let out a snort before glancing toward me. "We used your distraction and jumped on them. I ripped off the headphones, hoping that would do the trick like last time while Sylvia tackled El. It worked. After that I just helped Sylvia secure El until you, well…" he trailed off before shaking his head. "That's basically it, nothing ridiculous or crazy, I don't think any of us can deal with that sort of thing right now."

I nodded, noting with no surprise that a lot of the officers were here. Some of them were probably set up in wait by the memory device, some might have even been called in. I returned my attention back to Felix. "You didn't have to come at all. This was mostly between our family and him." Actually, with how he kept talking about Mother, it was very closely related…

"And let you take all the credit? Nah," Felix scoffed, causing me to blink and glance over, where I noted a faint smile on his lips. "Seriously though, I couldn't just let you two go in there alone. Yeah, it ended up turning out okay." He hesitated, probably thinking about how I went ballistic earlier. "But what if it hadn't? Three heads are better than two. Plus, you need someone to talk to now and Sylvia is in the same state as you. I don't think either of you are in the talking mood."

Well, he wasn't wrong. Now that I thought about it, Sylvia never said a word this entire time, not after I met back up with them. At least, not to me.

I guess she was dealing with it in her own way, but Felix was right. I was grateful to have someone to talk with, to have nearby as I organized my thoughts. I glanced over once more, seeing a distant expression on his face. "Do you want to go home? I mean, to your house?"

A moment of hesitation flashed across his features and I let out a weak chuckle. "I'll take that as a yes. Come on, I'll drive you there."

"Then what will you do?" Felix turned to me, serious. "Go home alone? Try to drag your father into the house by yourself when you are still shaken? Or not bother and just crash once you get into the driveway?" He shook his head. "No, I'll stay with you until you two are settled, at least. After all, my house isn't that far, as you might recall." The end was definitely said in a teasing tone and I just huffed, getting a smile from him.

We were now into the town proper and I noticed a lot of people rushing about, dressed in clothes that were, but weren't, familiar.

Military uniforms? Felix seemed to notice too, because he frowned and pressed his face to the glass. "What's the military doing here? It's only really been a day since the device was destroyed."

"Maybe they were in the wings, waiting?" I murmured, lost in thought. "They mentioned there was a hundred-mile radius, right? Past that radius, they might have been aware something was wrong. Maybe they were prepared to swoop in whenever?"

"Makes sense," Felix muttered as we watched the officials moving about. It seemed like they were evacuating the citizens. I glanced at the car radio. We never used it, Dad was always against using it actually, but Felix seemed to have the same idea, reaching forward and tuning the radio in to the local news which sounded like it was in chaos.

I could hear a female reporter, trying to sound calm, but obviously shaking as she spoke. "It's been a day since a sudden upsurge in incidents we have called the memory epidemic. Recent reports indicate that the U.S. Military is getting involved with the evacuation of those critically injured or in danger and the protection of all people in the…. Region…. Advise to…. Indoors." Static filled the end and I sighed as the radio shut off. Ah, right, this wasn't our car. I would have to give this back to Kelly if I ever got the chance. At least it gave us something. We headed back to my house, weaving through the traffic and officers. Thankfully, since we actually had a purpose and weren't just fleeing away, it seemed that the officers didn't bother us. I was grateful for those little concessions. We arrived at my house, the street eerily devoid of most of the panic of earlier. I got out with Felix and we both helped Dad into the house, noting it was unlocked. I didn't remember locking it, so I guessed that made sense. Dad was still out like a light, deep in slumber. I didn't really want to wake him, so that was fine by me. Not wanting to deal with helping him upstairs, we placed him on the couch with a couple of pillows and blankets. I was grateful for Felix's help, I didn't think I could have done that myself, to be honest.

"Will you be okay?" Felix asked as we stepped out of the living room into the main entrance. He was antsy, probably wanting to check on his family.

"Yeah, I'll be fine," I said, and I felt like I meant it. As I pieced through my thoughts, I found myself calming down. I was glad. I might have hated some of my memories, but I was grateful for the chance to know WHY, to understand why I was the way I was.

Felix nodded, a grin on his face. "Dude, I'll see you soon." And with that, he hurried out the door and down the street, probably just as worried about his own family. The car sat in the driveway, a reminder of just how insane the last few, well, forever has been.

I let out a long breath, heading to the kitchen. I grabbed something to eat and sat down, staring at the table. Light shone gently through the windows as I stayed lost in thought.

I didn't know how long I sat there, maybe a few minutes, maybe an hour, but the sound of knocking caught my attention and I tilted my head up from the slumped position I'd taken. Who could that be?

I walked over to the door, opening it up.

On the other side, standing on the top step with two military officers behind her, was Mother. No, the woman who pretended to be my mother. However, as I stood there, I realized I had no energy to bring my guard up. "What are you doing here?" I asked, holding the door open enough so they could only really see my face.

Mother stared at me quietly, a surprisingly tired and pained expression on her features. Her brown hair was tied up in a tight-ponytail though some pieces were already falling out. "Ki."

"Don't call me that." I pursed my lips, feeling a few dredges of anger well up. Who was this woman to call me that? She just took the place of Mom without asking.

She closed her eyes, letting out a breath as the two officers behind her shifted, tense. Why were they there?

"Kieran, can you let me in? I need to see your father."

"Why?"

"Just…" She trailed off before glancing back to the two officers. "Can you two stand back for a moment? I need to talk with—"

"Commander—"

"Just give me one minute, I will be fine." With that, the two backed off, moving down the steps and back enough paces to be out of earshot. She returned her attention to me, her expression filled with dismay. Why was she so upset? No, she was sad, but why? "Kieran. I'm sorry."

I froze, startled. "What do you mean?"

The woman reached up, as if to ruffle my hair, only to stop. She quickly dropped her arm. "I didn't mean to deceive you or your father for so long. It was just supposed to be a quick in and out." She shook her head. "Unfortunately, I don't have time to prove my point to you, but… Kieran." She recomposed herself before standing upright, catching my gaze with her own. "My name is Ilda, Ilda Requina, an FBI agent and a federal investigator. My task was to infiltrate a family and discover the truth behind a sudden change in the populace of the east coast cities. We'd gotten reports of people calling to relatives in those areas, only to end up with disconnected numbers. Anyone who went in either didn't come out, or came out with their memory ruined and confused on why there was a problem. I was given some items that they thought would protect me, along with the name you know as Rebecca. The items and name protected me… for a short time. … for a short time. It gave me enough time to speak with the police chief who spoke highly of your father. I went to meet him and discovered the absent aspect of your mother. I lied…" She trailed off. "I managed to acquire another version of the device he was working on in order to protect you. Not realizing it was a prototype, I tried to set it so that you both believed I was your mother and his wife, so as to keep an eye on things and remain under the radar, but…"

"It backfired." My thoughts swirled, finally connecting the last few dots, so that's why the military was here already. "That's why you could sometimes still remember, like me, but…" I bit my lip. "Then why are you here now? Why do you want Dad?"

Ilda winced, and my guard was automatically up, knuckles white from holding the door partially open. "He was involved in the… attack." I could tell she wanted to use another word. "He was a victim, but he was still one of the ones who orchestrated everything—"

It didn't take much for me to figure out where she was going with this, and it took everything in my being not to slam the door in her face and lock every part of the house. "You want to take Father away, after everything that's happened? You're going to take Father and leave us—leave us with—how could you?" The last sentence was said in a faint voice. Why did I have to deal with this? I was just a normal boy, not anything special. I didn't want to deal with this anymore.

Ilda eyed me quietly, despair clear on her face. "Your father tried to protect you." I stilled, returning my attention on her. "He tried to protect you. He had no choice." She took a deep breath. "I could tell, because I had parts of my memory that remained, thanks to your father, so I knew tentatively that I was supposed to keep an eye on things, but I wasn't sure what or why. I came to love your father and couldn't help but love you as my son." She smiled weakly. "Ridiculous, isn't it? But that's how it went. I guess I was grateful. I got to meet you two and, because I came in and interfered, bringing some of the military grade items with me, your father was able to create a way to stop you losing more of your memory and, slowly, reverse it."

I stared at her in silence for a minute before finally responding, "Why are you telling me this?"

"Because I want you to know, no matter what happens, I won't let any more harm come to this family, understood?"

"Then why do you have to take him?" I breathed. "You know he had no choice—"

"I know that, but no one else does, they want someone to blame for this crisis—"

"But they have the main people involved!" I cut in, glaring. "We took care of them earlier, at the old mansion."

Ilda nodded, expression even. "I know. You, Sylvia and Felix, correct? I heard it through the radio. You three did very well." She sighed, and I noticed that the officers had come back up the stairs, seeming antsy.

Ilda noticed as well and straightened her posture. "Kieran, please. I know you have no reason to, but… trust me."

I stared at her for a few minutes and let out a tired sigh, opening the door the rest of the way. The officers almost jumped through the open doorway, just as Ilda extended her arm out, stopping them from practically pouncing inside. She let me step to the side before lowering her arm, letting the men through.

I turned away, feeling all sorts of emotions swarming inside.

The two guards hurried out, dragging Father between them. A flash of anger shown on Ilda's face. "Pick him up."

The two guards hesitated before shifting their grip, holding him between the two of them so he was no longer being pulled across the floor. Ilda and I watched them head toward the car before Ilda turned back to me. I wasn't sure if I was just imagining things, but she seemed desperate and sad. "Ki, I hope someday you will be able to forgive me."

Those words stuck in my head as she turned, briefly glancing back before walking away. I slowly closed the door, only to find myself crumbling to the ground, staring up at the ceiling.

"Are you done yet?" I found myself asking, I wasn't sure to whom, but I felt I needed to. I didn't think I would be able to handle anything else happening. I was barely handling things as they were.

~ * ~

That's how Sylvia found me about an hour or so later. She opened the door and paused, noticing me staring up at the ceiling. I felt my neck crack as I finally moved to glance at her. Through the doorway I spotted the familiar police car. Oh, the guard we helped must have brought her back. I would have to thank him later.

My attention drifted back to Sylvia and it wasn't hard to tell she was done. Her expression was haggard and resigned. She closed the door and slowly slid down the opposite wall. I was promptly reminded just how young she was. She really was the same age as me. "Are we done?" Her voice was devoid of emotion.

I couldn't reply, just simply glanced toward the living room, an empty living room.

"Ki?"

"You know the woman who I thought was my mother?" I turned back to her, catching her just in time to spot the nod. "It turned out she was with the government. She came in to check out what was going on and accidentally ended up involved with our family. She came by a little while ago to explain that and to take Dad into custody."

Suddenly, anger flashed across her face as she shot to her feet, glaring down at me. "And you just let her take him? She lied to you! To us!"

"I know." I stared up at her and she seemed to calm, maybe noticing my expression, because she fell against the wall, shaking as she leaned against it.

"Then why?" she pleaded quietly. "Haven't we dealt with enough?"

I turned my attention back to the ceiling, my whole body numb and tired.

"Kieran!"

"What else could I do? They were going to take Dad, no matter what!" I surged onto my feet, anger and pain rushing through me, both from the thought and the sudden movement. "There was nothing I could do from the very beginning! She could have just barged in and taken him. The officers with her were ready to do just that. They wouldn't have cared about what I said." I cut myself off and took a deep breath to recenter myself. "She stopped them. She spoke with me, explained who she was and apologized. You weren't there, Sylvia."

"No, I wasn't, that's why I don't understand." She spoke softly, but the words stung. "Kieran…"

"Who can I trust?" My voice was quiet, and it caused Sylvia to freeze. I caught her attention and if she wasn't against the wall, she probably would have taken a step back, startled. "My mind and memory are a mess and I doubt yours is much better. Dad was collapsed and I doubt Felix's family is in much of a better state than ours. Mira?" I shook my head. "Everyone is barely keeping themselves together, where does that leave me?" I let out a breath. "Sylvia, I know you have no reason to believe me. Just like I had no reason to believe her, but that's all we can really do right now. Believe and hope things work out. What else can we do?"

She opened her mouth before snapping it shut, seeming to realize what I meant. She slumped back down, legs pulled up close to her chest as she quietly observed the wood floor. "We used up all our options..." she trailed off, before leaning her head against the wall with a dull thump. "At least those people will be behind bars. Dad might be as well though. So, where does that leave us?"

I had nothing to say. What could I say? I didn't know either.

I just wanted to go to sleep and assume that all of this was an elaborate dream the day before Mom's accident, simply so I could go back to much simpler times, when memories, madmen and FBI weren't involved. I let out a weak chuckle. Man, there was a thought.

Again, time passed before a soft growl echoed around the room. I blinked, glancing toward Sylvia as she curled in tighter. I let out a sigh and pushed myself to my feet once more, though I'm not sure when I collapsed back down, catching her attention. "Let's grab something to eat." I reached out to her. She hesitated before taking it, pulling herself up. There wasn't much we could do now, but we weren't going to just let ourselves end here. We dealt with too much to just let it end like this. I think Sylvia agreed because she followed me into the kitchen, grabbing what she could. It was a mish-mash of food, but it did the trick of calming our stomachs. We needed to figure out what to do. Where to go.

"Did your friend go home?" Sylvia spoke up, and I paused. Why did she say it like that? Sylvia was Felix's friend as well. I observed her closely, noticing her curling into herself and I decided not to ask. Maybe it was because of the prolonged period of being alone, did she qualify Felix as one of her friends anymore?

"You are talking about Felix, right?" I finally said, noticing as she relaxed a little.

"Yeah."

I nodded as Sylvia pursed her lips, deep in thought. "He was only changed recently. He's probably in the most stable condition."

"I don't want to be a burden on him—"

"I don't think you would be a burden." She chuckled. "You three are way too close…" she trailed off before shaking her head, finishing the last of our instant ramen. "Plus, I know his father. You do too. I think they wouldn't mind us staying with them as… as things get dealt with."

I glanced at her. It wasn't hard to figure out she meant Father. "All right."

With that, we finished up, cleaning up what we could and packed a few things. Sylvia didn't have much she needed to grab, so we were out the door and down the street as the sun completely disappeared beyond the horizon.

Had it really only been a day? I stared up at the rising moon. It felt like it should have been a lot longer. It didn't take long until we came upon Felix's house. One of the military officers was there, talking with Felix's mother. As we stepped up to the doorway, the man nodded and hurried away. Felix's mother spotted us and, for a moment, worry crossed her face before it fled. "Kieran, what are you doing here? Are you all right?" I hesitated and she shook her head. "No, never mind. Come inside. Felix and… and Harold are home."

Harold?

Sylvia smirked, spotting my confused expression before hurrying after the woman. I shook my head and stepped inside, grateful for the sudden warmth that wrapped around us. It was cozy, just like I remembered. Before I could do much, Felix's mother was pushing us into the kitchen, sitting us down before getting back to getting dinner together. "Are you two hungry? Did you need someplace to sleep? Felix!"

I blinked as footsteps raced down the stairs and into the room. Felix slid to a halt and blinked, spotting the two of us. "Huh? Why aren't you at your house?"

"Felix, that's not our business," his mother admonished.

"It's fine." Sylvia smiled weakly. "We just… We can't stay there right now."

The woman hummed before nodding and turned back to Felix,

who was watching us carefully.

"I'll explain later," I mouthed, causing him to nod.

"I'll get the spare bedroom set up." He glanced toward his mom. "Dad's still out, I think he's still recovering."

"Your dad?" I asked as Sylvia stiffened.

"Felix, where is Harold?" she asked, worry clear in her voice.

For a brief moment, a flicker of anger shown on Felix's face before it disappeared, startling me. Felix glanced at her before wincing. "Right, you would know him. He's upstairs, first room on the left."

Before I could say anything, Sylvia bolted away up the stairs. I turned my attention back to Felix as he said, "Do you remember the man who always stood with Sylvia? The one who was in my house all those months ago?"

"The first one who…" I trailed off, glancing toward his mother, who was busying herself with collecting blankets and other things. I guess she was letting us talk. Though, I will admit, it was strange seeing the once exhausted and barely able to move woman suddenly bustling around with renewed energy.

"Yeah, him." Felix pursed his lips before shaking his head. "Your father was right, not everyone came out of that unscathed. It took everything in him just to make it home. He hasn't woken up since. Mother's worried."

I have a feeling that was an understatement.

"I'm sorry."

"Don't be. I wouldn't change what happened. Well, I would, but I don't think any other way would have ended well, so…" he shrugged before shifting. "Though, I would have preferred…"

I thought of the flash of anger and frowned. "Wait, did you know he was your dad? I don't remember you talking about it when we were at the park."

"That's the thing." He pursed his lips, briefly glancing toward his mom before gesturing for me to follow. We stepped into the hallway before he continued, letting out a long-held breath. "He knew." I blinked as Felix clarified. "Sylvia and Dad both knew that… that I was his son and they didn't say a word." He gritted his teeth, hands clenched tightly. "How is that fair? That they knew who I was, but I didn't know?"

I stayed silent, unsure what to say to him. Sylvia hadn't remembered me for a while, at least, not until recently. I believe it was probably in the last few months she fully remembered as my memory got 'better' but… it's possible they remembered at least the basics before than which gave them an idea. After a few moments, he let out a sigh, seeming to slump. "But I guess I do understand."

"Huh?"

He leaned against the wall, arms crossed. "What good would it have done to know I was related to a Specter? That most of my family was in that state? I guess, I kind of understand why they didn't tell me, but—"

"But you can't help but feeling angry and hurt." I nodded, leaning against the opposite wall. "It's painful, when people don't tell you things, even after you realize they were only trying to protect you."

"Heh, yeah, sounds about right." Felix trailed off before pushing away from the wall. "I'll admit, I'm still angry at them, at my dad and yours. At Sylvia, but…" he ruffled his hair before grinning. "Hey, I'm not one to keep grudges for long."

I chuckled before peering up the stairwell. "So, now that I know you don't completely hate Sylvia, do you mind? If we stay here?"

"No. Never."

"Thanks." I smiled, feeling just a little better. This house, bustling with sounds and warmth, was much better than the dreary place I'd left down the street, even with the imperceptibly heavy atmosphere. Sylvia was right. "We might be here a while though."

Felix grinned. "Hey, that's fine by me. I think all of us need a chance to recover. We can make it a big get-together, bring Mira and her family over later—" He cut himself off.

I let out a breath. "Anyway, I'll help you set up the room, do you mind?"

"Do you need to ask?"

"Probably not." I headed back into the kitchen, walking over to

Felix's mother to help her with the blankets. I didn't think we needed that many.

It didn't take long for all of us to settle in. Harold woke up, to everyone's relief, about an hour after we arrived. After a long conversation that I did not want to get involved in between Sylvia, Harold and Felix, I got a chance to re-meet him.

He spotted me and quickly apologized before thanking me for being Felix's friend and trying so hard to remember him. His grip was solid as he shook my hand and I grinned. There was no way I would leave anyone behind if I could help it. I think he seemed to realize because he let out a hearty laugh and told us the house was ours until things worked themselves out.

Working themselves out was another story entirely.

Chapter Thirty

I was sitting in the living room, probably a day or two later, watching the news out of morbid curiosity. They were still talking about the upheaval the memory manipulation caused. The collapsing of infrastructure and the over-burden on the farms and factories that maintained food within the radius was a big issue. However, on top of that, it seemed the death count was in the hundreds, almost a thousand.

I shivered. Was that from just the electrical currents? Or the Specters? Or both?

Trials were under way for all those involved. Thankfully, the main focus seemed to be on El and Leonard. I frowned when they presented his full name. Now that I thought about it, Dad only ever said his first name. What worried me was that the last name... it was the same as Mother's maiden name. Sylvia seemed to notice as well. Disgust shown on her face before she peered toward me, worried. "Ki?"

I leaned back against the couch, only slightly averting my attention from the screen. "Yeah?"

"Are you okay?"

"Hm?"

Sylvia sighed and fully turned to me. "We can't just ignore it. That bastard... he was our uncle."

I turned toward her and felt my shoulders slump. "I know." She seemed startled at my words, so I continued, "I figured it out when I was talking with him. I just... didn't want to believe that my own family could..." Fingers dug into my arm at the memories, only to be pulled back as Sylvia leaned forward, hand gently taking mine.

Julie Boglisch

"Well, either way, he's not going to hurt you again. He's on trial and, even if, by shit luck, he manages to get out of it, I know some people." Her smile was cold, but it slowly shifted to warmth and comfort. "Just because he was our uncle doesn't mean anything. He is related to us by blood, but that's it. He's not family."

I pursed my lips and slowly let myself relax, returning my attention to the screen. "You're right."

"Of course I am." Sylvia lightly punched my shoulder. "Come on, let's watch and see that bastard get thrown in jail."

I shook my head, but couldn't help but relax a bit more, comforted at the thought of Sylvia at my side. However, my thoughts than turned to my next worry. "Then it's Dad's turn." I said, leaning back as I watched the trial once more descend into chaos, a shouting match from those outside, a few barging in.

Sylvia's expression dimmed. "Yeah…"

Neither of us said anything else as we watched. It must have been fun, trying to find people who knew nothing about this incident. They definitely had to move quickly, since this was international news in, well, a day. As soon as the machine fell, everyone was aware of the change. Ilda's involvement only sped up the process and allowed them to pinpoint exactly where they needed to be to make sure things went smoothly. I wondered how they found people who didn't know about it to be on the jury. Maybe someone from the opposite coast? I wouldn't know.

I just hoped those people would be lenient on Dad. I hoped they would understand that he was a victim, not a criminal. It seemed Sylvia agreed with me as we watched.

As we waited for the verdict, a day passed into the next. A few days after we decided to stay and two days after that short conversation on the couch, a military doctor came by to do a quick examination of everyone. It seemed they were going door to door to make sure everyone who wasn't evacuated was checked for problems.

I could only assume what those were. Thankfully, the examination was easy, a regular physical. Harold was told to go for a brain scan, along with Felix and Sylvia, which all three conceded to. I have a feeling those brain scanners were being worked overtime. It was a day or so after that they got results from their exams. I cringed at the analysis, but conceded it could have been worse.

Sylvia mentioned how, when she went in, there were a lot more people in much worse states than they were. The doctor was surprised to find out that the three of them had been Specters at one point, so…

It seemed that they wouldn't have any permanent damage, unlike the majority of people, but they would always have a bit more of a struggle remembering things, the synapses weakened from the exposure. But it would gradually heal itself if given time.

About halfway through the week, Felix went over to Mira's place to find out her condition, but when he returned, he was tight-lipped and almost on the verge of collapsing. I had a feeling it wasn't good news. After he calmed down, he told us that Mira was heavily damaged by the waves. She would always be struggling with multi-personality disorder and memory lapses. Her father wasn't much better, having been on death's door when he was rescued and helped. Her mother, well… Felix didn't get a chance to say anything as the woman saw him, yelled at him for getting her family involved and how dare he harbor the son of that man who helped cause all of this.

I heard that and cringed. I wondered how many other people were aware of who Sylvia and I were. Who we were related to.

Thankfully, Ilda did a good job keeping Father's name under wraps, even if his face was shown. Unfortunately, that meant that most of the people in town recognized who he was. Some didn't care, some… some were like Mira's mother.

I didn't think that would ever go away.

There wasn't much I could do for Felix. I knew he didn't hate me for, well, being me. But I could tell my, well, our presence wasn't going to help him much.

I let out a sigh as I slumped into the couch once more, more than a week after the events that put Sylvia and me in this situation and a few days after the trials began. I was incredibly grateful for Felix's family's kindness. I went by our house a day or so after Felix was thrown out of

Mira's place to find that our house was practically trashed. Windows were broken, the fence ripped and writing sketched or drawn into the walls. Rude and disgusting words about how we were filth, how our family shouldn't have been born. How dare we create something that brought death to so many...

To be honest, I wasn't sure how Felix's home avoided ending up in the same state. It wasn't hard to imagine that everyone realized we were there. I did note that the car was no longer in the driveway and could only hope that it was returned to its respective owner.

I shook my head, returning my attention to the TV. I turned it on before freezing. Standing on trial, Ilda right behind him, was Father. He stood tall, tired, but still Dad. It seemed some rest over the long week helped even in that situation.

"Sylvia!" I called up, my voice pitching up slightly in my hurry.

Footsteps pounded on the stairs as Sylvia practically flung herself into the room. "Kieran?"

"Dad's on," was all I said. Her eyes narrowed and she quickly moved to sit next to me, scrutinizing the screen harshly.

The trial was just like every other, screams could be heard from outside. Thankfully, it seemed they didn't use his name.

"Is it true that you were the creator of the memory device?" An attorney walked past the podium, watching him carefully. It seemed he had the stand and I was going to guess he was not on Dad's side.

"That is correct," Father said.

"And you used it to manipulate the minds of those around you?"

"I was not aware of that function when it was first created." Father spoke evenly, voice firm. "It was only created in order to erase the bad memories from my family so that I wouldn't have to see my daughter trying to commit suicide a second time. There was no intention of creating that device."

"But you did create it and then expanded on it."

"I did create it. However, I was coerced to continue working on it."

The conversation continued on in much the same fashion, the

attorney asking questions and my father responding. A while later, the defending attorney came on. Sylvia gasped, recognizing the guy. It seemed Ilda went through quite a few hoops to get someone good. I didn't recognize the name, but Sylvia and the others, who arrived not long after Sylvia, seemed to know him as well. Felix just shook his head, wondering how I didn't know the guy. I wasn't that interested in trials, so...

I could see he knew his stuff. Every question he asked, every piece of evidence he brought forth, made Dad out to be a sympathetic victim. Unfortunately, the truth behind Sylvia's attempted suicide and my being held by that man came out. Sylvia hugged me tightly when Dad told about how he found me and rescued me. I somehow successfully tuned most of it out, not really wanting to hear a recap of something I was trying to forget. However, it seemed my situation was what finally swayed the jury. It wasn't long after that when he was found innocent. Guilty of only minor infractions, but innocent for being behind this whole mess.

"Your sentence, as decided by this court of law, is a twelve-month probation period and a $12,000 fine—" Anything said after that, I ignored as I found myself slumping in relief, covering my eyes with the back of my hand as I let out a laugh, just so grateful. Dad was coming home. He wasn't going to jail.

Sylvia was crying, letting out hiccupping sobs even as she laughed quietly, probably just as relieved as me. I was probably doing the same, it was hard to tell, but we would have Dad back and that was what mattered. Things might still be a mess, but at least everyone would be together again. We could deal with that.

"That's actually probably the best possible outcome he could have gotten," Harold said, catching my attention. Felix's mother was smiling softly as Felix cracked a large grin.

"What do you mean?" I asked, dropping my arm.

He turned to me. "They put forth a good case of him being a victim just as much as everyone else, even if he was the one who created the device in the first place. Plus, he is still getting a punishment and the main culprits are jailed. I think people will be okay with this."

"Wait…" Sylvia slowly turned to me, realization dawning on her. "Ilda said…"

"To trust her?" I grinned. Sylvia scoffed, but a faint smile trailed on her lips. I turned to Felix's family and bowed my head slightly. "Thank you for letting us stay this whole time."

"Of course, dear, now I think your father should be heading home soon. Though I have a feeling that there will be a few people apologizing and helping with clean-up."

I didn't think so, but I didn't say otherwise as I stared at the screen, watching as he was led out, Ilda not far behind. You know? She actually did pull through. She told me to trust her and she was right. Dad was coming home.

Maybe someday… maybe someday, I could forgive her for lying to us, for forcing us to deal with all of this.

Someday…

~ * ~

The house was a mess. We got to work as quickly as we could, startled when one or two of the neighbors came by to apologize, passing over food or helping to clean up. I was grateful. I didn't think anyone would help, but I guess a few seemed to understand, even if the majority still seemed to despise us. A few people tried to attack us or throw vile words our way, but they were quickly dealt with, either pulled away or silenced peacefully. I was grateful.

We waited at the steps as the sun beat down overhead. It had been a day or so since Dad's verdict and Sylvia and I mostly spent the time cleaning up the house. The windows were still mostly broken, but I wasn't too worried as the warm summer sun cast a gentle glow over everything. The graffiti was gone from the walls, toilet paper and other items picked up and thrown out. The dust was cleaned from the inside and we were able to at least put plastic over the damaged windows. We would have waited inside, but both of us wanted to see when Dad pulled up, just to make sure we weren't going crazy.

There wasn't much fanfare on his arrival. A lone car pulled up to the side of the road and the driver stepped out. I stilled, noting it was Ilda, but Ilda only cast a solemn expression our way before opening the back door. I found myself standing up alongside Sylvia as Father stepped out. He seemed tired, but his expression brightened upon seeing us. He glanced toward Ilda, saying a few soft words before he walked over to us. Ilda watched, a faint sad smile on her face. She slipped back into the car, driving away.

That was the last thing I noticed as I darted down the sidewalk, Sylvia only a pace behind. We almost tackled Dad, causing him to let out a warm laugh as he hugged us both, startled.

"Hello, Kieran, Sylvia, sorry for causing you so much trouble."

"It's fine." Sylvia pulled back, a warm grin on her face as she rubbed her nose. "We got the bad guy." I didn't miss the way Father winced and Sylvia didn't either. "Dad?"

"Hm, Bad guy... I guess you would call him that." He sighed, pulling away slightly, hands on our shoulders. "I'm going to get this out of the way now."

Sylvia and I exchanged glances, before Sylvia said, "Does this have to do with him being our uncle?"

Father sighed. "Yes. To be honest, your uncle and mother were close. There was a reason I trusted him with this project. Why he was so passionate about it himself... why I could never fully hate him, no matter how much I might have wanted to. He truly did want what was best for people. He really did want to forget his sister's death."

Father's words were enough to remind me of some things the man said, sister, the way he hesitated before saying death, the way he kept talking about Mother in that fond tone. My earlier conversation with Sylvia came back and I found myself asking, "Then... why? Why did he..."

Farther seemed to understand. He put a gentle hand on my shoulder. "I think he just... I think it was too much for him. He wanted to help, but he took it too far." He shook his head and pulled me close for a second. "But he's not going to hurt you or anyone else again, all right?

I don't think any of us will forget what he did, but we can move on, right? I, for one, am starving."

I hesitated, before relaxing. Right, it was finally over. I pulled away from Dad and smiled. "Yeah, I think we all are, but… you're staying, right?" I trailed off, pursing my lips.

"What? You don't want me to?" He chuckled upon seeing my expression and pulled us both close once more, almost squishing the two of us against him. "Don't worry. I'm staying. I'll be right here, with both of you. After all, I think I have a year and a half worth of apologies for both of you."

"I'm looking forward to it." I found myself hugging him back before pulling away, allowing Sylvia to get his full attention. I thought those two had a lot they needed to talk about.

Personally, I was just glad to see all three of us home. Even with that last piece of news, I wasn't going to let it ruin our reunion. I walked inside, followed by the other two as they continued talking. It was nice, having the entire family together once more, without the fear or worry of something falling apart hanging over us.

I didn't think I felt that even before this whole mess started.

Actually, I hadn't felt this relaxed or relieved since before Mother's death. Mother… I smiled softly. *Sorry it took so long, but we're finally starting to move on, all of us.*

Don't worry, I don't think I'll forget you again, but it's finally time for us to stop living in the past. I, for one, am looking forward to it.

Epilogue

"Felix! Come on, hurry up!" Mira's voice rang over the hillside as I glanced up from the book I was reading. I could see the newlyweds hurrying up the hill, wedding bands flashing in the sunlight as they arrived. Mira was looking much healthier than she had when we were younger. The gaunt and tired expression she had for years was now gone. Felix was smiling brightly, his hair a mess as usual, but he had cut down to only wearing one piercing in his ears. They were both well dressed. I closed my book and stood as Sylvia blearily opened her eyes, having fallen asleep on top of her notebook.

"Hey, man, looks like you're still doing well. How's your father?"

I grinned, taking his hand in mine in a firm grip. "Good. Father decided to remarry the other day."

"That Ilda woman? He forgave her?"

"It's been six years." Sylvia yawned, stretching upward. "Is it that surprising? It took years for Mira's mother to finally let you two even SEE each other, right? And Father did actually love her, even though it was half fake. Now that they've sorted out how they feel, things are working out…" Sylvia trailed off, and it wasn't hard for me to guess why. She was still upset at Ilda even now. Personally, I no longer had any problem with her. She was my mother, just in a different way. She was there during that year, helping me even though she didn't necessarily have to. Just because her memory was erased didn't mean she had to play the good mother. She truly did care and I was fine with that. Sylvia… She'd gotten better but I knew she still struggled with trust issues. I wasn't sure she'd ever really forgive Mom and Dad. Sylvia perked up, continuing where she left off. "By the way, how was the honeymoon? It must have been spectacular with how beautiful the wedding was."

The two blushed as Felix draped an arm around Mira.

I chuckled, placing my hands behind my head as I leaned against the tree. "Mira, how are you feeling?"

Mira stared at me for a long time before her smile dropped and she let out a sigh. "I'm doing a lot better, but…"

"She still sometimes slips back into that time." Felix grimaced. "Just like a lot of the others. Speaking of, how is your research coming along?"

"Ask Sylvia about that. She's been doing most of the scientific stuff on it, I just engineer what she designs."

"It's still impressive though," Mira pointed out. "Ever since his probation ended, your father got a surprising amount of job offers, didn't he?"

"You've only reminded us of this a thousand times," Sylvia joked, causing Mira to huff and turn away, arms crossed. "Plus, I guess it kind of runs in the family."

Felix chuckled before turning to me. "Still, maybe one day, you two can come up with a way to reverse-engineer what your father did."

"I know…" I sighed. "I wish Father could work on it, but he was banned from touching anything memory-inducing again, so I guess it's up to us, right, Sylv?"

"Don't call me that." She spoke up with a yawn as she sat up, the reprimand half-hearted at best. "Anyway, enough about that, we have a party to celebrate and as annoyed as I am to admit it, we have an upcoming wedding as well, don't we?"

I rolled my eyes as Sylvia grinned. "So, let's celebrate. After all, our families are all back together, you two are finally together, which by the way, took WAY too long, and Kieran and I are about to become world famous on our own merit."

"Oh, so you did get accepted for that Master's program," Mira teased.

"You know it." Sylvia winked before jumping to her feet. "Now, time to get drunk!" She grinned, pumping her fist before hurrying down the hill. I shook my head as Felix yelped and followed with Mira laughing along after.

Even all these years later… some things never changed.

I glanced up toward the sun and grinned. "Well, not going to forget this, am I?" I turned down, placed my book in my bag. "Wait for me!" I called, laughing as I raced down the hill after them, the sun warming my skin and the fresh air practically singing of a brand-new start.

While my memory might fade with age… Whether for better or for worse, I didn't think I'd ever forget what happened. No matter what happened.

But I was okay with that.

I would rather remember everything that happened, no matter how difficult, than forget who I am for even a moment.

I feel like that was a feeling all of us held, everyone who survived that horrible time. After all, we could live to tell about it. It was our job to make sure it would never happen again.

Sylvia and I were going to make sure of it. No matter how long it took.

But for now, I was going to just enjoy the life I had, and the memories I was able to create of my own free will. Both the good and bad. I was going to cherish it all until the day I no longer could.

About the Author

Julie Boglisch is a twenty-eight-year-old writer who loves to write, draw, and drink tea. She has two adorable dogs and enjoys her free time watching YouTube.

Demon's Song
Requeim of Stone Book One

Alex always wished to see the Overlands, a place of sunshine and freedom. However, as a slave in the far corners of the Underlands, it was all but a dream. That is, until he's framed for murder and is forced to flee during a demon attack.

Searching for the answers to why he was framed and seeking a chance at the fleeting freedom he's always dreamed about, he journeys to the capital, meeting friend and foe along the way. But the Underlands are both beautiful and dangerous. Having a demon hunter on his tail and a witch whose sole desire is to become the high Seer around him, he's in for quite the journey.

Demon's Call
Requeim of Stone Book Two

Having escaped the city of Raynout, Alex, Rita and Milos find themselves journeying in search of Alex's mother and the answers she can provide. Their search leads them to the dangerous and unknown region of the north, where legend tells tales of its perilous waters. Along the way, they learn not only more about the Underlands, but about themselves as well as they struggle to come to term with who they are and where they belong. Meeting interesting new allies and a dangerous new enemy, the three of them must learn how to fully rely on each other... before the waters of the north tear them apart.

Epidemic
The Elifer Chronicles Book One

It has been forty years since America closed its borders and separated from the world following the Vietnam War. In the ensuing years, the country has developed in incredible ways, or at least, that is what Maxwell and Karina, a set of twins from a community deep in the forests of New England, have been told all their lives. In a town surrounded by larger-than-life trees and crags, they didn't have a reason to believe otherwise.

That belief is put to the test when they find their house ransacked, their mother missing, and their only chance to live is outside of the barriers they've grown used to. Barriers... that they never realized existed.

Retrieval
The Elifer Chronicles Book Two

Maxwell and Karina, twins who are the cure to a disease which is ravaging the country, find themselves journeying to the distant locale of Collern City in search of their missing mother. Meeting strange allies and dealing with dangerous enemies, they must learn to navigate the treacherous streets and discover more about what is going on behind the scenes in both the gated community and outside of it. Meanwhile, their guardian and friend, Lex, struggles to deal with his family's desires. He finds himself caught between his own wish to flee his home, never to return. and the wish of his brother, Caym, who desperately wants him to stay.

FOR THE FULL INVENTORY
OF QUALITY BOOKS:
http://www.roguephoenixpress.com

Rogue Phoenix Press
Representing Excellence in Publishing

Quality trade paperbacks and downloads
in multiple formats,
in genres ranging from historical to contemporary romance, mystery and
science fiction.
Visit the website then bookmark it.
We add new titles each month!

www.ingramcontent.com/pod-product-compliance
Lightning Source LLC
Chambersburg PA
CBHW051100030726
47504CB00006B/1716